PSYCHIC VOICES

Book 1

in the Mary Jameson Supernatural Thriller Series

by

J.P. Alters

This novel is a work of fiction. Names, places, incidents, and characters are figments of the author's imagination or are used fictitiously. Any resemblance to actual persons, living or dead, events, or locales is entirely coincidental.

Book cover design by: Christian Bentulan

Edited by: Susan Keillor

ISBN 978-1-7392374-4-8 (Paperback)
ISBN 978-1-7392374-5-5 (Ebook)

Contents

Acknowledgements

I'd just like to take a moment to shout out a massive THANK YOU, to all the wonderful souls who had my back during this whirlwind journey of writing and publishing (two times!) this book. Your encouragement and support have meant the world to me.

A special heap of kudos and gratitude, goes out to the fantastic Susan Keillor. She's not only the brilliant mind that edited my work, she's also a beacon of encouragement. Susan, you rock!

Can we also take a moment to appreciate the phenomenal talent of Christian Bentulan, my cover designer? Thanks Christian, for turning my book into a visual treat. Your cover designs are truly a work of art.

And of course, I can't forget my self-appointed beta reader; Elain Lee. Your feedback and support have been invaluable to me. You, my pal, are a gem. The same goes for my super proofreading buddy, Kala Whyte. Thanks for ensuring every i was dotted, and every t was crossed!

To my close friends and family, your unshakeable faith in me keeps me going. Your belief in me fuels my dreams, and for that, I can't thank you enough.

From the bottom of my heart, THANK YOU!

Best wishes,

JP x

Author's Note

Hey there, dear reader,

First off, a gigantic THANK YOU, for picking up and reading Psychic Voices! I know time is a rare gem these days, and that you chose to spend yours on my book warms my heart. I can't wait to embark on more reading adventures with you!😉

Before we dive in, I think it's important to let you know that Psychic Voices does touch on themes and includes language of an adult nature.These elements might be upsetting for some readers, so please take care of yourself, and only proceed if you're comfortable.

Fun fact, PsychicVoices, was initially birthed into the world in 2022 under the title: A Psychic Subterfuge. It being my debut novel, I stumbled a bit, and made a few rookie mistakes. So, I decided to give it a bit of a facelift, and re-launch it with some improvements.

You might've already ventured to my website and read up on my bio. If you haven't, here's a quick run-down. I'm a South-East Londoner, born and raised in a lively Jamaican/English household. Our family mantra has always been the Jamaican 'One Love,' embodying unity and, well, love. And that's exactly what I aim to radiate through my stories – diversity, unity, family, love… you name it.

Why not swing by my website and subscribe to my mailing list? You'll get the inside scoop on me, and my upcoming book in the series, which is set to hit the shelves this October. Just head to www.jpaltersauthor.com, scroll down a tad, and click that subscribe button.

I sincerely hope you enjoyed Psychic Voices! If you did, I'd be over the moon if you could leave a review on Amazon or Goodreads. Now for a little thank you gift! As a token of my appreciation for your support, I've got a short story from the Mary Jameson Supernatural Thriller Series, just for you.

Follow the instructions on the provided link: https://dl.bookfunnel.com/46u9t5uokp

And you'll have access to this exclusive mini-book, Psychic Training, on the house!

Best wishes,

J.P. Alters

PART ONE

Chapter 1

My face feels numb. Even as I drag my hand across my cheek, there's no sensation.

'Mother... park... run... can't get caught... new life,' more sporadic words burst out, as I collapse against a heap of clothes. A fly lands on my cheek, and I shoo it away. It's not alone; a swarm drifts over the dishes strewn across my living room floor.

My lips twist. A room for living? Hardly what *this* existence could be called.

Tears well up in my eyes again and my nostrils sting, signs the clutter around me must reek. Well, I don't care.

As I rock back and forth, my hair tangled in my fists, I glance at the anxious little girl beside me, then at my other friends. Gathering my fragmented thoughts together, I muster up some energy.

'Please, go with me. I need you all with me. Don't you care how much I'm suffering?'

'We do Mary, we love you so much. That's why we want you to stay.'

'Stay? Stay here in this daily fucking torture? Where I have people talking and screaming at me, day and night? No way. I don't want this life anymore, Little Mary. I've had enough of this shit.'

Jo steps forward, palms outstretched to me.

'Mary, please think about this. You have your whole life ahead of you. It could be so wonderful.'

A bitter laugh escapes me. I stop yanking my hair and instead, knead a lump on my forehead. Is this a new one? It makes no difference. God, I'm sick of this migraine. The noises will not stop. I do not have enough strength to smash my head against the floor, so rubbing it will have to do.

'If that's supposed to be a good thing, Jo, then I can't see why. There's nothing good about my life. It's fucking miserable, and it's only getting worse by the second.'

Tears crowd me, blurring my sight.

'I just want my mum.'

My whisper breaks, and I am so lost in my desolation I do not hear Dolores' soft outcry, or see my friends share glances. Instead, I hear the familiar; click, click, click. Then the white noise static of a radio station and the other voices take over centre stage again, and I lose control.

'Peter wants to know about Saturday… can we go on Saturday, Bill?'

'Tuna is nice, but I like chicken more.'

'You're stupid, and you will always be stupid. Look at you, just sitting there. Idiot.'

'Come and dance with me.'

The random conversation floods in, making me swoon. Breathing quick, shallow breaths, I roll over onto my side, curling into a tight ball of misery. Then, decision made, I move onto my hands and knees before struggling to stand up. Placing my hands on top of the nearby pile of dirty clothes, I push, my limbs shaking.

'I don't think I've eaten today…' I say aloud, then. 'When was the last time?'

Little Mary cries then, making me sorry for her. I can never bear to see children upset. Or animals suffer. Dazed, I touch the wall like a sleepwalker, then move.

'I'm sorry, Little Mary. I just want to be with my mum again.'

'OK, Mary. We'll go with you,' they say.

I smile, and my dry lips crack and bleed. Finally. I knew they would see it my way.

We are running so fast I have no time to gulp for air. My heart feels like a parasitic host is about to rip through my chest. The whistling, dappled trees flash past in my peripheral vision. My scabby legs and arms have all of my residual energy. If I can make it to my mum, then I won't be alone anymore.

My usual companions run beside me. Little Mary is sprinting just to my left, on the grass. Her large brown eyes are wide with fear in her delicate face. My dearest friend is small for ten years old, just like I was, when David first over-powered me and ruined my life.

Louise, an ex-schoolteacher, runs alongside Little Mary. Lou is measured and calm, but now she is in fast forward. Her long blonde hair is streaming out behind her as she pelts along as quickly as she can.

Kind Jo's portly figure lags, but he is chugging along the field and making steady headway.

I cannot see Dolores, but I know she will trail far behind the others because of her advanced years. She will find us, though. The others have fanned out.

They hid as soon as they realised David was coming. We all know what he will do if he catches us. Strained or shocked faces fall into a backwards blur as we push ourselves to the limit, then beyond. My lungs are screaming.

We can make it to the bridge. I trip over the sole of a too-worn trainer. The momentum I am running with does not allow me to stop. I grab at the air to help steady myself, but the action tips me even more off balance and I topple, flying onto the grass like a dead superwoman with no powers.

'Are you ok?' A lady pushing a buggy along the path stops to ask me. She looks concerned as she heads towards me.

'Quickly, he's coming, Mary. Come on, come on,' Little Mary hisses at me. She has an uncharacteristic undertone of hysteria in her voice as she hurries me up.

As I dig my already grubby fingers into the soil, my limbs shake with effort and fear, but I push up with the strength remaining in my torso.

The lady extends one navy striped arm in my direction, but I slap it away on automatic pilot.

'Fuck off.'

A fearful peep over my shoulder keeps me updated on my worst fear. David reaching us without my noticing and stopping me from entering my new life with my mum.

It will be worse if I accept help from an outsider. David does not like it when I am around others;- he does not trust them.

Snatching a look at Little Mary, I then scan in front of us for Louise, catching my breath as Lou's gym-fit shape merges into the grassy horizon.

'Lou! Wait.'

'Come on, Mary!'

'... please,' Little Mary adds, always polite.

Lou has gotten far away from us, and I do not want her to disappear from my line of vision. It is OK if I lose sight of some others, but Lou, Little Mary, Jo, and Dolores. Well...I just need them with me. We are tight. Always together, no matter what. Lou jogs back.

The lady withdraws her slapped hand and I notice she is wiping it on her jeans leg surreptitiously. She does not comment on the profanity her kindness garners. Instead, the woman looks in Lou's direction, then at me as I wave away Jo's helping hand to get off my hands and knees.

'No, Jo, I can do it.'

'Are you alright?'

'Sweetie, do you need some help?'

Staying silent, I glance up at her. She is mistaking me for a child, even though I am twenty-one and have just sworn at her. People often make that mistake until I flip them off or spit at them.

Although I stopped using mirrors a long time ago, I still have a pretty good idea what she is seeing. Smoke-grey eyes with dark smudges underneath, and long jet-black hair with an homage to Amy Winehouse's dragged-through-a-hedge-backwards style. Someone once told me I looked like a prison camp refugee.

The lady looks sympathetic, and she tries not to stare at the unkempt clothes that hang off my bones. Standing there, a waft of my sour-milk smell puffs up from my top, wrenching at my stomach and making me sway. Blood floods to my already flushed cheeks and I close my eyes, smelling myself.

'Huh.'

'Hurry.'

'I'm coming!' I call back to Lou, shame and Jo both lending me the extra energy it takes to finish returning to my feet.

Nodding at the woman, I blink, feeling relieved for the interruption into my gritty reality.

A man is jogging towards us, addressing the kind mum as he nears, 'Everything alright?'

The man does not acknowledge us and the two people share a look.

Fuck you both.

Back to an upright position, I wonder if I am imagining David is breathing down the back of my neck. Argh. I swipe a palm over my nape. At least the thought prompts me to get moving again so I can finish this and be back with my mum. It is unbearable not to have family around me.

We are still going fast, but we are tired. We came so far to get here. Any minute now I will collapse. I have been running almost by will alone. We must have run for at least forty minutes from my studio flat.

As I think about my bedsit, I can almost taste the acrid smell of the accumulated rubbish, dirty dishes, and fetid clothes which sometimes unmasks itself to my nostrils. A quick cuckoo "hello," before the reality goes back into hiding again.

Also… the walls are fucking green for God's sake, and I have always hated green. My brow wrinkles as I wonder if I was told to paint it by one of my friends. Or maybe I like to torture myself.

'Mary, come on.'

My friends call to me, snapping me back on task. Lou beckons us from ahead. Oh, thank God, she is standing by the gap in the fence. We swerve our path like a flock of birds in a V formation, racing towards Lou.

A prickle on the hairs on my nape alert me to David's impending emergence. He is nearly here. No, I will not let David get to me. He will ruin things. He always comes at the worst times, and I cannot feel any worse than I do right now. This has to end, because I need to get back to my mum. Sweat pours down between my sharpened shoulder blades.

My screams expel themselves from me in jittered mumbles, jogged out of me in confused skits. Fleeing like a March hare, I make a bolt for a hedgerow. Praying I will spot the right part of the bridge and end this torture before David is upon us and forces me to stop.

'You can't get away!' I hear him say, his voice like a rumble of thunder. Is that my imagination, or actually him?

'If I do not speed up, David will catch me,' my voice squeaks out as I throw another panicky glance over my shoulder. *Do not fall.* That is how the bad guy gets the good guy in the movies. David is definitely the baddie in this scenario… but am I the goodie?

An unexpected smile relieves my pinched features as I scrutinise the surroundings in front of me, spotting the bridge behind Little Mary. Jo and Louise are standing with her, and I walk towards them, confident Dolores will be on her way to join us.

'We're here. We're at the river.'

'I can remember when I first found this place.'

'…It called to me. The blue water called to me. It knew I would come back here one day. Maybe I belong to it?'

Silent, I breathe in the beauty of the trees. The warm sun feels nice on my face when I hold it up towards the sky, absorbing the golden rays. My eyelids drift down, and I hear Lou trying to calm Little Mary's sobs as they approach me.

'It's time now. Come on then, Mary, if you're all set. Let's just get this part over with.'

'Are you sure, Mary, really sure? What about everything I told you about me? What if it happens again to someone else?' Little Mary asks me again, in between sobs.

My friends are unhappy about this, but they are loyal and will support me. They are the best, which is why it's so difficult to say goodbye to them. As I sway backwards, I almost lose my balance, but then I refocus. There it is, the gap in the fence Little Mary has identified. I walk closer towards the wooden fence, and the doorway to freedom it encases. Allowing myself a sigh, a song flits into my memory: "Hard to Say Goodbye."

Little Mary is distraught. It is hard for her too. She wants me to stay. She stands close to me now, as she usually does.

'That's not down to me, but I'm sure it won't happen again anyway. Please be quiet, Little Mary, I can't concentrate when you cry like that,' I tell her absentmindedly.

Mary and I share a name and lots of other similarities. She reminds me of myself when I was a child and was first taken into the foster care system. Little Mary has a lot of horrible stories to tell. She also sings funny ditties she makes up herself. But not now…now she is crying.

The hairs in my nostrils begin to sizzle and the smell of sulphur sears into me. David is upon us: his emergence crowds me.

'He will not allow my plan to happen. It is now or never. Manipulating the fencing, I squeeze through the gap, stepping up to the flimsy wire barrier it conceals. With one leg thrown over with giddy abandon, I transfer my weight to the other leg. After a wobble, I steady myself, gripping the biting wire now wet with my blood. I need to balance so I can climb over and properly throw myself away. Away from everything, and away from David.

With both legs over, I tilt my chin up, and prepare to swan dive into my next incarnation. A bird… maybe an eagle? I think I will like that. Top of the food chain.

I perch. Ready to be rid of the pain in this soiled existence. I hold my arms out straight on either side of me and arch, standing on my tiptoes. For once, I find perfect poise. This is it; I am ready to be with my mom again. Still balancing on the balls of my feet, I concentrate and bend my knees in "ballerina-esque" fashion. First down. Now up.

Two sets of nameless hands snatch me out of mid-air. They wrench me away from my next evolution with rude abruptness, dragging me back over the fence.

'No!'

'*No. Get off me.*'

'It's OK now.'

My stance is ruined, and my thin skin tears on the wire. The fresh air I enjoyed before now burns like acid onto my many cuts. Four powerful hands wrestle me for control as I try to get back to my peaceful Nirvana.

I shout and scream. Police uniforms surround me, and I lash out at them, spitting, scratching, anything to break free of their grip.

As my view of my capturers increases, so my vision of escape moves further and further away from me. I see it dwindle as though it is the end title screen at the movies.

'No - *Fucking pigs.*'

'Le'megoyoubastards.'

'Miss, please, we're here to help.'

Pathetic stubbornness sees me scrabbling to return to where I had been perched. I was almost there. They cannot take me away from my peace, my freedom. I refuse to suffer this life anymore. I will not tolerate it.

They fight with me to reverse my impetus, but I cannot put up much of a challenge. Feeble in comparison, they carry me off with ease, as though I am a bucking packet of sugar. Upside down, I see the waiting ambulance and know what comes next.

'No.'

'No! Get off her you idiots!'

'Leave her alone!'

My friends scream at them in unison, but their frantic cries go ignored, and disobeyed.

I do not want to be sectioned again, I hate being trapped in hospitals and kept docile. All of the exertion proves too much for my stomach in addition to the running, and I spew up frothy yellow bile. It is the powdery acid from the coated tablets I swallowed this morning. I implode. Still in their arms, I retch, trying to protest a weak "no" in between heaves. No, please no, David is coming.

'Come on now, missy, try and calm down. We aren't going to hurt you.'

'No, no I won't. Get away from me.'

'It's all ok, miss, it will all be OK.'

They are speaking, saying something about my rights, but I do not care or understand. Beside myself, snot runs into my mouth, making me heave again. The smell of sulphur grows stronger as I am forced into an ambulance and strapped onto a gurney. A circle of faces surrounds us all.

'He's coming! Please, no. Help me. David's coming. You've got to let me go! Let me go. I need to be with my mum.'

A circle of blurry faces surrounds me, and I look from one to another, begging for help.

Stop this. Please. My anguish is abruptly silenced by a bee sting in my arm, and I look down. The ambulance staff have given me an injection, so I know the drill. In seconds, I will lose consciousness, and wake up weak as a kitten, sectioned in a hospital. The tranquilliser begins to take effect. Drowsy, my eyelids blink shut slowly.

'David… he's coming, let me go…' I whimper, as my world grows quickly smaller, then I lose consciousness. My tears leave their trails of clean down my face as I sleep.

Chapter 2

I do not want to leave. The Blue is always warm. My mum mouths soothing words to me, switching between French, Fon, and English. Then she smiles. Her chestnut brown skin gleams and she shakes back her long braids, nodding. The blue light makes her look like a bronzed Egyptian sculpture. I am whole again.

'Mummy,' I whisper.

She shimmers with love. Radiant with it.

I feel her joy and adoration for me at my core and it fills me with an answering candescence. The light expands outside of me, growing so bright I raise a hand up against the glare. When I blink my eyes open again, I am in alien surroundings. My eyelids slam down again in an immediate flash of refusal.

I need to be with my mum.

Someone is stroking my face with something cool and soft.

Mum? No, it cannot be. If I open my eyes, will the sensation go away? It feels so magical, like nothing I have experienced for years. Kindness. I don't want to chase this feeling away. Is it Heaven? Are my beloved friends here with me in Heaven, too?

A waft of fresh pine shampoo reaches me, and I understand what it means, but I do not react. Dammit, I am neither alone nor am I in Heaven. Resisting the urge to cradle my dizzy head, I keep my eyes shut and I remain silent. Information is power.

'An hour ago, this little lady showed up on a "one three six." She's lucky. No local hospital available for a Place of Safety. Dr. Sinclair agreed to admit her here, at The Rainbow Unit,-' a man's voice said.

'Her name is Mary Obosa Jameson. Her records say she's twenty-one. Mixed English/African and British born. She has a diagnosis of paranoid schizophrenia and she's treatment resistant. Hypermobility, IBS and suffering from malnutrition and dehydration and bloods show vitamin D and iron deficiencies. Superficial wounds and a few minor hematomas but no other physical health conditions.'

'What else does it say on her record cards? Any family? Next of kin? Nearest relative contacted?' A disembodied woman answers him, she has an Irish accent. Despite the clinical language of her words, the female has a hug in her voice.

'Ahh, poor thing. It says here that at eight years old, her mum died of cancer, and she went into foster care. How sad. She has no other relatives, no known friends.'

'Twenty-one and she's treatment resistant? Are they sure? -What've they tried?' the man interjects in a tone ladened with disbelief.

'Everything,-' the woman replies. 'Every medication they tried worked for a couple of weeks, then psychotic symptoms returned, stronger than ever.' She breaks off then,

'God, she's tiny. How much do you think she weighs?' A gentle tut punctuates her question.

Her voice sounds closer, as though she is peering at me while she speaks.

'Oh Ian, will you look at her? She's probably about six and a half stones. Can you see how sharply her bones are poking out? Is it possible an ED is also undiagnosed?'

'Possible, might just be self-neglect though?'

'Yeh, we'll keep an eye out, monitor the situation.'

Thanks for noticing my bones sticking out, lady, I cringe. They think I have an eating disorder. It feels as though I am under a microscope having cells stripped from me with a scalpel. The familiar flood of anger warms me. It rises inside, a slow tide of heated blood. From the tips of my toes, the sensation increases… it is them against me, always. *The bastards.*

After a brief pause in their conversation, I sense a presence looming in my space again. I tense, careful to keep my eyes still underneath their lids.

The man says,:'Uh-Oh. We'll have to watch this one, Sinead. It says here she's a fighter.'

'What, this little thing?'

'There's a bit of a forensic history here. Apparently, she attacked her foster parents a while back. Oh… it also says she can be verbally and physically aggressive towards clinical staff. Mary becomes violent, leaving others badly injured.'

'But she's tiny–and she looks so young, like one of those little porcelain dolls. She reminds me of my Juno. Hard to imagine she's going to wake up and come out swinging any minute.'

Her voice has a slight catch in it. For Juno? Or me? I wonder. They need not worry; I am not going to "come out swinging." I learned a long time ago physical aggression only makes things harder for me. It would prolong my incarceration and get me pumped full of tranqs. What they are talking about happened years ago, but I am not surprised it is in my records. If you are in the system and you fuck up even once, it stays on your record forever. It poisons how people view you in the future, and they can say whatever they want about you. Your record taints anything you have to say about anything. Bosh. That is me forever, stained with someone else's indelible judgement.

'What happened to her? How was she admitted?'

'Mary Jameson arrived with the police on a "one three six," hollering she was going to end it all. She was openly responding to hallucinations, and members of the public called the police. They arrived with an ambulance team to pick her up. She climbed over the fence to reach the river.'

'Oh my God–that close, aye?'

He sounds shocked.

The cloths soothing strokes continue, dipping in water, then anointing my skin. I stop enjoying its coolness on my hot skin, gritting my teeth, and resenting the intrusion, but I stay silent. It is important to know their intentions. Alerting them to my consciousness will trigger a guarded conversation.

The police ruined my immediate plans, but whichever shithole they have taken me to, I will escape. I will finish what I started and reunite with my mum. Whatever it takes.

I know smug sympathy will rest on their faces if I open my eyes, and I consider slapping it off. My limbs feel weak, and my brain is woolly, so I flex my small fists as a test. Nothing speeds the after-effects of sedation through the system. It takes time to regain control of my limbs again, depending how much was given.

When the woman speaks again, her tone is upbeat.

'Hmm, what a shame, aye Ian? Being so young and everything. Never mind, Mary's at The Rainbow Unit now. Sure, we've had other patients whose cases seem just as… challenging? Our Dr. Sinclair turned their lives around.'

'Yes, true. What about Scott and Miles? They were hopeless cases, end of the line types. That stinker Scott's got a job and flat, and Miles is ready for discharge soon. Dr. Sinclair is a miracle worker, I swear!'

I mentally scoff at the hero worship in the woman's tone. Who is it for, this bloke? Ian, or that doctor? What a sad bitch.

'Sinead, will you be okay with the rest of the paperwork?'

Unconsciousness attempts to reclaim me, and I struggle against it. Life has a shitty sense of humour. I had wanted to be an eagle or something and here I am, trapped like a bird with a broken wing. "Fuck my life," is my last thought before sleep embraces me again.

CHAPTER 3

Throat burning with thirst, I open my eyes, searching my surroundings to see if there is anything I can drink. After pushing my long hair from my face, I spot a jug of water with a beaker beside it and push up, so I can help myself to it.

Hands cradling my head, I wait for the room to stop spinning. After a quick sniff of the liquid, I test a bit on my lips. Confirming it is harmless H-2-O, I pour it out into the beaker. Although I am holding the container with two hands, the water slurps over the side as I drink it. Allowing myself one long belch, I wipe my mouth with the back of my hand, then stare at it.

Lifting both hands above the covers, I examine them properly. I can see they are still wounded, but they are clean. Turning them over, I submit my clean nails and digits to scrutiny with round-eyed wonder. Then, after lifting the covers and peering down, I suck in a quick indrawn breath and my mouth makes an "O." A night dress. I touch one of my unsoiled hands to the soft material now gracing my torso. It feels so nice against my skin… a night dress.

After a quick survey of my surroundings, I fold myself back underneath the heavy linen bedding. I haven't been this well-cared for since before my mum died. A thought burrs its way into my mind: Where are my friends?

'Little Mary, Jo, Lou, Dolores - where are you?' I dart my grey gaze around the corners, searching for them. For a few tense seconds, anxiety rises inside me, making my stomach clench. Then I release my fear with a shrug. I know I need not worry, because my friends are almost always with me. Sometimes they go away, but I know they will come back soon.

'Toto, we're not in Kansas anymore... swit swoo.'

I let out a silent whistle in an impressed breath. Have they taken me here by mistake? This place is ridiculously swish.

The last time they detained me under the mental health act, they locked me in a room on my own because of my risk of violence. However, my current environment falls under the category of "exclusive."

During my previous sectioning, I had slept on a bed as giving as a wood chip box. Urine had lingered in the air and bedding, so pungent the odour stung my nostrils. When I had left my room to use the diabolical communal bathroom, a sea of screams accompanied me. The owners were the strange individuals who roamed behind me.

The room I found myself in has struck me dumb. It is swanky, and here I am. In a comfy bed and dressed up in a soft night dress.

I look around me. The oak door is closed and matches the armoire, chest of drawers, and wardrobe. I can see it has no lock. Standard. It does not surprise me. The rooms are plush, but they would never allow a lock on a patient's door. Not in a million years.

Light floods the room and the large windows sparkle - clean. Tilting my head, absorbing the warm sunshine drifting through, I smile. I love the sun.

Gazing around, I realise there is another door in my room, wide open. How did I not notice that first? Angry at myself, I eyeball the doorway, wondering how I could have missed this. Scanning the room for potential weapons, I mumble to myself... if anyone runs at me, they will not catch me off guard.

It remains silent, informing me of its emptiness. I smirk, allowing my shoulders to relax, slumping down again in the bed.

'Stand down, Mary, stand down.'

Wanting to extend my view into the room, I angle myself but then catch sight of a shower and toilet. My mouth drops open as I process what it means.

'Holy shit. I have my own bathroom. Fuck me, this is living the life.'

Just then, I inhale the scent of lilacs... and toast. My tummy rumbles, making me aware I am starving. Thinking back to my last meal, my lip curls at the memory that occurs to me. The tin of beans with a congealed grey skin... when *was* that? The thought does not curtail my appetite and my tummy groans again.

Awe rises inside me, and I stuff it back down. What difference does it make? They boss you around, interrogate and jab you up, and someone in charge decides there is no more to do. Then they kick you out.

I relax back against the pillows again, no longer impressed. *Whatever* - and where the hell are my friends? I look round again, restless for my companions.

As I continue to absorb my new environment, I realise with a frown I can hear humdrum noises outside, but no screaming. Footsteps outside come closer to the room. My back straight, I sit up alert again, but the effort it costs makes me shake. My arms slide under the covers to disguise the weakness and I exhale a deep, slow breath.

There is a knock at the door and it opens–just a touch, then a man sticks his head around in, peeping into the room.

'Yeh?'

'Good morning, Mary. I'm a nurse; Ian–can I come in and have a quick chat?'

'Whatever.'

Ian comes into the room, silent on the thick carpet. He is close enough I receive a waft of his powerful aftershave.

I watch him, noting Ian does not get too close to me. He has stopped at the foot of my bed. Smart. He knows the drill.

I roll my eyes. Prick.

'It's nice to see you're awake. How are you feeling, Mary?'

'Alright. Come to tell me to fuck off now? Fine by me.'

My chin is sticking out and I grind my teeth, recognising his voice. He sounds like the mug who warned the lady about my violent past, when I was first admitted.

Crossing my arms over my bedcovers, I raise one defiant eyebrow, staring at him. Bothered.

Ian's eyes widen, and he takes a wary step back at my hostile demeanour. He shakes his head with vehemence.

'What? No, of course not, Mary. It's nothing like that.'

'I came to welcome you to The Rainbow Unit. Tell you a bit about us here and check how you are.'

'OK...'

I feel my shoulders relax again and I exhale, allowing myself to slump back against the plumped-up pillows again. Although I would have left if they had discharged me, the idea of some breathing space is welcome. A holiday from my shitty real life before I get back to my mum. The memory of feeling like a hunted animal is not pleasant.

David will want to stop me and will show up the second my shadow slips around the corner from this place. This hospital, full of sunshine and people knocking on doors before they come in. At home, David had been increasingly present lately, and if I leave, there will be a sneak attack on me, undertaken with swift and malevolent glee. I scowl at my visitor.

'Oh.'

'What?'

'We did "obs" on your vitals while you were asleep and need to check them every fifteen minutes for a while. Just to see how you're doing. Is that O.K. Mary?'

Ian shifts, pulling at his tunic.

Rolling my eyes again, I stick my middle finger up as an answer.

'OK then... I'm sorry about the intrusion, Mary. I'm afraid it's standard procedure in a psychiatric institution.'

'Why ask me then if I don't have a choice?'

'I hear what you're saying, Mary, and I'm sorry. A restrictive measure, but it's what we have to do, for now.'

Ian clears his throat. He sounds like a door-to-door salesperson with his foot jammed in the door. Another NHS politician. I shrug, glancing down at his ID card. It dangles from his waist instead of from a lanyard around his neck. Someone once told me that was because of the risk of strangulation. I can see the risk. Bullshit artists. Them and us. They are all the same.

'Whatever.'

I'm not a "happy camper," but there is no point in bucking against the rules. It would not serve me to kick off. I know the ropes, and where that kind of rebellion gets me. Lash out in anger, and the hospital puts you on a "one to one." It happened before, one member of the staff *always observing me.*

The constant monitoring from staff had made me explode with rage and I tried to make them go away the only way I knew - violence. They put me on a "two to one," and kept me medicated, docile.

I would be vulnerable under sedation. It took away my voice and my ability to defend myself against other patients or staff. It made me a prisoner in my body, and I liked it even less than the constant one-to-one supervision. No. I do not hit out whenever I am detained, no matter what. But that does not mean I have to be a kiss arse or deprive the staff of my witty repartee. I smirk.

'So... I mentioned before that we're in The Rainbow Unit? Well, allow me to expand a little?'

'Get on with your spiel, then.' I treat him to a saccharine smile.

Ian is not put off by my unimpressed tone and displays his even teeth in a wide smile. I wonder if he has an even temperament to match the teeth, or if he will be one of the tricky ones. Hmm, maybe that smile was why the other nurse liked him. I glare at him.

'The Rainbow Unit is an exclusive treatment and research facility set up by world renowned Dr Sinclair fifteen years ago. We use state-of-the-art resources to treat mental and physical health.'

'Are you a salesperson or something? What kind of commission do you get?'

I ask, unmoved by his words. Ian blinks at me and says nothing in response.

I snort at my humour. Goddamn, I am witty, and I have only just woken up. I'm here all week folks. Well… maybe.

The nurse continues as though I have not spoken, and my wisecracks go unacknowledged. He obviously does not see the funny side. I snigger to myself. What a shock that is.

'When you came in yesterday, Dr. Sinclair wasn't able to come and meet you. She had an emergency with an ex-patient. The doctor is free in one hour and wanted me to ask you to come meet her. Do you feel up to that today, Mary?'

I examine him. He uses a gentle tone, but his eyes are not soft.

Ian had been kind when he thought I was asleep, though. He had mentioned I reminded him of "Juno." I remember.

'No. It was Sinead who said that.' Little Mary's voice corrects me, making me jump.

'Sinead?'

'The nurse.'

Ian and my friend answer in synchrony. I whip around, searching for the owner of the sweet little girl's voice.

Ian's eyes narrow.

I smile when I spot her and sigh my relief, shoulders softening. Now my little friend is back, I can relax.

'Here I am, Mary.'

Her dimples show when she beams, and the crooked charm of it illuminates her plain brown wren countenance and makes me grin right back at her.

I glimpse Ian's expression and can see his eyes have sharpened on my face.

So what? I shrug to myself. They already know I am mentally ill. That is why I am in here. They have labelled me "crazy" since I was ten years old when David showed up during the first incident. Maybe even before that. I am sure they have read my file by now. Everybody here will either hate me, feel sorry for me, or fear me. Either way, they will know I am a hopeless case. Nothing can change that fact, there is no-one to help me. They had taken the only way I had to end my suffering and now David is aware of my plans. It will be difficult to try again. I am stuck here for a while.

'Who's this Dr. Sinclair then?' I give an unimpressed sniff.

Ian beams and seems to trip over himself to share the background of the doctor.

'She allows patients to call her Adelia. She's highly esteemed - a legend. Adelia's a psychiatrist, top in her field, *and* she's a neuroscientist as well. Can you imagine that? Dr. Sinclair has been doing ground-breaking research in the treatment of schizophrenia since she opened this centre.' Ian finishes, breathless.

Sycophant. My mouth opens, making a dry "O."

'Whoop.'

Ian does not acknowledge my sarcasm but sounds friendly as he asks me, 'Can I get you anything, Mary?' I stare him dead in his eyes that do not match his tone and stay silent in response.

Beside him, I can see Little Mary is speaking to me. She is leaning forward, but no sound is emanating from her. So weird, but that happens sometimes. Like, my psychosis is on the fritz. Shrugging, I turn my attention back to Ian.

'What about personal effects from your home? Do you need anything from there? I can organise someone to collect things for you?'

'No.'

Nosy bastard. I snort. If they find anything in that hellhole, they'll be lucky. It is a nightmare mix of dirty dishes, filthy clothes, rubbish, flies, and stench. My hand moves to my neck to touch the necklace my mum gave me. There is nothing I want from there. As long as I have –

'Where the fuck is my necklace?'

The sun has risen further and streams in through the window. It lights up the tiny dust particles sharing the large space between us.

Ian increases the gap further, as he steps towards the door again.

I shake my head. I need my necklace. Did I leave it in my stained nightmare of a bedsit?

I never take it off. I bite my bottom lip to stop the tears and wring my hands in consternation. That necklace is the only thing I have left of my mum, except for memories. When I went into foster care, they got rid of anything I arrived with. My foster parents told me everything I had brought with me was rubbish.

I shake my head. Click. Click. Click. Radio static turns on.

My heart sinks in a reassured way. Here it comes.

'Well, isn't this nice?' Dolores' voice flutters.

Dolores is not holding her knitting for a change but is still clasping her hands together.

Where is Louise?

'I'm here, Mary. I couldn't come for a while, sorry.'

I smile my relief at her. Cool and preppy in her appearance, with her sweater knotted over her shoulder.

'Ah, now this is really nice. Look, you have the T.V. and, everything… you see? Lovely. Enjoy some luxury here and get well quickly, Mary,' Jo's deep Ghanaian accent extols, as he moves to stand next to Little Mary. She has her head in her hands but has stopped mouthing words.

Jo always wears traditional African clothing. This varies between a striped smock or a bright purple, yellow, and black toga. He had told me they were his family's pattern and colours.

I hold out my hand, gesturing to Jo to approach my bed.

He comes and as Jo and I sit in silence together, I think to myself how good his bedside manner is. I feel calmer just by seeing him.

Ian pauses his flight from my room but does not comment on my guests, instead offering me refreshments. 'Something to eat, Mary? Tea and toast?'

I nod with vague eyes.

Ian seems to understand I am distracted by my friends, and I am glad he does not compete with them for my attention with anymore conversation. It annoys me when people do that.

Their chatty voices lower from a building stream to a babbling brook as they speak amongst themselves. Grateful for the familiar sound, I relax, laying back in my bed and shutting my eyes. I listen. My long lashes flutter against my pale skin.

I am relieved they are here, but it is probably best not to look shit-bug crazy when Dr. Sinclair comes to see me, if at all possible. My breathing slows and I keep my eyelids closed.

Ian leaves the room.

CHAPTER 4

I sit upright, shuddering for breath. I had been dreaming of lightning striking a field. Yellowed grass covers the vast field, and I had been running. Low and fast, zigzagging to dodge the blue bolts of lightning that struck down in powerful forks. I sprinted from tree to tree as I tried to find cover, but the limbs were bare, and when I looked at them, I became scared they might attract the lightning. Mouth dry, I scanned the empty horizon, then peered up at the ominous sky. I stood still and allowed the inevitable strike. As I did so, the sky turned a deep blue, and it flooded me with energy.

Then I wake up.

I see the cup and saucer standing on the chest of drawers as soon as I open my eyes. Ian had not woken me up when he brought back my tea. My mouth pulls down at the thought of someone was so close to me while I slept. I pull the bedcovers up over my chest. What is the matter with me? How had I not woken up?

The nursing staff forced me to rise early. I use my en-suite bathroom and open the matching oak wardrobe and chest of drawers to find they contain a plentiful stock of clean and quality clothing.

The other nurse stands, humming as she assists me. It is the nicer one; "Sinead."

'The last person here left their shit.'

'No. It's all yours, Mary. We ordered it especially for you. Wear whatever you like.'

My tone is terse, but Sinead gives a sincere laugh.

Returning to bed, I lay back, face screwed up and arms folded.

'Where's my other stuff? Where's my necklace?'

'That filthy lot? We had to get rid of it, I'm afraid. We kept the necklace though, lovey. I'll have a look in storage for you. Chop-chop now. Can you believe - the founder of this entire hospital, Dr. Sinclair, is waiting at the restaurant to meet you? She's cleared her schedule especially.'

Sinead beams at me with an expectant air about her and I keep my expression belligerent.

My bloodshot eyes narrow as her words sink in. "*Chop-chop now*." Piss off.

I treat her to the middle finger.

Sinead guffaws, but her face still does not lose its pleasant expression.

'Well, then. I'll just leave you to your morning ablutions, shall I? One hour, please, Mary. Dr. Sinclair appreciates punctuality,-' the nurse tells me with a smile and taps her watch as one last reminder.

Sinead leaves my room.

Putting my head back on the pillows, I shut my eyes, weighing up my choices. Ignore orders from that stuck-up bitch doctor and stay in bed. Or get up and do what I am told. What bullshit does this woman want with me? Guarantee, there is something.

I tap my toes under my covers as I mull it over.

When doctors tell you to do something and you blank them, they pump you full of drugs and diagnose you with something else. Then they smear "aggressive" and "risk" all over your records, making them less likely to let you out. Ever. Maybe it is nice here, but it is not fun to live in captivity. Being told when to get up, go out, take a dump. I do not know who is in here with me.

Sitting up, I resolve to meet this big shot doctor. Besides... the food they gave me was nice, and I want to see what else is on offer.

Remembering the wardrobe, I get up and flick through its contents. There are jeans with different coloured T-shirts, comfy knickers, and bra, inoffensive. Pulling out a few labels, I bite my lip. My mum used to like this shop; it is grannyish but not bad. Mum always said they were "quality." I smile, wiping my eyes with the back of my hand, then get dressed.

Ian comes to escort me to his boss ten minutes before we are due. Fuck it. Laying the brush back down, I give up my attempts to de-tangle my matted hair, and we leave the room to head for the dining area. Fuck it. Who cares anyway?

Seated at a table is an attractive woman in her mid-late forties. Tousled blonde hair, large blue eyes, and exquisite bone structure housed in an elegant frame. She is wearing black trousers, a white satin blouse, and an air of self-contained confidence that makes me itch to slap her.

I make a mental sweep of the room and its exits. One way in and another out. The doorways are clear.

'Good afternoon. You must be Mary? I'm Dr. Adelia Sinclair–you may call me Adelia.' Her upper-class English accent grates on me.

Flicking a check at her wristwatch, Adelia leans forward, like a rattlesnake striking at its prey. I veer back with a frown.

Adelia holds out her hand to me and I wave it away with a tut. Hell no, bitch.

We sit mute, facing one another head on.

Experience tells me this is a waiting game. A battle of wills designed to put me at a psychological disadvantage. A pissing contest. It will not work, though.

I smirk. It never does, not anymore.

Freezing in place, I am alert. In contrast, Adelia appears nonchalant, and wears a small smile of patience on her china-doll face. Her eyes remain trained on me, and I scan her back.

I catalogue her many physical attributes with disgust.

She looks like a French model, *and* she is a doctor. Must be nice for her.

I grind my teeth at the injustice of it all but remain unmoved.

'You look like a fucking marble statue.' I snort at my wit.

Damn it. Biting my bottom lip, I shift my feet, staring down. I could kick myself for giving in first. I wait until my breathing is less shallow and I feel more in control. Then I scrutinise Adelia's face again. Swallowing the ever-present anger, I acknowledge it never pays to piss-off the "top dog."

Positioning myself where I can see the room's occupants and exits, I clock objects likely to be a threat to me. My lashes are long enough to hide my covert glances around us, and my undercover looks confirm we are not observed by anyone. The raised border along all the walls will sound an alarm if struck. Staff will come at a run - rapid tranqs at the ready.

It is bright in here. I raise my eyebrows, seeing that like the luxurious bedroom suite, they have not bolted the furniture down to the floor. Good, I can hurl the chairs and tables in a scrap. My shoulders relax and I blow out.

Classical music plays from speakers in the ceiling, drifting down to me, and I see a small table where two people sit chatting– nurses or clients? Something I am never sure of.

What had I overheard a nurse say about an eccentric ward psychiatrist once? "Where does a tree go to hide? *In the woods*."

Through my various detainments, I had found that to be true. Psychiatric staff can be screwy.

In here though, it is the opposite. Everybody looks sane. Well, everyone except me.

Without thinking, I scratch my arm, wincing as I catch the broken skin. My nails are jagged at their edges.

'I will show you some of the unit while I tell you a bit about what we do here.'

She falls silent and just stands, watchful. The surreal nature of my situation occurs to me, and I nibble at my bottom lip. Where have all my friends gone? Is David still close by? It is strange I have not heard from them all. After all these years, they have just disappeared. Unless I did not wake up from unconsciousness?

Staring back at the doctor, my eyes squint, and my bony face puckers, as though I am sucking on a bagful of lemons.

Adelia, she had said… with her name badge pinned to her blouse and her swipe card hanging from her pocket. She looks like visiting royalty. "Queen bitch," I dub her. Life must be so easy for her. I bet.

'Hating you.' The aggressive edge rises in my voice.

Surreptitiously, I pinch myself, but nothing happens, so I dig my nails into the scarred palms of my hands. Is Adelia real? Is this happening, or am I still in my flat, surrounded by stench and misery? I question myself. Adelia remains in front of me, clear as day. As she regards me, I feel as though her blue eyes are peering into my soul, stripping it bare, layer by layer.

She smiles, and I am exasperated to see straight white teeth completing her perfection. Of course, she has the movie star teeth to go with her "Grace Kelly" movie star good looks. I close my mouth and feel around my fuzzy teeth with the tip of my tongue. I wonder when I last brushed my teeth, and how bad my breath smells.

Adelia does not seem to notice my sour breath but is staring at me quizzically. I push my small fists underneath my thin thighs, wincing at the pain this causes me.

'Are your palms sore?'

My mouth falls open. I did not even notice her taking her gaze off my face. I nibble at my lower lip. Without thinking, my hand flutters to my neck, then I clench it back into a fist so she cannot see the scars and deep gouges in my palms. My nails, torn and sharp, do their job.

'Mind your fucking business, yeh?'

'That is alright, Mary. We will dress the wounds for you. It will ease the pain and avoid infection. I should not have asked you in such a direct manner.' She tuts.

I do not want to discuss my hands. It will give her too much insight into my inner thoughts. I look around the room to see if anyone else is in the room or has overheard.

Adelia puts her own unsullied palm up in my direction.

Adelia shakes her hair back with a careless confidence that belies her deferential tone. Is she just fucking with me, trying to put me on the back foot by questioning me about my "self-harming?" Is she asking about it to humiliate me? Make me feel small?

I study her with narrowed eyes, trying to decipher her intentions.

Adelia brushes a non-existent crease out of her top, then smiles at me with her head tilted to one side. She looks kind and genuine.

Battling my increasing agitation and paranoia, I decide to take her at face value. Glancing down at myself, I jam my mitts into my pockets, forcing my foot to stop tapping.

'It's just a habit I have.'

My eyes stay downcast, but not through shyness. Fuck off. Do not *dare* to ask me anymore questions. I simmer with rage and fear.

'And when do you do it?'

'If I'm... not sure.'

She sounds curious and my tone is halting. When I flick a glance at her, I notice her eyes registering my restless foot.

My telepathy must be on the spritz because Adelia has not heard me tell her to fuck off in my mind. I smile at my humour, and the fear I am experiencing reduces. As it does, I feel less angry. She is not giving up on this, and I know they always make it a massive deal if I hide it in hospitals. Best to be open with this or it will bite me in the arse.

My tone is halting, but I know it is also abrupt.

Adelia frowns, and I think her pale skin takes on a green tinge underneath the fluorescent lighting. She looks like a pretty witch from *The Wizard of Oz*.

'Not sure? Not sure of what?'

'I do it if I'm not sure if things are real or not… Sometimes I get confused.'

'I am real.'

Silence warms my cheeks, and I avoid her penetrating stare, I am not used to conversation outside of my head anymore.

She pulls her ID card from her waistband, showing me her badge.

'See?' Adelia shifts, pulling her chair closer, and I tense in reaction.

Staring at our positioning, I note we have both sat far from the table. Adelia gestures for me to emulate her, and I scrape my chair along the shiny floor. Nails down a chalkboard.

I make no comment, but a certain quality in Adelia's voice triggers a vision of the past.

A mind movie regurgitates in my mind of a time I had come across a kitten. My eyes fill with tears at the memory, even though it was years ago. Tiny mewling and fur. Using my softest tone, I had called to her, as she had hidden under the burned-out car in the alleyway I had spotted her in. The kitty had shivered on the spot, then had darted away. I looked, but she had vanished, absorbed into the maze of industrial buildings surrounding us. A sucker for animals, I had never forgotten her.

Now, all these years later, I remember, because Adelia is using the same coaxing tone I had used with that kitten. Adelia leans forward, grabbing my attention back.

'Mary? I'm not sure if they explained to you, but the police picked you up. They were worried you would harm yourself. This is the Rainbow Unit in Surrey. It is a psychiatric treatment centre just outside of London. Do you remember anyone telling you?'

'I am the consultant psychiatrist in this ward. I believe you have met some of our staff?'

I nod my head. Well, I can remember overhearing them anyway. With a shrug, I tug at the collar of the T-shirt I am wearing to cool down. Adelia's scent lingers in the air, assaulting my nostrils with her expensive perfume. Sophisticated. It's probably the one called Chanel Number Five everyone has heard of, or something even more exclusive that only the "very best" people know about. The static increases in volume and I silently warn them not to destroy this moment of normality for me. "*Are you sitting comfortably, children? Then I will begin…*"

'There's Rose, our lady, for refreshments. She handles the Michelin star meals we provide. I employ Ian, a ward nurse, Sinead - another ward nurse, John and Jackie, support workers. Angie is ward sister, and there's Dr. Pfeiffer who is on call with this unit and is our medical doctor. Occupational therapists, OT's Clarissa and Duncan will support you. They organise activities and will help get you ready to re-join the community.'

'There are other patients here, all admitted under the Mental Health Act. You will meet some as we walk around, others you will meet later. This is an eight-bed unit.' Adelia's blue stare drills into mine. 'We have seven patients in residence because I have discharged one of our patients successfully back into the community.'

Adelia is smiling and I mirror her, anything to ward off the static.

What does she want, a medal? I yawn, mouth wide, and my ears pop.

Adelia continues without commenting. 'Although we are a private facility based in Surrey, we receive referrals from the entire UK. We are in the privileged position of having the choice of whom we admit, and we welcome you to the Rainbow Unit.'

Adelia smiles.

I refrain from speaking, instead, staring at the T.V. on the wall. An advert for a cleaning product is on. My heartbeat gallops. It does that sometimes, without provocation.

I can hear the static increasing, and it is distracting me. I gaze around the room, my eyeballs flitting this way and that as I search for "them." The clicking always comes with the voices, but even with the noise of the announcement, it still makes me jump as the first voice speaks to me.

'I'm scared.' Little Mary is whimpering from underneath the table.

Whatever is she doing under there? Feeling tired, I close my eyes. Ignoring Little Mary helps a bit, but then the voices of the others join in the fray.

I feel a light tap on my hand. I open my eyes to see Adelia has tapped my hand and is now standing up. Her lips turn up at the ends.

The talking stops as though by magic and I blink.

I can no longer see Little Mary under the table. Where is she? I rub my eyes, then regard Adelia with surprised gratitude as I enjoy the abnormal feeling of clarity. It reminds me of the feeling you get from menthol and eucalyptus cold lozenges. So. Clear.

Chapter 5

'Come along, Mary. We will go around to meet some of the others – but only if you feel up to it, of course?' she invites me.

I consider the choice for a moment. I need Adelia on my side, and I want to know more about where I am - and how I can get out of here quicker. Also, I accept I am still a bag of bones and cannot handle any trouble right now. I make my decision and stand up, slowly.

Adelia bares her perfect teeth again, then also stands. She resembles a glamourous hostess from a game show, but she sounds like someone official. Like I imagine a surgeon in the army would speak.

'We supply all our guests with basic wardrobe items. Hopefully, you will have found nightwear placed at the end of your bed, and your wardrobe and chest of drawers should be stocked with spring/summer clothing and accessories. Unfortunately, we have to guess at our patients sizing, so we have everything stocked in advance of your arrival. However, it is our ward nurse Angie who completes the orders. She is usually very exact with her estimates.'

Angie does what? I feel a bit woozy after standing up to follow her, so I put a hand to my forehead taking deep breaths. How long have I been here?

Adelia taps my shoulder and I flinch away, unused to being touched.

'Take your time. You are not at optimal health, Mary. In addition, you have been horizontal in bed for several days. It takes time for the body to become acclimatised to normal movement again,' she tells me.

I nod and take a steadying breath.

'O.K.' I tell her, then begin to walk. I need to get my shit together. Maybe she could offer me another meal or a drink? That might help for a start. I feel waspish. It is O.K. for her.

A bubbly middle-aged brunette walks along and interrupts Adelia with a wicked grin. I come to a halt beside them, steadying myself with one hand against the wall.

'Hi there, I'm Jackie Barlow a support worker here.'

Jackie holds her arm out to shake my hand.

You will be waiting for a long time there, sister.

I look at her outstretched hand with disdain on my face. I leave it there, hung out to dry in no-man's-land, then frown at the newcomer, crossing my arms.

'Jackie Barlow,' she repeats. As though I am asking her. 'You must be Mary Jameson?'

I shrug. Obviously.

Jackie continues to speak, 'Ah... Well, it is nice to meet you, Mary. I'm sure I'll be seeing you around. Welcome to The Rainbow Unit.' She gives me a jaunty wink as she leaves.

Adelia starts walking again, and I follow her slowly on automatic pilot. I look left and right with quick, sweeping glances and make sure my mouth does not hang open as it wants to. I have never seen such a shining haven of purity before. The polished parquet floors, the yellow walls the same colour as the cheerful flowers in a vase in my room, the tasteful pictures scattered on the walls. I sniff. The air smells like fresh bread, lilacs, and money... Shit loads of it. I smirk at my thoughts. Damn I am witt-eeeyy.

'At the moment, you're here under a section two of the Mental Health Act for a period of assessment and treatment for up to twenty-eight days. A community psychiatric nurse -they call them CPN's from the mental health team will come and see you for a chat about how things are going before you are ready to leave here.

'Yours has been in touch. Her name is Eileen Mcintosh. Eileen will be your care co-ordinator. After twenty-eight days has ended, you will either stay for further treatment, or you will be discharged back into the community.'

A song I remember pops into my head: Should I stay or... I blink the song worm away and struggle to refocus on what this doctor is telling me.

Shit, she is dry-up. I want to lie down again before this woman bores me to sleep while I stand.

I stop in front of a picture catching my eye.

'Is that a Van Gogh?' I ask her. 'I used to love this one. I can remember.' Sudden tears spring to my eyes. I do not know how it is familiar, I only know it is triggering emotion in me.

Adelia's face softens as she looks at the picture.

'You have good taste, Mary – it's called: *The Starry Night*. It's beautiful isn't it,' she states.

We come to a stop at a reception area with comfy sofa's, an expensive looking drinks machine, and some newspapers.

'Let's take a rest, shall we? Your mind and body have suffered from a great deal of trauma, and you will not have returned to your optimal health yet.'

Adelia guides me to sit down and a rotund woman with matted brown hair wearing bunny slippers stumbles past us. She looks like a sleepwalker shaken awake from an indescribable nightmare. Dazed and petrified at the same time.

'Well, good afternoon, Sharon. How are you today?' Adelia asks her.

I look at her. This is so bizarre. Adelia is speaking to this woman as though everything is just fine.

'Theykeepcomingformystuffstealingmypropertyburglarsthe lotofthemfuckingthievesIhatethemIhatethemfilthyscumallwant mystuff,' comes the strange answer.

I make a faint whistle under my breath. OK then. I am not the only one cuckoo for Coco Pops around here. Clearly.

Sharon sits down at the edge of the sofa. She is staring at the space in front of her, rocking backwards and forwards. Then she stops, all of a sudden looking angry and spitting out profanity. Her words are unrelated and disjointed.

I knot my eyebrows together and lean in, trying to listen and make sense of what she is saying. The frogs are doing what to Michael Jackson? Eating him? What?

Adelia seems not to notice the strangeness of Sharon's demeanour or conversation and sits a little closer to her while she addresses her, speaking to Sharon in a quiet, soothing tone.

I move further away from them both. That fruit loop is not about to attack me. I am not up to my full strength and cannot protect myself yet. Let Adelia take one for the team. My lips twitch at the picture. Adelia, with her perfect nose suddenly punched crooked like a prize-fighter. Good. Serves her right. Keeping me from being with my mum, the queen bitch.

Adelia begins to initiate conversation between myself and Sharon. Oh no.

'Sharon, this is Mary. She's new here.'

Sharon has calmed down but still looks like she is in a world of her own. She now appears to be tracking invisible flying objects in the air in front of her. Well, it is apt if that *is* what she is seeing, because she looks like a space cowboy. Lost in a completely parallel universe.

I tilt my head to the side as I regard her. I wonder if I look that out of it. Half chewed at pictographic images flickered into my mind of myself, sprinting in a field with the cold wet grass on the sole of one of my feet, because I had one shoe missing. I recall I had the sensation I was being suffocated by my clothes and had thought about ripping them off me. I had felt compelled to flee, to run away as fast as I could, to hide...to seek freedom. From David.

I purse my lips. Yup. Odds are I do look the same level of crazy.

A guy in chinos with bad breath and a polo shirt bounces up to us. He holds his hand out to Sharon while he addresses us all.

'Hi all. Sharon – we have the baking and cooking session startin' in a few minutes. You said you wanted to be reminded.'

Sharon gazes at him with her mouth open and stops talking to herself.

Adelia glares at the newcomer. Her cornflower blue eyes shoot icicles at him. Whoa. Note to self – do not piss Adelia off.

The guy catches the full power of her gaze, and does a quick two-step backwards, then slaps his hand to his forehead.

'Argh, I'm so sorry. Ladies, do forgive me! You must be the new guest we were expecting - Mary? Forgive me, welcome. I'm *Duncan* and I'm one of the OT's here. I work with another OT, Clarissa, and we plan all the activity for inside and in the community.'

'I always advocate for good manners at The Rainbow Unit. Civilisation is what separates us from the animals, and politeness is an important expression of being civilised,' Adelia tells us all.

Duncan nods quickly agreeing, then bares his yellow teeth readily. He remains where he stops, regarding Sharon.

'Would you care to join us for today's craft activity, Sharon?' Duncan waits with an air of expectation.

I step back and give him the side eye. Fucking sort your breath out, mate. Then I snort. He seems positive Sharon will join him. I doubt that will happen.

Sharon lowers her hands, and she looks at us and then stands up.

'Yes, I would. Good day to you both,' Sharon bade us - in a voice reminiscent of a seventeenth century governess.

I double take Sharon. I have to look again, just to make sure it is her speaking. My mouth makes a small circle. I did not see that coming.

Our companion then walks off, her hand resting on Duncan's proffered elbow like a stiff-backed character from a Jane Austen novel. She does not spare us a second glance.

I try to lower my eyebrows, but they seem to be stuck high up on my forehead and refuse to obey.

Adelia does not seem put off her stride by this interruption and begins to tell me about the area the Rainbow Unit is situated in, and the layout of the building and grounds.

'It is a previous stately home,' she tells me.

No shit. It is a monolith straight out of *The Great Gatsby*. A brief flutter of excitement rises in me as Adelia pronounces when I have recovered a bit more of my strength and she considers it safe, she will allow me to explore the manicured gardens. I will take any glimpse of freedom offered to me.

Adelia tells me she designed the landscape herself, and every section of it is perfectly symmetrical. There is a maze she configured, and Adelia herself personally chose every plant bedded in the five acres of land framing the Rainbow Unit.

Adelia says at first, she used her inheritance to fund the site. Then, after a while, her research attracted overseas investors who had financed The Rainbow Unit. Adelia explains there are many philanthropists who search for an enterprise such as hers, and they contribute financially in order to ensure the stability of the project.

'We produce positive, quantifiable results you see. People leave here, and their lives are completely changed. They are given a brand-new start. I give you a chance to make positive contributions to society.'

Another female comes to join us in the small breakout area. She is a neat young woman, Asian in her appearance, and looks about my age. I look for the ID badge on the chest of her pressed white blouse but am not able to see one. She sits down and her shiny black ponytail swings as she crosses one navy chino covered leg over the other. She is gazing at us with one side of her mouth lifting.

Her pristine appearance annoys me, and I eye her up and down without a word.

She has a dainty nose and almond shaped dark eyes. I can see in those eyes she is fully aware of her own physical perfection and feels superior to me. She arranges her symmetrical face into a smile, displaying her straight, white teeth like a model in a Colgate advert. It does not touch her pretty eyes. *Hate you.*

'Hello, I'm Somya,' she tells me.

She sounds smug.

I point an index finger at my chest and ask her, 'Me?' Is this person talking to me?

Somya smiles again, nodding with regal complacency.

'Of course, you.' She sounds amused.

I frown at the conceit in her tone, my mouth turning down. She is giving me a headache.

'Well, in *that* case… feel free to fuck right off then, won't you?' I tell her.

There is a brief and frigid silence after my words and I put my hand to my mouth in a mocking gesture of shock.

'Oh no,' I say.

'How lovely,' Somya comments.

'I do try,' I say, then giving her a tight smile I offer her the two-fingered salute.

Adelia ignores the hostile exchange and introduces us like two guests at a party.

'Sonia, this is Mary. Mary has just joined us here at the Rainbow Unit. She'll be staying with us for a while as she continues her journey back to health.'

I notice *Somya* does not correct Adelia when she says her name wrong and keeps smiling at her. Urgh. What an arse lick. I roll my eyes. I do not have the time or energy for all this fake shit. I just need to get the hell out of here so I can get on with *it*. Back to my original plan. Eyes downcast I wait for Somya to go away again.

'Hi Mary, nice to meet you,' is all she says.

'Tell Mary a bit about your experience here, Sonia, won't you?' Adelia invites.

Somya smiles at Adelia, but her smile evaporates when she turns back to me.

'I've attended one hundred percent of my talking therapy sessions and enjoyed every single one of my psych-ed sessions. I'm compliant with the medication Adelia has prescribed, there's only one more treatment left I have to complete and then I'm good to go!' she tells me, flicking her ponytail back over her shoulder.

Somya is not looking at me anymore. She directs her explanation to Adelia, who starts nodding halfway through Somya's brief report of obedience.

I roll my eyes. Good for you, Somya.

'That's right, Sonia is doing so well! Sonia is showing true commitment to her recovery during her stay here. She is "all in" and is towards the end of her journey now.'

'Wow, that's great "Sonia,"' I say in my most cheerful voice.

I give Somya a slow clap.

Somya smiles, accepting her due praise. Then I see her register my expressionless face and realise I am being sarcastic. Blood floods her cheeks. Her nostrils flaring, she squints her eyes at me.

I snort a laugh. Oooo – Princess Somya does not like being mocked. Her face is transparent, even to me. It broadcasts her thoughts clearly and is telling me, "You bitch." Good. She can suck it.

I regard Adelia and keep my face blank. Whatever she is selling here, she seems confident – and Miss Superiority two thousand seems sane (although, I know you never can tell, not really) even if she is a big time smug-bag.

Maybe whatever Adelia is doing here could work for me too… For the first time in a really long time, I wonder if there might be a different way out of my world of torture than the one I have planned. Is there a future for me after all? I dare not allow myself to consider the possibility.

Somya takes her leave from us with a polite murmur.

Adelia smiles unperturbed in response, and we stand up to continue the tour of the unit.

I take a deep, simmering breath before I start to walk beside her.

Adelia's gait is coordinated and fast as she marches down the corridor. I trot along behind her in badly timed steps, my discordant walk annoying me.

A chubby young woman with bright blue eyes and bouncy brown ringlets walks down the hallway in the opposite direction. She smiles at me, showing off deep dimples.

'Alright? Nice to meet you,' the young woman calls out in her South London accent as we walk down the corridor towards her.

In response, I pin an oversized smile to my face. 'Wow - So nice to meet you too,' I sing out in reply.

I know I drip saccharine sarcasm. Fuck her.

As we resume our walk, I hold up an arm in the air, flipping my would-be greeter the middle finger without bothering to turn and face her to check she has seen.

Suck on that you cheerful cow.

Adelia does not comment, but I tell myself I had better reign it in for a bit, unless I want to go on a one-to-one.

We come to a stop.

'Hi, Derek, how are you doing today?' Adelia asks a whippet thin man.

The man gives a brittle laugh as his eyes dart around the corridor. After his short laugh, he gulps then nods quickly.

'I'm OK. Thanks, Adelia,' then asks, 'Aren't I?'

He sticks his hands in the pocket of his brown corduroys and shuffles one Hush Puppied foot in front of the other. He appears to wait on tenterhooks for Adelia's confirmation or denial.

Today *is* a good day, apparently.

Adelia smiles and nods. She tells him in a slow voice, 'Of course you are, Derek. You're doing fantastically well.'

Adelia puts her open hand out towards me.

I step back, kissing my teeth in irritation, then I look down and stare at the reflection of this *Clark Kent* of a man in the shiny floor. What the hell? All of a sudden, my thoughts become jumbled and heat up my translucent skin.

'Derek, this is Mary Jameson. She joined us here a couple of days ago. Mary, this is Derek. We have been lucky enough to have Derek here as a guest with us for a few months now. Derek has made remarkable progress with his recovery. I am expecting great results.'

Adelia smiles at Derek and her blue eyes shine.

Usually when I first meet someone, I like to mark the occasion with a rude comment, middle finger, or if I consider them especially deserving – a good old-fashioned spit in the face teamed with a "*fuck off*."

I do not enjoy social situations, and I fancy I can sense Derek's matching unease. Derek's delicate cheekbones are stained pink, and he smooths his collar-length hair down the sides of his angular face with both palms flat. His eyes are dropped so low he would not be able to see any gesticulations I made anyway.

This would not usually have bothered me, and he would have gotten the same treatment as everyone else, but as Derek's eyes rise from the floor, I acknowledge that for some reason, I find I do not have the heart to kick this puppy, or to treat him to a rendition of my usual repertoire.

His eyes. They are soulful pebbles of brown, very much like the puppy I just found myself comparing him to. I am a sucker for animals.

'Hi, Mary. Welcome,' he mumbles in a soft, cultured voice.

My eyebrows fly up again. Derek is unusual for my experience. He sounds well educated. A frisson spikes through my heart and causes my face to twinge at the same time Derek's eyes slide up to meet mine.

'Your eyes are luminous,' he tells me, then blushes again.

Derek has an air of guilelessness outside of my experience.

Lost for words, my mouth falls open. I touch my hands to my warm cheeks in surprise. My eyes are "luminous?"

The grey in my eyes turns stormy. 'You takin' the piss?'

I plant my feet hips width apart and stare at him. Goddamn. You show any sign of weakness and guaranteed, someone always takes the piss.

Derek shakes his head quickly. 'Of course not!'

I squint, and study Derek. Hmm.

Adelia's smile vanishes, and she looks from my face to Derek's, her face tight throughout our interaction.

'OK'

'Thank you, Derek. We have other people to meet so we will leave you to it now,' Adelia tells him in a clear dismissal.

The hint is not lost on Derek.

I look at Adelia's narrow eyes and chew on my bottom lip. I know I am not great at picking up social cues, but this woman seems annoyed. I wonder why.

Adelia floats on regally down the corridor. At a loss, I put a hand up in weak salute to Derek. I half turn to watch him take off down the corridor in a fast pace. His steps will be jerky, I bet.

Derek had not said anything else, but when I look back over my shoulder, I see he has stopped, and his brown eyes watch us as we continue down the hall. Derek seems fixated.

I pivot 'round and have to hustle again to catch up with my tour guide.

Adelia's back is ramrod straight and I address my question to it as I reach her.

'Did I do something wrong?' I ask Adelia.

Not that I am bothered. She can keep that stick up her arse and swivel on it for all I care.

'No.'

My eyebrows lift at her tone.

'Really?'

I smirk at her. I call "bullshit."

Silence skewers us both with its awkward grip and we continue to walk along without a word.

I shrug, and Adelia comes to a stop outside another door.

'Are you ok, Mary? You seem quiet?' Adelia asks before tapping on the door with a delicate touch.

I frown then double take. I am confused. Am I mistaken or has she got a strop on?

'Er...I'm fine thanks...' Then test the water. 'I mean, if you are?'

I remember my strategy. Adelia might be weird, but she is the alpha here after all.

Adelia smiles and shakes her head. Her silvery laugh tinkles out in the air between us. Even her breath smells perfect. Maybe she chugs down those sweets I used to like that tasted like soap?

'Of course. I'm fine, Mary, bless you for asking.'

She claps her ringless hands.

'Well, you've met Derek and the lady who called out briefly to us was called Marcia. Come on, let's go in and meet another one of your fellow residents.'

Against my will, I know my smile contains some relief. I have been forced to put a pin in my plans to join my mum for now, but as psych hospitals went, this place does not look half bad. I do not mind staying here for a while.

I nod, telling Adelia, 'Alright, yeah. I can do that.'

CHAPTER 6

Adelia knocks on the door for the second time.

'Hi, Sophie, can we come in?'

Silence greets us first, but then we hear, 'Yes.'

We walk into a room similar to my own.

A young woman sits crossed legged on the bed, in bright red dungarees with a drawing pad on her knees and large headphones strapped to her braided head. She bears such a startling resemblance to the actress "Halle Berry," I am confused. Adelia calls out to the woman.

'Sophie.'

'Hey.' She looks uninterested.

Sophie's lips move, and I am so transfixed by her perfection I almost miss her reply when it comes.

I blink and step back, not wanting a comparison.

'Who's this?' Sophie asks Adelia.

Her tone is blunt, and she rests her gaze on me, standing in her doorway.

'This is Mary. She's new to our unit's family. Mary, meet our resident artiste: Sophie.'

Halle's doppelgänger lifts her head up and takes off her headphones. She looks at me with intensity.

Instinct tells me to make myself smaller, in case she identifies how defective I am, but I step forward, my hands on my small hips.

'Er, *do you fucking mind*? Your eyes are burning my face off?'

'Nice.'

'OK. Thank you, Sophie. Enjoy your day.'

Adelia begins to herd me out and Sophie replaces her headphones, shrugging in response. Instead, she looks back down at her pad, drawing again with the charcoal she grips.

'And I had expected Sophie would be the one to display an artistic temperament.'

'Yeh?'

'Let me tell you a bit about the treatment we offer here,' Adelia says as I fall into step with her.

My guide strides off down the corridor again, forcing me to hurry to catch up with her.

Chapter 7

This hospital is vast. My neck aches from all the rubbernecking I am doing. I feel like a tourist staring at the building… well, what I would imagine a tourist would feel like, because I have never actually been anywhere.

'So… I appreciate I have partially explained about where we are and what we provide, but I did not explain why we came to exist. I founded the Rainbow Unit because someone close to me was diagnosed with treatment resistant schizophrenia and there was no treatment available that was sufficient. Do you know what your diagnosis is?'

I nod. I should. God knows I have heard hospital staff discuss it enough over the years.

'Yeh–I know what it is. It's what you just mentioned. I'm a "treatment-resistant schizophrenic." They must've tried every medication there is.'

Adelia nods.

'That's correct, Mary. According to your medical records, other medical professionals do believe they have tried everything for you. But there *are* other things that can be done. There is alternative medication, along with new and innovative treatments. We use them here with our patients and they are only available to a select few. I will only conduct this with your understanding and consent, because I believe that will increase the effectiveness of your treatments.'

Coming to a halt, I admire a cosy reading nook. A woman with dirty blonde hair and wide-spaced eyes wanders past us. She wears Mickey Mouse ears and a comfortable-looking tracksuit. The woman is muttering to herself, and her slow hands snatch at things only she can see. As she nears us, her eyes flit between us, marking us and our actions with fear.

Adelia smiles, filled with serenity.

'Good afternoon, Patricia.'

Patricia stops in the corridor, flickering like an old-fashioned video put on pause. She appears arrested for a second or two but does not meet our eyes. Then she continues to pass, shuffling on down the hall.

'Patricia has not been a guest here for very long, so please excuse her lack of social skills. She is at the beginning of her journey to recovery. It is different for everyone.'

I shrug.

'Whatever.' Not interested. Who gives a shit about Patricia what's-her-face?

Adelia sits down with poise on the sofa, gesturing beside her. 'Please. Sit.'

'Why?'

'Because I want to discuss the treatments we offer. Is that alright?'

I know from my previous attempts during being sectioned under The Mental Health Act that if I try to run away from the treatments or the hospital, it will only make my stay in here longer and harder. Plus, I do not know what my treatments will entail yet. Even if I did somehow escape from the hospital, the police would only bring me straight back. Then a few burly staff will restrain me, pull my knickers down for a swift jab in the buttocks with a heavy sedative, and they will prolong my section. Indefinitely. No thank you. I sit down. I will be obedient. For now.

Pan pipe "musac" drifts through hidden speakers and punctuates her question.

I look down at my nails, trying to pick out some of the dirt and shrug my shoulders without looking at my companion. They always ask permission, but really, I have no choice, and we both know it.

'Treatments for schizophrenia in the past were a choice between electro-convulsive therapy, sedatives, or brain surgery–it was all we had before the invention of anti-psychotic medication,' she starts off.

My head shoots up and I drill into her with my eyes suddenly full of lead. She had better not try any of that shit on me. I say nothing, but now I am listening.

'The early anti-psychotic medication had a sedating effect on the individual but produced uncontrollable shakes, somewhat similar to the tremors those suffering from Parkinson's disease experience.'

'The meds still do that!' I am drawn in against my will and interrupt my "schizophrenia history teacher." 'I call them my "Shakin' Stevens" tablets.'

Adelia nods and waves with casual insouciance at someone in my peripheral vision walking past us. She continues,

'I know. That was part of the reason for me developing my treatment regime and founding this unit. I wanted to identify and utilise more sophisticated medication for schizophrenic patients. Medication that controlled symptoms without the physical side effects. My remit is more specific though. I focus on helping those individuals who are schizophrenic, who are also labelled "treatment resistant."'

I stare out of the French windows beside us, then at the elegant grounds just a few feet away, feeling a stir of hope. Then I clock the key card beside the doors and notice the reinforced iron threads running through the glass. My shoulders slump. A gilded cage, then. I am trapped again.

'Can I offer you some water?' Adelia gets up, gliding to the nearby water dispenser.

I turn back to my new self-allocated saviour and accept the recyclable cup of water with a vinegary expression on my face and no word of thanks.

Adelia frowns at me in confusion.

'Why?'

'Why those people?' Nothing in this world is for free.

Adelia smiles.

'Well, there were several reasons. I had personal experience with the inefficient treatment available for schizophrenic patients. That sparked my vision. A part of this vision was treating a few patients in beautiful surroundings. Everyone detained to the unit feels like a valued guest. Safe and well looked after, while they begin a journey towards recovery and reintegration back into society. We have a swimming pool here, a state-of-the-art gym, a sauna and a steam room *and* we have a full complement of staff.'

Holy shit.

Adelia looks at me, raising her eyebrows as though in expectation.

Gritting my teeth, I stare at her without expression. It takes effort because I am impressed despite myself. I place my empty cup on a side table next to us.

Adelia's face remains an undisturbed lake of serenity. She sips at her water.

'All staff here are permanent. I believe continuity is beneficial for a patient's recovery. I have already mentioned a few of the staff we have here. The OT's, nurses, support staff and our medical doctor. Well, besides those people, we also have a chef, a masseuse who visits us once a week, a cleaner and two regular security guards.'

Against my will, my mouth drops open in amazement. Hey, this might not be so bad after all. Sounds like I imagined a spa break would be. The "musac" changed to Beethoven and I like that better. Classical music always reminds me of my mum.

'While we offer group sessions here, I achieved most of the therapy on a one-to-one basis. I believe one-on-one treatment is the most effective because I target it for the individual. It is tailor-made therapy for up to eight guests in residence.'

Adelia is silent for a moment while she studies me. A stilted conversation in the background draws away some of my attention, but no-one approaches us.

I do not speak and stare back at her, raising my eyebrows. *Yes? Can I help you?*

'So, what will you be doing to me here, then? Nothing good ever happens to me. There has to be a catch.'

Adelia smiles, smooth as honey, before continuing.

'A catch? No Mary, not at all. I work with all the residents. Discussions like this one will form part of your treatment plan at least once a week. These "talks" will form the basis of your psych-education. I believe it's very important to understand mental health and the symptoms of the condition, besides understanding the impact within the wider context of society and its treatment. I do not believe in "dumbing things down" for people, but I expect you will learn to keep up.' Adelia almost spits the last words out.

OK, she is not a fan of "layman's terms."

'They'retakingmystuffthey'rerobbingallmystufftheywant mystuffandIwantitbacknowfuckingthiefsdirtybuggers,' a muffled voice came, rising from behind us. What is her name again? Who cares?

An alarm sounds and I gawk as three members of staff run in to approach the disturbed patient. I can see the woman struggle, but then the nurses calm her down and she walks with them in a halting manner, out the door. How bizarre. Damn it – a song worm starts in my mind. How bizarre, how bizarre. Ooh baby. Ya makin' me crazy. I stare at Adelia.

She gives no sign she is aware of the distraction.

'I deliver training in mindfulness and meditation. Those are tools that can help to manage anxiety. I undertake hypnosis, and I delve into a person's memories and give post-hypnotic suggestions to help you manage your mental health symptoms in a more adaptive way. I conduct cognitive behavioural therapy–or CBT for short, and we also build a Three-3D interactive hologram bespoke to each individual.'

It sounds like they go to a lot of effort here. When you are in section, the hospital staff dope you up on prescription meds, the psychiatrist talks to you for half an hour every few days while they type, and you get sent to a room filled with people for "ward round." I never bother to speak anymore during ward round. I just sit. Confirm my name and date of birth, then agree with everything they say. Tick that box. Check. Get out sooner. Check.

'Who gets to say who gets admitted here?'

'I, myself, have specifically chosen all of our patients.'

'Why?'

I inhale. Against my will, I feel lucky. I have "been chosen." Well, that is a novel experience. I narrow my eyes. Nothing is for free.

Adelia chuckles. She appears unphased by my blunt question.

'I chose you because you are under twenty-five years of age, are diagnosed with schizophrenia, deemed to be treatment resistant–oh and because you suffer from hallucinations. In short, because you are a perfect candidate for my treatment plan.'

One of Adelia's tousled curls strays out of her loose chignon as leans forward. It seems to add to her overall perfection. I note she is the antithesis of the cheery cockney I had just flipped off in the hallway. Leaning back, I watch her in silence.

'During our sessions, I will build up a picture of the predominant hallucination you are experiencing. I then construct a hologram based on its description; besides the information I collate.'

'A hologram? What's the point of that?'

I frown, trying to digest what Adelia is saying. A hologram?

This "psych-ed chat" thing is complicated. Scratching my head, I close my eyes. The details do not interest me, so I do not keep the boredom out of my tone. My sarcasm does not dull Adelia's enthusiasm for her subject, and she continues her explanation with obvious relish.

'I use all of this to enable it to interact with the patient like an avatar. This is a form of holographic therapy allowing the person who has the hallucinations to converse with a specifically designed avatar, or a brain/computer symbiosis. I monitor the various parts of the brain stimulated. I facilitate dialogue between the patient and the entity, so the patient can practice learning to control any future interactions.'

'Wow,' I breathe, exuding sarcasm. She needs to shut up now.

A fly crawls along the arm of the sofa, its fat buzzing accompanying it, and I swat it away. Although I hate flies, I will not harm it.

I have hit a wall in my concentration now and start to fidget. The sores on the palms of my hands itch and I refrain from scratching them. I examine Adelia. She is unconcerned by my boredom. I wonder how long they will sedate me for if I slap this woman into silence. No, I will not do it. I have been down that road and I hate the one-to-one it would bring me. I fold my arms and stare at her.

Oblivious to my inner musings, Adelia continues, 'The last form of therapy we use is a light therapy, and I'm told it's a very relaxing experience. We also invite discharged patients to visit and talk to current patients at "The Inspiration Group." I believe it's of paramount importance for patients to have something concrete to aspire to. Many of my previous residents are an inspiration.'

'I'm not fucking interested. Can I go now or what?' My voice is terse.

She sounds proud of her treatments, the unit and of her "previous residents." I roll my eyes, then stand up, reaching the end of my patience.

Adelia smiles as though I am saying something endearing and looks up at me with a sweet expression on her face.

'Of course, you can, Mary. I apologise for speaking to you for so long. I told you–Schizophrenia and its treatment is a subject which I am passionate about. Let me escort you back to your room.'

Adelia moves from sitting to standing in one smooth motion, fluid as water.

My bottom lip feels cracked and sore, and I resist the urge to nibble at it, following Adelia and moving into a standing position. Remaining silent, I wonder how long I can last here before they kick me out. Realising I am rocking backwards and forwards, I stop myself with abrupt force.

'It's OK, Mary. There's no rush. You'll stay here as long as you need to. Everyone's recovery is their own personal journey. There's no time stamp here.'

Adelia's cornflower blue eyes briefly skim my appearance.

'You look tired now. It is a lot to process. I will walk you back to your room so you can rest.'

I shrug. *'Whatever.'*

God, I need to lie down. The idea of lying in that comfortable bed with its thick cotton sheets and cosy duvet is like a water slide on a hot summer's day. I can hear my voice, low and gritty with fatigue. This woman and this massive place are both exhausting. Adelia is not kidding. It is a lot to take in.

Chapter 8

I scope out the restaurant and dining room again. It is spotless, and the furniture is all simple, quality items. I inhale the tempting waft of herbs. Garlic. Hmm. My mouth waters in response.

As I step further into the room, I glance around, weighing up its occupants. As I wait for someone to jump me, I am bracing my body with steel. I know the ropes; I know how this part goes. The weakest "inmate" here is always prey. The strongest get to set their own rules. Those who are in between fall in, helping others to enforce the will of the strong or whomever is in charge.

They have incarcerated me in enough institutions to know I do not enjoy being prey. So, I fight hard and fierce at the beginning. Then, once the others recognise I am someone on top of the food chain as opposed to the bottom of the pile, they will leave me alone, and I can ease up a bit. That is how it goes.

So, with this in mind… who the hell is this "*meeb*" and what is she doing stepping to me? Whatever she thinks she can get from me, she can forget it.

'Hi again,' the brunette cherub woman sings out to me.

I frown at her. The two of us stand still, regarding each other. The only noise between us is enthusiastic cutlery scraping. I remain silent, my arms folded.

She shoves a chubby, starfish handful of ringlets from her sweaty face, and two dimples pop up in her cheeks like corks bobbing on the water.

'My name's Marcia–but everyone calls me Marcie. We met before, didn't we? D'ya remember? In the hallway the other day.' Marcie's words bubble out at me.

Her London cockney accent makes me think of the chimney sweeps out of Mary Poppins. *"Over the rooftops, step in time."*

I blink at Marcie with a stony face, the long-forgotten aroma of decent food causing my belly to rumble loudly. I look at the food counter, salivating. *Move, bitch.* I'm hungry.

'No.'

I try to sidestep round her Humpty Dumpty shape. I cannot. The gap between her and some chairs is too small. Patricia stumbles past. She mutters as she walks, and I flinch as I realise what the other noises she is making. Patricia has an issue with flatulence.

Heaving, I stick two fingers in my nostrils to plug my nose and block the smell.

The girl, "Marcie," is not taking my hint and is still chirping away in my face. I shake my head.

'Yeh, yeh - don't ya remember? You were walking with Adelia, then I said "hi," but you prob'bly didn't hear me 'cause you didn't answer - but then when I looked back you were havin' a chat wiv Derek–we call him Dishy Derek for obvious reasons, and then-'

'Are you some kind of simpleton or something?' I cut sharply into her torrent of words.

Marcie takes a step back as she giggles. The sound is contagious, ringing out in the hospital restaurant.

It reminds me of a cartoon character I used to watch on Saturday mornings with my mum. *Popeye.*

My lips twitch of their own volition and I fight off the instinct to laugh. Straight faced, I stare into Marcie's eyes, giving her what I privately think of as my "Rottweiler" look.

'Do you have any cigs?'

Marcie looks like a "mark," someone easy to take from. I do not smoke myself but will grab whatever currency I can.

Marcie shakes her head, eyes round.

'Adelia doesn't allow smoking here. There're no-smoking rooms, and no smoking allowed in the gardens. No tobacco allowed in here at all actually, because she says it's a filthy habit that pollutes the health of everyone. I tried it once when I was about thirteen, but I coughed so much I thought I was gonna choke to death-' Marcie catches my eye and cuts her own story short.

'No, sorry, I don't smoke,' she summarises.

No smoking on site? What the hell?

'Probably why you're so fat.'

I stare her straight in the eyes with raised eyebrows and do not smile. Then I study her reaction.

Marcie lowers her head, and her loose chin trembles as though she will cry, but she does not. A moment later Marcie gazes over my shoulder, swiping her hair out of her eyes again, then nods.

'Yeh, I know, but that's OK.' Her attention is on something off to my left.

I cannot hear anyone approach. I whip my head around and look over my shoulder to see what she is looking at. There is no-one there. I remember where I am. Oh yeh. Psych ward. I frown at her then ask,

'Do you think you see something?'

'What?'

Marcie stops talking, nodding slowly. She is cocking her head to one side as though she is listening. Her dimples pop up again.

I flick another glance over my shoulder. None of my friends are with me.

'Oh. It's no-one real. Probably.' Marcie grins at me with a shrug. She is obviously taking my one question as an opener for a full-blown conversation. I stare at the food being dished up to others at the counter and my stomach rumbles again. It looks so good. I eyeball Marcie. Get out of the frigging way. She is still talking.

'Adelia has taught us all about "psychosis." So now I think I'm prob'ly seeing my main "hallucination." Her name's Teresa and she's an angel – a good one, though. Adelia is building a hologram of her for when we've got our sessions. Teresa likes you, though. She thinks you're really pretty, even though you can be mean.' Marcie delivers a flurry of words.

I roll my eyes. No shit and tell Teresa I am about to get worse. I am seriously "hangry." Marcie is lucky the threat of sedation and extended detainment is keeping me in check. Or I would have smashed her face in by now.

'Tell Teresa I said to stick it up her ass.'

Marcie gawps.

I want my dinner. I realise during our interaction, Marcie has shifted enough I can now get by her.

Pushing past her without a word, I march up to the counter to choose my food. I make sure I barge her with my shoulder as I do so, just to be certain I hammer home the point that I am not her target and do not want to be her friend.

I am not prey. Not anymore.

'Hi, my name's Miles,' a guy tells me as I sit down at the table.

I am not sitting next to him for companionship. I am sitting there because I can see the door and get to it easily from here.

His deep voice sounds kind, and I glance at his symmetrical face. I can see it was pleasing to the eye. The golden tone of his mahogany skin reminds me of my beloved mother.

Lowering my gaze back to my food, I wait for him to get fed up and leave. He does neither.

'Good for you.' Dismissed.

I hear him shuffle around in his chair for a few seconds, but he does not speak. Miles is opposite me, and next to a young woman. I recognise her as the stick-up-her-ass girl from earlier I met. She reminds me a little of a South Asian Lou… "Somya." That was her name. I remember. Funny how I can remember things again now the voices are not clogging up my mind all the time.

'Welcome to The Rainbow Unit.'

I do not look at him, although his voice is appealing. Miles sounds gruff, like a big, bashful bear.

I do not raise my head again or acknowledge his welcome. Instead, I continue to eat.

'Fuck off, yeh?' I do not look up.

'Just ignore her. She's not very nice.'

Somya's voice is cutting and proprietary. Her accent speaks of privilege, and I feel my hackles raise in response.

I lift my head and look at her. Neither one of us speaks, but Somya looks back at me steadily. I withhold the urge to mimic her. "Well, she's not very niiiiice."

After I hold her gaze for a few moments to make my point, I turn my attention back to my plate. Taking advantage of the fine cuisine, I gulp. When I finish eating, I will fill my pockets with food scraps. I scrunch the napkins in the palms of my hands, ready to wrap up some rolls and a few apples. Just as soon as I am unobserved. Survival. You have to be prepared, because you never know what is coming next.

Somya rolls her eyes at me and shrugs, then turns back to Miles.

The two of them look like a couple of "normals." They speak to each other in low voices that blend in with the general hubbub of the dining room.

'They're ready to leave.'

'You still here? I thought I told you to fuck off?'

This girl is persistent. Or desperate. Either way, I do not want her around me.

Marcie shrugs.

'Yeh, you did.'

She irritates me and her cheery voice is audible despite the restaurants' surrounding sounds. There is not much of a din here in the dining room compared to some, but there is still a fair bit of the usual eating noises - clanging dishes, chairs being scraped, people talking - and there is also low, calming music swelling all around us. Marcie's voice rings out above all of that, loud and clear. Chatting nonsensically.

Marcie half turns to me in her seat, her eyes wide and her hand outstretched.

'But it's OK. I decided not to listen. I remembered what it was like when I first got here as well. Miles and Somya were already here, but they wasn't as calm as they are now. They was all crazy and all over the place with their madness.-God, this one time, Somya was proper sprinting, starkers down the hallways–totally naked, an' she was screaming, "I am Aphrodite" (whoever that is,) at the top of her voice. Oh - and her boobs was just swinging all over the place, they're actually pretty perfect–obviously, they would be right? Then Adelia came out and just talked her down an' another time, Miles was crawling around on all fours like a mahungus dog, but at the same time it was even more weird because he was meowing in this proper loud voice just because–'

'Marcia–that's enough,' Somya cuts Marcie off in a firm tone.

I open my mouth to advise Marcie "no-one cares," but instead, I find that I take umbrage to the aristocratic tone Somya is directing towards Marcie. I scrutinise my would-be self-appointed hospital tour guide and hospital buddy. Marcie looks crestfallen, and her eyes point down towards her feet.

'Sorry,' Marcie mumbles. Somya's admonishment instantly quells her. God, here is another one that reminds me of a puppy. I roll my eyes.

Silent, Marcie continues to look down.

My mouth puckers up and I suck in my cheeks. Nope. It is no good, I cannot keep my mouth shut.

'Who died and made you God?'

The bossy cow. Alright, yeh, this girl can talk a glass eye to sleep, which is annoying as shit, but still… She seems harmless and she is just trying to fill me in.

'It's one of Adelia's rules. We don't discuss how we *were*–we look at what we aspire to. Thoughts become actions.' Somya speaks slowly, as though she is talking to a child, or to someone who does not speak the same language.

Actually, bitch, I can speak two languages–plus a few words in Fon. My mum was French African and taught me French, and a smattering of Fon as well as English. I just choose not to use many words in any language.

I shrug. 'And?'

Somya's eyes stare into mine, lips pursed.

'What if *my* thought, is that you should shut the fuck up and butt out of our conversation?' I throw the challenge out to her.

Somya gives me a dirty look, then drops her gaze.

'Very mature. Whatever.' She turns back to her dining companion.

'Yeh, that's right, it is "*whatever*." So how about you just mind your business and get on with your dinner, you stuck-up bitch?' I instruct her.

Marcie spouts some of the grape juice she is drinking from her nose as she guffaws. Her eyes are wide.

Somya and Miles do not look or speak back at us again, but I can hear they are speaking about what "optimal nutrition" looks like and are swapping juicing recipes.

Marcie shuffles her chair closer to mine and the legs scrape eagerly on the shiny floor. She keeps her voice low.

'They're both ok. They're alright, really. Both of 'em are being discharged over the next couple of weeks so they prob'ly don't want anything to slow that down or something. I know I do talk a lot. Everyone tells me, so I know it's true. Adelia has mentioned it to me before an' I'm s'posed to control it… take deep breaths an' count an' all that… I do try, but y'know…' Marcie breathes in deeply, closing her twinkly eyes.

I wait for her to speak, but she does not. I turn to regard her.

Marcie has the air of a child waiting for Christmas Day at 11:59 on Christmas Eve. She looks as though she might burst.

My lips twitch. She is clearly suffering.

'What? "*You know*" what?' I give her a license to speak.

Marcie blinks, then exposes her dimples again.

'I dunno what I was going to say. Sometimes I just talk for the sake of hearing my own voice. I s'pose about nothing. I feel like… it's probably because of the "ADHD." That's short for "Attention Deficit Hyperactive Disorder." That's what they told me I had when I was at school– well, on one of the few times I went to the poxy place, anyway.' Marcie giggles.

I feel my face answering her with a smile of its own and I repress it.

'Stop chatting breeze.'

My voice has lost its edge. We return to eating.

It has been years since I have savoured a meal like the one in front of me. The lady had said it was filet mignon in a mushroom sauce. I close my eyes, salivating at the aroma. Mmm. It has also been years since I have eaten with anything resembling company. Sawing through the meat with an awkwardness belying that I am unused to using cutlery. My mum would turn in her grave.

'This is some tasty shit,' I hear someone murmur.

I snort. That is true though, I have to admit.

CHAPTER 9

I push past the zombie woman standing in the corridor.

'You can fuck right off.'

The woman smells like unwashed body. My stomach revolts and anger bites at me like the memory of me sprinting into the park. I withhold the urge to slap her around the face for triggering that memory and causing me to heave. Instead, I clench my fists and hold my breath while I get out ahead of her taint.

Not so long ago, I smelled like her, but now, I do not, so she can piss off with her ripe self.

I plop down into the chair at the table the support worker guides me to. The low classical music playing in the background of the coffee nook is not what irritates me. What has me grinding my teeth in irritation, is that they have forced me to leave the solitude of my room to meet some woman I do not know, and now this bitch keeps staring at me.

'What?'

She offers me a tight smile but says nothing for a few seconds.

'What the fuck're you staring at?' Thunder on the horizon.

The support worker stands to attention at the door, shifting his feet, and he looks at the well-turned-out woman in askance. "John," his name tag reads. I interpret the question in John's gaze and feel incensed. No, John, do not do it, mate. You do not just jump in and jab me up with tranquillisers. Just piss off.

My red-rimmed eyes are watchful for the woman's response to John. My shoulders relax when I see her shake her head. So, I am safe for now, am I? Bastards.

My hands have started to scab over and are itchy, so I pick at the scabs on my fingers underneath the table separating us. This woman is triggering me.

Looking unconcerned, she grants me another brief smile before speaking.

'You must be Mary. Good to meet you.'

The woman has a clipped, Scottish voice.

I tut, crossing my arms. OK. This woman thinks she can handle me, does she? Well. We will see about that. Silence lurks between our stiff figures, while the two of us sit in the coffee area of the hospital.

I look out of the window, grinding my teeth together. I embrace the familiar rage I can feel creeping up inside and stoke it up. Stupid smug cow. Coming here, thinking she knows me. What does she want from me, anyway? I kiss my teeth.

'Hi, Mary. My name is Eileen McIntosh, and I'm your CPN. Do you know what a CPN is, Mary?'

I stare at her. Wordless. Fuck. Off.

Eileen leans towards me, tucking a strand of mahogany behind an ear. Her bobbed haircut is as precise as her tone. She brushes a speck from her suit jacket, then leans down.

On red alert, I shift in my seat, turning so I can see her hands and track their movement.

Eileen correctly interprets my sudden focus and retrieves a small card from a purple and yellow tartan patterned bag. She explains,

'Because they sectioned you under the Mental Health Act, it entitles you to someone to help oversee and coordinate your recovery. This can be a social worker or a community psychiatric nurse. I am also known as a "CPN" for short.' Eileen's voice is as direct as her green eyes, and both lack any warmth.

'No one cares? People here already tell me what to do. So how about you just piss off back to wherever you came from?'

I glue a frown on my screwed-up face and stare into her eyes.

She says nothing in reply and sits watching me with a calm gaze. She does not smile at me like Adelia had, and I sense she wants to deliver a sharp slap to my disrespectful mouth. At least she is not fake.

I tut and shift, restless in the chair.

'Urgh, whatever, just hurry.' I am getting one of my headaches and the stuffy, artificial air in this room is making it worse. 'Today would be good.'

Eileen's eyebrows raise, but she does not comment on my last sentence.

'I will leave soon, Mary. But first, I want to give you my card. It has all my contact details on it. Staff here also know how to reach me should you want to.'

My hands curl up in response. Hmmm. Bossy. That never goes down well with me.

'D'ya wanna stop staring in my face?'

The card remains where she leaves it on the table between us.

Eileen continues what she is saying as though I have not spoken. She has a script she needs to get out.

'I will call here for regular updates on how you are progressing towards recovery to check with staff how you're doing, and when they let me know you're near to discharge, I will come and visit you to plan for your discharge. We can look at any referrals needed to support you to re-join the community.'

"Re-join the community?" That is a joke. I've never been a part of any community except the one in my head.

After rolling my eyes, I shrug. Ah well, I snatch the card Eileen laid down with a gentle hand and shove it deep in my trouser pocket. The desperation for the return of my belongings wars with my need to maintain my stony façade. Well, one belonging in particular.

'They took my clothes.'

Eileen's elegant eyebrows rise, but she does not look bothered.

'When you were admitted here?'

I nod. Then clear my throat. A few days ago, I approached Sinead, but nothing happened so I have to try someone else. I need it back.

'My mother's necklace. I… I always have it with me. It's all I have left of her.'

Sinking back into silence, I realise I have forgotten to ensure that I loaded my voice with its usual aggression. My hands fall down the sides of the chair like two pieces of limp spaghetti punctuating my torso. My lip trembles and I bite it. Penance for its honest betrayal of my feelings.

Eileen's eyes are warmer. Her irises glimmer like the Aegean Sea. Although she has not moved, I think the CPN now appears to be leaning closer to me. She smells fresh, like cut green apples. When she next speaks, Eileen's abrupt tone is slower, melting into a soft Scottish brogue.

'I'm sorry. That must be very upsetting. I will ask the staff to find it for you and give it back.'

Eileen taps the table where she had put her card, as though it is still there, reminding me,

'Alright, Mary. I'll call and see how you're getting on in a few weeks and in the meantime, if you need anything else, or you need to see me, then ask the staff to call me. Nice to meet you.'

Eileen stands without further ceremony, taking her leave from me just as my hostility ebbs. It is just the usual line of bullshit they always feed to me. Maybe she is not the worst if she gets my necklace back.

Chapter 10

'What a shame. I'm booked for a massage today, Mary, so you'll have to wait.'

I turn to look at her. Her glossy makeup and black hair are as immaculate as her outfit.

'You make me sick.'

Somya raises one eyebrow.

'Jealousy is a hideous thing, dear.' Somya's voice is honey laced with arsenic.

'So's your mum,' I quip back at her with a tight smile.

I know my nostrils are flaring and my breathing is coming in short bursts as I try to drag more air into my lungs.

'Mary–please don't get upset. You know what happens when you get upset.' Lou arrives out of nowhere, the voice of reason, trying to calm me.

I know what happens when I get upset. David makes an appearance, and then everything turns to shit. Someone gets hurt, and I get into trouble for it. I look at Somya's taunting face. Hmmm… I consider.

No. Lou is right. Turning away from Somya's smirking face before I punch her teeth in. Already, I can visualise myself wrapping both hands in her perfect hair and yanking her head down to smash against my hard knee. Crunch. Claret everywhere.

Nope. No one-to-one with "Shakin' Stevens" drugs for me. I do not want that. The deep breaths I am taking are doing nothing to steady me, and whenever I close my eyes, I see red dots drift down behind my eyelids. Rage is descending.

'Ah. *So* sorry, sweetie. You wouldn't know, but you need to have a shower before you can take advantage of the masseuse's talents, anyway. It's called being "*civ-il-ised.*"' Somya slows her voice down.

I grind my teeth so forcefully they are in danger of cracking.

La chienne. I think. What a bloody bitch. I stride away, my fists clenching against the falsetto of Somya's amusement. God, I cannot stand her.

Following the knock on my bedroom door, Adelia's face pops from around the heavy wood.

'Good morning, Mary, I thought I would check on your well-being.' Adelia steps into my room and the sun filters upon her. It irradiates her features.

I sit up in bed, pushing my tangled mop of crow-nest hair out of my face.

'I noticed you are not taking part in any of the workshops we have run by our wonderful occupational therapists,' Adelia admonishes me.

I remain silent and pick the sleep crustaceans out of my eyes while I stare at her. Why is she checking up on me? What is it to her?

I shrug one shoulder.

'*And*?'

'And… it's your decision. However, I believe the workshops are an important part of your reunification with society, Mary. The longer you hold yourself apart from us and from your recovery, the longer you will be in here.'

That sounds like a threat. I squint at her. I am not in the mood today. This queen bitch is about a second away from me punching her in the throat.

Adelia takes a step backwards, but still faces me.

'There is a workshop today at midday to make sun catchers. It will offer you the opportunity to utilise your motor skills, follow instructions given, and to make something attractive. Mary, it is up to you.'

Adelia leaves my room.

Not really though, aye? I sigh... Fucking sun catcher. What the hell is a sun catcher, anyway?

Urgh. For God's sake. This is like *Sophie's Choice*. I look around the bright, busy room. Not all the Rainbow Unit's residents are here, so I guess they have other activities scheduled. I can either sit next to the "stick up their arse" Siamese twins; Miles and Somya - no thanks. Dirty blonde hair zombie girl, who is always away with the fairies. Nope. That fat miserable one with the dark hair. She is crazy as a box of frogs, and I do not trust her not to jam a pen in my eye as soon as look at me. There is a seat next to the OT instructing the class–what kind of wanker sits next to the teacher? Or the muggy verbal diarrhoea girl. Marcie.

I roll my eyes as I sit next to Marcie.

A grin bursts out over her face and I roll my eyes again. If I had been chewing gum, I would have popped it.

'Hey, Mary, I'm glad you came! We've just started – well, a few minutes ago we started, so they've just given us all the instructions - but I can tell you them anyway because I've done this before.'

'Take a breath, aye?'

Marcie cracks a smile and breathes inward.

I raise an eyebrow. Marcie does not seem to care what I say to her as long as I communicate. She continues on, happily relaying the instructions for making a sun catcher as though I have not spoken.

An exhalation. Then I focus on the iridescent materials on the table in front of me. In the background, I hear the OT Clarissa calling out instructions to "Sharon."

'I've done it before. It's not that hard really, when you get the hang of it.'

I look around the room.

'Yeh? Tell that to Sharon.'

I cannot resist.

In unison, we both look at Sharon.

'Sharon, dear, I keep telling you–we don't lick the glue pot. Please put it back down,' the OT advises her in a quiet tone. She has no trace of sarcasm in her voice.

Marcie's blue eyes meet my smoky, grey ones. Hers twinkle like stars. As Marcie giggles, I feel my lips twitch. This is so surreal. Head down, I place my attention on the task at hand. I will make a sun catcher. Because that will make all the difference between my mental health and my recovery.

After the two-hour craft session, I lift my finished product to inspect it, and Marcie does the same. Mine does not look half bad.

I look at Marcie's. It hangs limp and crooked from her fingertips. Her crestfallen face tells the story of her devastation.

'I thought you'd done this before?'

It does not look like she is the sun catcher expert. I take a swig of water from my Evian bottle.

Marcie stares at her ornament and nods.

'Yeh... it looks a bit... homemade.'

I spray my water out, looking aghast at my fellow crafter.

'Homemade?'

It circles itself like a dog chasing its own tail. I swallow a sudden gulp of water and tears brim up in my grey eyes like a mist. I take another swig.

Marcie holds it out towards me.

'I'd like you to have it. As a present.'

Her chubby starfish fingers offer me her gift and her face is hopeful. The sun catcher hangs lopsided and broken looking from Marcie's bitten down fingernails. Her face clears and she chuckles.

She tells me, 'It's all wonky, just like me.'

I am surprised to find my eyes mist over.

'Except from my mum, no-one's ever given me a present before. Thanks.' My voice is gruff. 'I love it.'

I give Marcie my sun catcher, and she hands me her effort with a brazen grin.

Marcie has the temerity to stare at my ornament as though she is holding a tiger from a piece of rotten string.

I pin my lips together to keep from laughing out loud, but then meet Marcie's sparkly gaze and I can no longer hold it in.

We both look at our exchanged pitiful excuses for decoration, giggling until tears run down our faces. Doubled over in our chairs, we convulse in laughter, hardly able to hold ourselves upright.

The OT, a muscular woman who wears gym gear, rushes over with concern.

'Ladies, is something the matter? How are you feeling?'

Marcie clutches at her stomach, her laugh peeling out. It mingles with mine.

CHAPTER 11

'Hi, Angie, do I have the all-clear for a garden visit with our newbie here?'

Angie puffs out her ruddy cheeks and looks me up and down before she nods, crossing over to where we stand in the corridor. The woman holds out her meaty hand to me, speaking to us in her broad Yorkshire accent. I stare at Angie, and my eyes widen as I notice her upper lip. Angie has a thick moustache. My mouth falls open as I take it in, in all its glory.

I look at Marcie, who, as always, looks angelic. Is she unaware of Angie's facial hair? She could have warned me. I feel a compulsion to stare at it. Should I tell Angie she has a huge moustache on her face? Does she even know? I swallow the urge. Nope. I want to see the garden, and I doubt she will let me if I annoy her. I avert my gaze and keep my lips pushed together.

'Mary, I'm Angie.'

She pumps my hand up and down with force.

'Hi.'

Whoa. That's a big fucking moustache you have there, Angie.

'I'm ward sister here. I was on leave when they admitted you, but I'm back now. Anyway… welcome.'

Her voice is shorthand. I can tell she is used to giving orders.

Angie grants me a quick grin, then looks at her Fitbit watch.

Keeping my own eyes trained to hers, I remind myself to shut the fuff up. Do not piss this woman off. I instruct my subconscious. Do not look at her moustache if you want to get back into the garden again.

'Adelia said you're doing well. She has given permission to Marcia or Sonia to show you around the grounds because you're still new, and they are both close to discharge.'

Angie's tone brooks no argument and does not invite conversation.

Alright, Marcia is Marcie's actual name, but do all the staff call Somya the wrong name?

I nod. Whatever, I am eager to sample the slice of freedom beckoning me.

The moustache is quite thick… my fingers itch to feel its softness and begin to stray up to my own upper lip. I clench my hand to stop them from obeying.

Angie stares into my eyes for a few seconds, then nods.

'OK then. You two come with me. I'll give the "*garden card*" to you Marcie. Remember, be back within two hours, and see a staff member when you return.' Angie moves off.

We follow her to a glass office, where she explains the garden visit procedure.

'For your benefit, Mary, I'll explain again how it works. You ask staff if you want to visit the garden. Dr. Sinclair decides who she clears for garden access, and if you receive permission, you come and request the card. You need to swipe beside the door, then push it for it to open. All the doors to outside are card swipe pass only. You won't be able to get outside without a card. Rules are: new patients go out with staff or established patients at Dr. Sinclair's discretion. After one month, this gets reviewed.'

'What happens after one month?'

'You could go by yourself. Whenever you like.' The ward sister holds the card out to Marcie. 'Or you might get your garden privilege revoked.'

Brilliant. Her words fall on me like a judge's gavel. Marcie takes the card.

Angie stares into my eyes again, as they round at her statement. Boy. They giveth, and they taketh away. Some things never change, no matter how fancy the surroundings are.

'There's a shared kitchen here to practice home skills with the outpatients. The kitchen is also card pass only, and security has fortified the knife drawer with a combination lock. If alerted by the alarm, clinical staff and security will attend.'

Angie looks at us. She rocks on the balls of her feet with her arms crossed behind her back.

Ok then. End of conversation. I fan my face. The room is hot and humid. Scared I may throw up, I elbow Marcie. Get on with it, for God's sake.

Marcie nods, taking the card, then links arms with me as she draws me away.

'Yeh. Thanks Angie, see you later!' she throws out over her shoulder.

We walk over to the French doors. They have ornate handles, but I can see the swipe box attached to the side of it.

'Do them both at the same time.'

'Huh?'

'Like this, see?'

Marcie shows me. She swipes the garden pass down the side of the little black box with her right hand, then pushes the door open with her left simultaneously.

Cool air rushes in at me and I breathe it in. It helps me to savour the freshness if I close my eyes, so I shut them, breathing in the scent. I had forgotten this. Hmm. Cut grass. I open my eyes to see Marcie grinning at me, her chubby cheeks dimpled.

'You remind me of a cartoon chipmunk.'

Pushing by her, I step outside into the garden area and look around me.

Marcie giggles. As usual, she does not take offence.

'Thanks.'

I feel my mouth drop open as I stare at the abundance of perfection all around me. It is like something out of a celebrity lifestyle magazine. "Inside the grounds of a mansion. Not too shabby.'

I remind myself I may stroll along the quaint path.

Marcie trots along beside me, spouting conversation like water from a hose.

'Adelia told me she designed this garden herself. She said she had a "vision of perfection" she didn't trust anyone else to deliver. There is nothing that woman can't do.'

I roll my eyes.

'Whatever.'

There is no edge to my voice.

'She's so nice to us all. She's a neurosurgeon and a psychiatrist– can you imagine having that brain? God, she's *so* gorgeous, isn't she? Talk about having it all or what? I wonder if she's married and what *he's* like? I bet he's like a superstar, mega-rich and, well, handsome. Adelia is *so* amazing. She gives us all this luxury, and she gets nothing in return.' Marcie speaks with fervour.

'Sounds like someone's got a bit of hero worship going on.'

Marcie links arms with me, and her rich chuckle warms me.

Without a word, I detach our arms, putting more space between us. My back is stiff, and my lips are tight.

Marcie does not notice.

'Probably, yeh.'

'I think she's wonderful.'

I roll my eyes again with a small smile. OK. Marcie is sweet. Like a little sister on a TV show. I flick a quick look at Marcie and feel my eyebrows rise. I realise… I do not want to push her away.

'You know… You're alright, Marcie.'

'Thanks. I wish I looked more like you, though. You're amazing too.'

Colour floods my cheeks.

'Me?'

I remain in step with Marcie, blinking back tears. My first compliment since my mum died. Someone thinks I am "amazing." Strange world.

Chapter 12

This part of the garden is new to me. It is pretty. The insects sing in the grass like an invisible orchestra, making me smile. It is a nice place for my "psych-ed" session with Adelia. I walk along with my teacher for a while in an agreeable silence, enjoying the sunshine.

'So... is it ok with you if we talk about *schizophrenia* for a while?'

I clench my jaw, steeling myself. Here comes the shitty bit.

'What's the point of that?'

I know I sound aggressive.

'Well, I spoke to you about my thoughts on psychological education when we met last week. I think it's important for a patient to understand about the effect the symptoms of their illness might have on them, and how society views them. It's an integral part of recovery and helps with insight and with context. I believe this understanding helps to form a good basis for rehabilitation.'

We pause by the garden bench, surrounded by fragrant roses that hang with heavy beauty.

Adelia gestures to a seat, then sits down. She waits but seems in no rush to get a response from me.

I shrug, then sit down with an abruptness causing my buttocks to slap against the cold, hard wood. Ouch. Even through my "boyfriend" jeans. That hurt. I squirm a bit on the seat to assuage my butt cheeks.

'There are three different symptoms of schizophrenia: positive, negative, and cognitive. The positive symptoms are things like; hallucinations, you can have different types of those; auditory, where you hear sounds, voices, noises, etcetera no one else can; and visual, where you see things that are not there.' Adelia allows her sentence to hang between us, and her eyes drill into me. They seem to demand a response.

'Like what?'

Adelia smiles. 'Like people on the TV talking to you, or a photo moving. Are you familiar with that kind of hallucination?'

I nod, but do not want to talk about it. Yes, I am. It is shit, and scary. This is what happens to me. No-one can see my friends.

Adelia continues. 'There are also olfactory hallucinations, smelling odours that only *they* are aware of.'

I use my fingers to untangle a large knot in my hair. I say nothing else.

'There are tactile hallucinations where people imagine they can feel things on their skin. Other symptoms are delusions or paranoid delusions. Examples of these are people having fixed beliefs based on untruths. They might believe they are the centre of a conspiracy to hurt or kill them, for instance. These can all form part of what we call psychotic symptoms.'

Against my will, she is piquing my interest. No-one explained this in such detail to me before. I had heard medical staff and social workers refer to my diagnosis, but I have never understood what it meant.

'Tell me if I get too technical–I am passionate about psychosis treatment. It's my favourite subject.' Adelia accompanies her shrug with a smile.

The doctor seems to wait for a response, so I give her an unsmiling nod. Whatever. My foot jiggles.

Adelia continues to smile, then takes a breath.

'The negative symptoms are the opposite of what I just mentioned.'

I do not understand and frown.

'Think of negative symptoms as the lack of, *or absence of,* emotions. When a person is experiencing negative symptoms, we see them presenting as depressed. They cannot derive pleasure or experience arousal and may self-neglect because of these symptoms.'

Adelia stares into my eyes.

I nod again to show I am still following. I am surprised. Her explanation fascinates me, even though I feel confused by her language.

'The third one is the cognitive impairment. Things people may experience are poor memory, attention deficit, or dementia. There might also be issues with a person's analytical skills. They interfere with one's ability to access their higher reasoning and to interpret complex information.'

I do not know what she means, but I think I get the gist. A picture of my fellow residents, talking to themselves and snatching at the air in front of them, pops into my mind.

'Like Sharon or Patricia?'

Adelia unfolds her long, linen clad legs and, standing up with a brisk nod, she fans herself.

'That's right. Shall we go inside for a drink? It's getting hot out here. Uncomfortable.' She turns to face the direction we came from.

'It's a long walk back to the building.'

Her pale skin suggests she is not a sun worshipper, but I should not assume. My skin is pasty at the moment, but I love the sun and never burn under its gaze. Moving to join her, I eyeball her, shoulders hunching over.

Adelia strolls down the path and continues with what she is telling me.

My twenty chihuahua steps to every one of hers. How the hell does she look so chilled while walking so fast? And she is still talking.

'If we think about an accepted concept of human existence, schizophrenia deconstructs it. To many, the ability we have as humans to experience emotions, our environment via our senses and the data they tell us, the ability to access higher reasoning, is what defines us as being a "human being."

'Then, if we say people who are diagnosed with schizophrenia can lack these basic human skills, does it mean society questions that schizophrenic sufferers are less than human?'

My jaw unlocks, dropping open at Adelia's last words. Do people think that? That I am not human? That "we" are all inhuman? I narrow my eyes, flicking a hard glance at her, my back ramrod straight. Does Adelia think that?

Smiling at me, Adelia pats me on my arm with a chilly hand.

'I don't think that just in case you were wondering.'

'Thanks for the disclaimer.' *Stuck up, bitch.* Bet she does think that.

'I'm telling you this theory to explain what others have seen as a rationale for the historical treatment of people with schizophrenia, and then I'll explain what we do here. Is alright, OK?'

She takes my silence as permission to continue.

'So, do you grasp society's previous perception? Of course, we are talking about the early nineteen hundreds.'

'Let's move onto the treatments. There was a movement called "eugenics" in the early nineteen thirties which was prevalent in Britain, the United States, and throughout Europe. The number of those diagnosed with schizophrenia was rising. There was an accepted belief that schizophrenia was a "Mendelian" gene or trait.'

'What does Mendelian mean?'

Adelia smiles at my question.

'A "Mendelian trait" is a trait passed down by our parents. It's called Mendelian because of a man called Gregory Mendel. He was the scientist who uncovered the theory of these types of genes. Mendel thought traits follow rules of only two versions of a gene: dominant or recessive. An example of these traits would be things like freckles, hair type, and blood type.'

I nod, my reluctant interest in what she is saying helping me to follow the information she is giving me. I remain silent as I let the implications of what she is saying soak in. Wait–had she said schizophrenia could be hereditary? My dad's history pops into my mind. Had he had it too?

Adelia continues, 'Nazi's, amongst others, believed schizophrenia was one of these Mendelian traits and if a person was ill, they could pass it onto their progeny: sons, daughters, grandsons, granddaughters, etcetera. A brilliant Berlin psychiatrist began research on those diagnosed with schizophrenia. He wrote a famous paper advocating sterilisation for these people. He believed they would pass on the genes for their condition. The same psychiatrist became the founder of a research facility that studied human genetics in America.'

A ladybird lands on my shoulder, diverting my attention from Adelia. She pauses as I pick it off with delicate fingers, then blow in gentle encouragement for it to fly away. I look back at my history teacher, trying not to show how rapt I am to what she is saying.

'Many countries were becoming more interested in the study of eugenics–and racial purity. In Germany, Hitler and others aimed to keep the general population free from people who carried any genes that meant defective offspring. They targeted those who had health conditions such as bi-polar disorder, schizophrenia, mental retardation, deafness, blindness, or alcoholism. At first, they passed a law to enable their sterilisation in psychiatric institutions they called: *Asylums*.'

Adelia sweeps her fringe out of her eyes, then swats with viciousness at a fly buzzing towards her.

I mouth the word. "*Asylums*." I had heard of those.

Adelia nods.

'Asylums were overcrowded, horrible places. Before the end of World War Two, they had murdered a quarter of a million using this rationale. They deemed psychiatric patients unworthy of life because of their likelihood of being a drain on society's economy. Hitler utilised gas chambers to carry out what they called "euthanasia."This was all a pre-emptor for the concentration camps, and their continued mass murder in the attempts to "cleanse" their race.' Adelia puts up quotation marks with her fingers as she walks and talks.

Swallowing, I am dry mouthed at the idea of such a ruthless and hateful society. Germany must have been terrible for anyone who was different. Europe and America seem to have held a similar view of those with mental health.

My ever-ripe imagination treats me to emaciated people with shaved heads, screaming in tortured agony for the betterment of society. I shake my head and blink it away.

People can be evil to each other. I know this already, but the depths of cruelty that Adelia's explanation speaks of shocks me. It makes me sad. I blink, tuning into what Adelia is saying now.

'Treatments for schizophrenia in the past were brutal. Those in charge of psychiatric institutions did not care about their patients' survival. They saw the patient as a drain who could never contribute to society. I wanted to solve this problem.'

We reach the French doors and Adelia swipes whilst I push the door.

We step through the threshold.

'Would you like a coffee?'

I nod.

'Would you like biscuits with it?'

I swallow my bewilderment.

'Sure.' I know my voice is cracking, and I clear my throat. It is years since someone has offered me biscuits with a hot drink.

I shake my head again, redoubling my efforts to focus on what Adelia is saying. Although unable to understand one hundred percent of her monologue, it is a pleasant change from people speaking to me as though I am five years old. A fast learner, I am reading between the lines to figure out what she is talking about.

Her earnest tone puts a lump in my throat. This lady wants to change things. She thinks we have something to offer. When Adelia falls silent, we slip into a serene silence. I look at her out of the corner of my eye, and she smiles when she catches my brief look.

I surprise myself again when I smile back.

Chapter 13

'So, you've seen 'round the unit a bit with Adelia, I bet–did she give you the tour and a speech? Your psych-ed session? Oh, yeh–what about the swimming pool? Have you been swimming yet?'

She is in her usual rush to get the words out.

I shake my head, unable to remember going swimming for years. I am not confident in the water.

'D'ya like swimming? I love it in there, even though I'm a rubbish swimmer.' It's better in the water 'cause I don't hear the voices when I'm in there.'

Since I arrived here, I am not hearing my own voices as much. This should be a good thing, but I miss my friends and feel lonely in their absence.

Marcie seizes my arm and I stare at her, and back to my arm, then back again with ice in my grey eyes. I do not like anyone touching.

Marcie removes her hand as though scalded but does not lose any of her bubbly enthusiasm.

'Let's go swimming.' Marcie claps her hands together in anticipation.

Lips pursing, I do not argue when Marcie drags me back to my room. What the hell, it's not like I have anything better to do.

Marcie's tangential conversation flows over me like the abstract tributaries of a river. Marcie speaks about her favourite songs and TV shows, then describes the time she walked into the local Curry's electronics store and spent two hours talking to the televisions there. She had been convinced she was receiving messages from the broadcaster meant only for her.

'The funny thing was–I don't even like Curry's!' Marcie ends her anecdote, cracking up with laughter.

I smile, but I do not join in with her peals of laughter. I am not sure why this story is so hilarious, but her good humour is pleasant to be around - even if it is off kilter.

The swimming pool reminds me of a glamorous holiday camp. There is a large water dispenser with sliced cucumber in it, and beside it on a silver tray, there is a hot water dispenser with herbal teas and accoutrement. The reclining sun beds are positioned around an enormous pool, and the changing rooms have slatted wooden doors to ensure a lack of privacy. I open the door of one to see a white towelling robe on a hanger and matching slippers placed side by side on the floor underneath.

'*Whoa*.'

Check this shit out. Unbelievable.

'There's one set in each of them. They're for us to wear and we chuck them in the laundry bin after each use. Come on.'

Marcie points to each thing she describes, and her ringlets bob in excitement along with her words.

My mouth drops open as I look around me. I have never been to a swimming pool such as this before–or any pool I could remember, in fact.

I dip my toe into the water. It is like warm silk. I close my eyes, savouring the experience. I feel my lips curve upwards in appreciation.

There was a swimming costume in my wardrobe, just as Marcie had told me there would be. She had instructed me to put it on and to bring a towel. She picks her robe up and throws it over her shoulder, along with the towel she had brought. Her swimming costume is a bright purple and as she tip-toes into the pool, a comparison between her figure and a Telly Tubby cartoon character slides into my mind with the harshness truth sometimes holds. I remain quiet, though, and do not comment on the resemblance.

I dangle my feet in as I sit at the edge of the shallow end, while Marcie lunges in doggy paddle style, thrashing around with great energy.

'Get in!' Marcie beckons with her hand. 'The water's lovely when you get in - come on.'

The door creaks open to admit Sophie and Derek. Feeling my face flame, I rush all at once to get into the water, so they do not see me in my costume. I have seen them both walking 'round together a few times now.

'Are they a couple?'

Marcie laughs. 'Nah. I think Sophie's gay, so I doubt it? Those two are just friends.'

Sophie is gay? Is Marcie sure? Maybe Sophie is she just picky. Looking as she does she can afford to be.

'Can you swim?' She hops, then tucks her knees up to her chest under the water. Marcie treads water.

I nod with caution.

'Hmm, a bit, but not like… well, or anything.'

I do not want to build myself up, then look stupid in front of an audience. Marcie is like a happy baby elephant in the water. Even though Marcie lacks any swimming skills, she seems at home in the water, and her enjoyment is contagious.

Marcie splashes me with water, and as the spray hits my face, I splutter with rage and shock. Gulping back both emotions, my small fists clench. Who does this girl think she is?

She spatters me again. I wipe the water from my eyes, then stand still, waist deep in the pool. Does she want to fight? In here? Confused, I stare at her, and my eyes narrow.

'Go on… splash me back then,' Marcie instructs me with a wide smile.

She seems to mean it and does not seem confrontational. I look around us, self-conscious.

Derek and Sophie come out of the changing rooms, and as I take in Sophie's perfect hourglass figure, I sink my shoulders below the water. How embarrassing is this? I have the body of a ten-year-old boy in comparison with a real-life Halle Berry doppelgänger. I sneak a look at Derek out the corner of my eye, and my mouth unlocks. Who knew?

Derek is wearing swimming trunks and his defined abdomen muscles are on show. He sits on a sunbed, and he and Sophie speak to each other in voices I strain in vain to hear.

Another splash hits my face. It shocks me out of my fixation with Derek's abdomen and makes me blink and splutter. I whip my face around to stare at Marcie, my lips tight with vexation. How dare she?

'C'mon - splash me back then!'

Marcie slaps the water at me with her hand.

She will not give in until I do what she wants. I tut. Child.

I splash Marcie back and wait, expectant for her face to change and for her to look annoyed.

Instead, Marcie chuckles loudly and frolics, walk-swimming in the pool in a circle around me.

I giggle in surprise. This is fun.

I spatter her again, palm flat in the water, and Marcie's laugh rings out in joy as she splashes me back.

'Water fight!' she shouts as I let myself join her at play.

Sometime later, Marcie and I salute the still dry Sophie and Derek as we leave the pool area.

'See you guys later,' Marcie shouts.

My quick breaths make a panting sound and I grind my teeth as I look at them, my small nostrils flaring. Sophie and Derek have their heads close together as they gossip. At the sound of Marcie's cheery goodbye, they break apart. They have a lot to talk about.

I can see Derek's face tints itself with pink as he glances at me.

'See you both later,' he calls out.

Derek does not raise his voice, but the acoustics carry his words to my waiting ears clear and strong. I have not been raised with males like him at the children's home. No-one was gentle or well-spoken. He does not seem the type to even shout. I take a deep breath in to steady myself. Get a grip, Mary Jameson. You're acting like some kind of lovesick idiot.

Sophie nods, holding her hand up in farewell.

Chapter 14

I am having a "bad day" and do not want to get out of bed this morning. The support worker, Jackie, is rallying round me in resolute cheerfulness and I realise I cannot remain in my cosy bed in peace. Then I remember. I am going to a picnic.

Marcie suggested a picnic. I have never been to a picnic before. It is Marcie's idea. My thick cardigan is in the wash, so I must wear the only other one. The ugly green one I ordered by mistake. Flipping hate green, but at least it is warm.

As I jog down to the garden, I am mumbling under my breath to myself, 'I cannot believe I have let Marcie talk me into this.' I greet Marcie with a smile.

Ignoring the butterflies of anticipation fluttering in my tummy, I help Marcie spread out our feast. Marcie lays out the picnic blanket on the soft grass while I place our snacks on top with reverence. I look over the items we took from the restaurant. Fruit, crisps, rolls, juice, yoghurts, fresh baked bread, cakes…I have never had such a banquet before.

I resist the urge to load up my pockets with food. I have learned now that here at The Rainbow Unit there is no sparsity here to be seen. Food and drinks are available around the clock.

We sit down, careful to avoid squashing our culinary bounty.

'What's the story of your dominant voice then?' Marcie asks me whilst we snack on crisps.

How have I never had these crisps before? I close my eyes. My mum had cooked a lot, I remember, but I had forgotten the taste of her food. I cannot remember her presenting me with any crisps when I had been small. I love Monster Munch.

When I open my eyes again to look at Marcie, I realise she is waiting. Also, she is quiet.

I shrug, uncomfortable. Little Mary's story is not my story to tell.

Marcie, never one to let an opportunity to share her thoughts pass her by, takes my silence as her opening.

'My key voice is an angel!' Marcie tells me in a breathy voice.

Her raised eyebrows tell me she expects a big reaction to her news. Tada!

I look at her with a flat gaze saying nothing and continue to suck on the pickled onion snack with glee.

'Yeh, you've said already,' I say.

Marcie frowns as though I have stolen her thunder. Her vague look tells me she does not remember telling me either.

'At the canteen?' I remind her.

Marcie shrugs. She has given me the unabridged version regardless.

'An angel has been coming to visit me every night since I was fifteen years old. Sometimes it's the bad angel that comes and it tells me to do bad things or says bad things to me. It's so scary when he comes - we won't go into that now, but about two years ago, the good angel came and put a baby in my belly.'

'But I thought you said the good angel was called Teresa? What – the good angel made you preggers? Doesn't sound too saintly to me, and how did she put the baby in there?'

Marcie expands. 'Teresa can just make the pregnancy happen with a click of her fingers, because she's an angel. Also, I thought it would have been a very special baby,' she explains with a sigh.

I look at my companion and scowl.

'Wait, I'm confused. So... what are you saying? That you believe that a good and an evil angel both came down from heaven and or hell – then one of them just magically popped the baby there?' I frown and point to her ample stomach. I ponder the logistics of Marcie's claims.

Marcie nods.

'Both,' she tells me, then strokes the corner of the picnic blanket.

I roll my eyes.

'And do you reckon this baby is gone now... or do you still believe you're pregnant?'

My hand cups a handful of strawberries and I bite into one of them, relishing the flavour crowding my tastebuds. Hmmm. It has been so long since I have eaten strawberries. They are plump and sweet. As I close my eyes, a picture of my mum doing the food shop floats into my mind. She used to squeeze the fruit before she put it in her trolley. It should be soft, that meant it was ripe.

'Well... sometimes I think I might still be pregnant,' Marcie whispers.

I snort.

'What - with like... the longest goddamn pregnancy ever?'

Marcie frowns, pouting at me, and I think how she has a chubby, angelic countenance.

'Well... it sounds stupid when you put it like that.'

Marcie seems to unwind and leans forward.

'Since being here and being treated by Adelia, they keep giving me pregnancy tests – one a week and it shows up as negative every time. I think the angels were both all in my mind... Well, *most* of the time I believe it's made up. But every now and then I think it might still be true, and maybe I'm going to be a mama after all.' Marcie sighs, then looks up into the distance with unfocused eyes. One hand rubs her belly, protectively.

I roll my eyes and throw a crisp at her forehead.

'Idiot. You won't be a mama. You're going to be medicated, that's what you're going to be. Medicated and sectioned forever.'

Marcie is unoffended. 'Well, I'm like you then, aye?'

Marcie grins, flashing her dimples.

'Yeh, I suppose you are,' I tell her with affection. She is a lot nicer than I am.

Marcie has not lost her grin and shelves her smile only so she can shove a doorstop of bread into her mouth at once. She chews her food with her lips open, smacking them together like a carefree child.

'What about you?'

'What about me?' I ask.

I put the stalk of a strawberry down at arm's length for an ant I spot. Bon Appetit my little "anty" friend.

'Well, I can talk for England, everyone knows about that, but I get lonely here, no-one talks back to me, and I don't have any friends here. Or anywhere… what was I saying? Oh yeh, anyway – what about you? Who's the dominant voice in your head? The main one you talk to the most or the person who speaks to you the most?'

Looking at my companion I consider my feelings towards her while I think about answering her question. Despite myself, I know I have a softness towards Marcie. It has crept up on me. It is refreshing not to feel like I need to be dead inside, or that I have to close myself off and fight for survival. She has told me what goes on inside her head, and I can see I am not the only schizophrenic in the village. Knowing that makes a change. Somehow, I feel less lonely. I shrug, deciding to open up to her a little bit. It cannot hurt, just this once.

'Probably, my closest friend is a ten-year-old girl called Mary. I call her "Little Mary." Well, she's been absent since I arrived here at The Rainbow Unit, but I see her every day.'

This is the first time I have spoken to anyone else about Little Mary and I look at my companion's facial expression to await laughter, or some of the teasing I have given to Marcie. Unlike me, Marcie does not treat me to either. In fact, Marcie looks back at me with an enthralled facial expression. OK, she is non-judgemental it seems.

We are near flowers, and a bumble bee "buzz buzzes" by Marcie's face. She fans it away as she nods with eager quickness.

'Go on. What's Little Mary like? Does she say mean things to you? Does she make you do things you don't wanna do?' Marcie leans closer to me.

With a wave of my hand I waft a fly away from my face, then shake my head.

'No, Little Mary doesn't do any of that. She's sweet. Since we met at the care home she's been ten years old. Little Mary was abused and had a childhood like mine. She had no-one to stick up for her when she needed it. I think that's why she likes me so much and wants to be with me. So, I'm not alone and nor is she.'

As I explain, I struggle to make sense of my own tortured mind. If what I had been told about my subconscious is true, it meant I produced Little Mary as a hallucination. But why? Is she serving some purpose part of my psyche needs to live out, or maybe she exists just so I can allow myself to have a friend I can interact with?

God, I am *so* fucked up.

There is a stone on the picnic blanket, and I flick it away, tilting my head up so I can soak up some more of the sun's rays.

'Was that like your childhood, Mary? Did someone hurt you when you were little then?' Marcie asks me with her usual lack of diplomacy.

I stare at her, my steel grey eyes drilling into hers.

Marcie's expression contains no mockery when I search her face. Her eyes look shiny, as though she is close to tears.

I look heavenward. God this girl is soft as butter. How she got through life in one piece is beyond me.

'Yeh. Shitloads of people, Marcie. At the foster home they placed me in they treated me like … well, just terrible. The best time that I had there was when they just used me as their servant, doing all their cooking and cleaning. There was always some reason, something I'd done wrong that I had to be punished for. They used to whack the shit out of me, and I wouldn't get dinner for days sometimes. Bastards. At least I stole a few bits of food to keep myself alive, and I could drink as much water as I liked. There was a lot of other… stuff, that they did. Silly spiteful shit, but… it still hurt.'

I do not want to talk about it anymore, but Marcie is sitting staring at me with her watery eyes. She is waiting for a conclusion to my story. Taking a breath, I oblige her by expanding further.

'But then… on top of all that, my foster father got all creepy, suddenly. Started wanting me to sit on his lap and to give him hugs. My foster mother would get so angry with me – as though I was doing something wrong, and it was all my fault? That was a lot worse than them just treating me like a piece of shit and making me do all the chores.'

Marcie sucks in a big breath, then chokes on her pear and coughs. Her eyes are now streaming.

'Oh my God! How old were you? Didn't you tell your social worker?' she asks.

I smile sadly and shake my head.

'I was about eight when they sent me there. The turnover was terrible, of social workers I mean. They never allocated me anyone, or if they did, then I didn't know about it. I remember a couple of officials showed up once, but only spoke to the foster monsters. They had me all spruced up, and had a bedroom looking lovely, but they never allowed me to go in there. It seemed like the social workers were always in the middle of case handovers, so they would send someone to cover my case most of the time. Anyway… you know how it would have gone. My word against the foster parents. A messed up ten-year-old girl, versus the word of two upright citizens. I knew who they would've believed, and then it would've gotten even worse at home.' My recollections are laced with venom.

'They wouldn't have listened.'

I nod. 'Nope, they wouldn't have.'

'So, what happened then?'

The events that happened next had led to further, long term trauma. I am not ready to share specific details of my past to that extent.

Shrugging, I drop my eyes to the end of the blanket at my fluffy slippers. Arranging my slippers beside the blanket, I line them up with precision, along the vertical green stripe.

'Dunno. After a while they didn't want me anymore. Then they sent me to a children's home for the next few years.'

Where it got even worse if that was possible.

My flat tone tells her, "End of conversation."

Marcie surprises me with her empathy, appearing to sense this. She asks no more questions, instead saying,

'My angels tell me to do things I don't want to sometimes. They tell me I have to eat certain things, or that I'm not allowed to eat certain things. One week I could only eat and drink things that were pink. I kind of liked that to be fair. I remember I went to Tesco's and found pink lemonade to drink, and I ate marshmallows, sweets, and pink wafers. Another week, I could only eat things that were round which was a right pain up the arse. I hated the time the angel told me I could only eat toilet tissue. It went on for ages, it was so gross.' She wrinkled her nose, then says, 'I thought it must be because there's something in the stuff the angel tells me to eat that the baby needs.'

Tears in my eyes, I nod, agreeing with her. Logical. I shake my head, clearing my thoughts, but when I look at her I know it is with the shadow of pity in my eyes.

'That must be tough – sticking to what someone else tells you to do?'

I cannot ever seem to follow orders; it is just not in my DNA.

Marcie nods. 'Yeh, sometimes. Especially if it's things I don't want to do.' Marcie also shakes her head, then pins a smile to her face.

Marcie's expression is cheerful, even in the now gloomy atmosphere.

'Anyway,'

'it's been tons better since I got here. The angels haven't visited me that much, and also, I'm learning to have dialogue with them now, so I don't have to do everything they tell me to – well, when I don't want to at least. That's been fantastic for me,' Marcie announces.

I give her a small smile, nodding. I am glad she has found a bit more freedom here. Whatever Adelia is doing then, it is working.

'Well, any improvement is great, I suppose,' I agree.

Who am I to judge anyway? I tried to throw myself off a bridge before they admitted me, so I had not been doing well myself.

Marcie's face clears, and she holds her hand up, waving with enthusiasm.

'Hey, there's Derek and Sophie – Hi, guys! Alright Derek, alright Sophie?' Marcie calls out her greeting.

Derek and Sophie stroll past us, deep in conversation. I squint at them. Those two are thick as thieves.

'Hi, Marsha. Hi, Mary – nice cardie,' Derek calls out.

Marsha? How come people do not seem to know other patients' names? There are only a few of us. Plus - "Nice cardie?" Yes, it would be - if I did not mind looking like a giant booger.

'Hey.' There is a lack-lustre amount of enthusiasm in my voice.

The chatting twosome pass us without further conversation.

'Miles leaves tomorrow – did you know?'

The presence of the other two does not derail her locomotive train of speech. I shake my head.

'How would I know?'

Marcie takes a quick breath in, excited at the opportunity to impart some information.

'We have to be there to see off any of the patients that are being discharged. It's the rule. They get a taxi for the patient to take them to their homes, and we all come out -with staff there as well, then we all hug or wave to them and wish them luck and that's it. Anyway... That's what we do....' Marcie's voice trails off.

I pushed my hair off my forehead and looked at the blue sky again. Whatever.

PART TWO

Chapter 1

I find my way to Adelia's office and sit ready for my therapy session, perching on the sofa with reluctance.

'So, we have scheduled you for your first 3D therapy session today, Mary. Is that alright with you?'

It is a rhetorical question. Might as well get it over with now, or it will get rescheduled.

I shrug. 'Fine.'

Adelia reacts, sailing over my sullen disposition with sunny pleasantry. 'Great! Well, please get comfy. Get your feet up if you like.'

Just two gal pals together. Yeh right.

'So… I believe I already know your basic details, but just for my records can we go over them, please?'

I nod, unsurprised at her thoroughness. Adelia is the kind of anal doctor who keeps her written records in exhaustive detail. I confirm my name, address, and other personal details in rapid succession while Adelia notes them down.

'Now, please, can you tell me? Do you ever see or hear anything inaudible or invisible to others?'

Tensing in my chair, I say nothing, my stomach clenching. Whoa. Straight for the jugular there, Adelia. I never answer this question because then, people would know I am mad.

Adelia leans forward, speaking to me in a gentle voice, 'It's fine to discuss these things with me, Mary. I understand your reluctance. You have trained yourself not to admit this kind of thing. But please, remember where you are and what my role is? You are in the best possible place to discuss this, and I am the best possible person you could discuss it with. Won't you tell me?'

She seems to understand my difficulty with sharing. It has been so long.

Silence grips us together like an invisible vice. Then I am surprised when I hear my voice, dry and raspy. The first to break the deadbolt.

'I see lots of people, but I have one primary group of friends that no-one else can see or hear. They come and talk to me a lot.' Except here, because this is where I am getting better.

Confirmation of my madness does not cause Adelia to recoil. She nods.

'Thank you, Mary. I know sharing that can't have been easy. Do they have names -your friends? What are they like?'

'Well… there are many voices, and I don't know them all, but I have a few main friends: Jo is a nice African man, he's calm; Dolores is an old English lady, very proper and gentle; Louise is a preppy, A-type personality, and then there's Little Mary, she's just ten years old and sweet.'

All at once I feel liberated, as though a weight is off my shoulders, releasing a slow breath. 'I've told no one about them, or even their names before.'

'Tell me a bit more about them?'

'What else do you want to know?'

'Tell me… is there one character in particular that you see more often? Or maybe there's one individual that you perhaps feel a particular affinity with?'

As I screw up my lips to help me concentrate, a picture of Little Mary appears in my memory banks.

I nod.

'Care to talk about this person?'

It is a struggle not to feel as though I am breaking Little Mary's confidence, but then I realise that if Little Mary is a character in my mind, then this is all in fact, my story and so… I am not telling Little Mary's tale at all. It is my story.

'There is a ten-year-old girl who I feel especially connected with.'

'Go on, go on… What's she like? In what ways do you feel an affinity with her?'

'Well, she's shy, funny, and caring. She had an abusive childhood.'

Adelia looks sympathetic and makes a clucking noise with her tongue. 'Terrible… what's been happening to her?'

My brows knot together, and I shift.

'I think it has already happened to her? Same as me. I mean, at least, I think it's all in the past now.'

The statement relaxes me, and I take a second to savour the mellow lighting.

'Sorry for misunderstanding, Mary.'

Her voice and demeanour are sombre.

Silence settles upon us again, and I think about Little Mary and the first time she visited me.

It had felt as though the walls of the children's home were closing in on me, crushing the spirit out of me. Every time I went into a communal area, it was an emotional blood bath. Kids closed ranks on me, "the weirdo." They left me nowhere to sit, and there was never anyone to be close to.

I had no ally. The adults turned a blind eye most of the time, and the other kids threw food at me while I ate with sniggering surrounding me. Each day was a test of endurance. Like a prisoner of war, I was trapped. Tortured. Surviving. At night, I had sobbed into my pillow, gripping onto the necklace my mum had given me.

One night, on my way back to my room I saw a little girl with long brown hair, her face turned to the wall. She looked a bit younger than I was, and so fragile she might break, and I walked over to comfort her.

'Hey.'

My eyes widened and lips parted at the mature expression in the girl's eyes when she looked at me.

'Hi.'

'Are you OK?' The set of her face and the way she held herself reminded me of myself. I already knew the answer to my question.

After some silence, the girl told me, 'My name's Mary.'

Scowling, I waited for mockery, but there had been none. Realising she was serious, I smiled at her.

'That's my name too.'

I had my other friends, Dolores, Jo, and Lou by then, and we all called her "Little Mary" to distinguish the two of us. Little Mary had immediately felt like part of our group, and she became a firm friend and my most frequent visitor.

'What happened to Little Mary? Can you say?'

I nod, although I feel a reluctance that I cannot voice. The silence in Adelia's room is absolute for a few minutes as she waits for me to explain further.

'I'm not sure how, but I know in the past, someone abused her. Little Mary has a fantastic imagination. She can rhyme anything you tell her, and she makes up little ditties off the top of her head. She sings them.'

I feel a compulsion to balance the horror of the little girl's story with some positive facts about her. We are more than our horrific past.

Adelia seems astonished.

'Your "Little Mary" writes rhyming ditties?'

She looks at me with an arrested expression, and I nod, proud of my friend.

'Yes, and she sings them. She does it all the time. She's brilliant, in fact–her vocabulary is amazing!'

Then I realise how I must sound. Little Mary is a figure of my imagination. I sound less and less sane by the second to Adelia.

My shoulders slump.

Adelia's quick eyes take in the change in my posture, and she pins a smile to her sculpted face.

'That is truly impressive, Mary. I am very interested to hear about all of your friends. Little Mary sounds like an interesting character.'

No, I say nothing.

'I'd like to hear more about her, maybe during our next session if that's acceptable to you?' Adelia brushes at her pressed jeans.

She has ironed a crease down the middle of them. *Why?*

I stare down at my nails. The edges are smooth and filed now, but they are still grimy. Nibbling at my bottom lip, I look at Adelia. She is spotless, in contrast. She is wearing clothes that look expensive. I glance down at her painted nails.

'Yeh, that's fine.' I stand.

End of session.

Chapter 2

'Will she let him go or what?' I mutter my comment under my breath, glancing around uneasily.

Ugh. Somya is acting distraught. Hanging all over that mutha grubba Miles and wailing. Unlike Miles, Somya does not seem to produce any tears from her eyes, despite the amount of noise she is making.

'I'll call you, and I'll write every day. I promise Somya–don't forget me. As soon as I can, I'll get a juicer and we can swap recipes.' He wipes a line of snot from his face.

For God's sake. I roll my eyes for so long, I nearly fall asleep. Tapping one of my slippered feet, I scowl at the two of them. Marcie sobs, completely sucked into the emotive scene and wraps her arms around her waist making a wailing noise.

Although all residents' attendance is compulsory, all staff do not have to be present. I flick my eyes around our small gathering, crossing my arms over my chest.

John and Jackie are present–why do I always forget John exists? Ian has also come to say goodbye. No Adelia, but she made a speech at lunchtime. Some bullshit. Miles: What wonderful things are in store for Miles' future. She is so sure… *yada yada*. Whatever.

Miles is now on the move, and my head snaps towards him, tracking his movements. Great. He hugs everyone, going from one person to another. Ugh, don't bring your cry-baby, snotty self over here, mate. I put one hand to my forehead. My head is hurting.

Miles makes as though he means to approach me, and my eyes snap as I wave him off with my hand. *Get away from me with that bullshit.*

He goes. Miles gets into the car, with the perfect Somya trotting along beside the car for a few seconds. Her hand is against the window and so is Miles'. Oh, the drama.

I kiss my teeth loudly and turn to Ian. He is the top-ranking staff member here at the minute.

'Can I go now or what?'

Ian nods.

'Yes, fine - but are you OK, Mary? It's a very emotive situation.'

I walk off, my hand in the air. Not interested, pal.

Chapter 3

The radio plays in the background of the reading nook, and I am soothed by its normality. I forget about the unrest that my therapy session has caused me, and I lose myself in the world of books. Pleasure fills me and I sigh, snuggling my feet up underneath me. How long since I have been able to do this?

'I'm sure I remember my older sister playing this bag of misery song nonstop one year. It drove me wild, but now I kind of like it.'

An attractive guy I have not yet met slides taut, denim clad buttocks into the armchair beside the sofa with an amiable smile. He must be support staff. The relaxed air he emanates means he must be a nurse or a doctor. I can hear him humming along with the radio.

I look at my new companion, taking in his large brown eyes and rich, gleaming brown skin underneath the bright lighting.

'Hi.' I go back to my book.

'Hey, there. You must be Mary. I'm Errol.'

I nod, but do not speak. Maybe he's replacing Miles? I shrug. Whatever. No-one cares.

Not wanting to encourage conversation, I decide not to ask Errol if he is a new staff member, a patient, or open up dialogue between the two of us.

Instead, I go back to devouring my book.

Errol sits with me for a time, but he seems to respect my wish for peace as he does not speak again. I become swept up in the story, and when I glance up, he has taken his leave.

OK, Errol, see you around then.

I walk back from the cosy reading nook, my gait easy. I slip my hand in my jean pockets, finding the business card Eileen gave me in one of them. Well. Good old Eileen was blowing hot air up my arse about my necklace. I touch just underneath my collarbone, where it would have been, blinking away a sudden mist.

Stopping at the nurses' station, I hand it to the nurse on duty there. I watch as they place it into the small pile of cards that are stored in an open container - above the phone for convenience.

It is a delay tactic. I am eager to return to the emptiness of my room.

Back in my room and laying back on my bed, I take deep breaths and stare at the ceiling. "Mindfulness" they call it. I concentrate on monitoring my senses, noting the texture of the material against my skin. The mattress supports me, cushioning my slender body. I am not simmering with rage and sadness. I do not care that my friends do not come to visit me here.

Grief, at their loss, threatens to unbalance me, and I head it off with more deep breaths and an angry swipe across my eyes. Back to practicing mindfulness.

'It's just too quiet, that's all.'

'I'm just not used to the silence.' Or to the lack of distracting chatter. It had often caused me embarrassment when I was in public. Again, I feel a simmering resentment that curdles my stomach. I do not want to own these feelings. Loss. Grief. Anger. Abandonment.

I look up to realise that Jo has arrived. As if he hears my call. A small smile of greeting graces my lips. He hovers in the doorway with a solemn look on his jovial face.

Although I love Jo, because of my friends' recent neglect, I am uncertain how I feel about him at the moment, and I stay silent.

Jo does not come to stand beside me to offer me his usual gentle solidity.

I stare at the friend who is like an uncle to me. The silence between us grows, spreading like mould as neither one of us speaks.

After a few minutes, Jo moves aside from the door. He remains silent. He has a strange expression on his even features I cannot place.

I frown. I have never seen that expression on his face before. What is causing it? I cannot interpret its meaning.

'Where did you go?'

I shrug at Jo.

'What do you care? Where've you been? Where've all of you been?' I berate him, my voice guttural.

Jo looks sad when I speak. My tone of voice is the one I use for others, not my friends.

'I care, Mary. Very much. We all do,' he claims. Then, 'What did you give to the nurses in their office?'

I consider ignoring his question, but Jo's tone is steel wrapped in velvet.

My face pinches itself together in response. 'What is it to you?'

Jo's brown eyes are full of reproach as I toss my head back like a filly stamping her hoof, but he does not rebuke me.

I relent, unable to bring myself to speak to Jo like that again. It delivers a sting of guilt that I find unbearable.

'A card from my allocated community psychiatric nurse. Eileen.'

Jo smiles.

'That's good, Mary. You need to keep it safe, please.'

Rolling my eyes, I treat him to a snort of disbelief.

'I doubt it. Anyway, there's a stack of those cards in the nurse's station. I saw them when I went past. Those nurses must come and go in droves. Eileen won't stick around, I bet.'

Pushing aside my bedspread, I crawl into the bed. I am thankful for the coolness of the sheets.

'Anyway, I feel destroyed. I need sleep now, Jo.'

It is not a lie, I am spent.

'Please come to see me again,' I murmur to him as I slip into a dreamless sleep that lasts the rest of the evening and the entire night.

A few days later I come out of my en-suite bathroom to find Dolores, Lou, Little Mary, and Jo standing outside the door. (They respect my nakedness even if they do not respect my wish for mental space.)

'Hi, guys.'

I realise I have not seen them for weeks now and my salutation feels awkward. I wonder again where they have all been since I got here? Lou smiles at me and I can feel their united love floating out to me. When it is just these folks, my close circle and me, I am safe and happy. I forget I am annoyed.

'I've missed you. Where've you been?'

'You look so well, sweetheart. Your hair's all shiny and long, and your beautiful little face is filling out nicely.'

Dolores is off topic as usual and steps forward first, accompanying her words with an endearing smile. The scarf she appears to be knitting vanishes as she moves towards me, clasping her hands in glee.

Strange... I always wonder where it disappears to when it does that. Back into my subconscious, I assume. Yeh, but when you assume, you make an ass out of u and me. Thank you very much ... I'm here all week folks.

Jo is standing, looking out of the window to allow for my modesty. I grab some underwear and put it on, then rummage through the rack of fresh smelling clothes that are hanging ready for me to wear. I grab a comfy looking jumper dress, putting it on.

While the dress covers my head, I hear Little Mary's pure voice trilling out, 'We're so glad to see you, Mary.'

I poke my head out like a turtle from its shell to see Lou smiling at me. She nods her agreement with Little Mary.

I smile, but I know seeing them makes me resentful.

'Where have you been then? And what about all the others?'

Lou smiles back but looks uncomfortable as I peer around Lou's shoulder with an enquiring expression.

'They're not with us. It is difficult to visit you while you're living here.'

I frown again at her choice of words.

"Difficult to come see me *here*?' Ah, is the product of my psychosis unhappy that I'm in such luxurious surroundings?'

My voice drips with sarcasm.

'What - do they prefer me in the squalor of my flat, perhaps penned in by days old rubbish and mouldy dishes? Why?'

There is no answer, just a sad head shake that reminds me of Jo.

I feel indignation as I remember feeling alone. In the past, I have been so isolated, surrounded by only the constant yammer of the many voices and personalities. Isolated because of them? So tortured, so hopeless. I have endured the many voices that have filled my mind, but now they have just cut me loose, abandoned me. They do not want me to be happy.

'None of you want to see me happy and well? Is that it?'

No-one answers my chilly question, but Little Mary steps forward. She holds her hand outstretched but does not touch me.

'We're all sorry, Mary. We just... we can't be here with you... not right now,' my small friend whispers to me. She directs her voice at the floor she is staring at.

I want to scream and shout as I hear Little Mary's words, but I cannot bring myself to do it. I jerk my head at Dolores. She was the first friend to come to me when I had no-one. The only grandmother I had ever known. She twiddles her string of pearls and is avoiding my eyes. She is elderly and vulnerable differently to Little Mary.

I feel anger swell inside me, accompanied by a sense of loss and betrayal that makes my bottom lip tremble as I try to contain it. It feels bullish for me to direct my rage at such a tiny person, especially after what Little Mary has been through - and Dolores' age and frailty also garners inside me a particular respect I cannot override.

Hence, I share my vexation between Lou and Jo. I vent it between the two, moving my stormy grey eyes from one face to another and asking them, 'You don't want to be here? Did it matter what I wanted? When I wanted to live a normal life? Without you all in it? Did I want to be the crazy person talking to herself, deafened by the noise of you all in my head until I couldn't eat or wash? Or sleep? Did I? Did I?'

My voice rises, my temper bouncing off the walls and being absorbed into the silence of the room. None of us move, as if frozen by my words.

I cannot believe that they have made me get used to them all this time, and now that I am experiencing something nice, they do not want to see it. "We can't be here right now." Yeh, right.

'We did not forcibly insert ourselves into your life, Mary, that is not correct.' Jo's voice is even.

'Whatever. *You're not my friends and* you never were. You don't care about me.'

My voice is dull and drops into the silence like a brick.

What difference does it make? They are all in my stupid head, anyway. None of this shit is real.

Little Mary sobs.

'No, Mary, that's not true. We love you but... it's better if we don't come to you while you're here. Maybe you can leave soon?'

'Leave soon? Why would I want to do that? You must be the crazy one if you think I'd leave here until I have to?' My voice cracks with my disbelief.

Jo and Lou step in front of Little Mary, and Jo places one hand on her fragile shoulder. I feel shame flare inside me, and it incites me more. How dare they?

Lou tells me, 'We can't explain... But the energy... it's not good for us, it's... uncomfortable?'

What crap is that?

'Uncomfortable...?'

In the past, I have often head-butted the wall to stop the river of voices that assaulted me with their stories.

My thoughts are clear as I turn my sour face to each of them. I had considered this group my die-hard, my family, but now it appears I had been wrong.

'You don't want me to be happy or, well... you don't love me.'

Tears well in my eyes as I realise that they just want... what they want, and to hell with me, it seems.

Jo makes a sound of distress, which is out of character. His African accent is more pronounced than it usually is, and his voice is soft.

'Come now, Mary, you know us. We love you and we have for many years now. You are our family, and you know this deep down. We want you to be happy... but in this place... we cannot be with you right now. You just don't understand.'

Jo's voice chokes, and he shuffles his leather-clad feet on the plush carpet.

'*What* don't I understand?'

The firm mattress bounces as I sit down on my bed.

'I *want* to understand, but you're not giving me anything to work with here.'

My shoulders slump and my back hunches over, exhausted again. A sharp silence creeps in between us, permeated by the motions of my head as it bounces from one face to another like an observer at a five-way tennis match. This conversation is so fucked up. *I* am so fucked up.

Lou stops biting her bottom lip long enough to speak again.

'Just get well soon so we can all go home, Mary. Please, and… and look after yourself,' she instructs me.

'You're not making any sense!' I burst out, clenching my fists in frustration.

'This place is helping me get better. You just don't like that because if I get better, then you'll all disappear back to the land of make believe or wherever you came from!'

I lay back on my bed, feeling emptied.

They turn away from me, about to leave, but Little Mary spares me a quick look over her shoulder, saying, 'We need to go now, but I promise we'll be back, Mary. I know you don't believe us right now, but we all love you, so much. Please try to remember that.'

A picture of Little Mary's fragile frame when she first showed up and spoke to me flitted into my mind. She had seemed defeated by the abuse she had suffered at the hands of the one who should have cared for her the most. My soft heart melts.

Maybe my friends do not mean to be so lacking in consideration? They cannot understand what it is like to be me. To receive so much from others, often against my will. All of my imaginary friends… They always take so much, but these four… they gave me every positive memory I ever had after my mum died.

'We've got to go now, Mary, but we'll try to stay close. We promise,' Lou tells me. Dolores wrings her papery looking hands.

'You're going then?'

Hand outstretched to Dolores, I blink away tears, rubbing my eyes as they vanish.

'I don't understand.'

Why have they abandoned me? It hurt. I replay the scene in my mind with the overlay of psych-ed. If my friends are nothing but a product of my imagination and they are not real, then did this inability they have to come and visit me mean I am getting better… or worse?

Chapter 4

Arms crossed and feet tapping, I am clear about my reluctance to be here. I was already having a bad day, feeling down and confused. I want to go back to my room and hide under the duvet. They do not allow that, because it is "reverse progress."

Instead, I am out here in the cold, watching Somya sob her tearless goodbyes to the nursing staff. I listen with disgust to her effusive gratitude, looking heavenward.

It is like an award ceremony. I have had enough of this phony crap. I turn to Sinead, who stands to the right of me.

'Can we go now, please? It's fucking freezing out here.'

My hair blows over my face, ruining my huffy head toss.

Sinead smiles at me and her red hair waves back cheerily at me in the wind.

'Ah, not much longer now, Mary. We want to give our Sonia here a proper send-off, don't we?'

I tut in response. "*We*" can't even be bothered to pronounce her fucking name right, so why do *I* have to stand out here and freeze my arse off?

Shivering, I make myself hold the words back and content myself with giving Sinead some side stink eye instead.

Marcie is completely sucked into the emotion of the farewell ritual. I suppose she has been around Somya for a long time, maybe a year? So, her discharge might affect Marcie. I can hear that Somya is not as fulsome with Marcie in her goodbye and praise as she is with the staff. I do not think Somya will miss Marcie much, if at all.

'It has been quite nice to see you progress, Marcia. Although we have not had much opportunity to socialise. I do wish you well and will say hello to you when I am chosen to give my talk at an Inspiration Group Meeting.'

God, she is so full of arse. I stick two fingers down my throat and make a gagging noise. She had said "Marcia." Patronising arse.

Somya approaches me slowly, her arms outstretched on either side of her.

I raise my eyebrows, staring into her eyes.

'Don't even bother,' I warn her, my chin tilting up and my hands on my hips.

Duncan moves closer to us, bidding me, 'Now, Mary, be polite please–you know that Dr. Sinclair insists on politeness to one another. Please say a *nice* goodbye to Sonia.'

I whip my head around to stare at Duncan. Frigging Nazi–and her fucking name is *Somya*? Why do none of the staff acknowledge that? Why does Somya not put them straight? It actually pisses me off even more that she never reacts when she is called by the wrong moniker.

Fine. I shrug. No matter. I cannot care less about this girl, anyway.

'Goodbye… *Sonia*.'

My smirk has its own communication.

Somya's long eyelashes flutter, and her lips purse together. Ha! bullseye–I see you. She *does* notice when she is called by the wrong name.

I regard Sinead again, the cold making me more assertive this time.

'God, can she get in the cab, and can we *go back inside* now, please? I'm friggin' freezing.'

Sinead nods, shivering herself. I see that her own lips hold a blueish tinge to them.

'Yes, sweetheart, two more minutes, I promise.'

I do not argue anymore but allow my chattering teeth to reply.

Somya gets into the taxicab, giving us the royal wave. She is crying prettily and dabbing her dry eyes with delicate fingertips. Blowing dainty kisses, she stretches her hand out of the window of the car.

'Goodbye, all. See you, everyone,' she calls out, her voice full of drama.

I stare at Sinead wordlessly, but I know my face is full of expression.

'OK, fine go,' she instructs my profile.

I hunch against the cold and speedily depart, my arms remaining wrapped tightly around my waist to harbour a tiny vestige of warmth.

'Flipping Somya, I couldn't give a flying Somya,' I mutter to myself as I stomp back to my room.

'Friggin' stupid rules. Seeing off people who are full of arse that I don't even know - or give *one* crap about and making me freeze my backside off,' I grumble as I look at the floor.

'These people get on my nerves.' I tut, complaining to the corridor on my way back to my room. I march, head down past reception and the communal areas. I have a rest period coming up with my name on it and I have earned it.

'Who does?'

'Shit, Errol.' I screech to a halt, my hand at my chest.

'You should wear a bell or something. You nearly gave me a heart attack. What the hell, man?'

Errol smiles his crooked smile, full of charm.

My lips twitch of their own volition.

'Your pal Somya gone then?' Errol's grin is full of devilment.

I snort.

'Goddamn–someone here actually knows her name. Yeh, she's gone–an' I'm pleased to say, she took that stick up her arse with her as well.'

Errol throws his head back and laughs. It is a deep, rich laugh that rolls towards me in warm waves. It triggers a smile in response. Interested in Errol now, I take in his gold tooth glinting in his mouth as it bares itself to me. Oooo, Errol. Got a bit of urban style going on there, have we? I am racked with shivers and my teeth chatter.

'True words. Anyway. Sorry, I'm knackered and freezing cold. I need a hot shower. See you around?'

'See you around, Mary.'

Just as Sinead's voice always has a hug in it, Errol's voice always seems to contain a smile. Thinking about it, they would make a much better couple than her and Ian… God, I must need sleep. What do I care?

Chapter 5

I breathe a sigh of comfort. The tepid cocoon of Adelia's room is cradling me in its embrace again.

'Now, I want you to follow the usual steps as I direct you. We will isolate every muscle in your body and tense them one by one. Let's begin with your eyes. Clench your eyelids together, tight as you can. Hold. Now. Relax...'

Together, we complete the ritual that is now familiar to me. By the end, I feel boneless.

'Tell me something about your father, Mary,' Adelia directs me.

I shift on her sofa.

'What do you want to know?'

'Well... I think you told me he wasn't a part of your life with your mum when you were little. Did you ever have contact with him?' she probes.

I put my hand up as if to slow the twitch of my right eye.

'Alright, Mary... let's start off small, shall we? What did your father do for a living?'

I keep my eyes closed. I can still smell lilacs. The scent seems stronger than it was before. Cloying, and it is making me feel sick.

'I think... he was some kind of fortune teller or something.'

The words are all but pulled out of me.

'A fortune teller, you say? How colourful.'

'He was a weirdo, yeh,' I translate.

'Did he ever live with you and your mother?'

I shiver.

'Is it colder in here now?'

No answer.

'Is the radiator on?'

Adelia remains silent, waiting for an answer to her previous question with the patience of a spider to a fly.

I sigh, thinking back to the little my mum has told me about my father.

'When I was a baby. We all lived together when I was a baby.'

'And where did you live? A house, flat, caravan?' Adelia seeks clarification.

'Mum told me that at first, we lived in a nice house, but then later… a flat. A council flat.'

'What happened to the pleasant house, Mary? Do you know?'

I shake my head.

'Not really. Just that my dad had an accident and that after that they lost the house and moved to the council flat. Mum feared Dad. She told me we couldn't see him. It wasn't… safe.'

I exhale. That is the most I have ever told anyone about my past.

'Thank you for sharing that with me, Mary. As I explained earlier, it's important I get to hear about your childhood experiences. It all helps me understand what has shaped you into the person you are today.'

Her voice is smooth as oil, pouring salve over my discomfort.

My twitch stops.

'Now, please, could you tell me about you? What did you like to do when you were small?'

A picture of me in the children's home flashed into my mind's eye, and my twitch starts again.

'I made things up.'

'Oh... You mean, you fabricated things - told lies?'

The question seems to echo in the room, and I fight the urge to open my eyes and check that Adelia's therapy room has not morphed into a cave.

Shaking my head, I frown.

'No. I mean, I wrote stories. Just short ones. I was often alone, and I read a lot, and liked to write.'

'Ah... you're a creative type, are you?'

'So?'

'No offence meant, Mary. It was just an observation. We have had lots of creative types as patients here over the years. Let's get back to you. What's your favourite colour?' she asks. Adelia's tone sounds warm and light.

Surprised, I burst out laughing.

'Random much?'

Adelia barks out a brief laugh.

'Mine is red. Anyway, thank you Mary, that was great... Let's leave it there for today's session, shall we?' she says, and begins the countdown steps to bring me back to reality.

When I open my eyes, the soft lighting greets me upon my return and the scent of lilacs is once again in the foreground. I feel lighter, and I am relieved to see it is not the cavern of my imaginings.

'Thanks.'

This is my favourite place, the reading nook. I glance around me, savouring the quiet, and the sight of books close by. My mum shared her love of books with me, and at first when she was gone, they were my only form of escape. Because the voices distracted me so much, I had not been able to enjoy reading for a long time. Here at The Rainbow Unit, I find that I have picked up the habit again. I can remain rapt for hours, content in a different world.

Adelia sits beside me with a book of her own but does not speak or say anything that encroaches on my pleasure. The two of us sit on the comfy sofa, in separate worlds alongside each other. It is nice to have company. Peaceful.

I rub my eyes. The words start to blur.

My companion glances at me.

'Coffee?' Adelia suggests with raised eyebrows.

I nod but withhold the courtesy of saying please.

Adelia walks over to the top end coffee maker and the rich aroma of coffee makes my mouth water.

I accept the glass mug without a word.

Adelia sips her coffee and does not appear concerned by my rudeness.

A picture of my mum's patient face appears in my mind. Her neat afro glistening under the kitchen lights as she passes me a homemade milkshake, reminding me, "Manners maketh the man."

'Thanks,' I tell Adelia in a gruff voice.

Adelia looks at me and smiles. Her eyes seem lit from inside.

'My pleasure, Mary, enjoy.'

Cor, she is easily pleased. I smile back at her. Adelia is not too bad, I suppose. For a doctor, anyway.

Chapter 6

I stare at Jackie in surprise as she peeps her head around the door, giving me one of her sassy grins.

'What do you mean, my therapy session starts soon? My last one was a couple of days ago and I didn't book one for this afternoon.'

'Yeh, I know, but that's not unusual here, lovely. Dr. Sinclair packs a lot into the patients' schedules so you receive the maximum amount of therapy. It will give you the best chance of staying well after your discharge.'

It now seems meeting Marcie is off the cards. I will have to explain to her later and hopefully, she will understand why I cannot come.

Getting up, I go with Jackie to my therapy session with Adelia. I get disoriented when I walk around the building by myself, so I am glad of Jackie's help.

'Come in, Mary,' Adelia instructs me with a gracious smile.

She gestures towards the sofa, then to the armchair. They look inviting.

'Take your pick.'

I choose the armchair. It would be cliché if I had lain down on the "therapist couch."

'Please, can you confirm your name and date of birth for me?'

I restrain myself from delivering my habitual eye roll. Predictable. I give Adelia what she wants, reciting my identifying information.

We complete the usual relaxation exercises Adelia guides me into, then converse. I am relaxed but decide to keep my eyes open.

'So, I know you're still quite new to our little family unit… How are you finding it?' Adelia asks in her well-modulated voice.

I nod while I consider my answer.

'It's been nice.'

The words surprise me, but they are the truth.

Adelia nods.

'And your room, the gardens–the staff and other residents… how do you find them?'

'Yeh, nice… good?'

Hopefully, that is enough. It has been a long time since I have been able to say anything is "*nice," or "good*."

It appears my statement is enough, because Adelia nods like a sage, then says, 'Good… good, glad to hear it.'

She prepares tea for us both, then picks up a remote control.

'I will adjust the lights in here to make it more comfortable, then we can talk some more… Is that OK with you, Mary?'

I nod. For the first time in ages, things *are* OK with me. Who would not want to stay in this luxurious home?

Maybe she can read my thoughts on my face because Adelia grants me another smile.

'So… I know the events that led to your admission here at The Rainbow Unit, and I don't wish to discuss them at the moment. Instead, why don't we begin with you telling me something about your childhood? Is that alright with you, Mary?'

Not really, I think with a frown. These questions are unfamiliar, and I am uncomfortable with the topic. I stay silent for a short time, my tongue glued to the roof of my mouth.

Adelia's cornflower blue eyes fixate on me and seem to peer into my soul.

This is her tactic again, staying silent to trigger the other person into speaking.

Bristling, I take a breath. Although Adelia is a stuffy "by the book" type, she is also nice to me every time I see her. *Really* nice, actually, and I notice she is the same with all the residents here.

I blow my hair off my forehead and some of it sticks. The room seems warmer, and I fan myself, uncomfortably hot. I am struck by an urge to please Adelia, and to unburden myself. I unglue my tongue with a loud *click*.

'My mum was lovely, but she died when I was eight, and they put me into foster care… that's when everything went… bad for me.'

Adelia nods again, then invites me to explain.

I expand… 'My mum and I, we were happy, and living a life with just us two. There was school, meals together, trips to the swing park... Then, when I was eight, my mum got cancer. She lasted for a few months, but they put me into foster care when she couldn't look after me. Then she died, and I had to stay there.'

In my mind, I begin to dredge up many past hurts and disappointments. Things that I had forgotten about until now. Nibbling on my bottom lip, I consider… am I ready to bare to Adelia?

'That must have been traumatic for you, Mary. Do you want to talk about it, expand a little more?' She sounds kind, but in a detached way.

I catalogue some details of my previous life–trauma in chronological order. I realise I could welcome the opportunity to expel it all… but not yet, and not everything.

'It was bad. My mum was all the family I had. She was everything to me.'

'You said they placed you into foster care? How was that?'

'It was shit.' My voice breaks.

'Really? How so?'

'They were mean.'

'Mean? How so?' she repeats, eyebrows raised.

My mind is made up. I do not want to go into this properly. I am not ready.

'They were abusive. They beat me, locked me in cupboards, and didn't feed me if I didn't do what they wanted. I had to do the cleaning, and they spoke to me like crap. Anyway, the guy got sick, and they sent me back to a children's home.'

'So, we have spoken about the voices you hear, your "friends" ... Was it at the foster home that you experienced them?'

'Nah, it was when I was about ten years old that my friends appeared to me.'

Adelia taps more into her screen, taking notes, and I feel a twitch of irritation.

'I want to determine who the most dominant character amongst your friends is.'

'Why?'

'Well, Mary, I intend to build an avatar that will allow you to interface with it. It will lend a face to the voices you hear and give you the opportunity to practice interaction with your "friends" or "voices." This should reduce the effects or distress that communication causes you. It will take some time, but before you are ready for discharge, your avatar should be ready.'

'My friends all have faces already,' I tell Adelia, shrugging. 'I'm confused.'

Breathing out, I decide to embrace the ambience of the room again. It is warm and snug in here and I find the lighting calming. My eyelids flutter down. It feels like I can drift off at any minute.

My eyes click open again, and my body jolts in its seat, as though I am stopping myself from falling.

'What happened–did I fall asleep?'

'What were we talking about?'

Adelia smiles but remains silent.

She looks at me as if she is waiting for me to speak again. I am unsure if I have even voiced my questions. Had I just thought about them?

'Er… is that OK, Adelia?'

She bestows a dazzling smile upon me.

I feel stupid but chuffed I warrant such approval.

Contentment settles over me. It is an unusual state and I welcome it.

Chapter 7

I know why my hands are shaking. Derek walks into the reading nook, his rangy stride now familiar. It triggers a butterfly avalanche in my tummy that I push away.

No.

'Hi, Mary.'

Derek perches in a seat a cushion's breadth away from me, and I imagine I can feel the heat emanating from his athletic body.

His puppy dog eyes burn into me, and a hot flush makes its way up my neck to rest like twin pink doves in my cheeks. Damn it, Derek. I resist the urge to fan myself.

'Hi.'

My hand feathers the page and I swallow. I have rediscovered my emotional side and am reading a novel by Sarah Shane. It is moving me to tears. Before facing my companion, I swipe the back of my hand across my eyes, then I fold the page over, so my place in the story is saved.

'What is it? What do you want?'

My voice trembles, although I am careful to keep my tone neutral. I look at Derek with stony grey eyes.

Derek runs a hand across the back of his head, then tugs at his earlobes. He is staring at me like a deer caught in the headlights, face flushed pink.

'I just wondered… hoped. If you might have some lunch? Or… sit with me during lunch, I suppose? We can't go anywhere. Sorry, that's stupid, I know, but I thought maybe we could… on a "just us" basis."

Derek is speaking quickly, and his words run together. My eyebrows bunch up as I try to make sense of what he is saying.

'What?'

'I've never been very good around people, worse around beautiful women like you, you probably think I have a cheek even asking you.'

'Beautiful women like me?'

As I repeat his words, I attempt to process them. Meanwhile, Derek pushes his hair back, squirming in his seat. He half rises, as though he is about to stand and leave. He disturbs a book on the shelf behind him, and it drops onto his head. Derek's face and manner grow even more flustered as he scrabbles around to put it back.

Then I understand what is happening here... *Derek* likes *me*… My mouth drops open. His words and flurry of clumsiness confused me, but now I understand I feel a stir of unfamiliar sympathy. He is more uncomfortable than I am. I put a hand on Derek's arm.

'Erm… but you haven't actually asked me anything, Derek.'

Then a second later, I bite back a smile. His words click into shining place again. Derek thinks I am "beautiful." Me. Mary Jameson. The girl the kids used to call "The Scabby Psycho."

'Will you go to lunch or dinner or breakfast with me one day please, Mary? Like… on a date.' Derek looks down at his knees.

A beautiful silence drifts gently down, settling between us like snowflakes. Delicate.

'I've never been on a date.'

My hand slaps over my mouth to retract the confession, but it is too late. Derek sits back down, moving closer, with one hand stretching out towards me.

'No pressure. I would just really like to spend some time with you. We don't have to eat if you don't want to–we could go into the gardens instead. I like you, and I think about you a lot. It's as though I need to know you more?'

'Alright.'

'Really?'

My voice does not sound like my own. It is scratchy and dry. I fan myself with my hand. Is it hotter in here? I surveil Derek. God, he's cute. His mouth is hanging open, and it makes me smile.

'Yeh, why not? Er… patients aren't allowed relationships in here, so we need to keep it on the down-lo. Maybe we should meet in the gardens instead?'

I am used to keeping one step ahead of the screws.

Derek agrees, reminding me of a nodding-head dog on the dashboard of a car.

'OK, great. That's great, thanks, thank you… today? Tomorrow?'

'Tomorrow. About two.'

Now I have put Derek out of his misery. I regain my composure. His voice sounds so hopeful.

A date… I will savour this conversation later, back in my room. For now, though, I reopen the book I had put aside when he first sat next to me.

Derek takes his cue and stands.

I glance at him, and my chest is constrained at the transparent pleasure on his face. He is wreathed in smiles, and I blink in surprise. This happiness is because of me?

'Thanks Mary, I will wait for you just by the water feature at two tomorrow then.'

I nod, then look down at my book, but I know the second he leaves.

CHAPTER 8

Adelia's treatment room is always just right. Temperature, lighting, sound. Adelia's room is a "Three Bears porridge" kind of room.

I inhale and exhale, on cue with Adelia's instructions. She is right. I *am* relaxed. I continue with my description of my friends.

'Lou is short for Louise?' Adelia asks.

I shrug, keeping my eyes closed.

'I dunno.'

'OK, that's fine.'

'Tell me more about your young friend, "Little Mary." The one who makes up the ditties.'

I feel warmth as I think about our friendship and I touch my smile, uncertain if it is real.

'She sings them, too. Little Mary's been my friend for years.'

'What does she look like?'

'Small, thin, brunette.'

'What else?' Adelia prompts me.

I remain silent, needing to think.

'She has brown eyes?'

'Have you remembered Little Mary's surname yet?'

'No, I haven't.'

We have spoken about Little Mary during the last few sessions, and even in my fuzzy state, I know I have already given much of this information.

There is silence for a while.

'What do you think it might be?'

'I said I don't know.'

'When did Little Mary come to you? Does she ever tell you any details about her own life?'

Adelia is such a stickler for details. Who asks if a hallucination had a surname. Is this usual? Silence meets my thoughts.

Her voice sounds thin and sharp like a reed, piercing my comfortable buzz with its edge. Suddenly, I feel uneasy.

'She has experienced abuse, like me.'

Has the temperature in the three bears room dropped? I shiver.

'Abuse? What kind?'

I plan my reply, staying silent while I think. Little Mary was about ten years old when she first visited me. I had returned from the foster home and was living in the children's home where I suffered terrible loneliness. Little Mary told me she knew what it was like to be abused and cast out. They had locked her in cupboards for minor infractions, drugged, starved. She did not get to see anyone and had no friends–except me.

The static sound clicks in my ear, and I breathe deeply again in relief, knowing my friends are nearby. My shoulders slump down.

'*Don't* tell her anymore. *Please.*' Little Mary materialises beside me, whispering in my ear.

'Why?' I ask out loud.

'Because it's part of your treatment.'

I note that Adelia's even, modulated voice, now contains a prickly barb in it I do not understand. It stings me, and I wince from it.

Little Mary speaks softly to me again. 'Don't tell her anymore about my story, Mary. It's not safe for you. Please.'

I remain silent, opening my eyes to stare at the ceiling. Had the paint up there always been chipped?

'Close your eyes again,' Adelia demands.

Is that Adelia's breathing I can hear? Strange, it sounds so loud and fast, as though she is running. That is weird. We are just sitting down.

'Did she tell you what kinds of abuse? What location is Little Mary from exactly?'

I sit up, and the spell of relaxation dissipates.

'Lie back down immediately.'

'No. I don't want to. I have a headache.'

We lock eyes. Blue meeting grey. Adelia's beautiful face is pinched and angry. Her nostrils flare and in the dimmed lighting, I can see her chest rising and falling heavily. I do not understand why. My voice sounds flat, and I realise what I said was true, I really do have a headache. It has been a while since I had one.

I run over my logic in my mind. Little Mary may be a figment of my imagination. She is likely to be an alter ego of my making in fact, but… she has asked me not to tell Adelia anymore and I do not want to betray her - even if she is just part of my subconscious. Plus, Adelia is acting weird. Does she have some personal reason for wanting to know about Little Mary in particular?

Adelia's right eye is twitching. Huh, it is usually mine.

'Go back to your room,' she barks out.

I stand, imagining I feel the knifes edge of her voice piercing my back.

This is strange. For all her kindness to me, I consider there might be something off about Adelia.

Chapter 9

The unit seems bigger and more confusing to navigate when I am alone. I open my door, peering over the threshold, seeing a mousy-looking woman muttering to herself as she walks past. I recognise the Mickey Mouse ears and note her slack expression. "Patricia."

Since seeing Patricia, I have not come across anyone else. This place is enormous. As I walk, I admire the pictures gracing the walls.

It is cold out here today and does not smell like fresh bread. Instead, I can smell fresh linen in the air. It evokes memories of a younger me, trotting alongside my mum and her basket of clean washing as she hung it on the line. I would hold the pegs for her, passing them one by one as she chatted. My mum laughed most of the time, and she made me laugh too. The clothes would swing, dancing in the breeze. Mum always hugged me when she was finished, saying the same joke every time:

"Come on, Peggy, let's go back in."

The memory makes me smile, and I stop to lean forward and inspect a framed photo of what looked like a medieval tapestry. I read the small plaque underneath it. "Safavid Courtiers Leading Georgian Captives." I step back, my brows twitching together.

"Captives." A shiver runs down my spine.

'Hi.' Marcie's cockney accent makes me jump. I turn to seek the owner of the voice.

'Hey.'

I look at my would-be companion.

'So, who've you spoken to today?'

My silent frown does not put Marcie off, and she steps closer to me. I shrug. It is getting boring by myself, anyway.

'Sophie… and Derek.'

'Ah. Sorry, yeh?'

Marcie's apology sounds genuine as my cheeks bloom and Marcie catches on. Despite her rambling speeches, there are no flies on this girl, that is for sure.

As the blood rushes further to my face, I slay Marcie with cool grey eyes, then walk off without a word and she scampers along beside me.

This is the most I have spoken with anyone in the last decade.

'So… D'ya reckon Sophie resembles anyone famous?'

'Halle Berry!' Despite myself, a chuckle escapes. I cannot resist saying out loud what we are both thinking.

'You should have a look at Sophie's art one day if she'll let you. It's amazing.'

I feel my shoulders relax, and I slow my pace, falling into step with Marcie. Our footsteps echo on the polished floor, accompanying Marcie's conversation like a high-hat drum beat that is keeping time.

'Derek is nice too–I think I heard he used to be some kind of computer whiz or something? There's also Sharon and Patricia… I think Sharon seems better… but Patricia seems the same as when she got here to me. They told me I was doing well the other day. I might be able to leave soon.'

Marcie pauses for air, but I do not speak in the intermission. OK.

'I'll get to come back and visit afterwards though–like Scott who's coming to today's inspiration group meeting. He was here a little while ago.' Marcie slows her pace and her voice lowers.

We reach one of the snug areas, so I sit down on the large sofa.

Marcie sits down beside me, and I see her shoulders are slumping. Her feet dangle off the edge of the sofa, not reaching the floor. She reminds me of a dejected child.

As I study her down-turned face, I sense the reason for it.

'Scott, aye?'

It is my turn to ask, and Marcie's turn to blush. She shakes her head, clearing the pink from her face like an Etch A Sketch.

'Scott was so clever. He was a Rastafarian and spoke about religion, politics and loads of nutrition like an expert. The nurses couldn't tell him sod all. I didn't know anything about what he talked about, but I liked to hear what he had to say–an' he had loads to say, proper wild and gobby, that man. Even when he got better, he was full of attitude. He did stuff just to piss off the staff. Like this one time, he used his art supplies to graffiti over the walls of his room. When the staff came to have a go at him, he just gave 'em a load of mouth.'

Marcie's lips curve into a tiny smile and her dimple threatens an appearance.

'No-one could tell Scott nothing without backing it up. He proper wanted to know reasons he should do what they said. The theory, the lawful reasons, the use of it, the ins and outs of a cat's arsehole–then he still might refuse.' Marcie chuckles. 'Anyway… Adelia helped him to get better. He stopped talking to himself so much, he slept at night, and he didn't believe that aliens had inserted his arm with a chip so they could monitor him anymore. They discharged him a couple of months ago. It will be nice to catch up with him again. Staff said he's doing well.' Marcie clears her throat.

I shift in my seat. The melancholy in her voice is affecting me, and I nibble at my lips.

One of Marcie's feet swings back and forth. The noise it makes as it scuffs against the sofa on its return journey puts my teeth on edge. I clench them, nostrils flaring.

Marcie is unaware. She sits staring into space like a life-sized robotic dolly with her batteries removed.

It unnerves me. Looking around the room, I stand up. I surprise myself by holding my hand out to Marcie.

'Come on. Let's go to group and go for a walk in the garden after.'

'Well… it is a nice day out today, I suppose. That might be nice,' Marcie responds, her voice regaining its usual vigour.

My voice sounds as rusty as my emotions, and I clear my throat.

Marcie looks at me in surprised joy, then nods.

As I smile at Marcie, an old song my mum used to play comes into my mind. Something about a new day…

Chapter 10

Looking at the plaque outside the room, I feel pleased that I have managed to find my way there. All by myself. "*The Circle Room*."

I open the door to find staff and patients in the room, with over a dozen people seated amongst the opulent decoration.

Ooo so fancy. I consider the most unobtrusive place to sit, chewing my bottom lip, until I notice Marcie standing up and gesturing to two seats together.

I go closer to her, and she whispers as she plonks herself down, then pats the empty seat next to hers. 'Let's sit here.'

'Cheers, did we miss anything, do you think?'

'Nah, we're still waiting on Sophie, and I can't see Scott yet.'

There are a couple of empty seats on the patient side of the semi-circle of chairs, and one empty seat on the staff side.

Sophie and Sinead arrive. Sinead walks over to Adelia, speaking into her ear. Adelia nods, then waves Sinead away to sit back in her assigned chair. Sophie saunters over to flop herself onto the cushioned seat next to my chair. She puts her head down and draws in the pad she has brought with her.

Adelia moves with her usual fluid grace. She focuses on the microphone but does not hold it. Holding her arms open wide beside her, she addresses the audience.

'Good afternoon group.' Adelia allows us to respond in kind.

I look around, feeling my stomach tense as the other patients deliver on cue in parrot fashion. Cringe.

'The Inspiration Group is, as you know, mandatory. However, our friend Derek is unwell today and cannot join us.'

'Ah.'

'We are honoured today to have our former patient Scott Gilmartin to speak with us. He is an "Inspiration."'

Adelia closes her eyes, clasping both hands to her heart to the soft round of applause.

A nerdy looking black man stands up and moves out of the circle of silken padded seats towards the small stage that holds the microphone on a stand. He picks it up.

I take in his glasses, short, neat afro, blazer, and spit-shined shoes. I wonder if he has come to enlist us in the geek squad and smirk to myself.

Marcie frowns, unamused.

'Who's that William Jackson lookin' mutha grubba?' she hisses out of the corner of her mouth. Her mouth drapes open and she appears to double take.

I do not have a clue who she is referring to, but I recognise she is making a joke and smile to please her.

'Good afternoon, Inspiration Group. My name is Scott Gilmartin and I'm here to tell you what a difference Dr. Sinclair and The Rainbow Unit have made in my life.'

'What the shit?'

'What?'

Marcie's eyes are like saucers, and I check if the other patients mirror her shock. Taking quick stock of their reactions, I can see Sophie is looking arrested by the man on the stage. Her hand is still over the sketchbook she is drawing in, and she wears a baffled expression on her face.

I survey the other patients. Patricia sits with a smile on her face and keeps touching her Mickey Mouse ears as though they are a talisman. She stares around, waving now and then in a mellow manner that suggests they have recently given her some medication. She covers her eyes, then she stares at her palms and repeats the process. I glance over at Sharon. She is twitchy and her face is wearing her habitual expression of equal parts fear and anger. Sharon is gawking at something invisible on the walls in abject horror and her face is melting into a silent scream reminiscent of the famous painting. I shake my head, turning away. They freak me out. Both, away with the fairies.

I put my attention back to the speaker. This guy looks like an accountant, not the clever and outspoken Rastafarian man Marcie had talked about earlier. Adelia is standing beside him, with a gracious smile pinned on her face.

'So… it's lovely to see you all. Thank you for giving up your afternoon to come and meet with me today. I'm here to speak with you at the request of our wonderful Dr. Sinclair.'

'Please, Scott, call me Adelia.'

Scott's smooth laugh reverberates through the microphone out into the silent room, and I am reminded of a compare double act on an American TV show. I hate those things. He sounds mild mannered. Not like the obstinate prick Marcie had described.

'Of course, Adelia, and thank you so much for having me today. It's an absolute pleasure to be invited.'

'It is my pleasure, Scott.'

'So… they discharged me a couple of months ago, and my therapy continued as an outpatient for another four weeks. Adelia here has given me a second chance at life. I now have a flat that I keep clean, I have a wonderful job, and I'm focused on bettering myself and helping others in my spare time. I'm a man reborn.'

My eyes widen at his suavity, and I give Marcie a side look. This guy flipped off the staff and graffitied his room? Maybe he was unwell at the time… or maybe Marcie had been unwell so remembers things differently?

I can see her brows tweak together and wonder if she is thinking the same thing. The mind can play tricks on you, I would know.

Scott is smiling, as though he is the star of a toothpaste commercial. He seems like a very bland man indeed. He applauds the staff with an urbane chuckle.

Adelia smiles back, full of grace, clapping at Scott's words.

The rest of the staff and majority of the patients spontaneously join in with the applause.

Unimpressed, I peep at Marcie again. She has a frown on her face and is stroking the back of her neck. She reminds me of someone who has lost her keys and is mentally retracing her steps.

Adelia stands up, spreading her hands on either side of her again.

'As you know, I invite some of our previous residents back to share with us the next steps they have taken on their journey. We are lucky that quite a few agree to share details about their progress once I have discharged them back into the community. I believe that showing what is possible for your future gives others hope besides a concrete vision to aspire to. Please, Scott, tell us what you're doing with yourself now. If you do not mind, please share some details about your new life with our other guests?'

'Anything for you, Adelia. I owe everything to you. I can't thank you enough.'

Adelia turns, holding one hand out to Scott. He grasps it with gratitude, closing his eyes as though in rapture. What is *this* shit?

Our guest speaker clasps his one free hand to his heart. I grimace. Urgh. What an arse lick.

Scott then explains to his contained audience he is now employed as a payroll clerk for a private company, and he volunteers at a local hospital in his spare time.

Well. Is Scott Gilmartin not just the hap-hap-happiest arsehole this side of paradise? God, he is peeing me off. His voice is now scraping at me, thin and mechanical, through the sound system. It is giving me a headache. I stick a discreet finger into one of my ears and shift on my seat, restless and trapped. Shut the fuck up, Scott.

'Didn't you used to be a designer?' Sophie's abrupt question breaks into his dialogue like a needle scratching a record.

My head goes to the right of me where Sophie is sitting. She looks as confused as Marcie does. Maybe Marcie was correct in her description of Scott's personality, after all.

Scott nods deliberately while he presses his palms together.

'Well yes, that's right, I did. But I don't need any of that now. I had an epiphany, and I have realised that my actual goal is to serve others. That's what my life is all about now and I can say that I have never felt this fulfilled before.'

Scott's maple syrup laugh is as innocuous as the rest of his intonation, and he is talking through his smile. He reminds me of a ventriloquist's dummy. I lean forward on my silky throne, squinting my eyes as I stare at our guest speaker.

Is that a twitch? His huge smile seems to flicker like a dimmer switch for a few seconds.

Adelia starts off another round of applause rippling through to the staff like a Mexican wave of approval.

I wriggle again, uncomfortable. This is like an award ceremony, full of plastic American "B movie" stars. There is something I dislike about Scott, but not that he is the contentious bully I had expected from what Marcie had told me. It is because he seems rehearsed and over the top… "pleasant."

My mouth is a moue of disgust. I shrug. What is it to me, anyway? If it works for him…

'Do you have anyone special in your life now, Scott?'

Adelia stares in Marcie's direction, and her brows slice into a frown.

'Goodness me, no. That nonsense doesn't interest me. My place is to serve others, I told you. I dedicate my time to making other people happy and helping to preserve our society in whatever way I can. That is my focus.'

'OK...'

My eyebrows shoot up and so do my friend's. Well, that is... *saintly* of him? I suppose.

Marcie shrugs, eyebrows fused together. 'Whatever.'

'Excellent. Well, I think all that is left for me to say, is that I wish you all the best on your journey towards health and value. I am so very grateful to Dr. Sinclair for her intervention. Both she and her wonderful staff have granted me a rebirth.'

Scott looks round the room with another commercial-grade smile pinned to his face, cutting off his lukewarm regard of Marcie to applaud. His appreciation punctuates the end of their conversation.

Marcie flinches but says nothing further.

Urgh so fake. I am repelled and fascinated. Scott has maintained his mega-watt grin throughout his entire talk. It is disturbing.

I look at Sophie. After her question to Scott, Sophie had retreated to her drawing and does not look up.

I steal a glance at what she is drawing. It is clearly a woman, with strong, attractive features and a wide smile. On the bottom left corner, I can see some writing. Curious, I read it peripherally, trying not to look too obvious.

My eyebrows fly up when I absorb what it reads:

"We are all in danger. Meet Derek tomorrow at 11 am at the pool. TELL NO-ONE!"

I look at Sophie's face. Puzzling. Her facial expression is unchanged. Her eyes do not even meander in my direction. Is this a joke?

After the meeting, Marcie links arms with me and calls out to where Adelia is sitting with sturdy Angie. She does not go any closer.

'Hi, Angie, can we have the garden card please?'

Angie glances at Adelia, who gives an almost imperceptible nod of her head.

'Alright, come and get it now mind, I have work to get on with,' Angie instructs us as she stands up to leave the ornate meeting room.

Marcie does not move, standing still with me for several minutes and I watch, uncomfortable at her visible pain. She is staring at Scott and even from her profile, I can see her eyes shine with tears.

Scott remains on the stage. He is shaking hands with members of staff with an ear-to-ear smile. Scott is speaking only to those gathered around him on the stage and is not glancing around the room. With the air of a second-rate, visiting politician, he pats Patricia on her Mickey Mouse eared head.

My eyebrows fly up to my forehead and I look at my companion. I see her jaw drop.

'Come on,' Marcie tells me with uncharacteristic direction.

'OK.'

My obedience is equally uncharacteristic, but I move along beside her without complaint to get the garden card.

Chapter 11

Marcie makes slow progress towards the garden doors. Everything about her was slumped downwards, as though she were weighed down. I surprise myself by asking, 'What's wrong Marcie?'

Marcie stumbles along, stopping with her hand on the door handle. She is frowning and quiet.

We unfold the glass doors out onto the grounds, and I breathe in the air's sweetness. It is a gorgeous day. So fresh. The birds chirp their cheerful song, making me want to smile. I stand still on the threshold, closing my eyes. Here, it is easy to absorb the warm caress of the sun, and the smell of cut grass. I can hear a grasshopper's singing. I open my eyes, taking in the glory that is all around me.

'Can you smell the flowers?'

It has been a long time since I enjoyed anything. I step out onto the grass in communion with Marcie.

She smiles at me with a nod, and I feel she recognises the feeling of appreciation flooding me. A kind of rapture that sings through my blood.

We navigate the path, and I am thankful Marcie allows me some quiet time to absorb the landscaped beauty surrounding us. It is perfect!

'So, what were you saying about Scott?'

'Scott used to be a bit of a git with staff, and he was also a sex addict. The guy was always sniffing around, after a bit, with us girl patients. Not nasty, just on it, you know?'

'Not really.'

I shake my head. I do not know. We stroll further along the path, and I notice the flower beds are colour coordinated. We are in the blue section. Is that done on purpose? Colour coding the flower beds?

'He was always chatting girls up, trying to cop off with someone. When he got well, he chased after Sophie first because she's... you know, "*stunning*" or whatever. But, too bad for him - turns out Sophie also likes the ladies, plus I remember she'd mentioned she was seeing someone–another patient? And it was well serious. Miles, Somya and everyone else that was there were nuts. So that just left me...'

'You need to spell out what you're getting at, Marcie. I'm not a mind reader.'

'We had something while he was here.'

Marcie remains silent after speaking, and I wait for her to add more. I scratch my head, hoping she does not expect me to pick up where she left off.

'We kept it a secret because staff are strict about that. "No patient relationships allowed." So, we kept it under wraps.'

My gaze doubles back to her as I remember Marcie's question to Scott. Mulling over the talk Scott gave, I think about the quality of his interaction with Marcie. Whoa, that must have been gutting. The guy had acted like he did not know Marcie from Adam. Cold.

'It was like he didn't know me. It's a bit gutting to say, but maybe he just forgot about me?'

We walk along further with the sun warming our backs. I am uncertain what to say here. Am I meant to comfort Marcie or to listen? I keep quiet, unsure.

'He didn't seem like himself at all… he was a dedicated Rasta, his dreds were gone and the numbers job? He told me he was shit at maths and he always said that he had dyscalculia.'

'What's that mean? Dyscalc–whatever you said?'

'Sorry. It's a condition where numbers are difficult to deal with. It's sort of like dyslexia, but with maths? They thought I had it at school.'

Marcie gives a little gurgle of a laugh. A tame version of her usual full out belly giggle.

'Maybe he was like that when you knew him. He could have been confused, and acting different then?'

'No.'

'Nah, I don't think Scott had been. I don't think he was always a flake like I was. Deep down, I've always been the same me, sometimes not well, sometimes well. Scott told me that mentally, he had always been fine, with no issues until he hit thirty because of all the weed he smoked.'

'He was proper clever and talked about corrupt systems and fighting against "them," and knew all about that kind of stuff, but he was a bit of a puff head as well. He said it was nature's gift, put here for us all to enjoy, only it seemed like he was sensitive to it, or had some bad shit or something because it turned him funny?'

Cursing my lack of social skills, I rack my brains for something to say. I want to help Marcie make sense of the differences she saw in Scott.

Marcie smiles but looks melancholy as she plucks a flower. Twirling it between her bitten down fingernails, she sniffs it absentmindedly.

'Anyway, Scott was brass balls confident. He knew what he wanted. He acted like he thought he was "Billy Big Balls" all the time. Scott… just seemed to know himself, you know? He didn't seem to care what anyone thought about him. Today was so weird because it was as though… it just wasn't *him* up there today. It wasn't him at all.'

'It does sound as though he has changed.'

Marcie kicks at a stone along the path, then says with more energy, 'Also, what's weird is that he *hated* hospitals. He kicked off a lot at the staff because of that. He used to slag off hospital staff for representing a "tier of power." That's what he called it. Scott said everyone worshipped consultants, and he couldn't stand the fact that what they said went. Dunno why, I think he had a terrible experience once or something, but anyway, he hated hospitals, and he *could not stand* hospital staff.'

Marcie falls quiet again, then murmurs, 'And now apparently, he loves them…'

We stroll on, and Marcie allows the silence to prevail, appearing to be immersed in her internal world. My lips part as I remember Sophie's note, and I glance at Marcie from the corner of my eye. Should I tell her?

The note said, "*Tell no-one.*" This is the first confidence I have ever been drawn into an implicit agreement with, and I am loath to break it. I'll find out what it's about, then I'll talk to Sophie. Marcie is nice. I don't think there is real danger, but if there is, I will warn her.

We are in a psychiatric unit, and Sophie is also a patient… maybe this "danger" is part of her… what had Adelia mentioned the other day in recovery class? "Delusions."

Maybe the note and the talk about *danger are part of her delusion*. I bite my lip. Should I meet her after all? Is it safe?

Chapter 12

We are standing near the steps of the pool and are just about to jump in when Marcie leans close to my ear, whispering, 'Dishy Derek's here.'

Derek appears, dressed in shorts and a T-shirt. He pauses on the threshold of the changing area, looking around.

By now, Marcie realises I am attracted to Derek, and has dubbed him Double D for "Dishy Derek." Damn it, not when I am in my swimming costume again! Is this punishment for something I've done before, perhaps?

I wrap my arms around my waist, silently cursing my porcelain complexion. I can feel heat rising up my neck, ears, and face and know I am bright red. My eyes are glued to the floor. I have got most of the matted clumps out of my hair, and now tie my hair into a ponytail. I wish my hair was down so I could hide my face. Derek addresses me in low tones.

'Can we talk?'

My eyebrows twitch, and I look up to see Derek's tightened features. He glances at my companion.

'Er, sorry that was rude... I... you're welcome too, of course, er... Marshey?'

Derek has not offended *"Marcie,"* with his mispronunciation and she chuckles, giving him an easy shrug.

'It's Marcie.'

'No worries, mate, that's fine. I'll be in the pool having a swim when you've had your chin wag.' She jumps in with a splash.

Double D and I look at each other, and he gestures to the seating area. We sit down.

'What did you want to talk to me about, Derek?'

'Is everything alright?'

Derek stares at the floor. I watch him warily as he rubs the back of his neck, then pulls at his earlobe.

'We all used to be something… before we came here, you know?' he starts quietly.

I do not know what I expect him to say, but not that. Yes, I know. I used to be called crazy… and I was frightened all the time. Thank God, things change. I nod.

'I was... am a computer expert. IT was my life for years. I worked with cyber security for about fifteen years. I loved it. In my spare time I did things I probably shouldn't have. I took a lot of drugs, and I also accessed information illegally. I saw things I could not unsee. It all contributed to my anxieties and paranoia. Things got terrible for me. I was… unstable.'

What? Dishy Derek took drugs? Does he mean… is Derek telling me he is a "hacker" and that's how he had seen things?

'Do you mean secrets?' I lean closer. 'What did you see?'

I grin and study the secret object of my affection. That Derek took drugs surprised me. I am also round eyed at the news that Derek is a hacker. I wait for him to expand with raised eyebrows.

Derek guesses my incredulity and smiles back at me.

'I'm not proud of my previous actions. But yes, I took drugs– stupid thing to do. It triggered psychosis, then they diagnosed me with schizophrenia. They tried some of the usual anti-psychotics on me and they didn't work. I was a cyber security specialist before they admitted me to this unit. Actually, I was well-respected in my profession. I could hack into practically any system.'

My mouth falls open. Derek is so clever. 'Really? I can barely start a computer.'

Derek pushes his hair back from his face, staring back at me with a sheepish grin. His large brown eyes sparkle like iridescent pebbles in a pond, and I find I am unconsciously drawing even closer to him.

I am so near I inhale his woodsy scent, mingled with chlorine. I shut my eyes briefly. Mmm, he smells so good! I realise he is saying something.

'Sorry Di... Derek, what did you say?' I catch myself before I let his nickname slip.

Derek smiles with patience.

'I don't blame you for tuning out. You're probably bored now; I shouldn't have gone on telling you about my computing knowledge... but I wanted to explain that computers and I have a history. I have always felt a compulsion to plug into whatever system I can connect to almost as soon as I'm aware of it.' Derek drags a handful of his hair back again, his eyes shifting left to right.

I frown, then shrug.

'Er... OK?'

Derek seems to think it is urgent enough to separate me from my companion, and to interrupt us before our swim. Although I do not know him very well, from what I have observed, I should have thought that is out of character for him.

'That's what I did, you see.'

I shake my head, still not understanding what he is getting at.

'Sorry?'

'I hacked into this system, into Adelia's electronic files, and I don't like what I found there. I don't like it one bit,' Derek announces in his deep voice.

Surprised, I lean forwards, saying with an uneasy chuckle, 'What did you find? Is Adelia avoiding her taxes or something?'

'No.'

Derek's brown eyes are solemn as the grave, and he looks around us again.

'There were records on us, and on some of her previous patients.'

I smile in relief. 'Oh, Derek, is that all? Obviously, there are files on us! I mean, I'm not a genius or anything, but even I know they keep tabs on us wherever we go. We are in the system. A hospital patient needs records for sure - how else would they know all our medical information?'

Derek treats me with a pitying look. 'No, Mary, not the kind of files Adelia has. They're exceptionally detailed. These records go back to way before they admitted us to The Rainbow Unit. They contain too much information. There's stuff in there about our childhood, education, relationships–and that's another thing. None of us have anyone else outside of here… there are no *next of kins* recorded for any of us current patients, or any of the patients who Adelia's admitted here in the past… As though she deliberately picked people for the unit who were all alone in the world.'

I feel a shiver travel up my spine, transferred by his last sentence.

I think of the passion that Adelia spoke with when she had talked about helping people to recover. That would be very difficult to fake.

After a moment I suggest, 'Maybe she just feels a bit sorrier for people who don't have anyone? Or maybe she's trying to cut down on lawsuits. She'd have to pay out if our treatment goes wrong.'

My chest swells as I catch the smile softening Derek's features, albeit briefly.

Then he shakes his head.

'There were also references to video recordings. I think I recognised some names of people who used to be patients here, Mary. It looked like Adelia had video files on them in their homes. Why would she have recordings of them in their own home?

Are they aware? Why would they have agreed to this? I cross-referenced the names with their files. These are people who were from all walks of life, and some of them real big shots - *Type A* characters who maybe cracked from the stress. Now they all work in menial jobs, or jobs that are the total opposite of what they did before… Something's wrong here. I can smell it, and I'm worried.'

What Derek is telling me stirs an eerie sense of discomfort. 'Like that guy who came to speak to us–er...' I search around for the speaker's name.

My brow clears when it arrives on my tongue.

'Scott!' I name the Inspiration Group guest.

'Scott was apparently totally different before.'

I am tempted for a second to explain in what way he is different but change my mind as I flick a look at my friend. I decide to keep quiet and not expand.

'His records were there too and you're right, I only knew him briefly, but from what I had observed, his behaviour is completely changed.'

Derek's proximity triggers my newly realised erotic imagination, and I surreptitiously inhale his woodsy scent again. I blink as I realise Derek is continuing to talk, and I have missed what he is saying.

'Huh? Sorry?' I feel stupid and blush a tender pink.

Derek's eyes hold mine without effort. I am silent, spellbound.

'I'm going to do some more digging over the next couple of days. I want to find out if there are video recordings and what is on them - but I just need you to keep an eye out for anything strange… I'm asking you to be careful, Mary, please.' Derek's hand reaches out, and with the lightest of touches, strokes my hand.

I feel a frisson and nod. I would probably agree with anything Derek asks me to do. At the moment, I am in a very vulnerable state. With my eyes low, I wish again that I had my hair down to hide my face.

'You comin' in or what?' my friend shouts out with unrepentant glee.

I feel myself grin in automatic response and I look at Derek.

'Do you want to join us in the pool?' I ask, the last part of the question coming out in a choked voice. I almost suffocate with shyness.

He smiles, but regret hangs like a transparent cloud over his face.

'No, that's ok, but thanks for the invite, Mary. Please remember what I told you. Be careful, yes?'

I nod, still feeling uncertain of what I need to be careful of, but again, feeling I will agree to anything he wants, in order to make the frown leave Derek's face.

I flinch as a splash of water slip-slaps at my bare legs.

"Fuck's sake, Marcie."

"Come on!" Marcie calls out.

'I'll tell Marcie what you said,' I warn him. 'I do not want to keep this from her.'

'Yes, fine, whatever you think best–but please tell her not to tell anyone else, yes? Staff cannot know. No matter what.' Derek leans in when he speaks, and his gaze bores into mine.

'See you around.' Derek leaves me with a smile and a promise.

'Bye,' I whisper, biting my lip as my eyes cling to his departing figure.

I turn, then use the steps to join my friend in the pool.

Marcie sticks two fingers down her throat and makes gagging noises, dramatically doubling over, and heaving as she walks around inside the pool.

'Getta room!'

'Oh, shut up you.'

'What did Double D want, anyway? Did he invite you upstairs to his room?' Marcie wiggles her eyebrows.

We have taken a pause at the end of the pool, lounging on the steps, and catching our breath. I snort and flick water at her.

'No, pervert. He thinks we're all in danger here, that something dodgy is going on here at the hospital, and that Adelia is part of it.'

'What a crock.' Marcie's laugh peels out.

I smile.

'Well… in fairness, I probably didn't explain it very well, but it did all seem weird. Apparently, Adelia's got some files on us in her computer system–oh, and there was a reference in her emails or something to some video recordings of ex-patients that Derek said he'd look into a bit more. I dunno. It did seem "dodge" What do you think?'

Marcie screws up her face and pouts her rosebud lips.

'I think Derek is a hottie, and he's clever an' all that–but we are all in here for a reason an' you should remember that. Maybe we should tell staff and they can up his meds or something?'

I shake my head vehemently.

'No, please don't do that. I sort of promised I wouldn't. He's not hurting anyone, and I can't decide if he's imagining things or not. You said that Scott changed a lot from when he left.'

Marcie nods, her face solemn, but then she chuckles.

'Somya and Miles won't change that much, though. They always were stuck up Adelia's backside at the hospital, an' they'll probably stay right up there after their discharge.'

Our giggles ring out in the echoey acoustics of the swimming pool for the next few minutes as we swim and splash each other in the carefree joy that seems to have become our pattern.

Chapter 13

I stare into the mirror in my room. I pinch my midriff. For the first time in as long as I can remember, I have some flesh to pinch. I cup my chest then gawk. I have boobs. Not much of a rack–but there is something there certainly.

My reflection is wriggling its eyebrows. This is new. I imagine myself with sultry curves, and Double D catching sight of me, then being astonished by my sexiness.

'Hubba Hubba.'

Cracking a grin allows me to see that the shade of my teeth is improving. They are nearly white again. I cannot remember when they were last this light.

A knock at the door makes me jump, interrupting my inspection of my new physique.

'Come in.'

I know by now whomever is there will wait for permission to enter. It makes me feel safer.

Sinead's red head pops 'round the door frame. The smile leaves my face and I look at her without expression. Sinead's chirpy voice sings out to me. She puts me in mind of a lark.

'Good morning, Mary. I've come to take some obs and give you your fifteen-minute reminder for your therapy session.'

'OK,' I say, withholding my thanks.

My mum would be so upset with me if she could hear me. My eyes drop.

Sinead steps forward and listens to my heartbeat. Next, she takes my pulse. She types into the tablet she carries.

'OK, well, enjoy your session then, Mary.'

Sinead does not seem to care about my rudeness.

Fifteen minutes. I breathe in quick, shallow breaths, then shrug. Spotting my hairbrush, I pick it up from the dressing table. My hair still gets stuck, but at least it does not get stuck until halfway down the hair shaft now. Progress. It's all about the progress. Now, I can tie my hair back, then use the brush to smooth over the top. I nod at my reflection. Maybe I would not win any beauty competitions, but I am good to go.

As I fling open my door, my gaze alights straight on Sharon, and I veer back from her. She is pacing again and talking to herself with increasing energy. God, can this woman actually just *fuck off?*

'Do you live out here or something?'

Sharon does not answer. Her mouth and eyes are wide open. As usual, her own inner world of horror absorbs her.

'You'll wear a hole in the floor.' I test her. No reaction.

Then I shut my door with a tut. After hovering inside for a while, I stare around me, feeling protective of my room. Opening the door again, I glare in warning at Sharon for a few seconds without speaking. She had better not dare to go in there.

Adelia will not like it if I am late, so I stalk off to join her.

It feels cold in here today for a change, and I fidget, unable to settle. Adelia does not seem affected by our environment and gets straight into our session.

'Today we are going to go a bit further into your past, Mary. How do you feel about that?'

I have my eyes closed as I lay down, and I hear the "swishoo" sound of denim, as Adelia crosses her legs.

I adjust the collar of my t-shirt. It feels like it is strangling me now I'm lying down on Adelia's massive sofa.

'Fine.' My voice sounds edgy.

I open my eyes briefly to look up at Adelia. She is nodding with an approving smile. Her blonde ringlets nod with her like a halo, and I sigh, admitting to myself that I would love to look like her. I would love to *be* her. I am inadequate.

I close my eyes and breathe in as Adelia is teaching me. In. One, two, three. Out. One, two, three. I savour the silence, as well as the pervasive scent of lilac disinfectant that dominates the room.

'It will be interesting for you to listen without questioning what I say. As the minutes go by, you will notice how comfortable you are with whatever I say. You can listen without questions coming into your mind. Do you understand?'

I nod. Yes.

'That's good, Mary. Now, we are going to start off by some simple relaxation exercises, followed by some conversation. If you find this acceptable, please could you raise your right hand?'

Adelia pauses, checking. 'Is this acceptable, Mary?'

I raise my right hand.

'Good. I would like you to relax here. You are safe and comfortable. It's possible to relax. You find it easy to relax. We will breathe together, and as we do, why not allow yourself to feel more and more at ease. You will feel safer, and more comfortable. You will, won't you?'

Adelia takes me through some muscle exercises, and, once she establishes I have entered the desired brain wave state, Adelia asks me to remember.

'Tell me… do you have any nice childhood memories? An early one, perhaps?'

I nod. The "Peggy" memory springs into my mind. It is one of my favourites. Another pushes it out. I smile. I have not thought about that one for a while. My eyelids flicker as I picture my mum's smile-creased face.

It was snowing outside, and I had wanted to play. My mum had wrapped me up like a mummy with her endlessly long scarf. It was a home knit, ugly. I could feel the scarf's scratchiness on my neck as my mum had looped it around my torso, then over my shoulders and in the shape of an "X." My mum had tied it around my midriff on top of my thick Aran jumper, then she had pushed my wooden arms into my Parker coat.

The many layers of clothing had severely limited my mobility. My mum had moved my limbs for me. She slipped my sock padded feet into wellies that had risen to my knees, then buttoned up my coat to my chin.

Then she had dropped a kiss on the small piece of forehead visible under the bobble hat.

'There,' she said as she pulled the hood up over the hat. I squinted, trying to push the hat up a bit to allow more vision, then hobbled out beside her in the dense snow. I walked like a cowboy without a horse.

The icy wind blew into my cheeks, and I sucked back a gulp of air. After twenty-four hours, it had finally stopped snowing, and now a pretty white blanket lay over everything.

I blinked at its beauty, then fought my layers so that I could stoop to collect a ball of snow. I had lost my balance and fell face down in the snow. My small feet had risen into the neck of their rubber prison as I dropped like a collapsed ironing board.

Eating snow, I moved my eyes up.

My mum had looked down at me, her expression one of comical horror. She had shrieked, then found herself in the same predicament as she fought our powdered foe to come back to rescue me. She had crouched down and tried to lift my dead weight body as I lay struggling to be free.

At first my mum had muttered and tugged at my waist. She was trying to hoick me up by my coat, pulling at me with futile energy. Then the momentum had sent her off balance. Mum had flown backwards into the snow pile. I had lifted my head up off the snow, and then giggled, my gap-toothed grin displaying itself.

'It's not funny, Mary!' my mum had told me in her cross voice.

Although I tried to stop myself from laughing, the snorts and chuckles had pealed out of me.

A huge belly laugh burst from her.

The two of us had laughed until ice cold tears had run down both our faces.

I laughed so much that I had freed myself from my snowy prison and I wrapped my arms around my painful tummy.

Back in Adelia's office again, I wrap my arms around my waist. For different reasons now. The laughter had faded, but the coldness of the snow had remained, seeped into my bones.

'How does that memory make you feel, Mary?'

'Warm in my heart, but also sad at the same time… it makes me miss my mum. Makes me miss being happy.'

'Thank you for your honesty, Mary.'

There is a slight pause.

'And what about your father? Was he a part of your life, Mary?'

I shake my head. 'No.'

The word is unvarnished.

'Was he ever there–in your life?' Adelia continues her line of questioning.

I nibble at my bottom lip and can feel my hands clenching.

'This is a safe space, Mary, you're still perfectly relaxed. Let's breathe together for a while before we end the session. You've done well.'

I allow myself to hear Adelia's instructions, and her calm voice sinks into me like golden raindrops as we finish our therapy session.

Chapter 14

It has been a long day today. Strange that some days seem long like that, but others fly by. This one is dragging, and I twiddle my thumbs and clock-watch for most of the day.

I close my eyes and lay back. I am spread out in my comfortable bed under the covers, as I practice the deep breathing techniques that Adelia has taught me. This will help me to relax.

I visualise a square. In… one two three four, hold… one two three four, out… one two three four, hold… one two three four. I listen to the sound my breaths make, tuning out everything else.

The sound of a scrape draws my attention and I sit up. I locate the sound. Someone has slid a piece of paper underneath my door. There is not much space under the door, so it does not protrude very far.

I sweep a few stray hairs out of my face and get off the bed to pick it up. Unfolding it, I can see it is a note. At the bottom, is written: "From Sophie." I scan the content.

"Derek and I need to speak to you. Things are wrong here and we are all in danger. Please meet us tomorrow morning at the pool."

My eyebrows raise. Well, the drama never stops here, does it?

Marcie nudges me and I follow her guileless blue gaze across the pool area to the sun loungers. Sophie and Derek sit, heads together. They look like they are deep in conversation.

Tasting bile, I feel my stomach clench. Marcie is staring directly at Sophie.

'Look at that.'

'Sophie is *well* pretty in her baggy little overalls, but can you friggin' believe it? She's even more perfect without her clothes on – holy cow, she's smokin' hot.'

I try to ignore Marcie's stage whisper and pursing my lips, I stare at Derek. Maybe he was not all that into me after all. Wait – did Marcie not tell me she thought Sophie was a lesbian? Is that true though? Who would bother to look at scrawny me with my teenage boy body, when the super gorgeous Sophie is about?

Derek reacts as though I am speaking my questions out loud. As I fix my eyes on him, his head swivels, and he levels a look at me. Hot and intense.

My stomach dips and I catch my breath. Damn it, Derek. Stop making me lose my shit.

'Cor, Dishy Derek's a bit of alright in his swimming togs, aye?'

'Slightly, yeh.'

Marcie continues to prattle on - but I tune her out.

Derek stands up and we face each other. I feel a polarised magnetism pulling me towards him. He moves towards me as if on runners.

I notice Marcie's chubby fingers gripping me, stopping me in my tracks.

She gestures down with her other hand and following her silent direction I look down. I had been about to walk right into the swimming pool. God, how embarrassing that would have been.

Derek stands on the other side of the pool, also flanked by his friend, the perfectly formed artiste. He treats me to a grin, and I see he had been about to do the same as me.

I chuckle.

We walk around the blue rectangle, meeting at the middle.

Derek's gaze holds mine.

'Well. This is slightly awkward.' Sophie's wry voice cuts into our silent communion.

Marcie giggles.

Derek and I do not break eye contact. We share a smile, then he clears his voice.

'We want to talk to you about what Sophie has seen,' he tells us.

Derek's face is stripped of all its joviality. He takes on an air of gravity and it settles over all of us.

We fall silent.

Derek keeps his voice low, staying close.

'Let's get into the pool. Although I think they won't be able to hear or record us out here, I think it'd be even harder in the pool... but stay close when we swim so you can hear what we've found out.'

We walk with a forced casualness into the pool, stepping down into its lukewarm caress one by one. The water is cold today, maybe the heater is broken. My inhalations are shallow, and I have to clench my teeth against their chatter. Shit that is cold. Derek comes closer, speaking.

'It gets warmer once you get your shoulders under... Tell them what you found, Sophie.'

Sophie is poetry in motion, and performs an elegant breaststroke as she fills us in.

'I told Ian my charcoals were finished, and I needed a certain kind to finish my portrait. All I had to do was pretend I was having a bit of a meltdown, then he thought I needed them. I knew there were none in the office and that Ian would have to go to the storeroom at the other end of the corridor to get them.'

The water gently laps at her words.

'And what?'

'He left me alone in the office.'

'Big deal. There's foof all in there you can hurt yourself with. That's probably why.' I had heard the triumph in Sophies voice, but I remain blunt as usual.

'Yeh, but maybe we could hurt *them*.'

I snort, then choke, as I swallow some water. *Please,* with the drama.

I splash around inelegantly. I still have not gotten the hang of this swimming thing. It is a struggle to swim and talk. I speed up so I can reach the shallow section again. Then I can put my feet down. Maybe I should just move my arms while I walk along the bottom of the pool. Will they be able to tell?

'I told Sophie what to do on the computer, step by step, and she could access the company records from the office computer.'

'It was so creepy, what I saw.'

Marcie rolls her eyes. She has been hanging around me for too long.

'What... More files that mention videos of boring ex-patients kicking back in their own homes?'

I smile to myself at Marcie's irreverent summary of Derek's concerns, but do not dare look at her again while I swim. I am impressed that she can quip, while she "doggy paddles" her way along the length of the pool.

'Well, yes, there is that... but there's a log of the effects of some kind of therapy. It details any way the patient changes after their discharge. I think it's something Adelia starts while we are here in our one-to-one therapy. Then she continues it when we are let into the community. There is all this data for all the differences in the patients' behaviour she's managed to create. It looked like... a journal of an experiment.'

'How do you mean?' I ask, then agreeing, 'Adelia *does seem* like she'd be really arsey about keeping records.'

I feel drawn in against my will, but I do not think that data recording is necessarily sinister.

'Well, take my old girlfriend for instance. Rachel. She was the first person I searched for. We met in here and I got to know her inside and out. Rachel told me that she always knew she was a lesbian and that she'd never fit in with her strict Christian, Jamaican family. She was a good looking, sporty type who had her own e-commerce line for sports gear. She herself mostly shopped in men's sections online because that was the style she had always been comfortable in.'

'So?' I ask again.

I hear myself using an unimpressed tone of voice. Contrarily, my heart is singing. I now have confirmation that Sophie is gay. I had just heard it right from the horse's mouth. Sophie is gay and so will definitely not be into Derek. Derek is safe. He can be mine. I release my breath and concentrate on not swallowing water as I did so. I had not even noticed I had been tense until my breaths start to come easier again.

'So… I found a video of Rachel. She was dressed in a frigging blouse and skirt. They sat her down in her armchair and she looked like a Goddamned choir mistress. She was even wearing tights for God's sake. Unless she's had a lobotomy, there's no way on earth she'd do that willingly. She was basically dressed in the church clothes her mum and dad had forced her to wear when she was little. It was the stuff I know her nightmares were made of.'

Marcie and I stay silent as we swim along. We flank Sophie so we can both hear what she is saying.

'So what, she changed her fashion style? Big deal.'

Check me out, the voice of reason.

'That's not all…I fast forwarded the footage. Rachel was in a chair sitting still doing nothing for hours.'

'And?'

'And… she has ADHD – attention deficit disorder – do you know how hard it is for someone like Rachel to sit still?'

We stop for another breather at the other end of the pool, and I hitch my elbows over the edge of it.

'Not really.'

'Flipping hard. Rachel was always moving. She didn't stop. That's probably why she was so sporty – because it helped her to use up some of that energy.'

Marcie kicks her legs out, saying, 'I have ADHD too - look, I'm a mermaid.'

I snort, then splash her.

Derek is quiet mostly, although he chuckles at Marcie's comment and my reaction to her.

'Staff approve of politeness and don't mind us getting along, but anything even approaching a romantic relationship is not permitted here at the unit. Us patients tend to keep any close friendships to ourselves. The staff never knew about Sophie and Rachel, although a few of us patients did,' he tells us.

'They had something special,' he states simply.

Derek turns his head to face Sophie, and I see his eyes shine with sympathy and something else. Then he turns to me.

'You look so worried,' the words burst out of me as I study his face properly. I sigh. He is so sweet.

He nods.

'I am worried, Mary, because I don't want anyone to get hurt, and I feel so drawn to you. I don't want to lose you before I've gotten to know you properly. I'm not exactly sure what is happening here, but something stinks. There are all those dodgy recordings of some old patients. Then there's how changed people become after they leave. I mean, it's so weird. Scott was a different person at the Inspiration Group meeting, and by the sounds of it – so is Rachel now, but why are they so dissimilar to how they were before? I don't like it. I think we should all leave.'

My mind plays devil's advocate, going down a rabbit hole. Escape from my mental health detainment? They would send the police to round me up again. Then they might tranq me up and keep me locked up for a few years. Maybe not here next time though. Maybe in one of those usual shit holes. All of us. Away from each other. Glancing at Marcie, Derek, and Sophie, tears fill my eyes at the thought.

Derek's comment sticks in my mind, and I mull it over. The motion of us in the water causes waves of gentle lapping to begin again.

'I want to get out of this place. Badly, and I want to find Rachel and check what's happened to her.'

Although her tone is low, I can hear that Sophie's voice is shaking.

'I don't feel safe, and I'm scared. I've decided that I'm going to tell them I want to be discharged from my section tomorrow. I'll call my CPN, Teresa. Then the hospital will have to either discharge me or take it to tribunal to keep me here. I'm mostly confident that I can pass a psychiatric examination now and they won't be able to keep me detained... Mostly...' Sophie mumbles.

Well, good for her - that makes one of us. I am still seeing my "friends." Albeit a lot less frequently than before, but they still turn up every now and then. I cannot predict what will trigger a visit from one or all of them. What if all of this conspiracy theory is nonsense because Derek and Sophie are just unwell?

'But what if this is all just because we are still crazy?' Marcie breaks in.

I breathe in relief that Marcie is framing my thoughts into unvarnished words.

'That's exactly what I was thinking. I dunno guys. The unit... it's really nice? There are plenty of crap hole hospitals out there with weirdo creeps in charge of them, but the staff here seem to want to help, and the facilities are the absolute bollocks. Maybe all this is just, you know... er, "crazy people" talk?' I ask, throwing hinting out the window.

How do we know what is true? How do we trust each other – or ourselves when we have learned our minds cannot be trusted?

'Let's face it. We're all in here for a reason.'

Sophie shakes her head.

'No, Mary, I'm not having any of that. I know when I'm better, and I know I'm sane now. I'm out of here, I don't care. Like Derek said, Rachel and I... we had a real love for each other. It was deep. After she was discharged, I didn't hear one word from her. She answered none of the calls I made to her from The Unit.

'No-one could convince me that Rachel just left and didn't give two shits about me as soon as she went. It started me off wondering. I thought something must've happened to her, so I waited for my chance.

I planned to have it out with her when she came to speak at the Inspiration Group. Only... I was taken aback when Rachel came to give her talk and didn't give me the time of day. She treated me like I was just *anyone.*' Sophie paused and cleared her throat before continuing. 'Rachel saw me there, but she acted as though I were nothing to her, a stranger.' Sophie pools some of the water in her palms, scooping it up to her face. Then she wipes her eyes. They are swollen, and I wonder if it is because she has been crying.

'That's just like me and Scott!'

I feel my face gurneying into the silence.

'Scott and me... We were hot and heavy when he was here at the unit, but when he came back to speak at Inspiration Group, he didn't wanna know me, a no-one. He spoke to me, but it was like I was a total stranger as well. Just like you said Rachel was with you. Alright, so me and Scott, we never had the "once in a lifetime romance type relationship."' Marcie throws up quotation marks in the air but keeps her arms low so that she does not lose her balance and slip fully into the water.

'We were close in our own way though, and at one stage we couldn't keep our hands off each other.' Marcie swipes a flattened swirl of hair off her face.

What the hell Marcie, you just added fuel to the fire? I wrinkle my nose at the picture in my mind her last sentence conjures, then peep at my three comrades. The mood in our small group is sombre.

'Well… I thought we were close anyway.'

I move further into the water. Without thinking, I move my arms back down under the water, and slip my hand into Derek's. Looking up, I see his eyes are clinging to mine just as our hands are.

'I'm out of here tomorrow,' Sophie repeats her intention. She pushes off from the pool wall with the powerful precision of an Olympic athlete.

'Is there anything that woman can't do?' Marcie muses out loud.

Derek and I giggle, breaking the tension.

'Probably not,' I reply, then push off myself, but with far less grace.

Part Three

Chapter 1

'Hi.' I sit down at the dinner table opposite Derek and next to Marcie, who turns to me straight away.

'Chicken en croute with veg tonight. My favourite.'

'Hmm, I love it too–didn't we have that last weekend aswell?'

'Sophie's gone.' Derek breaks into our banal conversation with a bald statement. Marcie and I gawp at him, and Marcie is the first to speak.

'Gone where?'

We both glance around the room trying to spot Sophie, then I realise Derek means "gone, gone." He looks devastated.

I put a hand on his arm and try to cheer him up.

'Sophie might just be into a drawing right now, or lying down in her room or something? Or maybe she's gone for a walk?'

I am out of practice with socialising, but I hope I sound reassuring.

Derek's face looks tense, then he shakes his head, denying the possibility.

'No. She isn't here at all, Mary. I ask the staff. They said Sophie was discharged today. At her request.'

'But Derek, that's great.' Marcie sounds jubilant. 'That's what she said she wanted? How come you sound so worried? Derek?'

She switches from my face to his, as though seeking answers. I know there are none written on my face because I am keeping it carefully blank.

'Yes. She did say that was what she wanted… but to just leave without even one word to me, even you or Marcie? We were close, and she said she liked you guys. To think that she would just leave without speaking, when she knew how worried I was about everything that I think has been going on…'

'What? So, what do you think happened? Adelia pushed a video in her face and suddenly–whoop - she's a goner?'

'Mary.'

Derek clenches his jaw and I grin at him, trying to force some levity into the conversation. His face, and Marcie's awkward chuckle, both inform me I have missed the mark, and my joke has fallen flat. Oops.

Metaphorical tumbleweed drifts down the table between us as my comment hangs in the air. Feeling bad, I decide to mollify Derek. He is closing his eyes again, and I watch a vein throbbing at his temple. Shit. Derek is really upset, interrupting my apology.

'Derek, I—'

'This is serious, Mary. Why can't you get that into your head?'

Derek's middle-class voice is verging on aggressive, and I feel my back straighten in response.

'There's no need to get shitty with me, Derek. I'm just saying that it might not be this big, terrible drama. Sophie may just have gotten what she wanted, that's all. We *can* have a difference of opinion you know. But… I didn't mean to make fun. I know you think this is serious.'

'It *is* serious, Mary. Why won't you listen?'

With a scowl, Derek stares at me, then Marcie, then back to me again, rapping out, 'Do we have a "difference of opinion?" Weren't we in agreement that there is something fishy going on here?'

I consider his words, and my next ones, carefully, not wanting Derek to be upset with me. Against all odds, I like him. I sigh, nibbling at my lip before I speak.

'It's difficult to say... but I believe that *you* believe you've seen some evidence that strange things are going on here. And that Sophie also saw something. Whatever you saw got you both really worried. It triggered suspicions and anxiety which you both shared–and that increased it.'

This sounds like at the end of "Scooby Doo," where they explain the crime. "And I would've got away with it too, if it wasn't for you meddlin' kids."

Anyway, I hope I had been inoffensive, although Derek's expression translates that I had not avoided it. At least I had not just come straight out and said, 'It's all bullshit, you just *think* you've seen all this crap, but you haven't, because you're still not well.'

'My God, you sound just like her, just like Adelia. I can't believe you would think that. After everything Sophie and I have told you we've seen.'

'But that's the thing, Derek. *I* haven't seen it. Only *you* have.' My tone is quiet as I spell it out to him.

Silence falls upon us like a guillotine.

Marcie and I turn back to our plates, then continue to eat in silence. In my peripheral vision, I can see Derek's face fall. I notice he is just pushing his food around his plate and my heart sinks. He does not look up or speak again throughout our meal.

* * *

'Afternoon lass,' Angie bids me as she sits down beside me in one of the small velvet chairs.

I am sitting in the vestibule, waiting for my massage. My shoulders are so tense, I am almost desperate for the masseuse to arrive. Funny when I think back to the Mary of a few months ago.

When I was first admitted, I had not even allowed anyone to touch me with my clothes on, and now here I am, looking forward to a masseuse to come and give me a back rub in my undies.

Angie's moustache is no longer even noticeable. Well, not as much anyway, I'm not blind. But boy, how things change. The nurse holds out her hand to give something to me.

'Here you go.'

'Your CPN has been down in our storage area, going through the boxes of patients' belongings. She said to give you this.'

Full of wonder, I open my hand slowly, and Angie drops my necklace back into my palm. My hand flutters to my neck.

'I can't believe it. I thought she'd forgotten about it.'

Tears prickle my eyes as I fumble with the clasp. I am so eager to have it back on, that my hands cannot manage the task. Angie laughs.

'You're joking, aren't you? That Eileen was a right pain. She kept moaning at us every time she called here to check on you. Like we don't have enough to do. In the end, we told her we were too busy, and to come down and look for it herself. And blow me down, that's what she did.'

'She turned up early Saturday morning at about seven o'clock. Stayed all day 'til she found it. Must have more time on her hands than we do,' Angie mutters under her breath.

Touched, I still do not trust myself to speak. An overwhelming gratitude floods my heart for this, Eileen's reported act of kindness.

I nod, my mouth and hands quivering as I put on my necklace. Once it is on, I touch it with reverence.

Eileen *is* alright after all.

Chapter 2

The cosy nook has an abundance of cushions, and I settle in amongst them, feeling resplendent. With a sigh, I reflect on just how much I have missed the quiet of my thoughts all these years. The ability to feel solitude. The voices in my head had meant that I could never concentrate enough to read any books over the last few years. I always had the constant wearing of other people's voices in my mind. They threw me off my train of thought and distracted me. It was exhausting. Experiencing a split in my attention all the time.

Now, here in The Rainbow Unit, I can breathe again. My thoughts are my own, mostly.

1984 is a book I remember from school. It was on the GCSE list and getting to the end of it had been another thing on my bucket list. Something that I had not even thought possible. Until now. Devouring it, page by page, I am steaming through it. Miserable though, it is turning out to be.

'Can I have a word?' Derek whispers in my ear, out of thin air.

'Argh! What the hell, Derek? You made me jump out of my skin.'

I flinch, dropping the book on the shiny floor as I do so, and it makes a slapping sound on the hard floor.

Although I "tut" my irritation, I am pleased to see Derek. Since our exchange at the dinner table the other night, Derek has kept a low profile, and we have not spoken. I have missed him.

Derek crouches down beside me to apologise, and his aftershave wafts up to tantalise my nostrils.

'Sorry, beautiful.'

Oh, goddamn.

Derek leaves his haunches and sits on the sofa next to me. His furrowed brow smooths briefly as he grins.

My heart picks up its pace. My shoulders relax and I unclench my gritted teeth. God, he is so cute. I sigh. All this mooning is just no good. I really need to stop it. Soon.

'What is it?' I note my tone is softer.

'Sorry I made you jump, Mary, but I really need to talk to you.'

Derek moves closer to me, speaking in a low tone.

My pulse raises as I look him over. His face looks set. It is serious. Or at least, Derek thinks it is, anyway.

I look around the reading nook. Most of the unit's patients are still sleeping. It is still early, and I have seen no one else around. I nod, then pick up the cup of hot chocolate I had made myself.

'What is it?'

'I found some more stuff on Adelia's computer.' He looks left and right.

Moving closer to me on the sofa, his shirt sleeve brushes my bare arm.

I frown.

'You're still doing that shit? Digging around? Why bother?'

'What do you mean, *why*? Don't you ever wonder what happened to Scott to change him so much? And what about poor Sophie? She wouldn't just leave and never come back. You know that deep down, you're just too scared to admit it to yourself.'

His whispers harbour an edge of desperation, and I turn to face the object of my girlie fantasies. After placing my cup down on the table in front of us, I take both of his hands into mine and stare into his eyes. His hands are icy.

'Derek, I think you had a really clever idea about what might be going on with the ex-patients, but if I'm honest, what I really think is that Scott just got better–and that Sophie is just out in the community, living her best life. She's back at home now, and moved on with her girlfriend maybe, so she's probably just trying to get some distance from us and this place or whatever.'

My tone is gentle, hoping to avoid upsetting him.

Derek's head rocks back as though I struck him, and he is absorbing the blow.

'Are you serious? Don't be so naïve, Mary, this whole set up stinks. Can't you see that?'

Derek takes his hands out of mine and grips my small shoulders with force.

My eye twitches and my nostrils flare as I fight off an urge to punch him in the face. Taking a deep breath, I shift backwards, then turn away to pick up my hot chocolate again and blow it. I am out of his reach. I shuffle my bum to the back of the sofa and sip. It is delicious, just the right temperature.

Derek smooths his curtained hair down either side of his face. He whispers to himself in a low voice. I cannot understand the words. For a while, he seems unaware of my presence, and then his eyes fly back to mine.

'Sorry,' Derek says in a mournful voice that hurts my heart.

I drop my eyes. Maybe he is having a relapse? Maybe I should tell someone?

Derek takes a deep breath.

'I found the videos. The one that Sophie watched and some more. I want you to watch the videos. Please. I found loads. They were all connected to files from previous patients. Each folder is of a person they've treated at the unit. They never relapse and get admitted again. They're supposedly well again, but they were just sitting in these empty, sterile looking flats... Waiting. Their records say they're doing shitty jobs and nothing much else.'

Derek runs out of breath and looks at me expectantly, a sad distance stretching between us.

'Erm... Derek, I hate to break it to you, but that's what people usually do? I'm actually looking forward to doing boring things like that. Having my flat clean, getting a job, and just chilling in the evenings. Kicking back and not doing much at all. Not being consumed by the voices of the others anymore. Peace. Sounds pretty much like bliss to me–how about you?'

Derek closes his eyes briefly.

I can hear his breathing. It is coming fast and heavy and I feel my stomach clench in response... When Derek opens his chocolate brown eyes, they drill into my grey ones.

'Listen to me. Please. I am not having an episode here. I'm just not good at explaining things... not a good talker. Adelia has videos of previous patients on her drive. These are not people "kicking back," or "chilling." These are like... robots with their batteries taken out. They are sitting with no TV, no music, nothing. Just sitting in their living rooms, in an armchair, and staring at a frigging wall for hours on end like a waxwork dummy.'

Derek's hair is flopping forward, and he pushes it back.

'They were all distinct personality types before. They were individual, unique–but now they could be the same person. It's all in their files. I read it. People just like Scott. The rest might have been anything before they came here, unemployed, or architects, artists, human rights activists, criminals, and rebels. They were all different, but now it's like they're the same person–don't you get it? It's like... they discharged them, and they've had their personality wiped. Everything that made them unique has gone somehow.'

I swallow, leaning away from Derek. I stare at him, then shiver.

'You're creeping me out, Derek.'

Derek's face looms closer. I can smell the coffee on his breath.

'I'm sorry. If it helps... I'm creeped out too.'

'Adelia has these files on us all. I think I told you before, they go back like–forever. She even knows about a warning I got from my supervisor when I was doing my computer coder training. Why would she need to know all that? How did she even get that information?'

Goosebumps raise up on my T-shirted arms, and I rub them. Derek's face looms closer, and he rubs the back of his head, making his hair stand up.

His breath smells of coffee. Uncomfortable, I cross my legs, folding my feet underneath me on the spacious sofa, and Derek continues.

'Then there's the money trail. Adelia had these massive payments in her bank accounts from different countries. I looked up the organisations and they're to do with some kind of military or militia. All over. Why would these companies be subsidising her? I couldn't work it out.' Derek's tone peters out as he finishes.

I frown and shift closer.

'But… What are you saying, Derek? What do you think it all means?'

I press him for a logical explanation. What Derek has suggested sounds like a conspiracy–if it is really true.

'I don't know… but so far, I've found out that Adelia has researched her patients to hell and back. Their whole lives investigated before they transferred here. Then they all seem to have had a complete personality U-turn after discharge. They live like monks when they leave here. Then there's the money Adelia is getting paid by bigwigs in different countries. Millions at a time. I didn't even bother to attempt adding up the amount of money she must have, but I don't know what it was for because it looked like they get nothing in return.'

Derek shakes his head.

'It's like there are all these hanging threads of wool. I can knit them together, but I have a long way to go. Not everything is clear to me at the moment, but it's coming. Already, I know enough to guess that Adelia is dangerous, and what she's doing to the patients is wrong. She's not curing us. She's... changing us somehow?' Derek stops again.

I stare into the distance with a frown, mulling over Derek's farfetched theory. Adelia had mentioned receiving funding from people, and were we not supposed to change? Of course, I have no proof Derek is not just having a psychotic break, and he fits what I understand are classic symptoms. Paranoid, spouting conspiracy theories. Derek wants me to watch the videos, but I do not know if I should chance it. We had learned in psych-ed that we need to "elegantly challenge," the delusions people might harbour. Not outright tell them it was untrue, but not go along with it either. What if I did not see what Derek saw when I watched it? What should I say?

Maybe the computer records and the videos are all hallucinations in Derek's mind, triggering Sophie, too? Marcie, God love her, had told me she used to believe she was being visited by good and bad angels. They told her what to do and often had sex with her during the night as she drifted off to sleep. Marcie had been so petrified of the prospect of the visitations that she had drunk gallons of coffee every day to try to stay awake. She said this had made her ADHD symptoms more problematic for her, because she was running at one hundred miles an hour, all the time exhausted.

I was hearing voices, seeing people, and living like shit. It is just like Marcie said... We are all in here for a reason. That reason is our mental health.

I sigh, nibbling at my bottom lip.

'I'm not crazy.'

My eyes fly to his.

'Mary, I'm not stupid either, and I know what you're thinking. I have a PH. D in computer science, with a deck load of qualifications in cyber security. I, one hundred percent, know what I'm talking about.

'Look, I know you're thinking it's all part of my mental illness, but it isn't–this is all real, I promise. I could show you, but I've already been a no-show for two of the Inspiration Group meetings and I can't skip another one. You know they're mandatory - it would definitely be pushing it. We just need to get out of here. We need to just get our stuff and go.'

Taking my hands in his, Derek holds them as though he has the petals of a flower laying on his palms.

I gulp. That is what my other friends told me. To leave. They dislike it at the unit. My eyebrows knot together again. Could it be that my other friends are symptoms of my mental illness, telling me to leave so I avoid recovery? How can I be sure? Maybe I should talk to someone about it? Maybe Sinead, she seems nice... for one of them.

Facing away from Derek's intensity, I take another sip of my hot chocolate. He distracted me from it, and now my drink is lukewarm and not very nice. I swallow, grimacing.

'But... '

'But what?'

'We're under section, so we can't do that? They'd just send the police to collect us, and then it might be even worse. They might take us to a shit hole hospital next time, detain us for longer, put us on one-to-one or sedate us. So, we can't leave, Derek.'

Part of me is glad I have this reason to fall-back on. My gaze falls upon my book, and I pick it up again. I will get another hot chocolate. This time, I will get some marshmallows to put in it as well.

'I'm sure that Sophie will be in touch soon, Derek. Give her time. She'll call or write to one of us. She's not the type to just leave without ever contacting us. You wait and see.' I reassure him with a small smile. Sophie would call next week or something. I bet.

Derek does not argue the point. Without another word, he turns on his heel and leaves.

I watch him go, following the stiff outline of his back with a sigh. Maybe I'll check with the staff for myself if a couple more weeks go by with no word from Sophie. She had seemed quite nice, and I can tell that Sophie means a lot to Derek.

There is a nip in the air, and I shiver further down into the collar of my jacket. The day is still bright, but the weather is turning. As we stroll around the yellow area of the gardens, Marcie asks me, 'Have you seen much of Double D lately?'

I trip over my own feet, as I walk along the path.

'No, I think he's annoyed with me. It's making me feel a bit gutted. More than a bit, actually.'

'Huh. Poor sod, him and Sophie were well tight, they were always together. It'd be the same as if you went and blanked me off. It would break me.'

I grin at Marcie's trademark candour, nodding.

'Shame we ain't allowed any mobiles or internet access here,' she chirps.

'Yeh, it's weird.'

Our conversations do not require me to speak often, but that is cool. I am used to Marcie by now, and if I want to speak, then I do. The idea of Marcie leaving the unit and cutting all contact with me makes me shudder. I snatch a quick look at her cherub cheeks. She has become so dear to me. What *would* I do?

I look ahead of us. I can see the French windows and the lights are on. Is that Derek I can see sitting down, all hunched over? I turn my eyes away from the dejected angle of his shoulders and nibble on my bottom lip. Poor thing.

'I think I'll ask someone about it.'

'Yeh, why not? It can't hurt, can it?'

'Angie, are you sure there have been no letters or calls from Sophie?' I put the question to Angie when I find her in the lounge.

Angie stops replenishing the cups and saucers for the herbal teas and looks at me.

She shakes her head, and as she does so, I note that her mouth droops downwards beneath her moustache. She answers me in her blunt way, training her gaze on me.

'No - why?'

I frown and shrug. Derek built up a very close friendship with Sophie, and he is fretting because he has not heard from her since her discharge. If I explain this, and my sense of unease to Angie, she will report to Adelia.

'Why are you pulling at your top like that? What's the matter?'

'Nothing's the matter. Sorry.'

Shit. Why not just wear a sign, Mary? I stop tugging my T-shirt down, smoothing the hem flat over my waist. I did not realise I was doing that.

Angie scrutinises me.

'It's just that, Sophie was so sure that…'

My voice trails off. "That you are all dodgy and that she was not safe here," does not seem like it would be a superb choice of words.

'She said that she would keep in touch with us.'

'Did she?'

Angie's already small eyes squint, disappearing even further.

A few months ago, I would have told her to go fuck herself and stormed out of the lounge. Now, I shift my weight from one leg to the other, feeling like a naughty pre-schooler being quizzed by her teacher.

'Yeh, she did, and it's been a few weeks since you discharged her. I haven't heard from her and nor has... anyone else,' I tell Angie.

Against my will, Derek's words stay in my mind. Derek is keeping to himself, and I have ruminated on Sophie's last conversation with us. She had been sharing her suspicions about The Rainbow Unit and Adelia. Then they discharged Sophie back into the community, and none of us have heard anything from her since. Something about that does not feel right, but I do not know what that "something" is.

Angie's eyes widen again, then she speaks in a voice that seems heavy with regret.

'Ah...'

'I'm sorry, love. This happens all the time. You patients seem to bond when you're inside The Rainbow Unit, but then when you get out, you go back to your old lives or onto new ones. Things must feel... different when you return to the community.'

I shake my head. Surely, Sophie would not just drop us all, drop her close friend Derek without a word? A thought occurs to me, pausing my breath, and I step closer to Angie.

'What if she's not ok back at home? What if she's having a relapse or something and no one knows? Or what if she's really confused again? What if she's hurt or lonely, or can't cope out there or something? She might need help?'

Angie shakes her head and "tsks." Then, she claps me on my shoulder, in her steady way.

'She's fine, Mary. Sophie still has her outpatient therapy sessions three times per week. Dr. Sinclair could tell if she were displaying any symptoms of relapse, I promise you.'

My heart is beating erratically in my chest, drawing my attention inward for a few seconds. Then Angie's words sink in. Wait... what? Tears of hurt prickle at my eyes. Poor Derek.

'Where do the outpatient sessions occur?'

'Here, at the Rainbow Unit,' she confirms. 'I told you, sometimes whe—'

I cut off Angie's words, drilling her, 'What? So, what are you saying? That Sophie's been here a dozen times, and she hasn't even bothered to come and see anyone? Why would she be like that? She's supposed to be... you're telling me she's just shit on all of us?'

On poor Derek? I think of him then, feeling angry as I picture his thin, worried face taut with anxiety and sadness. He is imagining the worst when all the time Sophie is coming back here, "happy as Larry." What the hell was going on here? Sophie and

Derek had been close. Friends. Fellow conspiracy theorists. Surely, she would want to set her friend's mind at rest?

Angie pats my back in her offhandedly kind way, then remembers our places and steps back from me, straightening her facial expression and her broad shoulders.

'Please don't get upset by this, Mary. I'm sure it's not personal. Sometimes discharged patients just don't want to face reminders of a time they were in a terrible place mentally. Maybe that's why Sophie hasn't been in touch with anyone here. She might make contact with you, but it will be when she feels she can do it without setting her mental health back.'

Never one for much chit-chat, this has been the most Angie has said to me since they admitted me. Out of breath and out of interest now, the nurse turns back to her task of setting up cups and saucers near the hot water for herbal teas. She begins to re-stack drinking glasses from the trolley beside her. End of conversation.

I know Angie might have meant her finishing suggestion to be a comforting one, but hearing her words causes my irises to magnify with tears. I do not think that Sophie and I were great friends or anything, but I know Derek still considers her one. Sophie had been close to Rachel. Marcie had been close to Scott. They had all thought they were important to each other. It seems like they had all been wrong. Or maybe all of this propaganda is just a load of old shit. I think about the strength of my affection for Derek, and my tummy rolls over. I consider my feelings for Marcie. My first ever friend. At least I know Marcie will stay true to our friendship. I would stake my life on it. I can trust Marcie not to crap on me.

Without saying goodbye to Angie, I leave the lounge. As I kick at a non-existent stone, I sniffle to myself, making my way back to my room. Fuck that bitch, Sophie, then.

Chapter 3

I sit in The Rainbow Unit's dining area, my chin up as I give my friends the cold shoulder. Dolores stands beside the chair, wringing her papery hands together. Lou is pacing, backwards and forwards, and Jo is standing still, with the air of a meditating monk. That look usually prompts me to speak, but I fight the urge. I will not cave. They completely abandoned me for three weeks now. It is out of order.

Against my will, I tap an index fingernail against the table in time with the pan-piped "musac." The tip-tap sound makes me raise my eyebrows. My broken stubs have grown for the first time in forever.

I look up to see Sharon, who usually talks to herself, is leaning forward across the table. She is staring at me. Hostility encased, her face framed by a gap in her unkempt hair. Yes Sharon, can I help you? I bristle, turning to confront her.

'What the fuck are you looking at?'

Sharon's thin lips are curling up into a snarl. I can see she does not like me, and my fists clench. Red alert.

Sharon's gaze creeps over my shoulder. I track it, finding myself looking directly at Jo. I smile at him on automatic pilot, then whip my head back to Sharon. Well, that is weird. Sharon is still focusing her attention in Jo's general direction.

I turn back to look at Jo again. He shrugs. Funny. I shrug too.

Sharon speaks in a low, hissing voice, 'Disgusting. Mixing with the likes of you. Don't think I don't know–you're all after my stuff. Fucking drug dealing criminals, the lot of you.'

I frown over my shoulder, back at Jo again.

I turn my attention back to Sharon.

'Who?'

'The Blacks.' Sharon spits out the word.

My upper lip peels back into a snarl in an instant.

'Hmm… racist *and* crazy. Wow, aren't you just a delight?'

I can feel my face is burning, and I hold my cutlery tight in my hand, at the ready.

Out of the corner of my eye, I can see other people in the room have stopped talking and eating and are now just observing Sharon's interaction with me.

She drags her browned talons into her hair, ripping out clumps of her dry hair at a time. Although she remains in one place, Sharon rocks backwards and forwards.

She is winding herself up, I can tell, so I slowly begin to stand.

'Shut up, shut up… Coming in here, pretending you're not working for them. Acting like you're all nice… I know you're in with "them" … you're just a filthy spy and you work for them - I know you do.' Sharon's voice volume is rising to a crescendo and now, she screeches the last words at me.

I can tell that Sharon is now worked up to the biting point, and I know from experience what is likely to come next in her repertoire.

Sharon throws herself across the table separating us, and as she does, grabs handfuls of steaming food from her plate to lob at me.

I drop the cutlery I had planned to use in my defence against her, so I can fend her off properly. Catching Sharon as she lunges at me, I dodge hot missiles made from a full English Breakfast.

Staff run to my aid as I wrestle the heavy Sharon back off me.

'DirtystinkingBlacksIknowyou'reinwiththemstealingallmy thingsdirtyBlacksthievesrobbingmeallthetime.' She screams as she sprays my face with her vile saliva.

Sharon's rage is making her strong, and she resists the efforts of the staff who try to intervene between us and carefully prise her off of me.

Revolted and enraged by the spit on me, I slap her hard in her face. Once. Twice. My hand connecting with her cheek so hard that it makes a "clocking" sound, and Sharon's teeth click together as her head flies back.

'Get the fuck off me, you filthy bitch.'

Heat builds inside my stomach, and then I hear the clicks. Click, click, click. It has been a long time, but I know *He* is coming... and soon.

'Calm down, little one, please,' Jo intercedes beside me.

Ian and Sinead drag Sharon off me, and hold her between them as she screams, trying to claw her way back onto my face.

The staff murmur to Sharon, in respectful tones, at the same time struggling to move backwards with her towards the door. Sharon is strong and frenzied in her movements and they are losing their grip.

As the alarms sound, Adelia arrives as if from nowhere. She strolls up behind the trio, flicking at the syringe she holds. I watch. My breath is still heaving in my chest and baked beans plopping off of my face and onto the table. Adelia leans forward and whispers in Ian's ear. He nods, then shifts a little to allow her space.

The tangy tomato sauce stings my eyes. I wipe them with the back of my forearm.

When I open my eyes again, Sharon is on the floor and seems docile, at peace. The support worker, Jackie, and security guard, Terry, have also materialised and are kneeling beside her. Adelia observes Sharon's vital signs and nods with a smile. A gurney appears from nowhere and they carry off my would-be attacker.

Jackie stays behind to clear the mess up, in partnership with the "dinner lady" who serves the food from the counter.

Adelia walks around the table to stand beside me. She pats my tensed arm.

My shoulders relax as she arrives. Her gentle tap lowers the barometer of my anxiety and anger.

'Are you alright, Mary?' Adelia asks, her voice full of solicitude and her face sympathetic.

Gratitude wells up inside me, striking me dumb.

Adelia offers me a handful of soft serviettes.

I take them from her, swallowing as I wipe my sticky face.

'Yes, thank you, Adelia.'

The residual adrenaline caused by mine and Sharon's altercation has made me vibrate all over. To stop the tears I feel welling up in my eyes, I bite the inside of my lip. Do not dare to cry. What kind of woose am I turning into?

Adelia removes the serviette from my hands, and guides me unresisting, to the door.

'Come with me, Mary. Let's go have a little pow-wow in my room.'

As I follow Adelia out, I spot Derek sitting in the corner and raise my hand. He is biting his bottom lip. That is funny, that is what I do when I am worried.

In Adelia's room, I sink into the seat, embracing the instant relaxation that washes over me.

Adelia smiles at me over steepled fingers.

'I'm so sorry about what just happened, Mary. Sharon still has a way to go towards her journey of recovery, I'm afraid… I hope it hasn't soured you on us here?'

I shake my head without hesitation at her question.

'Here, let me get you a hot chocolate.'

She gets up, gracing me with another smile.

I can feel myself light up in response to her kindness. Do not get sucked in. Hold something back, I tell myself–but I know it is too late.

'Thank you.'

It truly was my lucky day when I woke up in The Rainbow Unit.

Chapter 4

'Did you hear?' Derek's voice intrudes on me, making me jump. I am lying down on the lounger in the swimming area.

As I sit up with a smile, my hair falls out of its haphazard slipknot and into my eyes.

Derek perches on the cushioned pad at the end of my lounger, and smoothes my hair out of my face. I smile, pleased to see him.

'You look excited.'

'Yeh.'

He reminds me of one of those nodding head dashboard dogs. There is that puppy dog thing about him again.

Derek's eyes sweep over me, noting I am not wearing a swimming costume. I tut. He is probably also noticing that I do not have a book or magazine either.

'What are you doing?'

I roll my eyes. Nosy.

'I'm trying the meditation thing Adelia taught me in my last therapy session. I got bored staying in my room. It's supposed to help ground you in the moment or something. You take these deep brea—'

Derek cuts me off with a nod of his head, waving away what I was saying with an elegant hand. His eyes are extra shiny, and he seems wired.

'Yeh, like mindful meditation. Anyway, let me tell you my news.'

'What?'

'Haven't you heard–about the next Inspiration Group meeting?'

I can see something has happened that has piqued his interest. His face is flushed, and he has the tiniest tic in his smile.

'No, what happened?'

'Sophie is the next speaker.'

Derek produces the fact like a magician produces a rabbit out of a hat. "And now for my next trick, I shall make handkerchiefs from thin air - Tada!"

Derek's news sinks in and as it does, so my mouth hangs open.

I close it.

'So?'

Derek seems about to blow, and nostrils flare as he replies, his tone an octave higher. 'What do you mean "So?" So... you know that we both thought that Adelia and The Rainbow Unit are involved in some kind of conspiracy against the patients, then she goes missing straight after she asks Adelia questions about some of the previous patients in her therapy session?'

It is my turn to wave away Derek's excitement, and I cross my arms over my chest.

'Mary?'

I do not make eye contact with Derek until I feel his warm breath on my cheek.

'Mary.'

Derek asks again, then tips my chin up, tilting my face to his.

I allow his soft hands to guide my face, my eyelids drifting down.

'Yes?'

Derek's lips answer me, his kiss like the fluttering of butterfly wings on my tense mouth. Hot hands cup my face, and smooth back the hair with a quiet reverence that makes my heart pick up its pace.

'You are so beautiful.'

Well, that is off topic. If I strain away from him, I can observe him in silence. There does not seem to be any sarcasm in his expression. I am wrapped up in wonder… He really seems to like me.

'Sophie's coming to the next group session. It's this Thursday. We can ask her exactly what happens to the patients when they leave here. She can be our eyes and ears on the outside.'

I grant him a grin, and he frowns at me while smiling back.

'What?'

'You're cute–do that again.'

Derek shuffles closer, and his eyes lock onto mine as I turn to face him, full on.

As he leans in to close the space between us, I stop breathing, afraid to move. I do not want to break the spell.

Slowly… he moves *so slowly*, and I inhale his earthy musk, my eyelids shutting again as I quiver. My lips part under his, accepting his kiss with a relaxed ease that I never thought possible. Goose bumps grace my bare arms, my skin unbearably sensitive, as though every part of his presence is irradiating me.

Derek pulls away and I notice there are speckles of gold in his brown eyes. He clears his throat, but when he speaks, his voice is husky, and his words make me tingle. 'You electrify me.'

I swallow and move away, striving to leave Derek's embrace, but he reaches for me. I inch further away, shaking my head as I gape at him. Sudden fear squeezes my heart and my hand trembles as I hold it up in the space between us.

'No. Don't,' I say.

'Why? What did I do wrong?'

Good question. I really cannot say. I just know I need to get away from him. Standing up and turning on my heel, I head towards the door on legs that feel like jelly. I stop at Derek's plea.

'Wait!'

'The group. What do I ask Sophie? About the outside?'

I do not turn around to look at him, I cannot.

'Whatever you like,' I say, then resume my exit.

Chapter 5

The scent of chlorine from the pool is strong, and I look around me, breathing it in.

'I love that smell,' I murmur.

'So, who d'ya reckon your hologram thingy will be of then?' Marcie asks me through the thin barrier of the changing locker.

I pause for a second, one leg hovering half in and half out of knicker elastic.

'Erm… Well, I have a few friends, and they're all different, but I think probably Little Mary?'

'Why?'

My motions slow down as I consider my answer, pausing to pick up my swimming costume from the changing room seat.

'Because I think that she maybe speaks to me a bit more often than the others do. Although… not since I've been here.'

'Is it… What's she like?'

It is not just because of that, but our relationships are something I cannot easily answer questions about. My relationship with Little Mary is complex.

'Well, that's not it, no. They're all my friends, but the others are grown-ups, and Little Mary is about ten. She's funny and cute as a button. She cries when I get hurt or upset. She's polite, loyal, and clever.' I think a bit more, then add, 'Oh, and she has thin brown hair and freckles.'

This is more than I have ever shared with anyone. It doesn't feel like a betrayal. I feel that Little Mary will not mind my opening up to my newfound friend.

Adelia explained to me during our psych-ed sessions that we diagnosed schizophrenics commonly suffer from symptoms of "psychosis." Psychosis means we hear voices, see things other people do not, and smell or feel sensations others cannot. Apparently, a person who suffers from psychosis might be suspicious, or believe things happen that aren't true. Adelia explains it as this: Some people actually live inside their own personal nightmare, but for others, life is a beautiful dream.

I consider the information I've learned, seeing in my mind's eye a picture of Patricia snatching at butterflies with her vacant smile. Then Sharon, with her screaming paranoia. I continue with my answer.

'The other thing is because of what Adelia has taught us, I think Little Mary is likely to be a product of my imagination. When I first saw her, she told me terrible stories about how she was locked in cupboards at home for hours and hours in the dark. How they beat her and was starved for days. We have that in common. We are the same… so probably, in reality, Little Mary is some subconscious part of me that represents a past trauma. Something I need to work out–and she *really* doesn't like it here.' I finish with a short laugh.

Marcie's changing cubicle slams against itself as she flings open her door, making me flinch.

There is a thudding against my door a millisecond later.

'Mary?' Marcie calls through the door in soft contrast to the knocking.

I shut my eyes, realising I have said too much and knowing how soft Marcie is.

'Mary, I am so sorry,' she tells me.

Marcie's voice is thick with tears. I smooth the hair back off my face, swallowing the emotions threatening to overtake me.

I open my cubicle door, and when I speak, my tone is flippant, but I avoid her eyes. 'Are we going swimming or what?'

Marcie says nothing as I navigate around her into the pool, but she does not splash me immediately as she did before when we went swimming together.

She waits at least ten seconds and then splashes me.

My surprised laughter rings out, sending its happy echo out into the pool area.

I look around for a spare seat at a table after I am served in the restaurant. I see a few empty spaces at one table, then tense up when I see Sharon. Nope. Not today, witch face. Although I think I am seeing a change in her demeanour towards me lately, I do not trust that she will not be triggered by some unknown urge to attack me again. She is not talking to herself as much as before, but her habit of looking above my head or to the left of me as she grimaces in my direction unnerves me like nails down a chalkboard. Plus, she is a racist cow and I itch with the urge to throat punch her whenever I see her. I will not get sedated because of her.

Adelia notices my alertness, and stops walking, positioning herself in between myself and Sharon while she guides me to a table.

'I'd like to speak to you about something happening next Friday,' Adelia says.

'Why? What's happening next Friday?'

Adelia continues to walk again.

'We will discuss it, but it will be a special day.'

We scan the large room for two seats together, and are greeted within seconds by John, the support worker. I am surprised when I see him and think how I always seem to forget John exists. He is just so... bland.

We both smile at John as he greets us. Politeness, always.

'Hello, ladies, I'm just leaving so there's a couple of seats over at that table to the left if you'd like?'

'Thank you, John.'

'Please.' Adelia offers me a seat first, tapping my shoulder to gain my attention.

Patricia and Marcie are already seated at the same table, and while Patricia's gaze slides away from us, Marcie's face dimples into a greeting.

'Hi,' she chirps, her air of perkiness imparting itself to me.

I smile. By now, Marcie and I have enjoyed some lengthy conversations and I am at ease in her company.

'I am just telling Mary that next Friday is a special day for you, Marcie.'

My friend's smile dims, and her dimples vanish from view as she ducks her head.

What is this about?

Adelia stands up, clinking her knife against the thick plastic of her glass. All the residents are present - we all have the same mealtimes. Everyone stares at Adelia in expectation except Marcie, who is keeping her gaze downwards.

'I would like everyone to celebrate. Our time with Marcie here will shortly end. Next Friday, Marcie will begin the next phase in her journey to wellness. Please join me in a round of applause for Marcie. May she be healthy and productive in her new life,' Adelia announces.

She has put down her drinking apparatus and claps, surveying the room as a queen surveys her subjects. We all applaud on cue, and I wrinkle my nose, remembering my nickname for her. Queen bitch.

Tears fill my eyes and I grope for Marcie's gaze. Say it is not true.

Marcie's sad blue eyes tell me Adelia's declaration is true and will go ahead. I will say goodbye to the best friend I have ever known. In one week. Closing my eyes, I try to ignore the gurgling in my stomach, along with the heart wrenching emptiness rippling through me. I stare at my friend. She looks back at me, affection and worry on her transparent face.

I do not want to spoil this for her, and I do not want her to worry. As I decide this, I smile, straightening my shoulders. It will be OK. Although I will miss Marcie, I want her to be happy.

CHAPTER 6

It is always warm in my room, and it is annoying me that none of the windows open. I pry my eyes open, fanning myself with my hands. That never works. I shoot a glance at the window. Jackie has already come and opened my curtains once, then tried to jolly me into getting up.

The day promises to be beautiful. The sun is suspended in a crystalline blue sky and the birds are chattering away. It appears to be a lovely day.

It is all a lie.

Today is the day I have been dreading all week. It is the day I say goodbye to my best friend in the world, at least until I can join her on the outside.

Pulling the covers up over my head, I toy with the idea the whole thing is one giant hallucination. Am I really here? Does any of this exist outside my mind–and how can I know if this is real… or just a construct that my poor damaged mind has come up with? "I think, ergo, I am." I had read that somewhere, or maybe I had seen it on YouTube or something before they admitted me. I am not sure, but I think it means that because I can think, I must truly exist.

If the quote relates to me, however, it would be more accurate for it to say that because I feel as though my heart is being ripped out of my chest and pulled out through my anus, then this experience must be a real one.

I curl up into a ball, drawing in deep, shuddering breaths as I seek to manage my emotions. It is warm under my duvet, and my breath smells. I wrinkle my nose in disgust. Gross. I tug the duvet down so I can get some air.

OK. I need to face the day. For Marcie's sake. Better get this shit show underway.

Pushing myself upright in the bed, I propel myself off it, striding into the shower. Maybe if I can get all my tears out now, there will be none left, and I will not cry in front of everyone. In front of Marcie.

My friend is sobbing with such force that her ringlets are bobbing up and down like sets of auburn bungee cords, touching her shoulders, then bouncing back up again. I wince at the strength she grips me with, and pat her awkwardly on her cushiony back. I am still uncomfortable with this proximity.

'It's OK, Marcie, we will see each other soon. You'll come to see me when you come for your outpatient therapy, won't you?' I plead.

It seems impossible, but more tears gather inside me. They are welling up with the force of Niagara Falls. I am holding them back with steely resolve, pinning a tight smile on my face as I separate myself from Marcie to peer at her.

She is nodding as though she might not stop.

'It's OK, Marcie. It will all be fine. This is a good thing,' I exclaim in my most enthusiastic voice.

I know my facial expression must be making a lie of my words, because my heart is breaking.

'You're all recovered now, Marcie. You've smashed it! You get to start a whole new life back on the outside of these walls, and I will join you as soon as I can. You'll see. When I'm better, then I could get a job and we could share a place, just like we planned. It's going to be the best time ever!' I tell her, warming to my theme.

'We'll be like sisters? Who are best friends?' Marcie asks. Her bottom lip trembles.

I nod, eager to foster any small glimmer of hope to hold on to and cheer up my friend.

Actually, I mean the last part of my pep talk. For the first time in my life since my mum passed away, I feel as though I have someone of my own and something in my future to look forward to. All I need to do now is keep getting well, do everything the staff tells me to do… and not mess things up.

Marcie gives me a watery smile that is more of a grimace and is painful to witness. Gulping, it is her turn to pull back to look at me, then she says in a reed thin voice, 'Sorry for blubbering. I've soaked your nice white T-shirt.'

I shrug, telling her, 'No problem.'

My stomach churns as I swallow my sadness again. I will keep this T-shirt, never washing it, so I can feel close to Marcie when she has gone. Fear at the imminent loss of my best friend threatens to overtake me, and I fight it back. Ignoring the impulse to clutch at her and beg her not to leave me here by myself, I stick my chin up. I will not do that to Marcie's kind heart. It would be selfish and would make it more difficult for her to leave. After all, I will have the other residents and staff with me, and Marcie will have no-one. The least I can do is put a brave face on for her, and not add to her worries.

She clutches me again for one last time. The cab driver gets out of his large car and taps his wristwatch. I can feel Marcie shaking through her tight denim jacket, and I wince at the strength of her hold.

'Come on now, ladies, this is a great day! This is what it's all about, a fresh start for you all,' Jackie says, wiping her eyes.

We both nod.

'Promise me you'll call to let me know you got there safely? And that you'll put up the sun catcher?'

Marcie's dimple makes a brief appearance.

'Promise you'll keep in touch?' I whisper, quiet desperation in my voice.

'I promise! There's nothing that could stop me. You're the family I've always dreamed of.'

Marcie breaks into sobs again.

The support worker, John, finishes loading the cab with Marcie's belongings.

'Well, then, ladies…' he booms as he approaches us. 'That's the last of it.'

Marcie is the only thing left unpacked into the now full to bursting vehicle. I stare at the spacious estate car, packed with Marcie's personal effects. Adelia has organised a new flat for Marcie, and it is already furnished. During her stay, however, Marcie has accumulated clothes and accessories she wanted to keep.

I push Marcie gently away from me, towards the car.

'I'll see you soon, Marcie.'

Marcie hiccups through her tears and for once, she cannot speak. She raises a hand as she collapses into the cab.

'Bye, Marcie.'

We all wave her off down the driveway. It is as I turn to leave that I realise Derek is absent. I have been so distraught I have not noticed until now.

Walking toward my room to pick up my swimming costume, I decide to check the pool to see if I can find him.

'I thought you'd be here,' I tell Derek as I slip into the pool beside him.

The water is warm and smooth. It soothes me somewhat.

Derek's smile is a quick, jerky motion that mimics his usual smile.

I frown and try not to be distracted by his athletic physique.

'What's up?' I ask, simply.

'I wanted to talk to you about what I found out today,' Derek rasps.

I can see his Adam's apple moving as he speaks.

'I need to tell you about the lights,' Derek says.

I raise my eyebrows, not expecting to hear this.

'The lights?'

I look up at the ceiling spotlights. What could they possibly…?

'Not those lights.' Derek cuts my gaze off with a small, and more relaxed, smile, interpreting what I am thinking.

'What then? Is this where you were earlier? When I was seeing Marcie off? We could have done with you being there, you know. It was really hard to say goodbye.'

There is a lump in my throat, and I swallow it, trying not to allow a whinging tone to enter my voice. I hate whingers. In a short space of time, I have come to rely on Derek to "be there" for me. God, I am stupid. I resist the urge to dig my nails into my palms, to make them bleed. How did this happen?

Derek strokes my face with a gentle tenderness, staring deeply into my eyes. At first, I flinch away, but then I sway towards him again.

Derek blinks, clearing his throat.

'I'm sorry I wasn't there today, Mary. Marcie seems like a lovely girl, and I hope you know I'd do *anything* for you. It's just that this was too good an opportunity to miss. Our schedules were therapy free, and I think they didn't monitor our attendance at the discharge goodbye. At least, I hope they won't. Anyway, I needed to do a bit more digging around.'

God, not this again.

'OK… did you find anything?'

My voice is weary. I can half guess the answer already, and Derek does not disappoint.

He nods, yes.

'It's difficult to understand, but it looks to me like there's a journal about some sort of light treatment. I'm uncertain, but I think there're special lights turned on in sequence. They trigger a response in whomever they subject to them.'

'I don't get it?'

'I could be wrong, but it seems like… Adelia turns on these strange lights, and something clicks in our brains, making us do what we're told. Maybe… If Adelia tells us to "hop on one leg" with no lights, we tell her to go to hell. If she tells us to hop on one leg with the light show going… then we say how high.'

A shiver runs down my spine as I swim, not connected to the temperature of the water. Well, that is another creepy Derek idea. I have never heard about a set of lights making people turn into American chat show contestants, though.

'Why do you think that?'

'Because there's a record of when they're being used and of whom. Adelia gives an instruction, and then there's a written recording of what the outcome was.'

But… Adelia devotes herself to helping us. Her passion is genuine, and more than that, her actions show we are important to her. Adelia is always available. She practically lives at the unit, here most of the time to treat us, her patients.

'Why would she do that? She's the only one who cares about us? Adelia just wants to help us.'

I wonder again if I should tell someone? What if Derek is having some kind of psychotic episode and drawing me into his madness? What if he needs help? I nibble at my lip, unsure what to do.

'Look at all of this luxury they've given us.' I grunt, striking out towards the middle of the pool.

The swimming pool is warm, and the water feels like silk as I swim in it. If I am honest, I have gotten used to the comfort that surrounds me. I do not want to leave for an uncertain future, running from the authorities. Everything Derek has explained makes sense in a very sinister kind of way, but do I really trust what Derek is telling me he sees is *actual* reality?

I do not want to escape from my section, leaving this nice place to go on the run because of the rantings of a madman. Even one as clever and gorgeous as Derek.

My internal musings cause me to splutter, and I mess up my stroke rhythm again. I tut, annoyed. My swimming style is getting better.

'I'm not a scientist, so I can't figure it all out, but I know she's doing something to us. Maybe it starts when we're here… but I do know that when we leave and come back, we are different people.'

Is that a bad thing? I wonder.

'The lights are the key,' Derek states.

Chapter 7

I walk, heading down to the nurse's office, deciding to visit the gardens. Thank God they let me go out there unsupervised now. I will go to request the garden card. A walk outside will cheer me up and take my mind off my loneliness.

As I pop my head into the nurse's office to request garden permission, Angie calls to me, 'You alright, Mary? Why the long face?'

I turn to face her, then step forward.

'Angie, are you sure I have received no letters or calls?'

Angie looks at me, then shakes her head. I can see that her mouth is turning downwards beneath her moustache. Déjà vu much?

'No, love, sorry.'

I frown, nibbling at my mistreated bottom lip. This is Sophie all over again. Except this time, I am a lot more affected and confused. Marcie had been so adamant she would keep in touch. I was certain she had meant it, but it has now been weeks since they discharged her, and I have heard nothing from her. Not one word. Just like Sophie. Marcie has ghosted me.

'I just don't understand.'

Angie's eyes seem heavy with regret for me.

'Ah, sorry, lovie. I told you before, it's different when they're in here... Different for them.'

I shake my head. No. I am not thick. Marcie and I were close. I had felt the realness of her friendship. She was genuine.. Surely she would not just drop me? I consider the possibility Marcie might not be ok back at home alone. She may be relapsing, or could be unwell again or even hurt herself? I remember worrying about the same thing happening to Sophie. It seems like such a long time ago now.

I rest an anxious hand on Angie's stocky arm without thinking. Angie stares down at it, flicking my hand off her like a pesky bug. I remember the rules. Staff are amiable and polite, but they discourage touching staff for any reason at The Rainbow Unit. Staff may choose to touch the patients, but the patients cannot do the same. Boundaries. Rules.

'What if Marcie's hurt? Or if she is lonely and can't cope out there?'

Angie shakes her head again, then reaches forward to clap me on my shoulder. Again, I feel déjà vu and remember how Sophie did the dirty on Derek.

'Is she going to the outpatient sessions with Adelia?'

'There, there. Marcie is ok, Mary. I promise you.'

A heartbeat pulses in my chest and then Angie's words sink in. I feel tears prickle at my eyes.

'Is she?'

Angie nods.

'Yes, and I understand it is all going well. As expected, really.'

My shoulders slump in dismay.

'As expected,' I repeat. 'I just don't get it. Why would she have cut me dead like that? She's supposed to be my friend?'

I suck on my wobbly bottom lip, and my face flushes with embarrassment. I feel like a child who has just realised Father Christmas is not real. Say it isn't so.

Angie pats my shoulder again in her offhandedly kind way.

'Please don't get upset by this, Mary. I'm sure it's not personal. Sometimes discharged patients just can't face the reminder of being in a terrible place mentally. I bet that's why Marcie hasn't been in touch with you. Maybe she will contact you at some point? When she feels able.'

I know Angie means this suggestion to be a comforting one, but hearing her words makes my vision blur with tears again. I had thought Marcie and I were friends. The best of friends. It seems I am wrong. What Angie is saying is that mine and Marcie's friendship is just a painful reminder to Marcie. Something that she wishes to forget. Not a relationship she wishes to keep.

OK. So be it. I shrug off Angie's afterthought of platitude, then shuffle to the door. OK, that's fine. I have other friends. Sort of.

A montage of memories I shared with Marcie, kaleidoscopes in and out of my mind. The swimming pool, the walks and picnics, the giggling and chatting. Screen shot of myself in my room alone, painstakingly writing postcard after postcard to Marcie—just as we had promised to do, enter my mind. I have been writing to Marcie every week, but I have not received even a one-line postcard in reply. Well, from what Angie just said, I should stop doing this because communication with me is the last thing Marcie wants.

I stumble away, snivelling to myself as I make my way to the gardens.

I swipe down on the flimsy box, and push the door out into the garden, but then stand still, staring at it with blurred eyes. I feel like a sleepwalker. The green light blinks at me from the side. It is unlocked and waiting for me to open it. I do so, and automatically inhale as the secret world of perfection presents itself to me. It never fails to shock me with its beauty.

I remain still, taking in deep breaths to centre myself. Just as Adelia had taught me. Mindful breathing. I close my eyes, then open them again. The grounds are so peaceful. Restoring. If I can just put things into perspective.

My breaths come slower now. The main thing is that Marcie is OK, and soon I will be too. I am stronger now than I have been in years.

As I potter through the grounds, admiration for my surroundings overtakes my angst for my friend.

'Hello, Mary,' a sweet voice says from behind me.

I spin 'round to greet my friend at the sound of her voice.

'Dolores!' I gasp.

I have not seen or heard any of my friends for at least a couple of weeks now. Since we had the conversation in my room, that ended up confrontational and distressing. The overwhelming need I had felt to communicate with them had faded, but I am still pleased to see Dolores. An automatic smile overtakes my features, lighting up my face as a rush of affection embraces me. She is just who I need right now.

'Dolores.'

Dolores does not smile and "vanish" her knitting as she usually does. It is hanging from her fingers as she glides forward all at once. As though she is on an unseen skateboard that tugs her along. Boy, my imagination is funny sometimes.

'You're in—' Dolores' voice goes silent suddenly, as though someone has struck the mute button on a remote control. So funny when that happens. I smile at her.

'What? Dolores, I can't hear you?'

Dolores stops talking for a few moments, and presses one finger to her lip, appearing to think. Then she speaks again.

'Mary, dear. The others want me to keep quiet in case it makes things worse, but I can't. Please, love, just trust me that—' Dolores' voice disappears again, and I shake my head, bewildered.

'What are you trying to tell me, Dolores?' I rub the back of my neck. This is getting weird.

Dolores throws furtive glances left and right, as though she expects someone to "jump scare" her at any point.

'Please, dearie, don't be angry with me. I only want you to be safe.' Dolores cranes closer to me, and I can see the wrinkles in her paper-thin skin. She lowers her voice to a whisper.

'It will not get better for you yet, and I don't want you to suffer. I just can't bear it, no matter what they say is for the best for you in the long run. You need to—' The rest of Dolores' message cuts out again, leaving me in a quagmire of confusion. What the hell?

My features migrate into uncertainty as her sense of urgency transfers itself to me. I open my mouth to question her again.

'Is everything alright?' Adelia calls out from behind me.

I am so intent on listening to Dolores that the sound of Adelia's voice causes me to first shout out in shock, then jitter into the air by several inches.

'Argh!'

I whip around to greet my consultant. She halts her approach suddenly, looking at me askance.

'Sorry, Adelia.' I apologise for my skittish behaviour.

Adelia raises her eyebrows, and I know she expects an explanation.

'I thought I was alone out here, I guess. You made me jump.'

Did she hear me talking to myself? I take the risk of appearing insane so I can throw one last glance over my shoulder at Dolores. Both she and her knitting have disappeared.

I shrug and return Adelia's cautious smile.

'Oh. I see. Angie told me you seemed upset. Would you like to walk with me for a bit?'

I wonder where Dolores has gone and hope none of the others appear while I take a turn around the garden with Adelia. At least Adelia cares I am upset.

'Of course. Thank you.'

'I just wanted to check you were OK. Also, I'd like to speak with you a little about our view on "friendships" while you're here at The Rainbow Unit.'

I drop my gaze, flushing as I think about my steadily mounting feelings for Derek. Immediately after I blush, I remember what Marcie told me about Rainbow Unit rules on romantic relationships. They veto them.

I nod but stay silent. Wary.

'I appreciate it must be very unsettling for patients when they first arrive here with us. We have had many… *unique* personalities here, but as you know, all my patients have a diagnosis of schizophrenia and most display symptoms of severe psychosis.'

By now, Adelia and her staff have made certain that my education regarding my diagnosed condition is up to scratch, and I can easily follow what she means. I understand that people who have schizophrenia often suffer from psychosis. People like me, who speak to "friends" or others who aren't really there, and people like Sharon or Patricia, who clearly see and hear things others cannot see. Things that often seem to petrify them or things that make them furious. Sharon in particular.

'When the unit first opened, we had patients who responded to our treatments and who forged seemingly strong relationships with each other. We had a man and a woman here who had formed a romantic relationship. I later found out the relationship was also… consummated somehow.' Adelia clears her throat delicately.

I do not speak, but my cheeks ring out, advertising my thoughts about Derek's hot lips kissing mine.

'The female of the couple was ready for discharge first, and apparently, she swore she would keep in touch. Visit often, call her boyfriend.'

I can feel Adelia's gaze burning into me as we stroll along. I know what is coming next.

'She did not.'

I nod.

'Sound familiar?' Adelia asks in a rhetoric fashion.

That is what I was thinking. Adelia does not expect an answer and continues to speak. Her well-modulated tone soothes me as we walk.

'The male of the couple responded badly to what he viewed as a rejection. In a brief space of time, he transitioned from stable and almost ready for discharge to someone who was suspicious, extremely low in mood, suffering from delusions and paranoia and prone to erratic and violent outbursts.'

'He became convinced we were withholding his girlfriend from him, accusing myself and my staff of wild conspiracies against him that were responsible for her lack of contact. When he realised - as you did - that his previous paramour was well and still returning regularly for her outpatient therapy, he was utterly distraught. Unfortunately, it was too much for him to process and he took his own life.'

My gasp pierces Adelia's monologue, and I stop, rocking on my heels in shock. The ending of the story is a blast of ice-cold water to the face.

Adelia's eyes bore into mine and she sweeps an errant curl back from obscuring the line of her pure cheekbone.

'He had become dependent on his relationship with her, and when she withdrew all contact with him, his coping strategy for his emotional well-being all collapsed abruptly, like a house of cards.'

What a shit story. Thanks for that. Mouth dry, I ask Adelia, 'And what about her? What happened to the woman who had left?'

Adelia shakes her head, full of regret.

'She felt responsible, although she did not need to. I'm certain she had just wanted to move on with her life. As Angie mentioned to you earlier, we have found that even though a very real affection exists between patients when they live here together, there appears to be a need for the discharged patient to distance themselves from their mental illness and anything–*or anyone* they associate with that illness. The discharged patient *cannot* cope with contact with loved ones from their past and they seek to disconnect from it. We theorise it is too much to bear psychologically. In addition, that is, to the demands of therapy, returning to the community, and starting a new life.'

'In response to these pressures, the previous patient finds it easier to break the affectional bonds and to cut all ties to their previous mental condition–except for attending their outpatient therapy sessions, of course, which is a condition of all discharges here.'

'What did the woman do? When she found out?' I repeat my question.

Dreading the answer.

'She took her own life, too. One would assume she was overcome with guilt and loss. We found her in her flat the following day. I won't tell you the details of how we found her, but it was a tragedy my staff have never fully recovered from. That's why we take great pains not to encourage close relationships amongst patients here. They can be very... complex in their dynamics and the ramifications concerning patient recovery and discharge are... profound.'

My top lip sticks to my teeth. I clear my dry throat. Well, Adelia was a proper ray of sunshine today, was she not? What a terrible story.

I absorb the details in the context of my friendships. Sophie and Marcie are now discharged. I had been so sure that Marcie at least would remain a friend. However... Probably, the man in Adelia's story had been just as certain. He had been wrong, with disastrous results for both of them.

My heart bleeds for them, these unwell, star-crossed lovers. Doomed.

Now there is just me and Derek left...

Adelia and I resume our promenade in busy silence.

Chapter 8

'Mary hasn't eaten her dinner again today. You go this time, Ian.'

I lay in a foetal position in my bed, wearing the white T-shirt I had on the day that Marcie left. The mini calendar is on my chest of drawers, and I stare at it, wiping away the tears that drip down my face. The calendar does not lie. So-called "*friends*" do, but a calendar does not.

I still have heard nothing from Marcie or Sophie. Not one dickie bird to be heard. Nada. Nothing. I only have Derek now. And then… there was one.

Ian is knocking outside my room, interrupting my hunched misery. He calls me from the other side of the door.

'Mary… Mary, I've bought you something to eat.'

Unable to respond, I remain silent, staring at the wall. It is becoming difficult to see, as the natural light fades into evening.

'Mary, it's your favourite, and the cook made it with pork crackling as well, especially for you. Roast chicken.'

Last month, the promise of my favourite meal would have lured me from my darkened room. Today, the homey meal I once dreamt of, holds no power. Yet another week has passed since

Marcie left, and she has not called or written. My friends Lou, Jo, Dolores, and Little Mary have vanished again as well.

My shoulders curl up into a tighter ball. No-one cares about me.

'It's not good for you to be going without food, Mary. It's been two days now since you've eaten. We don't want to worry Adelia, do we?' Ian asks.

God forbid. I glance at the door. Ian always has an overly sympathetic tone in his voice. That asshole is as fake as a six-pound note.

'Fuck off, Ian,' I say, snarling.

I have no energy, so my words are little more than a whisper.

'I'll eat when I'm fucking hungry.'

A pause.

'OK, well, I'll leave a cold meal in the canteen for you.'

I hear Ian plod off back down the hall. He does not sound happy for a change. Well, he is not the only one.

A picture of Derek and Sophie explaining their conspiracy theory bursts into my mind. I wrap myself in an even tighter ball under the covers. Sleep's embrace awaits me like a faithful friend, and I slip into it with gratitude.

Chapter 9

I am in The Blue again. I love it here; it is so warm. Safe.

'Mummy.'

I feel myself rush towards her presence, but know I am not moving. In an instant, we meet.

'Hello, Peggy.' My mum's voice is full of the love I remember.

'Mum.' The word brims with love and yearning.

'I miss you. I want to be with you, Mum. It's so lonely here and I have no-one,' I burst out, my voice breaking.

I know she understands, and she soothes me.

'No darling, that's not true. You are never on your own, I promise you. Oh, Mary, my little poppet, you can't be with me yet. You still have so much good to do and anyway… I'll always be here for you. Un nyi wan nu we.'

'I love you too, Mum.'

The Blue around my mum pulses, and I feel her love reach me in a warm shock wave that fortifies me.

'Mary, listen… If you can stay here for a little while longer it will all make sense. I will come back and explain things when the time is right, but for now, I want you to look after yourself and to keep your strength up. Trust your friends. They will look after you as much as they can. You have wonderful friends, Mary. Please don't ever feel lonely. So much love surrounds you. You just need to accept it.'

I know she believes what she is saying.

My mum takes hold of my hands, and I stare down to see the familiar rich chocolate of her skin. In contrast to how they look, I can feel that her hands are the same sandpaper skin from my childhood memories. I had forgotten that until now. I laugh. It is skin that still tells the story of her hard work and love for me.

'What are you, Mary?' On cue, my mum starts the mantra she taught me from a tiny age.

I smile, warmth and familiarity blending into one.

'I am fearfully and wonderfully made.'

'You certainly are, Mary. You have so many gifts, and so much grace. Please, darling, remember what I said?'

I nod, recognising the fading with a sinking heart.

'No, Mum, I need you to stay with me–please don't go.'

I clutch at her with desperation as she releases me.

'Mary…' I hear a smile in my mum's voice. 'I'm always with you.'

The light that houses us throbs and increases like a forty-watt bulb plugged into a thousand-watt power. It blinds me, and I shut my eyes.

I open them to see my room… and my dear friend.

Little Mary is beside my bed. She is shifting her slight weight from one foot to the other. She wears a pensive expression on her face.

I sit up, my hair falling over my face. Pushing it back, I rub my eyes like the child I had been while I dreamt.

'What's the matter, Little Mary?'

It's been a long while since I saw my small friend. Despite my anger towards her and the others, the bond between us is still strong.

Little Mary twirls her long dark hair, looking at me in silence. Her brown eyes are like saucers.

'I miss you, Mary.'

She punctuates her words with sorrow, and I rush to reassure her. 'I was just thinking the same.'

I tilt my head to one side, considering the absence of my friends. The conundrum. Am I more or less sane? What does it mean, and whose version of reality do I believe in the most? Maybe Little Mary can answer.

'How come you and the others don't come by to see me anymore, Little Mary?'

Little Mary twists her hair again, sending furtive looks over her shoulder. My words root her to the spot she is standing in, and her mouth and chin tremble.

'Little Mary?' I coax.

My friend covers her eyes with hands that quiver, shaking her head.

What on earth?

'I saw my mum today,' I share with her.

I have learned distraction techniques from Adelia's sessions, and I seek to ease Little Mary's obvious discomfort, and to take her mind off whatever is causing her distress.

Little Mary claps her hands together, her smile radiating her face.

'What did she say?' she asks.

I frown, struggling to recall. It is always so hard to remember details about what she says to me after I leave her. I feel calmer after I dream of my mum but find it difficult to know why.

I peer up at the ceiling as though the answer is written there. It is not.

'You'll try to remember?' My mum's worry worn face flashes in front of me but is transformed. Made calm and beautiful by the love her features project.

I nod, experiencing a surge of adoration for her. I can still smell her scent of lavender in my nostrils.

"Olfactory hallucination," Adelia had explained.

'I don't remember most of it, but I think she said to stay here? Also, something about my having good friends?' I speak slowly, the cogs in my memory foggy from the medication I am now prescribed daily.

Little Mary's face drops, and she stares down at the floor.

'What is it? Is there... anything you'd like to talk about... from your past, maybe?' I prompt her.

If Little Mary is a product of my imagination, as I suspect, maybe I have traumatic memories stored inside that I need to bring out into the open and discuss. It is possible that is why I have not mentally healed, because I keep all my traumas zipped up inside.

Little Mary dithers, then looks at me and nods. Her face seems paler than usual, but I think that could just be the lighting. It might also be because my eyes are still getting adjusted to being awake again, after being with my mum in what I think of as "The Blue."

My companion comes closer.

'They diagnosed me with a mental health disorder at a very young age. I didn't fit in. Not with my peers at school, and not with my family,' Little Mary says in her well enunciated accent. She keeps looking over her shoulder as though she fears someone will walk in on us at any moment.

'My grades were poor because I couldn't concentrate and was nervous all the time. I had a terrible stutter, that's why I made up my ditties; it helped. Then, there were the scars on my hands. If I got upset, I made what they called "chicken scratches" on my hands. Repetitive scratches that I revisited until they became deep gouges in the tops of my hands. It was my way to externalise the pain I felt internally. The more anxious or sad I became, the more I dug my nails in. Blood would pour out of my hands, and everyone would run screaming from me.'

I curl my fingers over my own scarred palms. My cuts are finally healed.

'I caused a huge scene during an assembly, picking scabs until I fainted. All the children were hysterical and there was a big panic. Parents called the school to complain about me.' Her head droops like a wilted flower on a stem.

'I was an embarrassment to my family, so I was home schooled after that.'

The words are plain and gloss over the shame and loneliness she must have felt.

'And then?' I invite her, although I am not sure I want to hear.

Little Mary studies the tips of her shoes but does not speak for a long while. The silence stretches out between us, and I fill it with scenarios in my imagination.

'And then… I got punished even more.'

The raw pain Little Mary conveys in her last sentence makes me frightened to ask anymore. However, I need to know.

My voice lowers to a whisper. 'What happened?'

She raises haunted eyes, staring into mine.

'You know some of it already. I got beaten, locked in cupboards, forced to stay in baths of cold water in the dark, starved and drugged, made to…' Her voice trails off, then suddenly Little Mary is in my face, and she replaces her reticence with urgency.

'We all still love you, Mary, and we won't let anyone hurt you, no matter what. I swear it,' my diminutive friend promises, in a fierce, guttural voice that is forced from her, then turns and runs.

I blink like a sleepwalker coming to as she vanishes. This is intense.

Chapter 10

My conversation with Little Mary percolates in my mind. The longer I stay here, the more I learn about my psychosis, and the more confused I feel. Little Mary's memory is not the same as mine. It is similar... but I did not pick at my scabs in school—or did I? Maybe I had done it when I lived with the foster monsters, and I had forgotten? Sheesh. My brain is so fucked up.

Is it a good thing I am having these frank conversations with my friend? My hunch says it is. What would Adelia think if I told her?

My friends rarely come to see me since my admittance here. More so at the beginning, but it seems they only speak to me to ask me to leave. As if I can just walk out and defy a mental health act detainment, anyway. Over the years, they have been there for me. Keeping me company, encouraging me when I am sad, saying that things will get better, telling me they love me. Yet, they have been absent in the last few months. They do not want me to be *here.* To get treatment and to get *well.*

I mull it over as I walk.

I step into the restaurant to the sound of applause. What the hell? My stomach rumbles, reminding me I am not eating properly again. I head towards the counter, my gaze fixing on what food is offered. Chicken Wellington with steamed veg. Yes. I like that. Marcie had loved it, too. Marcie. My lower lip wobbles. I firm it. No. I need to pull myself together. Since coming here, I have turned into such a twanny. Weak. I must get my shit together.

'More Chicken Wellington for you, Mary?' Rose, the dinner lady, asks.

I look at her. Her chubby face is smiling down at me with encouragement. She is a feeder. I probably disappoint her with my skinny self.

I nod.

'Yes, please.'

She looks happy as she heaps my plate up with food.

I move to sit down and realise Dishy Derek is at a table, sitting next to Adelia. He seems morose. Great. What now?

'Hey,' I greet him.

My plate smashes down on the table with a bit too much force, and I notice it garners me some attention from staff. *Fuck off.*

Using my fork, I cram large mouthfuls of food into my mouth, shovelling it in, suddenly ravenous.

I can see Derek in my peripheral vision. His head is hanging down. He always reminds me of a puppy. I stop filling my face and let the food go down. *God,* I love puppies.

Derek remains silent, and the sound of classical music drifts down to us from the ceiling speakers. I like it so much better than the pan pipes they also play.

After a few minutes, I stave my initial starvation off, and turn to look at my solemn companion.

I shoulder him gently, whispering in his ear. 'What's up with you?'

Derek raises his head, staring into my eyes.

I tune the background noise out as I gaze back at him. A flash of insight assails me, and I guess what he is about to tell me. No. Not Derek, as well. It is more than I can take. Derek's large doe eyes are swimming with tears, his lips trembling. He is biting his lip between his squared teeth. He takes a breath.

'Adelia just made the announcement. I am going to be discharged in one week's time.' Derek sounds as though they have given him a death sentence.

He really believes his conspiracy theory is true, so in his mind it is. I feel my heart clench for him, for the fear and sadness I can see in his expression.

'I will miss you, Derek.'

More than he knows. I am mindful of staff listening and observing. They do not encourage relationships at the unit, and romantic relationships are flat out prohibited.

Derek knows this, and nods. Picking up his fork with a quivering hand, he stares at his plate. He does not look up again, and does not eat another mouthful, pushing his food around the plate. I do the same, appetite gone.

Chapter 11

The day is almost here, when I return to being completely alone again. My last friend is leaving me. I might as well get used to being on my own.

After swimming, I slink off to the restaurant by myself, avoiding Derek's company. Now, I am sitting at a table alone in the near empty room, fighting back the tears that threaten to overwhelm me.

There are still another couple of hours left before my next therapy session, and I do not want to cry in front of the staff who are dotted around the seats.

Adelia would hear about it. She would ask prying questions of me if they report I have been bawling my heart out in public. From experience, I know she would ask me the probing questions that sear me to my soul. Like scabs being ripped off an open wound before it is ready.

Well, I am not up for that. My chest swells, and my eyes burn with the effort of holding back the gut-wrenching sobs I am pushing back.

The radio that plays in the background seems in synch with my mood.

My lips tremble, swallowing. I do not trust myself to speak yet.

'Oh, we never know where life will take us…' My table mate is singing along with gusto in an off-key voice. It is Errol. He does not seem to care if anyone overhears him.

As I scan the room, I feel my lips twitching at his lack of self-consciousness, and his out of tune singing. Errol is lucky enough to escape attention. If I swallow, it forces down my sorrow. I clear my throat.

'Hi,' I say.

It has been a while since I saw him last, and I almost forgot he exists. My companion has compassion in his eyes and holds up one of his hands in the peace sign.

I switch my attention back to moving my cordon bleu lunch around. My tongue is sticking out the side of my mouth a little as I concentrate. I am getting good at going unnoticed. If I push the vegetables to the edges of the plate in different directions, then it is not obvious that I am leaving most of my lunch. Staff dislike it when you lose your appetite, and the next day it always seems like you are given a lot more.

I realise I care enough that I do not want to disappoint *them*. Shit. My brows shoot up towards my forehead. When I think back, I have changed so much my past-life me is becoming a cloudy memory. Delightfully hazy in its recall.

Errol interrupts my revelry, whispering in my ear, 'I used to feel like that, too.'

I flinch but hold back an exclamation. Jeez. I did not see him move.

'Like what?' I ask.

'As though the past wasn't really real anymore because I was becoming a whole new me.'

The corners of his mouth drop with an abruptness that leaves his face a study of seriousness.

'Bastards.'

My eyebrows fly up again, then I send a quick scanning glance around us. I am like a schoolgirl fearing detention if we get overheard. We are not.

'Who're bastards?'

I hiss the question so quietly it is nearly incomprehensible.

Errol's mouth twitches at my uncharacteristic temerity.

A thought occurs to me.

'Hey, how did you guess what I was thinking about?'

'Huh?' Errol asks, looking confused.

'A minute ago, I was feeling as though my past was unconnected to the me that I've become… then you said something like you knew, or you'd felt the same… oh, I can't remember exactly what you said, but the gist was that you know how I feel?'

My inability to explain annoys me, and I tut, knowing what I mean.

Errol grins, shrugging.

'Did I?' He scrunches up his nose and scratches his head, his neatly combed afro moving as one unit.

I nod, my eyes on him, conscious a headache is growing, and pinching the bridge of my nose to relieve it. Adelia and I have spoken about the noise I used to hear - the static clicking. She explained it is called "tinnitus." It is annoying, but I can tune it out and tolerate it with practice, using the different distraction techniques that they teach us here.

I am not in the right frame of mind to employ any of these techniques, and the growing white noise is not helping my headache. I give up trying to pretend to eat and have no more interest in conversation.

'Sorry. I have a headache and I need to lie down.'

Errol looks sympathetic, and I stand up, scraping my chair back. He nods, holding up a hand in salute as I leave the table to go to my room.

I can remember when I used to get lost in the corridors, but now, after several months here, I am at home. I can navigate the gigantic building and grounds without effort. The only place I an unfamiliar with is the Cloud Wing because it is closed for refurbishment. Like a homing pigeon, I make my way back to my room. I open the door, then collapse on my bed like a fallen angel. The static and clicking are back again today. Maddening in its intensity.

I will approach a staff member for a painkiller if it gets any worse.

There was still some time before my therapy session. I had checked the clock on the restaurant wall before I left. Adelia does not like it if we miss our sessions. As I think about Adelia's smile of approval, dropping into a straight line of icy disappointment, I speed up, deciding to take a nap to clear my head. That way I can have a little sleep, and then have a bit of time to wake up and freshen up again all before I go to see Adelia.

Chapter 12

I stand on the entrance steps, shivering. Possibly with cold, or with shock. I have been avoiding Derek for most of the week, hoping if I distance myself, his departure will not be as painful as Marcie's was.

I was wrong. Now that I am here, I find I cannot bring myself to let him go. I know my fingers are gripping him like a vice and I do not care that I am getting snot all over his nice, padded denim jacket. God help me, I am so in love with this man. How did this happen? How am I going to survive here without him? With no one?

Derek is holding me at arm's length, his red-rimmed eyes scanning my face. He appears to be absorbing every feature. He hiccups on a sob, then drags me back to him again, despite our audience.

'I will see you again soon, Mary, and I'll think of you often. I will picture you wearing your favourite green cardigan,' Derek whispers for my ears only.

'What?' What the hell is Derek talking about? That is so random.

I fucking hate green–*and* that green cardigan. That is why I have only worn it once. It had looked blue in the catalogue–it was a poor photo, or I am a touch colour blind.

'Remember all our conversations, Mary? The time we spent, talking about what happens after discharge. Remember me sometimes. Please... take care of yourself.'

I cannot respond; I am crying too hard. Instead, I look up, nodding, dumb with grief.

Derek cups my hands, then winces. They are small blocks of ice. He holds first one, then the other in between his warm hands, rubbing them and blowing on them to chivvy the cold away.

'It's time, Derek,' Angie says.

She steps forward, gesturing to the waiting cab. I know it is irrational, but I want to slap her in the face.

The cab driver shifts, shivering in the cold, and eager to get going. Staff have packed Derek's belongings in the cab. Only Derek himself remains to enter the vehicle.

Will I see him again? Will he discard me like the others, once he is back on the outside again living his best life, living his *real* life?

'Remember,' Derek mouths.

He still believes there is a conspiracy against us. Will he be OK out there? What if he relapses or hurts himself? What if someone hurts his crazy ass? He is so vulnerable. Tears brim up again, and I curl my fingernails into the palms of my hands. Do not start that again, Mary.

Derek gets in the cab and closes the door. I shut my eyes, so I do not have to watch him drive away. When I open them again, he is gone.

Bereft, I draw in a shaky breath, then glance around at the others. And then there are three... Patricia is windmilling around with her arms outstretched.

'Airplane.' Patricia never says an actual sentence, so I guess she is making progress during her stay after all. She is oblivious to the biting cold and has shrugged her coat onto the floor as she spins in circles. At least she is happy.

Sharon now seems more lucid, but not happy at all. She watches me in return, her face screwing up as though she is sucking on a massive lemon.

I feel my face pucker in response. Racist bitch. I still have the urge to punch her in the face whenever I see her, and my eye twitches. I drag in another deep breath to calm myself. They do not allow that kind of behaviour at the unit and might set me back with my discharge reunion plans.

I satisfy myself with a look of dislike for Sharon, telling her: eat my screw face, you biaatch.

My stomach gurgles with a warning. Oh no. I clutch my tummy as it cramps. I need the loo again, and quick.

Angie and Jackie both watch how my hands are clasped over my stomach, and they know what it signifies. IBS is back in play. Right on cue. Angie gives me the nod. I am free to go back to my room–to my toilet.

I am now alone. Again.

Chapter 13

My stomach is off. It has been churning and gurgling all night. I leap out of bed and run for my en-suite bathroom.

Ten minutes later, I return. Drained, I lay down, weak and exhausted. I could not eat my dinner again last night, and I missed Adelia's therapy session *again*. What is the point?

Sophie is gone. Marcie is gone. Derek is gone. I am alone. Sort of.

My friends from *here* have deserted me, but some of my voices are on their way back. Familiar and unfamiliar. Some are sweet, a few were not. Like nasty old Dominic, who has come back on the scene. A dirty old man who has been with me since I was ten. He delights in telling me sickening secrets or offering me his lewd insights. Dominic makes my stomach curl like a salted slug. He is one of "the many." The growing "many" that live again inside my muddled head. They have been gone for months, but now they are trickling back.

I grip my head again to shut out the noise. The buzzing in between their voices irritates me. The radio static noise comes, as though the frequency is not quite tuned in. I shut my eyes and breathe, as Adelia has taught me to do.

"Distraction is a great tool," Adelia always says.

Although the clicking noises accompanying the static agitates me, I accept them like an old friend. My head follows the sound, keeping time with the clicks, tracking them like a tennis match. Left to right, and back again.

I chant over the din: "Melamelamelamelamelamelamelamela melamelamela," and my head pounds, throbbing in time with my heartbeat.

As I accept the overload, the orchestral discord sweeps away my sorrow, and I am grateful.

An army of voices join each other, gathering strength.

My stomach churns, then spasms, and I rush to the toilet, muttering as I go in response to the voices. My words come in broken spurts as I move.

After washing my hands, I drop back into bed, like a stone.

I wonder if they will let me do what I used to do and "zombie out" on prescription meds. Since being here, I have not once got my drooling "Shakin' Stevens" tablets on.

A knock at the door punctuates the rush of voices, as well as my misery.

'Good morning, Mary.'

They have sent Sinead. I probably like her the most, but I still cover my face with a pillow.

'Go away.'

'Mary, sorry, lovie. I need to come in to check you're ok,' Sinead tells me.

I take the pillow off my head and stare at the door. So annoying that there is no lock.

'No. I want to be by myself.' The irony. I am anything but.

The door opens and I stare at Sinead with my mouth open.

'Get out of here,' I shout at her over the swell of the voices.

Energy fills my sagging body, and I throw my pillow at her.

It lands short of Sinead, and she steps over it without a pause in her stride.

'Now then, lovie, come on… don't be like that,' Sinead tells me.

The nurse is standing over me, hands on her hips and her head tilting to one side.

'I know it feels bad right now, but you are doing so well - you can't give up,' Sinead says.

She still sounds like she has a hug in her voice.

My eyes fill with tears and the strength leaves my body again. I wilt onto my one remaining pillow. Why not?

'Just go away,' I say, but without force this time.

Sinead takes that as her cue and pulls up a chair beside my bed. Sitting down, she smoothes the hair off my forehead.

Her hand feels cool on my heated face. I do not knock it away.

'Now then, first thing… you need to eat and drink. If you don't feel up to coming out of your room, how about I go and ask cook to knock up some of your favourites for breakfast?' she asks.

Mealtimes remind me of my friends. I have lost them. They have either gone, and no longer give a shit about me, or gone because something bad has happened to them. Either way, they are not here with me. I am back to being alone, and things are not good.

I cover my face with my duvet.

Sinead pulls it back down.

'No, love. Don't give up. You've come so far. You can do this. Just tell me what I can get you? How about a glass of ice-cold water with a tray of some croissants and fruit? Hmm? Doesn't that sound nice?' Sinead tempts me.

It does sound nice. My mouth salivates at the mention of water, and I realise that I am thirsty.

I clear my throat. It is dry.

'Thirsty,' I rasp with a nod. 'And my belly is off.'

Sinead does not recoil.

'It's probably just a touch of irritable bowel syndrome because of nerves. I remember you had a bit of the same thing when you first came, and then again after…' Her voice is certain but trails off at the end.

'After Marcie left,' I finish for her.

My voice sounds like a rusty nail in a coffin.

Sinead agrees.

'It's OK, Mary. It will work out, you'll see. Things always get better if you just hang in there.'

I glare at her as she stands up. Really? Although I disagree, I do not comment. My mum always told me, "If you have nothing nice to say, then say nothing at all."

'I'll be back in a few minutes with your breakfast. Lucky you, aye? Breakfast in bed, no less.' She smiles at me, then leaves.

I think about my friends. If I get better again, maybe I can go to find Marcie outside in the community. Or Derek. With a sigh, I decide to get up.

I step out of the shower to towel dry myself, then wipe the steam from the bathroom mirror. The door is open, and I can see that someone has left a tempting tray of fruit and croissants on my armoire for me.

The voices have quietened down. Manfully, I square my shoulders. I can get the brush all the way down my hair now. There are no knotted clumps of hair left. The staff have helped me to cut out what had refused to be smoothed, and the result is good.

I wipe the condensation away again so I can see my reflection again. Black smudges under my eyes and across my cheekbones have once again become prominent. I have little in the way of a cushion of fat. If I miss a couple of meals, boy does it show. Derek. My life is so empty without him; it all seems so meaningless.

I swallow my grief. Sinead is right, I have come so far. Once I am discharged, I can see Derek and Marcie again, maybe even Sophie, too. That will give me something to look forward to.

After drying, an idea occurs to me, and it brings a whimsical smile to my face.

I will wear the green cardigan with the large pockets that Derek had mentioned. How had he even known about me having it? He must have remembered the one time he had seen me wearing it at a picnic.

My lips twist. Now I know I must be in love. I fucking hate green.

Walking over to the wardrobe, I find and drag it off the hanger. Then I press the cardigan to my chest, like a mother hugs her baby to her and inhales. I must not have put it in the laundry baskets. It still smells like food. The picnic… Marcie. Sophie and Derek walking past. Tears choke me. It also smells like Derek. His warm, woodsy scent enters my nostrils, stealing its way down to my heart. That is stupid. He had not been near me that day. Must be my imagination.

I put the cardigan on, snuggling into it with my eyes closed, and slipping my hands into the pockets. My eyes open again as my fingers touch a piece of paper. I stare down at what my fingers have found. What is this?

I unfold the paper, reading what Derek has written there.

'My dearest, beautiful Mary. If you are reading this, then I am no longer here. I have tried to explain everything that I have discovered here at The Rainbow Unit, but I know you don't believe me.

'That's OK, I understand my Beautiful. I would have trouble believing me if I were in your position, too.'

My eyelids flutter, and I lift the paper closer, breathing in.

'Derek.'

My gaze skims the rest of the letter.

'I want you to know that I love you and mean it with all my heart. I have never said that to anyone before in my life. If I am not here and they tell you they have discharged me, then know that the first thing I would do would be to call and ask to speak to you. If I returned to the unit as an outpatient, then my priority would be to see you.

'I would need to check that you are OK, that you are safe and well. Please believe nothing which is to the contrary to what I am telling you–because it is just not true.'

But he has not contacted me, has he? Derek has gone, forgetting me. Just like Marcie. A fat tear rolls its way down my face.

'I repeat, Mary–do not believe them. I know everything I told you I saw was through my eyes, or through Sophie's, so I understand why you don't believe me. But I know that you are in danger. If they have taken me, you will be next, and I can't bear that to happen. I beg you to please see for yourself that what I have told you is true, then escape.

'I've opened a firewall in Adelia's records and included the step-by-step instructions I gave to Sophie all that time ago. It will lead you to the video. I have also included instructions on how to access the data on Adelia's research. Your best bet to do this without anyone finding out is to do as I did. Fake illness when they hold the next Inspiration Group meeting and go to the nurse's office computer.

'Please do this, even if the speaker is due to be Marcie. Even if it's me.

I have managed to check and my phone was never disconnected. The bills must have been paid automatically, so my number should still work. I have left my number underneath, please call me. What we have is real. I love you.

'Yours forever, Dishy Derek.

'P.S. Yes - Marcie told me!'

A trembling smile surfaced on my face, love swelling in my heart. For Marcie, the gabber mouth, who could not help herself, and for Derek. "Yours forever."

Sighing like a lovesick schoolgirl, I clutch the paper to my heart. My Derek. I had someone of my own. "Forever."

There is another folded piece of paper. It looks like instructions, just as he said.

I scratch my head. I cannot remember the last time I have used, or even touched a computer. It would have been at school. Would I even be able to follow these instructions? Will they make any sense, or will I find they are all nonsense or beyond my understanding?

I swallow. "Yours forever." OK, I owe Derek this much. Partly out of respect for his wishes, but mostly because of his declaration of love. I will fake illness and follow his request to the letter to see where this leads. Then I will know and be able to say that I have honoured his request if he ever asks me. If I ever see him again.

PART FOUR

Chapter 1

I stare at my reflection in the mirror, practicing my smile, before I leave for my therapy session with Adelia.

'Hi, Adelia,' I tell my mirror self, baring my teeth.

That looks sane enough. I am so near to discharge; I cannot ruin it so close to the finish line. Outside of my room, I pick up my pace, needing to be on time for my one-to-one session.

'Good morning, Mary. I am pleased that you could join me for your session today,' Adelia greets me.

Her silky tone seems to smother the voices I am hearing, the conversation cutting off like a vacuum bag seals off oxygen.

Adelia insists on politeness, and although I have already bid her good morning, I also grant her a quick smile. For good measure.

Adelia frowns. My smile is too quick - she is probably thinking it is a nervous twitch. Or maybe gas. She gestures to the sofa.

'Please take a seat, Mary.'

I no longer harbour any hang-ups about lying down on the psychiatrist's couch. On the contrary, I welcome the chance to rest my weak limbs.

Adelia performs the identity check with me, as she always does.

'Can you confirm your name and date of birth for the record, please?'

I give Adelia the information she needs, then sink further into the sofa. The familiarity of the routine soothes me, and I sigh, feeling my shoulders relax.

It is nice that Adelia has a brief conversation with me before she begins the therapy part of our sessions. I like it.

'You are feeling better today than you have been over the last week, Mary?'

I nod, keeping my eyes closed.

'Yes.' The voices have seemed to recede again once I decided to get up.

'Have you been hearing any voices? Seeing anyone that others cannot?'

I take a deep breath in, holding it.

I am torn. On the one hand, I think Adelia may suspect that I have been hearing things again. On the other hand, she might not, and I might get out of here quicker if I lie. I bite my lip. Decisions... decisions... Sod it. You've got to be in it to win it.

'No. Nothing,' I tell her.

The silence that frames our conversation seems to grow.

'Are you certain?'

Her voice has taken on a steely quality.

I swallow. Shit. Does she know? I want to leave here, and this woman holds the keys.

'Yes, I'm sure. I haven't seen or heard anything unusual. I've been sad, that's all.' That's all? "I felt really sad..." That must be the fucking understatement of the year.

'What about Little Mary? Where is she?'

I feel my brow furrow.

'I dunno. Why?'

My tone is sullen, but I am suddenly not in the mood to jump through hoops. Adelia's questions sometimes piss me off.

Adelia does not like to be questioned, and her tone drops by an octave in response.

'Because it is part of your therapy and that is what we are here for. Now… I will ask you again. Have you heard anything from Little Mary over the last week?' She presses me.

I breathe in and realise I no longer find the smell of lilacs in here pleasant. It is cloying and gives me a headache.

'No.'

'Alright, Mary. That's fine. Ordinarily, you undertake your sessions lying down on the sofa. However, today I would like to encourage you to sit up–just for a short while, please.'

Unmoving, I raise my eyebrows. 'Why?'

'Because you are nearing the time of discharge and so today, I intend to show you a prototype of the Three-D hologram I have been building of your most prevalent voice, the entity you refer to as *Little Mary*. It will be the first time that I see her as well.'

'OK,' I say, then sit up. Will she look like *my* Little Mary?

The hologram flickers on, unclear. Adelia makes some adjustments on her PC screen. The face of someone who looks a lot like Little Mary flickers into my view, projected into the air.

I blink. Shit. This is so weird. She does look like her–sort of, and a bit like me. I stare at Adelia, who is also transfixed. She swallows, then in a sharp voice, checks, 'Well. Is this an accurate representation of your Little Mary?'

I nod. 'Sort of… but her face is a bit thinner, her cheekbones stick out a bit more, also - she has larger eyes, and they're a different brown. Darker.'

Adelia makes some further tweaks, and I peer up again at Little Mary's face, suspended in mid-air. I feel goosebumps raise on my arms. God, this is freaky - even Adelia looks unnerved by it. I nod.

'That's her, or as near as dammit, anyway,' I say, feeling as though I am identifying a suspect in a police line-up. My friend's likeness blinks out.

'Alright, Mary. Please lie back down now.'

Adelia takes me through a relaxation ritual, and my breathing slows. Every muscle in my body is now relaxed.

'I want to hear more information about your Little Mary,' Adelia commands.

For fuck's sake, not again. Can we just get off this? I take a breath, my nostrils flaring.

'What do you want to know?'

After a brief silence, Adelia speaks. 'What is Little Mary's surname?'

'I don't know.' That is the truth.

'What abuse has Little Mary suffered? What things upset her?'

Fuck's sake. 'Her family... they said mean things, beat her, locked her up... drugged her.'

'Is Little Mary your age?'

'No. She's ten.'

There is another brief silence.

'There is an edge to your voice, Mary. Why is that?'

My answer contains partial honesty. 'I think... I think it's because I feel protective of Little Mary, and I don't want to let her down. I want to keep her safe.'

'*Have* others let her down, do you think?'

I nod.

'Who?'

'I think... Her family. It is her family who abused her.'

The silence grows. Am I talking about myself? My past? The monstrous foster family letting me down? Or perhaps... my mum for dying?

I visualise my namesake in my mind's eye.

'Does Little Mary have any identifying characteristics? A lisp, a mole? Anything like that?'

More questions about my friend. Little Mary does not want me to discuss her with my therapist. I know that. I squirm, feeling uncomfortable and disloyal.

'Where do you think she comes from? Which area? Does she have an accent at all?' Adelia fires out.

'She's well spoken. English.'

My voice is even more clipped than Adelia's.

'OK, Mary. Let us end our session today at that.'

I draw in a relieved breath. Yes, let's. I do not want to answer any more of these questions.

Adelia follows the usual verbal steps for the end of our sessions. As she suggests, I feel no resistance in my body. All my muscles are relaxed.

With a shuffle, I sit up straighter, pushing stray hairs off my face. My hair is so long and static. It is escaping the ponytail that I have now taught myself to brush it into. I hope it is not an indicator of my internal struggles. That my rebellious hair follicles are not an outward sign that I am returning to how I was prior to my section at The Rainbow Unit. A tortured, frantic woman. Living in nightmare squalor and filth. Spending my days confused, frightened, and distracted. Shit, no. I am not having that.

I bid Adelia goodbye–always politeness first, then go to the nurse's office.

Once there, I see Ian and Errol sitting down. Ian is speaking with intensity in a quiet voice to Errol, but Errol is grinning in his usual laconic way.

As I approach, I raise a hand, offering a faint smile of apology to them both for interrupting their conversation.

Ian looks up, flustered, and I wonder what he is saying to Errol. Or who it is about. Were they discussing me?

'Hi, Mary. It's lovely to see you up and about again. How are you doing?' Ian greets me.

'Not bad, thanks.'

'Ah. I expect you're feeling lonesome here, what with the numbers going down and all. I understand we are due to have four or possibly *five* more residents with us in the next two weeks. Won't that be great?' Ian has a megawatt smile on his face.

I nod, but no answering smile graces my face. Wonderful. Just chuck some of us out, get some more in–what is the problem?

'Anyway... What can I do you for?'

I roll my eyes. Ian is so obtuse. Anyhow. What difference does it make if he is sensitive to my feelings of loss or not? It does not matter.

'I would quite like one of those massages?'

Ian nods in approval.

'That's right. You should treat yourself.'

I agree, giving Errol a brief smile. Should I apologise to Ian for my previous rudeness? I wrinkle my nose. Nah. I find I cannot bear the saccharin awkwardness that even the idea presents. Instead, I stare up at a point in the ceiling. Tra la la.

Ian grabs the handset and dials an internal number with quick hands. I listen to him speak as he connects with someone. He holds the phone away from his face, covering the mouthpiece with one hand.

'You're in luck! There's a one-hour spot in ten minutes. How do you fancy that?'

I nod. I do not know what this will feel like, but I want to try.

'Yes, that will be good. Yes, please.'

'Great.'

On my way to the massage, I smooth my hair back, dragging my fingers through the loose part of the ponytail. It is knotty *again*. How is it *so* knotty?

'Urgh,' I mutter as I walk up to the door.

The last time I had been here that stuck up cow bag Somya had beat me to it. God, she had been an asshole. How was *she* doing? Somya, Miles, Sophie, Marcie, and Derek. All gone, and I am next in line to leave.

One hour later, although my hair is even more knotty, the masseuse had made certain my body did not follow suit. Boneless, I have a newfound appreciation for the benefits of a Swedish massage.

I stroll back to the nurse's office to request the garden card.

A swim would probably do me good right now, but the pool reminds me of Marcie, so I have avoided it since she left. Ian is now alone in the office, and after enduring a few minutes of his chit chat, I take the card and go for my walk in the gardens instead.

I smile.

'Beautiful day, isn't it?' Errol asks as he materialises from behind a collection of pretty blue forget-me-nots.

'Yeh. Nice,' I say.

I do not mind Errol. He is alright.

'They've booked the next Inspiration Group now, ya know,' Errol tells me.

I say nothing, but my eyebrows lift. That must have been what he and Ian had been talking about. Was it soon?

'It's being held this Thursday.'

My fingers touch the carefully folded piece of paper in my pocket. I have kept Derek's letter with me since reading it. I now have this letter and my mum's necklace. Well… It seems like "the time is nigh" or whatever the saying is. I owe it to Derek to try. There is another question I have to ask, although I do not want to hear the answer.

'Who's the speaker?' My voice is rusty.

'Marcie.' Errol is blunt, but he sounds melancholy. Why is *he* sad about that?

'You OK, Mary? It must feel shitty, not hearing anything from Marcie since she left.'

That is what I like about Errol. Whenever we speak, he seems down to earth. Plain speaking.

'Yeh… but I'm not too bad about it now, thanks Errol. I'll be OK.'

I believe my own words. I will be alright. I can see Errol nodding in my peripheral vision and he looks concerned.

'Yeh, you will be. Just… watch out for yourself, OK?' he says.

Well, that sounds cryptic. I glance at my companion.

'How do you mean?'

Errol does not speak for a while.

'Only that... just like outside of here, we all have a different side to us. We don't show everyone all our cards... Not everyone at The Rainbow Unit is what they might present to you. You know that anyway, right?'

I mull over his words, but do not answer. I trust the staff here at The Rainbow Unit, although I have learned throughout the course of my life that what Errol said is true. No-one shows you all their cards.

Finally, I nod.

'Yeh. I know that.' Although, it is shit to hear from someone else that this place is no different.

We do not speak again, but Errol stays with me during the rest of my walk, and I continue to absorb the restorative beauty that surrounds us.

The next Inspiration Group is coming, and I will be ready.

CHAPTER 2

'Is your IBS playing you up again, Mary?' John asks me.

I nod, making a big show of looking sorrowful while I lay in a foetal position, tucked up in my bed.

'Yes, I think it is.'

John continues to take my vitals, writing the information on the tablet he carries.

He shakes his head.

'There's nothing much really, temperature's fine. Your pulse is erratic, though.'

That will be because I am shitting myself.

'Oh. I've been to the loo about six times already. I've been having terrible cramps all morning, John,' I explain.

I hunch over more, curling into a ball under my duvet.

John nods, staring down at me, then puts his hands on his hips.

'We have recorded in your file that you get irritable bowel syndrome when you're upset. I think your friend is due to speak today, isn't that right?'

I shrug.

'That's what Adelia said at dinner yesterday.' I look down at my blanket.

John flicks a look at his watch.

'Inspiration Group starts in fifteen minutes. I'm sorry, Mary, but I think it's best if you miss today's Inspiration Group.' He shakes his head again, looking regretful.

I make my lip quiver.

'Oh no.'

John nods again, offering me a sympathetic smile.

'Yes. I'm sorry, Mary. I know you're probably disappointed. I can give you some medicine for the pain before I leave. I also have some solution to prevent dehydration that I'll mix and give you before I go. At least it will help you feel more comfortable. If you need help, please press the buzzer there. We are all in the Circle Room obviously, so there will be no-one in the nursing station, but don't worry - we have the buzzers connected to the Circle Room also, so we will know if you call and will come to you just the same.'

I glance at the round call button that is placed within my arms, and stare at him with large eyes.

'OK, yeh. I think you're right, John.'

I am sort of disappointed. Marcie is coming here to the unit. My first ever friend. My best friend will be right here, and I will not see her. I twitch and consider changing my mind and pulling a miraculous recovery.

Derek's face flashes into my mind's eye. Derek. Who also loves me. As I love him... No... I owe it to that love to see this out. Even if it all turns out to be a misunderstanding, or one big crock of shit. I will see it through.

John exits the room.

After waiting about five minutes, I fling the duvet back, sitting up to push my hair out of my face so I can see. It really is getting out of hand.

I jump up out of bed, not bothering to change and scraping my hair into a tight ponytail. I sling my dressing gown on over my pyjamas, padding barefoot around my room. Stealth mode activated.

CHAPTER 3

My heart hammers against my chest as I look around. OK, so I am in the nurses' office and the coast is clear. I take out Derek's instructions, unfolding them with care.

After a couple of seconds of looking, I spot the PC. I am not au fait with most technology, because the voices distract me, and I get confused when I use anything electronic. Consequently, it seems to take me ages to locate the power button.

It makes a noise. Shit. I flick a quick check over my shoulders. No-one arrives with a syringe in hand. I am still fine. I stare at the instructions and the paper shakes in my hand. God, it is hot in this hospital. I wipe sweat from my forehead and it makes the paper slightly damp.

F1. Command prompt

F11. Boot up

What the hell does that mean? Oh. I realise that Derek has written handy explanations down the side. They are keys on the keyboard, usually at the top of the keyboard. Got it.

I follow the rest of Derek's steps with painstaking care, my lower lip firmly between my teeth. Then I sit and click. Moment of truth, baby. This should be a video file. Or not.

The previously forgotten face of Somya materialises on the computer screen. SP96 it said. Oh, yeh–remember that asshole? What is she up to?

I lean towards the screen. Something is wrong. I realise what it is. Somya is not moving. Not even to flick her shiny princess hair like she used to. Not to pick her nose or fart. Not a goddamn thing. Literally. I look around me, then at the small clock on the bottom right. What the shit? I have been watching Somya for fifteen minutes? No way. Creepy. I close her file, then follow the instructions again to open another one at random. This one says SP12. This time, I do not recognise the face, but they are as still as Somya. I touch the screen. There is a timer on the top right of the recording, and it is moving. *Day 142 Hours 7 Minutes 4 Seconds 12, 13, 14, 15.*

One hundred and forty-two days? Since what exactly? Maybe since discharge? Is this person an ex-patient? This guy is not moving either. I shiver, remembering Derek's fear when he described what he had seen. "Like a robot with its batteries removed," he had said.

That is the nail on the head. I stare at "SP12." He looks young, and his expression is blank as he faces the screen. What the actual fuck? This shit is freaky.

I follow the steps again, more confidently this time. Another one. SP5. Same unnatural stillness. And again. SP62. The same. SP97. I suck in a whistling breath, like I have been punched in the gut.

Sophie. No. She is sitting in an armchair. Her posture is ramrod straight in a way that it had never been whilst I had known her here. She is not lounging around, hunched over her sketchbook or pad. There is no sketchbook and charcoal in the video, and I can see no art materials in the background. In fact, there is nothing in the background.

Sophie is dressed in a beige blouse with a black skirt. She is in a completely neutral environment that contains no personal effects. No other people either. Most noticeably, there is no girlfriend Rachel in the background, and Sophie is not wearing her headphones. No headphones. She is encased in silence. Sophie thrives on a chaotic environment. She loves–I take a sharp inward breath.

Oh my God... What about Derek? What about Marcie? I click out with a rush, and the screen goes blank. As I wiggle the mouse, my heart thuds as a thought occurs to me. Shit. Please no. I hold up Derek's last communication to me. My clammy hands have made it transparent, and the biro is fading so that I have to squint and tilt my head to read the instructions. Fuck. *Fuck the heating in this hospital.* Why can they not open some windows and let some fresh air in, for God's sake?

I blow out. Calm down. Another check of the time, then scan the corridors that lead to the office. I am OK, there's still time. I use the breathing technique and rub my bare foot on the floor to ground myself again. Everything is alright. I follow directions again and click. There is an unfamiliar guy on the next screen. He's young and black. In fact ... All the patients so far have been black, or minority ethnic. Hmm... I keep going, one eye on the corridor.

SP98. Another young woman I do not recognise — hang on... I double take the monitor, then become paralysed by what I am seeing. I *do* know her. It is Marcie. She is alive. But in name only. That *is not* my Marcie. I stroke the screen, one solitary tear falling down my face. Marcie. My breath is fogging her likeness, and I wipe it with a hand that trembles. Her eyes do not twinkle. There is no smile on her face and her dimple is not there. She is not talking or moving in any way, frozen as a corpse at a wake. Her hair is tied back so tightly that she appears bald. Marcie has slimmed down, and she looks so alien now that I had almost discarded her recording with the others that I do not know.

Marcie? I stare at her; SP98. She remains unmoved from her position, and only the rhythmic breathing attests to the fact that she is alive. How is she so still–and why? I break eye contact with Marcie. I will not waste any more time looking for Derek's video.

Marcie's recording almost crushes me. I need to find the email invoices that Derek had spoken about. In for a penny, in for a pound, as they always say.

Here we go - Six million pounds incoming from a company called NexGene Defence. Six million from Waverley Arms. Six million from GenCorp Military. Six million seems like it is Adelia's magic number. *That loathsome bitch.* I do not get it. What is she doing to us and why? Adelia acts like she cares so much, and she is a doctor. Had she not taken an oath or some bullshit?

Pushing guilt away, I doggedly perform the actions that Derek had taken the time to lay out. I had not believed him, or Sophie.

The research data that Derek had mentioned... I close my eyes. It is too much to take in. They had been telling the truth. All that time, and Derek had still loved me, even though he knew I did not believe him. I have to help them.

The time tells me I have just under twenty minutes. Then everyone will be back from the Inspiration Group. Should I warn the others? Sharon and Patricia seem to be doing better, but realistically, what would their response be–could they help? I shake my head. Not likely. No, and I know I will be next. For now, I need to focus on how to defend myself. Find a way to get free.

I know where the slide out pass key drawer is in the desk. I try it. Locked. I get on my knees to have a better look. It is a flimsy key lock. Thank you. I shut my eyes briefly in gratitude. Yes. I use one hand to yank it open with force, whilst controlling it with the other hand to stop it from rattling.

Garden? No. Then I will just be trapped in the garden when they search for me. The walls are too high, and I know they are made with smooth concrete that is disguised by the beauty of the foliage. I cannot climb it, but I can take the card for the kitchen. If I could get a knife, then sneak out the front somehow? A weapon is always good. At least then if it came to it, I would have a fighting chance.

Decision made, I jog to the kitchen in silence. If luck is on my side, I will jimmy the sharp knife drawer as easily as I had the desk drawer.

The swipe is smooth, and I push the door open, then head for where they keep the "sharps."

I shut my eyes, hope evaporating. Luck is not on my side. It is a combination lock, and they have reinforced the drawer. Why have I never noted this before? Maybe I could have memorised the code or something?

Shit. I push my hair back off my face. It is still in its ponytail, but so many strands of it are stuck to my head I feel I'm strangled by hair.

I yank the drawer repeatedly, two hands on the handle and one foot braced on the metal unit. Maybe I can pull it open with brute force.

'That won't work, Mary.'

'Argh!' I jump, whipping my head around.

Crap. My heart picks up even more speed. I did not hear Errol come in. This is it. He has caught me. I wait to see what Errol will do, staring at him like a doe caught in headlights. Maybe I can fight my way out of the room.

'You won't be aware of this, but the drawer has a motion sensor that has now tripped the *silent* alarm. That goes off first, to allow staff the element of surprise so they can catch whoever has tried to force it open. Then, after four minutes, the regular hospital alarm is triggered and goes off out loud.'

Errol looks at the digital clock, then back at my ashen face. His eyes bore into mine.

'You now have three minutes and forty seconds.'

Mouth open, I focus on the clock, my eyes blurry with sweat and lack of sleep. Huh? Is Errol letting me go? Three minutes?

'*Mary.* You need to move. Go now. Run back to your room, but make sure you stay low. They'll be looking for you.'

I swallow, believing him. Taking to my heels, I skid to a stop, hearing the footfalls of a barrage of Crocs all heading in my direction. I sprint in the opposite direction, making my way back towards the nurses' office.

Errol trots beside me.

'Remember, they might be in the nurses' station by now - so you'll need to go down onto all fours down the next corridor, so that you can duck below the window eye level.'

Without hesitation, I follow Errol's suggestion, assuming the mountain climber position so that I can still continue the journey to my room at some speed.

'Urgh.' A shaky grunt escapes me from the effort, and I bite down on my lip to silence myself.

Sweat is running uncontrolled from my head, dripping down my nose and off my chin. Fuck, it is hot. I desperately want to remove my dressing gown. My arms and legs burn, and I am reminded of my run to the river. Before they admitted me here. I had thought life was grim then. Boy, had I been wrong.

'*Kill her. Kill her, Mary. You need to do it, do it now. Please kill her, Mary. Make her dead. She needs to die. She has to die.*'

What the fuck? So many voices erupt all at once that I nearly jump out of my skin. Still on all fours, I freeze, and my muscles protest.

'Kill her! Do it!'

There are too many of them, assailing me all at once. They shout the same commands. Their emotions swim through me, amplified. Fear, rage, sadness, fear, rage, sadness–like an emotional triangle being played as an accompaniment to the orchestra of voices. Breathing through the nausea, I try to refocus my blurred vision. I need to get to my room. I can do it.

At the corner I pause in a crouch position, then brace my buckling knees, as I see there is still a clear path to my room. The staff are still looking around the unit for me, although I can hear that they are seconds away from where I am hiding. One of the guards is describing me bluntly to the others. Nice. I am the scrawny one with "all that black hair." Wait - did he just mention surgery?

'*Mary? Mary, do it now. Kill her. You've got to kill that bitch. She deserves it. Kill her.*'

I sneak into my room, closing the door with stealth.

There is no lock, so I scan the room for tools to barricade the door with, and my eyes light on the armoire.

'*Kill her. Kill her. Mary, do it. Kill her.*'

My skull pulses as it tries to contain the orders of the many, all at once. Bile rises, and I swallow it, then push back my hair. Sweat has stuck it to my face like fly paper. I can use the armoire. It is heavy and will slow them down while I think of something.

If I stand behind the armoire, I can heave it with all my strength. I do this, then collapse into a trembling ball in front of it. Inside my mind, the assertions of others gather momentum and strength, and my own ebb. They are all giving me the same command.

'*Kill her.*'

They are adjoining to one another, like a snowball gathering and leading to an avalanche. The "fear-sadness-rage" triangle increases its vibration, reverberating throughout me, until it blends together with all the voices, seeming the sole inhabitant of my body and mind.

I curl into a ball with my head quirked to one side. A petite statue with its head cocked, listening out for the sound of the staff's advancing steps over the cacophony of commands.

'*Kill her. Kill her. Kill her now. Kill her. Kill her.*'

I wipe my palms on my dressing gown, then put my hand up to my throat. Fear drums inside me, and a fresh bout of sweat dances its way onto my upper lip and forehead. The bedroom closes up to suffocate me, and I try to gulp in more air. It does not work, and I flap a limp hand in front of my face. It makes no difference. *The heating is always on here in this fucking hospital.*

I grind my teeth, needing to stop myself from joining in with the screaming.

'Mary Jameson, my name is Mary Obosa Jameson,' I chant in a low voice. Be careful. They cannot hear me.

I blink. It seems to help to block out the voices if I say facts out loud that I am sure about. If I focus.

'I am a patient here at The Rainbow Unit. It is a psychiatric hospital in Surrey. My name is Mary. I am twenty-one years old. My mum died of cancer when I was eight years old,' I finish in a whisper.

The last fact still gives me a lump in my throat and makes the damaged part of my heart throb. Although I had lost my mum years ago, how I still long to be with her.

That is it. I am all out of facts. All out of distraction.

I nod, wiping clammy hands on my dressing gown as I make my decision.

The fear and anger transfer itself to me. It is contagious. They are right. I cannot let everyone down. I must act. Too much is at stake.

I get up, my heart heavy as the steps of the hospital staff close in on me. OK, it looks like I have to kill that bitch. How will I do that?

'Mary. We are here.'

'Oh, Jo! Thank God, I'm so glad to see you.' I sniff, stifling the urge to run to my friend and sob into his arms. Fear makes all my words run into one.

'Jo, it is all true–what Derek and Sophie saw, I saw it too. Now the staff are coming to get me and give me a brain melt, then I won't be me anymore. Please help me, Jo.

Jo makes calming noises as he nods, holding one hand up.

'OK now, Mary, be still now, child, be still. All will be well. Just stay calm and listen to me. Do what I say, alright?' he asks, his tone serious.

What else would I do?

'They will knock in a minute. Do not fight with them. You have to let them take you.'

As the horror of Jo's instructions sink in, my eyes grow wide, and my hand flies over my mouth to stifle my automatic refusal.

'No, Jo.'

Jo nods.

'Yes, Mary. It is the only way. Listen. They will be more relaxed around you if they think you have given up. They won't use restraints and then you can escape.'

Chapter 4

'Jo! Guys!' Mary says into the tense room, whirling from one face to another like a spinning top. 'You aren't making any sense, Jo. Please just help me. *What shall I do?*'

Jo stands with a sad-looking smile on his face, with Lou, Dolores, and Little Mary all wearing the same expression as Jo's to various degrees.

I look from one to another. My movements are unconscious in time with the knocks that pound against my door.

'They're here,' I hiss to my friends, then look at the door with the desperation of a rat caught in a trap.

'Mary, we know you're in there. Please open up, it's for the best darlin'.' Sinead's voice is audible from between the heavy wood that stands between them. It still holds the hug in it.

I can picture what Sinead looks like as she says the words, all down-to-earth concern and hands on her hips. My eyes water.

I catch sight of my taut expression in the mirror, eyes blinking like those of a china doll. Blank in my ashen face. God.

I spin back to my friends and stretch out my hands with my palms up.

'There's stuff on this video that Derek led me to, and I think I heard them mention surgery. I think they want to give me a lobotomy, for Christ's sake.'

Lou steps forward with her hands outstretched. 'Shush, shush Mary, everything will be OK. It's alright, don't worry, sweetheart.'

I frown, shaking my head, shouting, 'It's not OK, Lou. She's going to cut out part of my brain to shut me *the fuck up*.'

My breath comes in ragged pants as I stare at my friends.

Dolores steps forward towards me. 'Please, darling, just try to calm down. Everything will be OK. Listen…' Dolores leans in as though she is about to drop some pearl of wisdom.

'Let them take you,' Jo insists, interrupting whatever Dolores had been about to share.

My mouth opens and shuts with no words. Confused by the sudden taste of salt on my lips, I lick my lips, realising I am crying. With the back of my hand, I wipe my mouth, then stare at it as though it belongs to someone else. My arms feel so weak. My entire body does.

'I don't know what to do.'

Little Mary stands, wringing her small hands and whispering to herself. She looks as disturbed by my predicament as I am, and Jo steps forward again, solemn.

'Mary, listen. Let them take you. Trust us. It will all work out. We will help you. Just let them in and go voluntarily with them. Walk down the hall–give them no wahala–no drama.'

The rapping at the door is stronger now, more than one fist knocking.

My time is up.

With one last look at the faces of my friends, I take a deep breath, then begin to heave the furniture away from the door.

'Coming,' I call out, with a lead stone in my stomach. This might be the last time I see them, or recognise them–who knows what a lobotomy does to a person like me?

Is this what happened to Derek? Or the others? My friend Marcie, somewhere staring into space like the person on the video Derek had shown me. No longer bubbly and giggly. A robot shell of Marcie, a human machine that awaited orders.

I shiver and Little Mary rushes towards me, appearing as though she is about to throw her thin arms around my waist, then stopping just short and staring at me instead, her small hands curling into fists beside her legs.

'We love you, Mary,' she tells me as she hiccups on tears.

After another dry swallow, I inhale. OK. I have decided. My friends are telling me to trust them, and I do.

I do nothing to stop the staff from forcing the door open. The furniture snails its way clockwise into the room as they gain entry. Sinead, Ian, and the security guards see I am not struggling, and Sinead shakes her head slightly when the guard holds up the restraints. We leave the room together, my chin pointing down and my mood sombre. Staff close the door to my bedroom behind us with an air of finality. I walk along the hallway with the unit staff, giving no sign I am aware of anything. My friends walk in front of me, Jo keeping pace with quiet authority.

My eyes water with gratitude and love. Their presence always makes me feel calmer and less alone.

'How?' Shit, I did not mean to say anything out loud.

I notice Sinead looking at me sideways, then sharing a pitying look with her colleagues. No biggie.

Lou takes over the instructions from Jo.

'We will walk up past the nurses' station.' She points to the staff member whose name I can never remember.

'John never locks his pass card onto his key ring, he always just shoves it into his left trouser pocket.'

John? Who the fuck is John again? Oh. I look to the right of me, using my hair as cover.

'Grab the card out of his left pocket, then make a break for it–hot-foot it into the nurses' office and shut the door. The door entry device to get in is flimsy. As soon as you get in there, get one of the mugs they keep on the shelf in there, then use it to smash the swipe device off the wall. That will make sure they can't use the other cards to get in after you straight away.'

Little Mary and Dolores slow down and now walk beside me, pushing in between me and my captors. Little Mary falls into step beside me.

Jo expects my next question: 'What then?' and continues with the instructions.

'Dial nine to get an outside line. Then use the phone to call your CPN, Eileen.'

I do not want to provoke any concern about my presentation with the staff so do not dare to voice my thoughts. No matter. Jo again correctly guesses what I am thinking behind my frown.

'She is not like the other staff members. Eileen will listen to you, and she will help,' he tells me.

Little Mary skips up to him, putting her small hand in his large one.

'Tell her why, Jo. Tell her why. Mary doesn't have much time.'

Jo looks at me with a world of sorrow in his eyes.

'I know Eileen will help you because she is my wife. Just tell her that "Caleb" told you to call her. Tell her I said she needs to get here with the police. Even faster than she drove to the hospital the time when her Uncle Eddie cut half his thumb off when he was using a jigsaw to cut our kitchen sideboard down.'

'But that doesn't make any sense, Jo? Oh whatever, fuck it.'

The door is coming up on the right in front of me. Sucking in a quick breath, I do as they told me to, making my move. Snatching the card from John's pocket, I sprint to the office.

Gobsmacked, my companions have little time to register my actions before I have let myself into the office and pick up the mug laying on the desk. Straight away, I smash the door entry system, locking them out.

I rifle through the cards and locate Eileen's, where my friends told me it would be. Grabbing the phone, I dial. The staff are peering into the toughened glass, cupping their hands at the side of their heads. I turn my back on them and grip the receiver.

'Eileen speaking,' a clear, pleasant voice answers.

Oh, thank God.

'Hello, Eileen, it's me: Mary Jameson. I need your help. Please don't hang up,' I start.

Silence rings out over the phone for a second, then, 'Why are you calling me on a Sunday, Mary? Where are the staff?' Eileen asks in a slow voice.

I take a deep breath.

'They're outside and they're coming. But please listen - I need your help, Eileen! There's a conspiracy against the patients. Adelia is experimenting with us. Please believe me, help me.'

Although I am passionate, my voice is limp and tired. Eileen sighs.

'Look... I am honoured you feel you can come to me, but I should tell you that people with your diagnosis often think that others are conspiring against them. It is common for patients to believe that there are plots to harm them. I should also tell you I don't actually work on Sundays...' Her voice trails off, as if she is about to put down the phone.

She does not buy my story.

'Please don't hang up, Eileen. Listen, *Caleb* told me to call you for help. He said... you need to get here faster than the time you drove to the hospital when... when your Uncle Eddie chopped his thumb off with a jigsaw, or a sideboard or something.'

I stumble over the Uncle Eddie story for a bit. The hand holding the phone handset is shaking. If I cannot get Eileen to listen, I am on my own. Dead.

'*Caleb* told you that?' The CPN's whisper fans the flames of my hope.

I nod into the phone, then continue in a rush.

'Yes, no–well, actually my friend Jo. He told me he was your husband and to say all that came from Caleb. But I don't know why Jo said that name, and I don't understand why a puzzle game could cut off someone's thumb either - but please, if you don't come right now they're going to chop out part of my brain to shut me up.

'Then I'll never find out what she's done to the others, and I won't be able to help them. Sophie was a boss artist, and now she doesn't have her sketch pad, and Marcie was so sweet and funny, and her dimples have gone, and Derek…' My voice broke. Derek loved me.

'And Adelia will do it to more of us because no one gives a shit about us down here. Oh God, please, Eileen, please believe me, we need your help. I'm begging you, please.'

Eileen swallows before she asks slowly, 'What does your friend Jo look like?'

Quelling the urge to scream down the phone, my brows wrinkle. There is no time for this shit, but I need her on my side. Biting my lip, I answer with care.

'He's big. An enormous bear of a man, really, and he's always calm and nice. His real name is Joseph Abeiku Saloman. He's African, he's from Ghana, and he's a doctor. He wears purple and silver, and sometimes black, traditional clothes.'

My eyes are shut as I picture Jo. When I open them, I see the person I have just described standing in front of me with a wry smile on his face. Whoops. I cover my mouth at my unflattering description. Sorry, Jo.

'Tell her I am here with you, and I said to say that I still look like a man who enjoys too much "kelewele," Jo instructs me.

I repeat what Jo said and hear Eileen suck in a breath.

'Jo?' she asks, in a voice drowning with tears.

I nod into the receiver again on automatic pilot.

'*Yes.* That's what I've been telling you, lady. Jo's here with me now and I'm going to die in here if you don't come *right now.* Jo says you aren't like the others and that you will listen and come to help me. Well, I need you to help me *right now*.'

The banging starts outside. They are striking the door, using one of the heavy armchairs as a makeshift battering ram. The office door is secure for now and the reinforced glass is holding, but I know it will not last for long.

Then I will be gone, lost like the others, and all my hopes of rescuing my new friends will disappear with me. Derek, Marcie, Sophie. All the other faces on the videos I have seen.

'Bring the police with you and come *now please*–as soon as you hang up this phone, because I don't have long, please you *have to*, I beg you.'

I hang up. Either Eileen believes me, or she does not. I pray it is the former rather than the latter, but either way, there is one more call I want to place before they take me.

The door rattles on its hinges and I know I do not have too long. There is only one number that I know. It is burned into my memory. After dialling the number, I listen into the earpiece, crouching under the desk space. I grip the handset with such ferocity that my knuckles lose all colour and turn white with the pressure. Silence meets me and the only sound I hear is my racing heartbeat.

Derek does not answer me. He is gone too, then.

Ian and Sinead push the door open, then peer around the corner, as though expecting me to hurl missiles at them.

I do not. Instead, I walk towards them with the air of someone about to hold their hands up to accept the wrist restraints. Like someone who is giving up.

'That's right, Mary, you come with us, love. It will all be alright, you'll see.'

I stumble alongside them, shaking so much that I can barely walk.

'You'll see, Mary, we'll get you fixed right up, and this will all be over soon. Adelia knows what she's doing,' Sinead tells me, blind faith in her voice.

The fear whooshes through me like a forest fire. It turns my limbs into jellied eels that are incapable of holding up my slender form any longer.

As Sinead speaks, I feel an injection in my arm, then red dots form in front of my eyes. They close my picture of the hospital corridor shut, like a cinematic lens, and my head connects with a solid "clonk" sound on the hard floor. The red of my blood spreads out like a stark banner, announcing my vulnerability.

Chapter 5

Urgency needles me that I have to get up, to leave this place at once. Then I am in The Blue again. I am safe.

'Hello, mon coer. I want to show you something,' my mum tells me; her chocolate colour skin is radiant as usual in the light of *The Blue*.

Anything. I nod.

'Yes, Mummy. What is it?'

My mum steps towards me, holding her hands up in front of her with her palms facing mine.

Instinct guides me to do the same. The closer my palms get to hers, the stronger the feeling of absorption. Prisms of light fractured shards of energy spike out further and further, until our energies melt into one.

Then… I am transported. My mum's memories are displayed to me as though they are mine, and I watch them as though it is my personal showing of a subtitled movie at a drive-thru cinema.

I know my mum is called "Sandra Obiemwen Aisosa Cherif," and that she was a naïve university student when she met my dad David at the supermarket, where she worked part time. Sandra thought David was very dashing, and she had known immediately that it was her destiny to be with him. From a Benin family, Sandra's parents did not permit dating. They had been religious and strict. Marriage with an English man who was not religious would have been out of the question. Sandra had been attracted to David but was reluctant to engage with him. She was very shy and unused to male attention.

'Not a problem for your father.' My mum smiles.

'He was a force to be reckoned with once he had made up his mind. David told me I was the one for him. He said he had known it as soon as he had clapped eyes on me–and I believed him. Your dad proposed on our second date, happy to make our relationship formal.' My mum continues to share the rest of her story, and I listen, rapt, to how it had progressed.

'We got married, and one and one had soon made three. You came along a year later and my parents passed away not long after. We had never told them about David's occupation. Your dad and I let them think he was a travelling salesman. In reality, though, David was an accomplished medium. Renowned in the psychic field, he had made a good living with the use of the gift he had been blessed with and he supported us well financially.'

My mum continues to smile, feeling my surprise. A medium?

'We had a lovely house with a back garden filled with roses. Things were great. David was so loving and kind. When you were born, he had doted on you too, but then tragedy struck.

'There was a terrible accident. David was the victim of a drunk driver. He suffered irreparable damage to his spine that left him unable to walk, riddled with pain and subject to terrible migraines. He became dependent on strong painkillers. On top of all of that, he had lost his skill for mediumship. David was inconsolable, and sank into a deep despair, seeming to withdraw more and more each day.

'With a young baby to look after and no income, I could not afford child-care, and could not work. We drew benefits and although we should have been entitled to support for mortgage payments, they denied it to us and due to the slow-moving bureaucratic process, we fell behind on the mortgage payments. The house was repossessed.

'The local authority re-homed us, but it was in a grotty two-bed ground-floor flat. At least it had wheelchair access. It was in the middle of a Southeast London estate that had a terrible reputation for anti-social crime.'

My mum stops narrating, and instead allows me to see that when my dad lost his ability to converse with the other side, he also stopped communicating with mum and me. He had become more and more distant. Brimming with anger and resentment, my dad, David, turned us away.

I become involved in the events, aware that they are past, but also current. My dad is consumed with regaining what he has lost, and with the idea of being able to commune with the spirits again. Spurred by his obsession to reclaim his abilities, David reads about the occult, and that is when he discovers voodoo.

Mum shows me how Dad gets hundreds of books, scattering them all around the flat. I see them as two individuals now, separate from their role of mum and dad. David and Sandra. Sandra is thinking there are so many books the combined content must contain every voodoo ritual ever imagined. From a devout Christian background, this recent practice is something the young Sandra finds strange and frightening.

David practises voodoo, putting all his faith into the occult. Strange, edgy people call at the flat at odd times in the night, laughing and demanding to speak with him. I see when they look at Sandra holding her baby, she instinctively clutches me close. That is when things become very dark.

David is a confirmed recluse. He is a scary and unkempt lodger. A man who is cloistered in his room, coming out only for the occasional snack and for errands. Sandra stays in the master bedroom when she is indoors, and I sleep in her double bed, snuggling into her side. David takes over the back room. Sandra says that at first, the door remains open, but one day she returns home from the weekly food shop and David is nailing egg boxes to the wall with the lights on and the curtains closed.

Sandra notices a lock on the door when she knocks to offer David some dinner. As before, there are the occasional phone calls for him, but she can never hear what is being discussed. By that time, she does not feel safe to get close enough to overhear.

There are pungent smells and unusual noises that stray from David's room, and Sandra suspects he is keeping animals in there - although she never actually sees any. Sandra tells me the strange sounds she hears keep her unable to rest or sleep at night.

For several months, Sandra cannot relax from sundown onwards, and remains bolt upright when in bed. I notice sweat on her upper lip as she strains to listen out, long into the night. She installs a sturdy chain on her bedroom door, and she arranges for a phone extension beside her bed.

The night arrives when a tapping at the door awakens Sandra.

The delicate woodpecker tap on her bedroom door at three AM causes Sandra to break out in a cold sweat. Sandra sits up straight, cuddling me to her breast.

'Sandraaaaaaa,' comes the whisper.

Sandra's breath stops in her throat, corked by fear. She does not answer.

'Sandra… can I come in?' comes the slither.

She dares not reply, but her heart beats wildly in response.

I see her hand shoot out, flash fire quick, to pick up the phone handset. Her left hand dials "999" for emergency help, whilst she cradles me with the other arm, the earpiece with her chin and shoulder. There is no dialling tone. Disbelieving, Sandra stares at the buttons on the phone and cuts off the call. She tries again with the same outcome. There is no dialling tone. No outside line.

The gentle tapping begins again, continuing non-stop, until the sun rises to peep through the sunny yellow curtains. The sound increases in its strength until it reaches a crescendo that sees Sandra swaddling my blanket around me to soften the noise. I view her entire body quaking in rhythm with the door that now shudders in its frame.

The hours of marinating in fear drives Sandra to scream out loud, and the noises stop, mid rattle. The silence is worse, and Sandra is so scared that she pees herself. Momentarily paralysed by the fear that holds her, she stays in the bed now warmed by her urine. Sandra does not trust that it was safe to leave her room and go to the bathroom to clean herself up.

'David?' Sandra calls out, her arms gripping her baby.

Her husband does not answer, and I watch as Sandra stands at the side of her bed on shaking legs.

'Ddddd,' she stutters out, then takes a deep breath and tries again. 'David, please. Are you there?' she asks.

'I am,' he replies.

Silence waits outside the door that stands between them.

'What are you doing, David? What's going on?' Sandra prays he will offer reassurance.

'I need you to give me the baby, Sandra,' David tells her.

Trembling legs step back, away from her bedroom door.

'What?'

'What do you want her for?'

'She's important to me, Sandra… for the ritual,' David tells her.

Reaching up, Sandra rubs her blurry eyes, 'what ritual? Why's she important?'

Another reed-sharp voice joins him.

'Please, Sandra, open the door and give us the young one.'

'What? No way - who the hell are you? Get away from my door. Get away from my baby and me, you weirdos,' Sandra shouts.

After shuffling from one foot to another for a while, Sandra decides. She places me down on the bed, creating a makeshift sling with my baby blanket. Sandra places my relaxed form close to her, wrapping me to her chest and tummy, then searches her room for weapons. The door judders in its frame again, amidst chuckling and calling out to her, and Sandra whispers a prayer of thanks that some instinct made her purchase such a sturdy set of chain and locks.

The sun still looks in from the window.

Sandra goes to her chest of drawers, removing the small cylinder of money that is held in place by an elastic band. It is all she has scrimped and saved. I know she is thinking: Only £300, but that is better than nothing. Then, Sandra takes the small carving knife she also keeps there. Sandra is breastfeeding, so is wearing a bra. She tucks the small roll of money into the bra beside her breast pads.

Sandra does not hesitate. Creeping on stealthy feet to the window, although her hands shake violently, she pushes the metal window forward on its hinge, praying for a silent exit, as she climbs out. Their flat is on the ground floor, so Sandra dangles her feet down, then releases her grip of the window ledge.

As soon as she feels the cold of the concrete beneath the pads of her feet, she takes off running. I am in a sling, and Sandra presses me into her while she runs as fast as she can. She is petrified I will slip through the bottom of the blanket she has knotted, as she weaves her way through the estate in her floral nightie to the bus stop with one arm still securing me and her eyes flicking this way and that for her would-be pursuers.

When Sandra reaches the police station, she collapses on the square tiled floor, begging them to help. The police officers make her a cup of tea, then call social services.

'We're sorry, madam, but because there is no evidence of any crime committed, we aren't able to take any action.'

Distraught, Sandra turns to plead with them. 'But I think David's dangerous. Those people he hangs around with, I don't know what they'll do.'

'We'd be happy to pop round and have a word with David for you?'

Sandra shakes her head, but then looks in hope at the social worker.

'You said that the flat is in joint names?' the social worker double checks.

Sandra nods, her shoulders slumping.

'Then the local authority will not re-house you because legally, you have a property to use. Although what happened sounds strange and frightening, David has not done anything illegal. Because we concede that his behaviour sounds very suspicious, we can check in on you periodically. I guess that because you're married, David is on your baby's birth certificate?' the social worker asks.

Sandra nods dully.

'Well, then, I should advise you that because David is on that birth certificate, in the eyes of the law, he has as much legal right of access to your baby as you do, Sandra.'

Sandra sits, absorbing one blow after the other, still in her nightie with breast milk filling her painfully full breasts. She removes the money roll before it becomes soaked but leaves the small knife in place.

Sandra has let go of the idea that David is still the man she married, and she now lets go of the idea that the authorities will help her. She has very little money. No job. And no home. No one is going to help her until it is too late. It seems like the police will not step in until he has hurt either me, or her, or both.

'Is there a hostel or something I can go to?' she asks, cutting through their depressing rhetoric.

'There is, but it's only for women who have suffered abuse,' the policeman tells her.

Another closed door. Sandra swallows. Then, as an idea occurs to her, prays that God will forgive her in her time of need.

'But he has abused me. David hits me all the time,' Sandra states, looking down at my tiny face. I feel her plea. "God, forgive me."

Desperate times call for desperate measures.

'Really?' the woman from social services questions. At Sandra's hesitant nod, she asks, 'But why didn't you mention that before?' with a frown.

Sandra swallows, putting a hand to her forehead.

'I wasn't thinking clearly, and I didn't want to say, admit it–but now I… I see I have no choice. David… he hits me all the time. I'm fearful of what he will do to this baby if he gets his hands on her. He's not right in the head, you see, and he is hanging around with some scary people. I don't know what they want to do with her either,' Sandra tells them, looking at the two police officers and then looking the social worker in the eye.

'Please help me. Help my baby,' she adds. The desperation in her voice is real, and those present recognise and respond to it.

The social worker nods, then pats her hand as she speaks. 'Don't worry, Sandra, I know somewhere safe. It's not luxurious, but you can go there, and no-one will know where you are. We keep all the identities of our ladies a secret. The location and phone number are on a "need to know basis." We will look to move you out of the area. You and your baby will be safe.'

The policewoman with the hard face seems to soften.

'I have some clothes you can wear from the lost and found for now,' she offers Sandra.

I mewl, and the adults all gaze down at me, waving my tiny hands.

'She's getting fractious,' the social worker comments with a soft smile.

'Sorry, my baby needs feeding.'

Everyone excuses themselves, allowing her privacy.

The memories fade away and Sandra the individual becomes Sandra my mum once more. I feel a tear escape from my eye.

'Mummy,' I murmur in a cracked voice. I smell her soft odour, her warmth and her overriding love for me.

When I open my eyes, they swim with the remembered feeling of closeness and safety. I am surprised that I am not injured by its loss. I blink as I go from twenty-one years into the past, and a dingy police interview room, to the radiant Blue and my mum right now. A great surge of love explodes inside me, shooting bright colours out like fireworks of energy.

'Your father is stuck here because he has unfinished business with you. He is not all bad. He fell out of alignment with source because in his physical existence, he concentrated on what he lost, and he was willing to use your mediumship light to get it back. Your father passed over soon after we left, and immediately regretted his actions. He cannot cross over, because he continues to focus on fear and rage, instead of embracing his love. Your dad loves you, but like many not connected with the Blue, he shows it in unhealthy ways. He can be drawn to you when you're in danger and will protect you. That is what happened that day with your foster father - your father took over your body to protect you. Because he has not embraced the Blue, your dad is still guided by his fear that you will be hurt, and rages against anything that might hurt you. Don't be scared of him. Call on him when you need to, mon coer. *He is misguided, and dangerous... but he won't hurt you.* Trust me. Trust the path and don't resist against what is meant to be.'

'I will try, Mummy.'

'Remember that your Benin name means "hand of God." Be guided by that. Be as He was–be *love* itself and do not allow fear or anger to throw you out of your path.'

She grins, then prompts me, as she always does.

'What are you?'

'I am fearfully and wonderfully made,' I respond on cue.

My mum beams at me, and I see the Sandra who had met David and fell in love.

'That's right, Mary. You remember, my dear heart. We all have the seeds of greatness in us, favour surrounds us. You are so very loved. Never feel alone.'

I absorb her joy, inhaling her familiar smell of lavender.

The Blue light that surrounds us grows so bright, that I close my eyes momentarily against the glare. Then I wake up.

Chapter 6

I open my eyes to realise my head is spinning and that they have strapped me down to a hospital bed. They are prepping me for surgery that will remove part of my brain, and likely strip me of my entire personality. Nausea rolls upwards in waves, making me aware that other than the sickness, I have no feeling in my limbs yet. Oh, yeh. The tranquilliser is yet to wear off, so I cannot move. Great.

Adelia is standing over me, looking down.

'There now, Mary, you'll be feeling better soon. You just had a slight knock on the head. And a little something else, of course.'

Like a trapped animal, I scan the room for someone else and croak out.

'Sinead? John?'

Now I can remember his name, the irony.

'Oh, they won't be around for ages. At my instructions, the staff who escorted you here have gone on break, and when they have finished, they will alert the theatre staff to ready themselves for surgery.'

'Why?'

'Why? Well, to allow me some one-to-one time with you, Mary. I have a few questions in my mind that I want settled before surgery. Oh, and we are in the "Cloud Wing," so don't worry, we are away from prying eyes.'

Adelia smirks.

The pieces of everything that I have learned all shift in my mind, and all at once, slot together perfectly with a click.

'I know,' I tell her, ice in my voice.

Adelia raises her eyebrows and purses her lips. She looks unconcerned.

'*You know,* Mary? What do you *know?*' she spits out.

Her question is a simultaneous query, as well as an insult.

'I know what you've been doing for years. But I don't know why.'

Adelia looks behind her. We are alone.

'What exactly have I been "doing," Mary? Enlighten me.'

'You take us in when we're sick. You hypnotise us, make us turn into zombie assholes. Then you sell us. You're despicable,' I throw the words at her.

Adelia tuts.

'Au contraire, my little gutter pigeon. I have been "*fixing*" you. You should thank me, dear. You not having the grace to show appreciation is even more of an indication of how much you require my help. You are damaged. A broken cog in a piece of dirty machinery. You need—' Adelia breaks off what she is saying, then continues, 'I am *here*, and I *will* save you and others like you from yourself. Whether you like it. *Or not.*'

I pull at the restraints, but still affected by sedation, my muscles show no sign of obedience and I lay impotent in their binds.

Choked by rage, all I can do is squint at my captor, hissing out my words from tightly pulled back lips. 'We trusted you. *I trusted you* and you *used* us all. How could you?'

'Ah, I am so sorry that you cannot see what a great honour this is for you. I have given you a great privilege.

'You probably will not remember, but I explained to you when we first met. I do nothing but give to you all. And you all–

what do you do? You *take*. Nothing but take, take, take. Draining everything you touch. It's *you people* who are *using* our society. I assist you all to readjust your thoughts so that you can no longer do that. It takes a lot of work and dedication,' Adelia contends, raising one slim hand to her heart with a sneer on her face.

'How could you do this to us? And *how* did you do it?'

'How? I have links who alert me to potential subjects. Treatment resistant schizophrenics. Sectioned patients, who no-one is interested in. You know the type. Then I have your background investigated and I learn everything about you, ready for our one-to-one therapy sessions. That informs me of your most impactful experiences and tells me how to program you optimally. How to keep you just where you belong.'

'Where do we belong?'

She smiles, a faraway look in her eyes as she answers quickly, 'Dead. Or in servitude.'

Adelia meets my eyes, and I shiver as some of the cold from her blue eyes transfers itself to me. She permeates the air with her hate. Adelia is proud, and she has not finished her gloat.

'I input certain trigger phrases during hypnotherapy sessions, then when you're discharged I bring you in for "light therapy."

'The lights are my real research star. I elaborated on technology that was already started by others who went before me–but I adapted it, honed it.'

She studies her nails and removes unseen dirt from her index fingernail.

The voices in my head hush, allowing me the time to process and plan questions. I know I need to keep her talking, to stall her for as long as I can, hoping I can think of something.

'Program us? How? What the hell can you do with some poxy lights?'

'Lights? Ha, you cretin. Those "poxy lights" are the product of years of painstaking research, trial, and error. I have perfected cutting-edge treatments based on *optogenetics*. I introduce a gene to your systems when you get your depot injection. Then, when you return as an outpatient two days later, I sculpt a laser beam into a hologram with a light modulator and that awakens the gene.'

'But… what does the gene do?'

Adelia straightens her spine and shakes her hair back. There is acid in her facial expression.

'Do? It alters your perceptions, your memories, and your behaviour. The light pulses allow different neurons to be targeted and activated and that controls what you see, hear, and think. Oh… and how you act. I rehabilitate you into useful members of society instead of the *pond suckers* that you are without my intervention. I am your creator, and I remake you into the image that I see fit to sculpt.' Adelia's arms stretch out.

Some feeling returns to my hands, and I struggle against the restraints that still hold me down on the bed with such desperation that I feel the ties bite into my wrists.

'Let me go, you psycho.'

I hear clicking noises, then static. No, not now. I cannot open myself to the voices now. It will make me even more vulnerable. Panic rushes at me with hot sickness.

Adelia peers down at me, and snorts.

Staff had also applied head restraints, restricting my head movements. I flinch at the venom I see in her face and squeeze my eyes tightly shut. My heart sinks. There is no escape.

Then, finding the strength to open my eyes and return Adelia's stare, I clench my jaw, grey eyes stormy. This queen bitch. She can go to hell.

'*Why*? What would make you do such a thing? We are people. We have rights. Human rights, for God's sake.'

'"Why?" My dear, what an utterly stupid question.'

She leans closer, her expression taunting.

'Because you are all aberrations. My father was a prominent German scientist who emigrated to the UK after the second world war. The British gave him safe passage and a new identity here because of the promising results he brought to his field. He studied eugenics. From an early age, I have known about genes, how some people are genetically superior and how some people are defunct genetic misfits who will perform no benefit to our society. My father raised me to know what my duty was, that my mission was to use science and my magnificent brain to save society by delivering us all from those who have nothing to offer. That is why.' Her voice slices into me and I close my eyes to it.

The voices are coming. They dribble through to me like a trickle in a dam that is no longer plugged with a finger. Soon, they will assail me, and I will be lost.

Adelia brushes a speck of imaginary dirt from her top.

'I cleansed you. The luxury here ensures that you don't struggle as I release you all from all traces of your previous "life." I reprogram you because you cannot do it yourselves. When you leave, I assign you a new purpose, somewhere to live. *Basic* accommodation because anything extravagant would be wasted on the likes of you. I give you jobs that hold meaning and use to society. None of the futile pastimes you had before.'

My lip curls back in a snarl as I meet Adelia's china-blue eyes.

'And the money? I suppose that had nothing to do with it? It was all about your goal to create a better society without us.'

Might as well hear it all.

Adelia shrugs, but her lips purse. Then she arranges them into a facsimile of a smile.

'I needed funding. All brilliant scientists need that in order to continue important research. There are mercenary organisations who are very interested in the work I do here and offer a certain level of patronage. Military dignitaries from two countries are also helping me to bankroll my results. They were galvanised by the recordings from the flats. There are so many applications for the use of the subjects in the future. You should thank me–I've given you all such drive, such purpose. I still await confirmation, but it would appear that your friends will serve your country before the year is out. Of course, neither they nor you will know it. *You* won't be aware of much at all after surgery, my dear.'

I close my eyes against the tide of nausea that rises inside me. Sophie's pretty Halle Berry face, with her neat A-line skirt and blouse on, peers back at me from behind my eyelids, closely followed by Marcie's laughing blue eyes and Derek's puppy dog ones. Oh my God. What has she done to my friends?

I regard her, simmering with hatred. 'We trusted you, you bitch. You made us believe you cared, and then you sold us to the highest bidder,' I hiss at her.

Adelia's face remains unmoved. I wonder how I had ever thought her beautiful. She resembles a waxwork dummy, stiff and expressionless. The woman is devoid of emotion. Creepy.

'You wipe out everything that makes us special. Then you sell us like cattle.' One solitary tear trickles down my cheek and I grit my teeth. I want so badly to smash her face in, but I still cannot move.

Adelia tilts her head to one side and contemplates the ceiling. Then she looks back at me, eyebrows raised.

'Well, now. That is a particularly vulgar way to view the situation. However, I am not surprised at your rather limited interpretation of your reassignment. I have *saved you all*.'

Adelia spreads her arms wide and shakes her head.

'Think about the misery and squalor of the life you led before I brought you here. I found you, I cleansed you, then corrected you. I have saved you and so many others throughout the years. Why, I've lost count. There were a few specimens who could not adapt to my evolved gene technology. Unfortunate because the crop numbers could have been a lot higher. No matter, I can always learn from these negative results–there is no such thing as failure in the name of science.'

'There's so much work to be done. I wonder if I could still activate the neurons even with a lobotomy. The finished product would be so much quicker, and the risk of program rejection would be less…' Adelia makes a moue with her mouth, then smiles.

'Hmmm… the possibilities are endless.' I can hear the static clearing but dare not take my attention from Adelia to see which one of my friends has come to me.

'Ah, well, I need to scrub up for your big day, don't I?' Adelia speaks as though she is a bridesmaid, speaking to a bride.

My "big day." *Happy living death day to me.*

I have run out of things to ask or say, and the feeling has still not returned to my arms and legs. A lifetime of horror flashes before me.

'One more thing.' Adelia returns, and her voice is so unexpectedly close that it makes me flinch.

Wordlessly, I gawp at her as she asks, 'How did you know?'

Adelia brings her eyes closer to mine, reminding me of a snake studying a mouse. Her bone structure is prominent under her thin skin, making her look reptilian.

With a shiver, I wonder again how I ever thought her beautiful? The hatred in her cold regard is now so obvious that she looks like an alien. Why had I not seen it?

I snatch at the chance to slow Adelia down.

'Sophie had a relationship with one of your "correctees." She knew her girlfriend would never willingly behave in the way she was, and that something had happened to her to make her change so much. Derek hacked in your computers and found all your dirty secrets. The files on previous patients, the recordings, the financial transactions, everything. We aren't just patients, Adelia. We are *people*,' I explain with satisfaction.

Adelia shakes her head.

'No, not that, dear child. I do not care about that. Some of you have learnt a few parlour tricks and accessed my computer illegally. Even a dog can learn to catch a ball. It's of no consequence. No, what I was referring to was… *how did you know about what I did to my daughter, Mary?'*

Chapter 7

My breath stops and my blood runs cold. Adelia's intense gaze holds my horrified one in its grip.

'You knew, didn't you? That your "*Little Mary*" was *my daughter?* That's why you need neurosurgery. I don't know how you know the details of my early experiments with Little Mary, but I could not have you sharing your stories now, could I?'

No. It cannot be.

'Little Mary is your daughter?' I ask her in an uneven voice when I can trust myself to speak.

I did not see that coming.

Adelia heaves a gigantic sigh.

'Hard to believe, isn't it? She wasn't exactly a chip off the old block, was she? I knew as soon as she was born to me that she needed fixing... Well, I tried, and I tried, but I could never correct her. She was so worthless. Although... some of my best ideas for experiments came from the initial testing I conducted on Mary, so I suppose she did have some use.'

Oh, my God. The horror of being brought up by this monster. Being alone with her, day in, day out, where Adelia could do anything she wanted, away from any staff or outside eyes. I gape at her, the creature that she is, as I understand the depths of terror that Little Mary, my beautiful, kind, clever little friend must have endured before she came to me. How? I do not understand.

Adelia peers at me with distaste etched on her delicate features. Sharp fear interrupts my thought process as she speaks. I am tied up, and anyway, I still cannot move my limbs properly. When she speaks, her voice is laced with barbed wire.

'You remind me of her.'

'No… it can't be. Little Mary… she's a product of my subconscious. She's from my imagination.'

Adelia's laugh tinkles out.

'She was a figment of your imagination? Ah, that explains some of it. Still… strange coincidence, though. You described her to a T, Mary. The avatar was the absolute image of her. Why, you even knew about the time she spent in the immersion tanks, when I used conditioning to reinforce my instructions and withdrew food for a few days at a time. The experiments failed, of course, because of *her.* Defective. Oh, and those God-awful little ditties she used to make up. Such a complete waste of time. I never understood.

'Mary was so stupid that it was an insult to my superior genes. Obviously, she inherited her drabness and instability from her father. Mary, *the little idiot,* was always seeing things that weren't there. Jumping at her own shadow. The drugs I injected her with never helped at all. Total embarrassment to me. I had to keep her existence a secret much of the time. It was so inconvenient. I made the mistake of bringing her to work once, and she completely humiliated me. Can you imagine? My progeny, a treatment-resistant schizophrenic. A defective mutant.

'She must have inherited the DNA from her father, the useless troglodyte that *he* was. We should have never paired. He was beneath me. Alas, my family funds had dwindled, and I needed to marry to replenish them. Oliver was at least from a wealthy family. The last of his line, and so desperate for me, it was pathetic. I agreed to marry him - his money helped me to set this place up. He had no further use after that, except to hold me back. He had to go too.' Adelia mentions this as though she is telling me about something arbitrary, like a trip to the shops.

I know the word for people like her. It comes to me like a whisper carried on the breeze.

'You're a psychopath.'

'Hmm…' Adelia pretends to consider my words. 'I prefer the term "visionary."' Adelia smiles at me, baring her teeth.

I fight against fresh waves of nausea and close my eyes.

'Mary. We're here with you now. Don't speak out loud and don't open your eyes,' Little Mary instructs me.

My friend's voice materialises from beside my right ear. Luckily, I am too exhausted to jump.

CHAPTER 8

I open my eyes as soon as I hear Adelia's steps leave the room.

My family is in front of me, waiting for me to look at them. Errol has also joined the gang. A tear trickles down my cheek. Despite the terrible reality of the situation, I breathe a sigh of relief at the sight of them.

I struggle to assimilate all the statements that Adelia has made.

'She said you were her daughter,' I whisper to Little Mary.

My throat is so dry, and I fight dizziness.

My friend's head droops like a wilted flower and, if it is possible, she grows even paler.

Little Mary nods.

'It's true,' she says.

'But… I thought *you were me*… A product of my subconscious mind, I mean.'

My empty stomach churns as overwhelmed, the events of the last few hours swim in my mind.

'I don't understand,' I murmur, shaking my head.

'Everything I ever told you was true. The only thing I didn't tell you was that Adelia was my mother. I couldn't tell you, because it would have put you in too much danger if she had found out you knew.'

Little Mary's voice contains a mature, melancholy tone that I did not recognise before.

'But... she said...' I struggle to formulate my question.

Little Mary watches me search her face, then the faces of my other friends. With a gentle smile, she correctly guesses what I want to ask.

'I am non-physical, Mary. Adelia murdered me and made it look like I had taken an overdose.' Little Mary glances at Jo, Dolores, and Lou.

They move closer to me, hovering with an air of wary hope, mixed with regret.

'We have all died and passed onto the next form of existence. Remember when Jo told you Eileen was his wife?' Little Mary clarifies.

I cough, choking on the air that expels itself.

'What? Why?'

Their explanations have made me confused, and I make a mewling sound of distress.

Dolores comes forward to calm me and to simplify. Her papery hands are wringing themselves now but are without her knitting.

'We crossed over to the non-physical but were not ready to join The Blue and go into the spirit realm. We all have something left undone. You see, dear... You are like your dad. Your mediumship light shone so strongly it drew us to you. We felt your existence because your light called to us. It is so powerful, and so pure.'

My mouth drops open and my gaze flits between them, one to another. No way. What the hell? I am calling spirits - *Like my father had.* Dolores is not a figment of my imagination? *Where did her knitting keep going?*

'We all have unfinished business here on this plane. I felt I had let down my daughter when she needed me the most. She has crossed over now, and I could have joined her, but I did not feel ready... worthy. When I hesitated, you called me to your side, Mary. I found you, and I no longer felt lost. When I looked at you,

I saw so many similarities to my Lily. Her forceful character, her kindness and humour, and, of course, you are both so beautiful.' Dolores' eyes twinkle at me.

I turn to stare at Jo, and my mouth drops open. If I am talking to ghosts. Jo is... dead? With a sad expression, he takes his turn to speak.

'I knew you would come here, to this place of torture and horror, and I wanted to help you. To guide you, and to keep you safe. You were just a child. Also... I must admit, I wanted the chance to see my Scottish rose Eileen again, and for her to know I was OK. I know she misses me and has not yet let me go.'

It is Lou's turn next, and she steps forward in her usual direct manner.

'You won't remember me, but I taught you when you were living with your foster parents. It was only for two days because I was a substitute teacher, but I could never quite forget you. You haunted me. I had felt in my bones that there was something bad happening to you, but I did nothing to explore, to help. I knew there was something... and I told no-one. I was and am, so sorry, I...' Lou, flounders, shaking her head. Tears run down her face, and she flutters her hands as she searches for the right words to finish her story.

'One day when I was at the gym, I died from a heart attack, and just as I was going... I saw your sad little face flash in front of me. You called to me, a psychic beacon. You looked so scared and withdrawn, and there it was... my chance to make it right. All those years of guilt, gnawing away at me. I felt an urge to go to you, and the next thing – hey, presto. There you were, sitting in the canteen at the children's home at the table all by yourself. I was desperate to befriend you, to help you in whatever way I could. Then I... decided to stay with you, try to help you where possible.'

Am I a medium, or is this all a product of my imagination? Adelia had spoken about Mendelian traits. Is my mental health condition one of those, or is mediumship my genetic legacy?

'Am I just completely psychotic?' I ask them, voice husky with tears.

Little Mary puts her hand near mine.

'No,' she firmly tells me. 'But even if you really suffered from schizophrenia, and all of us are a symptom of psychosis, Adelia's plans are real, and no individual on this earth deserves the living hell that Adelia plans to put you, and everyone like that through.

'Outside in the community, there were sometimes a couple of dozen voices calling to you at once and we know you suffered, but in here… there are hundreds of unaligned souls, still trapped in their suffering. The energies of the resounding pain they feel have lingered, and the psychic torture Adelia inflicted on her patients amplified those energies. There have been so many, batch after batch of patients. Subjects she identified. It's excruciating to experience en masse, and we knew you would not have survived such a psychic battering for long.' Little Mary suddenly appears older than me, mature as she discusses the unexplainable.

'But *who are they?* Who do the voices belong to? Adelia erased the mind of the patients, but their bodies are still alive?' I hiss, head spinning.

'The voices you heard before were all previous patients. They were unwell when they were admitted here, and the *treatment* that Adelia subjected them to only made things worse.

'Their energies are fierce and damaged, but they mean you no harm though. They are desperate to get their message through to you, but their minds are too jumbled to make much sense anymore. They are not in alignment, and they want revenge for everything Adelia has done to them, taken from them.

'All of them were patients that Adelia could not turn into automatons. Or patients that she just deemed as unworthy of her time. People like me, who she could not erase *effectively*. So, she discharged then murdered them. In every case, there was scant investigation. The authorities just wrote it off as an accident or a "tragic suicide." Most of them have lost their consciousness–they have gone mad with suffering and cannot come back to alignment with themselves. We experienced their pain too. Their terror and their hunger for Adelia's death.'

Dolores shudders.

'But then, how are you here? And where have they gone now?' I ask, confused.

'Errol came forward to help. He showed us how to connect our energies together, to focus them so that we could divert them from you. We are intercepting them for the time being, blocking them on your behalf. When you arrived here, there were so many energies… all vying to communicate with you–warn you, plead with you, *command you* to kill Adelia. It was automatic how we stood together in their way, and in doing so, we alerted Errol to our presence and to our positive intentions for you.

'We discovered by fluke that if we focus our intention together, we can do that sometimes. To keep your mind clear, we stopped them from communicating with you. Errol isn't like the others, though, dear. He wanted to help, so we let him through. Thank God we did because he taught us so much. Like how to block others, or to allow.'

Dolores fingers her pearl-string necklace, looking about her as though she half expects the owners of all the voices to flood the room like a tidal wave.

'Wait–Errol's dead too? But I thought he worked here?' I regard the face of my new friend Errol.

He shakes his head. No, oh God, no.

A couple of thoughts occur to me.

'But if you could do that all this time, why didn't you help me before? When I was going crazy in my flat from all those other voices? Why couldn't you step in then and help me–why did you let me suffer? And why couldn't you just warn me about Adelia, tell me exactly what she was doing here, or even that I should listen to Derek and Sophie, and believe them?' My voice chokes on the last question as I picture my absent friends.

Lou answers me.

'We couldn't, Mary. Hun, we didn't even know we could block them for you until you came here. We found out by accident because we were so desperate to protect you–we knew you were in a vulnerable place. You had been on the verge of ending your life in this current physical form. While that would have been sad, what goes on here is so much worse.

'Those who died here experienced torture and a prolonged suffering of a huge magnitude. Adelia would have committed you to that… eternal suffering, and we just could not have that. We love you. We knew we had to do whatever we could to stop that from happening to you. Unfortunately, it takes most of our energy and focus to act as psychic buffers, so when we do this, we cannot communicate with you either.'

'That's why we can't speak to you for long now, but we needed a clear channel so we could tell you, our plan,' Dolores explains.

Jo says, 'We cannot simply warn you, because there is a force that stops us from telling you in advance about certain events. It is a cosmic law that we cannot say or do anything to influence the choices you make if it alters your future from the one that is supposed to be. We try to help where we can, but we do not know if it will work or not. Despite knowing this, Little Mary tried to warn you when you first got here, but you could not hear her, then Dolores tried again one day when she came to you alone.'

'In the garden,' I whisper. Then, 'Errol. No.'

I am having a hard time keeping up with all the revelations my friends are telling me.

There are universal laws shitting all over me… and Adelia had killed Errol? Cool, handsome Errol who always says it like it is. I remember what Derek had said about names crossed out on a list. "*Something beginning with E,*" he had said, but he could not remember the name. *Not Eric.* I realised. It had been *Errol.*

Ian's face, chatting away to Errol in the office flitted into my mind, captioned by the saying I had once overheard: "Where does a tree go to hide–in the woods, silly!'' Ian was not talking to Errol; he had been talking to himself.

Errol steps forward, interrupting my thoughts with his laconic smile. Shrugging, he leans closer.

'Don't sweat it, Mary. It's OK. C'mon, you've got to focus on you now. Let's just get you out of here. We have very little time.'

I nod. OK. Let's do this.

'The guard has left one strap slightly loose. If you can just focus on freeing that hand, you could rotate your wrist, then you will get your entire arm out,' Errol instructs me.

I stare at Errol, remaining motionless. My mouth is hanging open.

'You have hypermobility, Mary. You can do this,' Jo says, moving closer.

I nod again. Yes. That is true. I know that. *I am double jointed.*

'Come on, come on, you can do it. We have little time,' Jo continues to urge me.

Pushing the revelations to the corner of my mind, I focus on getting free. Bending my hand back on itself, I strain to reach the ties with my fingernails.

'When you've got your arm out, Adelia has her equipment all laid out, ready for surgery. You can grab a knife from there, then cut yourself free.' Jo's steady voice guides me, as always, with kind assurance.

I do not hesitate. Trusting him, I do what he bids me to.

As soon as my torso is free, I sit up drunkenly, snatching at a scalpel. My fingers are numb and clumsy from the aftereffects of whatever they shot me up with. Fumbling with the knife at first, I tuck my tongue between my teeth, attempting to hold it in my grasp. The knife slices through the remaining constraints as though they are butter. I stumble off the bed, moving towards the door on cotton wool legs. My limbs feel too weak to hold me straight away–what the hell did they inject me with? After a second or two of teetering towards freedom, I drop to the floor like a dead bird falling from the sky. Shit.

'I'm made of fucking jelly.'

I flex, forcing myself to scramble up again, tottering towards the doorway like a toddler. This time, my baby gazelle legs hold, and I am jerking across the room, moving like a glitched computer character in a zombie game.

With laboured breathing, I use my hand to steady myself against the wall, and stumble from the theatre. Adelia's exclamation of outrage pursues me.

Chapter 9

'Come in here,' Little Mary whispers to me.

Mary, Jo, and Lou crawl alongside me as I enter the room on all fours as silently as I can. I know now that they do not need to do the same, but it helps me feel less alone. Errol and Dolores wait in the room for the rest of our clan.

My lips are numb. I purse them together while I concentrate. I cannot make the slightest sound. If Adelia hears me, that is it. The door is open, and I hold my breath as I slowly push it closed, sliding along the bottom lock as stealthily as I can. Clunk. Lock engaged!

'Mary…' Adelia's voice is cordial, but her tone is discordant, like nails down a chalkboard, or a fork scratching a plate.

I shiver with fear at the proximity of Adelia's vicious wildness. Where is someone else? Maybe they will be back soon, and I should call out for help? I dare not close my eyes in case Adelia materialises on this side of the door like a demon from a nightmare.

She cannot find me. It will be alright… Eileen will be on her way to help me.

Maybe… please God, let her be on her way.

My back pushes against the wall beside my friends, fighting back waves of dizziness. I flex my fists again, testing them, but my fingers are slow to respond, and I cannot form a fist. My hands still feel alien, and pins and needles stab their way upwards. Can I fight? No. I am still too weak. Sick and dizzy, I have not yet regained the feeling in my body. I cannot punch, but maybe I could throw something at Adelia. A chair? I nibble my bottom lip, shaking my head. It is no use. I cannot even lift my arms properly, let alone a chair. What have they given me and *when will it wear off?*

Little Mary crouches down in front of me, and I close my eyes briefly as her spectral hand gestures I should wipe the dirt-stained tear tracks. I feel the synchronicity of our paths. That so many times my little friend has done the same thing that I am doing now. Hiding from her evil mother. I know now that Adelia had found Little Mary every time–except the one time when Little Mary had found me. I frown… there is something in that. Something I think I should remember. From a dream, maybe? My forehead hurt worse than the time I had bought the stupid Sudoku book to distract myself from my "hallucinations."

I put my hands up at my throbbing temples with effort. Remaining still, I hold my breath again, then slap both of my clammy palms over my mouth to stifle my scream. The sound of delicate panting ranges closer. It is her.

'Mary, you do realise how pointless this childish hiding is, don't you?'

Adelia is right outside the door.

I imagine her lascivious face peering at different angles into the sphere of glass at the top of the door and tremble. Shit. Do not woose out now, Mary Jameson. Get your shit together.

Lou puts her finger to her lips, and Jo's fingers reach towards mine in reassurance.

'Mary, don't be rude,' Adelia says conversationally.

A shiver draws its icy finger down my spine, and I wipe beads of sweat out of my eyes with shaky hands.

Little Mary's eyes hold mine. I recognise Adelia's phrase from the glimpses of Little Mary's past that she had shown me before I came here. *That evil bitch.* I know what comes next.

I sweep my gaze around the room, inspecting it for any makeshift weapons that I can find, and my heart jitters as I spot something else. The air zings, and I *know* Adelia sees it at the same time. The patio doors on the other side of the room. They are open. Propped open by a mop and bucket. I can race 'round to the end of the room and I might reach the door and close it by the time she runs through next door to meet me. Or… I might not make it and in my weakened state, Adelia can chop me down like wood with just a push.

A picture of myself, moonwalking on jelly legs as I ran out of the theatre, pops into my mind. It has been a bit longer now, so I might have more control over my limbs.

I sense, rather than hear Adelia leave her post by the door, and I unclick the bottom bolt. Yanking back the door, I flick a look over my shoulder. Just in time, I see Adelia's white face appear at the patio doors in the room I am leaving. Adelia strolls towards me.

My friends and I take off at top speed. Although I am not up to my full strength, I push what energy I have into steadying my legs. My bare feet conduct good suction on the glossy floors and even in my vulnerable state, I think I have a good chance of outrunning a forty something woman who has had a desk job all her life.

Adelia's measured steps echo behind me, as she advances with slow confidence. In contrast, flat handed and determined, I motor down the endless corridors, my friends flanking me. My eyes remain glued to the sign that promises "exit," but I am at the other, unused side of the hospital and pray the security guard's office is near.

It is.

With a stop so abrupt I bang into the door, at first, I am too out of breath to shout out for help.

Adelia also stops just short of the security guard's office, removing a hypodermic needle from her pocket. She uncaps it with a slow flourish.

'Help! Please, someone help me!' I shout into the air.

An aura of malevolent calm surrounds Adelia, and her lips twist into a tight smile.

'Now, now, Mary. I dislike histrionics, they are so vulgar.'

Oh fuck, my head is still swimming, and I feel weak as a kitten. With a hand to my head to steady it, I register my heart, banging against my chest like a frightened bird in a cage.

I am dizzy as hell, and nearly within her arms' reach. The years of armour I have built around me are stripped away, and I am ten years old again. Alone in a room with my foster dad, with no-one to help me.

As I shake my head, it clears my thoughts like snow globe glitter settling.

No. I am weakened, but I am not ten, and I am not defenceless.

'Help me! Someone, please!' I shout, raising the alarm as loudly as I can.

Where in God's name are the security guards?

Too late.

Adelia reaches me.

'Be quiet,' she commands me.

Her hand whips out, and she slaps me. The force of her blow ricochets my head back, hitting the door behind me. My mind spins and I drag myself straight again, blinking to clear the stars that blur my vision.

'Don't you touch her! Don't you hurt my friend!' Little Mary screams.

Her mother blinks, and steps back half a step with a confused look on her face. "Mother, may I take two pigeon steps backwards? *Yes, you may.*"

Blinking like a drunken sleepwalker, I rub the back of my head, then stare at the blood on my fingers that the action leaves. Oh shit. My legs sag underneath me, and I collapse into a ball on the floor.

Jo and Lou move in front of me, lending me their invisible strength. Errol remains at my side. Friends until the end. *Family.*

My head flies left and right as I seek a way out, desperate.

'Someone help me! Help!'

Adelia overcomes her momentary distraction.

'*Someone help me.*' She mimics my voice cruelly.

Adelia stands still while savouring my fear for a few seconds, then takes a pigeon step forwards.

I press myself back against the door again, as though trying to push through it by the process of osmosis. While I manoeuvre myself back, I continue to clench and unclench my hands. They do not consistently respond. *Please God, help me. Mum, help me.*

'Ahhh. You're hoping for help, aren't you? Unfortunately, the security guard ate something that didn't agree with him. He went home about an hour ago. I told him not to worry about leaving us alone because I would arrange for a replacement.' Adelia glides forward again. She is a few metres away, but I can smell her sour, sweet breath.

'Whoops… Looks like I've forgotten to do that.' She takes another step forward.

'As I told you earlier, Mary, it is just us. Think of it as our last one-to-one session.' Adelia smiles, displaying all her teeth. "My, what big teeth you have, Grandma."

My friends are speaking, but their words are indistinct. They have not moved from their place in front of me, and I can see they stand together, and are clasping each other's hands. Adelia is unaware of them. Whatever discomfort she had felt when Mary shouted at her has gone.

Her eyes shine wildly.

As I gulp for air, a smell of sulphur permeates the hall and I disregard it. I shut my eyes, swooning as the arm with the needle raises and –

Sulphur? My eyes fly open again. My friends have linked hands with each other, and their chanting now unscrambles itself to me. I understand. They are calling out to David.

Chapter 10

The hairs at my nape prickle, and I know what they are doing. They are summoning *my father* to help me, although they fear him almost as much as I do. David is here now, and I feel his rage and fear swelter inside me. Violence will ensue, and I understand what happened all those times before. In his own way, my father had protected me.

My mother's words repeat themselves to me. David is misguided, but he loves me and will protect me. I do not have to be afraid. I open myself to his energy, accepting him, the good and the bad. *No resistance.*

Fearless now, I hold Adelia's madness-tinged eyes and stare her down. My pupils enlarge to fill my grey iris, regarding her with a new, sharklike gaze.

Adelia, observant even in the grip of madness, recognises a fellow predator and is immediately unnerved. Instinct makes her back away from me.

I remember again what my mum had told me, and lift my chin. Mum said not to be scared. That we attract what we are, and I am love. It is where we originate from, and it is always inside me. Mum always says that a source of pure love eternally surrounds us, and we are surrounded by favour. This source always waits for me to allow it to connect.

David did not cross over because he had felt he needed to make up for what he had not done in the past. He felt he had done wrong against my mum and me, and failed to protect me because he lost his way and was driven to the verge of insanity by his desperation. David loves me, but he is a spirit consumed with rage, despair, regret, and his fears for me. He is a misguided father, loving me despite the emotions that control him.

Whenever I am at my most out of alignment, I draw David. When I allow myself to be taken over by anguish, fear or anger, David comes and reflects that. When I feel vulnerable, he will come, and will do what he considers I need him to do to keep me safe. He is here now, and I understand he will lend me his strength. My father will protect me.

And still, I rise… I get to my feet, stronger now.

Adelia looks me up and down. She cannot understand what is different, but she senses that she herself is now in danger. I see Adelia's petite nostrils flare, a deer picking up the scent of a wolf.

David's spirit joins mine, and my recovering body pushes away from the exit door with confidence. I stride towards Adelia. Even though I have not regained all of my physical acuity, I double my small fist.

Without hesitation, I lash out at her with an unexpected and unnatural force. Adelia is lifted off her feet, flying backwards and landing with a thud. Her body slides down the corridor.

Adelia's exclamation melds with David's deep guttural laugh.

Adelia cuts off her cry with the abruptness of a record needle being lifted. She stares at me in shock.

'H-h-how are you doing that?' Adelia stutters.

Although I am not solely in control of my physical form, this time my consciousness remains throughout my father's occupation. An observant passenger in a canoe with no paddles, and I anticipate a doozie of a white river rafting experience ahead. At once, Adelia recognises I am different, a threat. My father is driven by negative energies. As is Adelia. Just as the same pole repulses a magnet, so is the incorporeal part of Adelia.

She turns, tottering back up the corridor in a bizarre reversal of roles.

David's strength and rage billows inside me, and I embrace his anger and hurt on behalf of my friend, my most beloved Little Mary. For all the times her mother had hurt or scared her. As I dwell on them, these thoughts fuel David's energy.

We join. My friends remain close, and I know they lend me their strength. Now, I am aware of my best friends, but also of the others who had screamed at me earlier… Jonesy and Tanisha, Devon, Wayne, Paulette, and many more. *Who are they?* They march with me as Adelia stumbles back. The syringe crunches under my feet as I stride towards my enemy, buoyed by the power of my companions.

Yes! I can beat her.

'Help! Someone help me!' Adelia's shrill call bouncing off the walls like an unreturned swing ball serve.

Her daughter screws her small face up.

'That's what all of us said. That's what I begged when it got terrible: "*Help me, someone help me*," and you used to laugh and mimic me,' Mary says with sadness.

David inside pulsates with the thrill of his free dominion over my body. I know now that I usually fight his occupation tooth and nail. I remember how before, I hammered at him until I pushed him back from the chasm he had scraped up from.

Now, I allow myself to open the channels I had not previously acknowledged, and as I do so, I accept the gift that my mum had shown me is part of me. This is my heritage, and I am now strong enough to claim it.

I am close to Adelia now, standing over her with my lip curling and fists clenched in a menacing way. She will never do this to anyone again, I will make sure of that. I advance closer.

The door at the end of the corridor swings open, with such force that it bangs against the wall.

My head flies towards the door to find the source of the intrusion into justice.

It is Eileen, the CPN. She came! Eileen's' eyes are wide as she enters the room, taking in the frozen tableau. Her arms pop up as though someone is pulling a rip cord in her back. Uniformed police and another man, who also raise their arms and focus on me, flank Eileen. I realise what they are seeing. *I am a threat.*

CHAPTER 11

I gaze back at Adelia and perceive an imperceptible smirk on her face. Adelia scrabbles backwards in a way that I consider theatrical. I watch her, cocking with my head to one side.

'Please, Mary, don't hurt me. It's OK, I understand,' Adelia pleads. Her voice drips with saccharin.

Adelia turns her attention to the police, her blue eyes wide and guileless.

'Thank God you're here, officers. This patient had a severe episode of psychosis and attacked me during a therapy session.'

My mouth drops open and I struggle to hold back my father's frenzy of rage and violence towards Adelia. *Wait, Dad. Please.*

I look at my friends and see that they still hold hands. Their heads are dipped toward their chests. A low hum emanates from them, and I sense a vibration inside me answering them. Jo comes forward.

'Turn and talk to Eileen. Tell her I am here with you. Tell her I said this is "*her time to shine*." Use those exact words. She always used to say that when she got called on to help with problematic cases.' Jo speaks with urgency in his voice.

Time is running out for me.

My father tries to seize control again to eliminate the threat to me. I look at Adelia, my lips curling. My fists scrunch themselves up again.

'*No, Mary, don't let David take control now — focus*! Repeat what I just said to Eileen, and for God's sake, do it now,' Jo demands.

I obey my friend, turning to the newcomers.

'Jo said to tell you he is here with me, Eileen, and that now is "*your time to shine*." He told me you always said that when you got called to help with problematic cases,' I repeat to the CPN.

I restrain my father, whose intentions rage inside me, and register that Eileen's expression changes. Before my words, Eileen had been beseeching me to stop my attack, but now her eyebrows knot together, and she stares at me aghast. I can tell she is now listening. Really listening.

'What?' Eileen asks.

Jo steps closer to me and speaks again, his words gathering more momentum as he warms to his theme.

'Tell her again that I am here and just repeat what I am saying exactly as I say it, Mary. You have run out of time and if you don't, this… monster woman will win,' Jo instructs me.

With a nod, I turn back to Eileen, ready to obey my friend to the letter. Adelia has drawn herself up and has regained her confidence. I am just another disposable patient; she can do what she wants to me, and no one will believe me. I am in the system, and everyone knows that once you are part of the system, you lose what little credibility you may have. Forever.

'Say that we never had children, although we wanted to. It was because I could not. Tell her I said I was always sorry about that, and that at the end I wished we had adopted a child to love, and so she would have had someone with her when I was gone. Tell her I died of cancer on October the sixteenth ten years ago. I left this plane twelve months to the day after they diagnosed me with cancer, and I spent the last month of that life in a hospice.

'I knew she was there by my side every day. Tell Eileen I miss her smile every day, and I used to love that dimple she got in her cheek when she grinned. Say to her she got a tattoo on her left buttock when she was a teenager. It was a dolphin, and we joked about it because that was my favourite animal.'

I translate Jo's statements as a pouring of verbatim information, hardly daring to steal a breath in between. Eileen's tears produce at first an uncomfortable silence in our observers, but then... the atmosphere changes to something else.

As Eileen wipes her eyes, the female police officer and two male officers stare at me with identical expressions of incredulity on their faces. They put down their arms.

Jo steamrolls on, wanting to be certain that I win Eileen's full trust and belief.

'Please say to Eileen that I always wore slippers and insisted she also wore them. I had a thing about moccasins with fluffy insides, and about keeping warm. I would put the heating on even in August, and it used to make Eileen angry, because she was always hot and liked the windows open. She used to like seventies music and loved to sing along to the Bee Gees–she had a terrible voice, and every night no matter if we had argued, I would always hug her before we went to sleep because I said, "*Tomorrow is another day.*" Tell her everything as I say it, Mary, quick as you can,' Jo says.

I had forgotten to translate and instead I had been listening to everything Jo had told me after "*the fluffy slippers,*" so I rush my speech to catch up with what Jo had said.

As I repeat his last sentence, Eileen finishes my words with me, and we say the words "*is another day*" in unison. The police officers' mouths all unclick, hanging open.

Silence.

'*Arrest her at once. Can't you see this filthy trash is lying*? She's one of "*them.*" I demand you get rid of her at once!' Adelia spits out her orders, breaking our communion.

The spell of entrancement that had lain on the four members of the jury splinters, and they blink alert.

'No,' Eileen tells the police with firmness. Her voice is clear as she turns to the police officers that stand beside her.

'I want to hear what else Mary has to say. You may not believe me, but everything Mary just said about my husband was true. She had no way of finding those things out–except from hearing them from either me or him. I've met Mary twice and I know damn straight that I did *not* tell her. My husband was an extremely private man, and there is no way on earth he would have told her such personal things about our lives. He would not have discussed them with anyone.'

Eileen turns to me, her eyebrows raised. She still looks dazed and awestricken.

'Let's hear from you what's been going on at this hospital then, Mary,' Eileen bid me. Her voice is gentle.

I take a deep breath. There is a lot to get out, and I know I have to say it fast.

'Well, first, I know this is going to sound crazy… but Adelia is into this thing called "eugenics," and she believes that all people with mental health conditions are ruining society. She has links with someone who tips her off when they find a schizophrenic like me. Someone who is treatment resistant, with no family or friends in their life, that is.' I swallow at the words, then look round.

Adelia observes my audience with wide eyes and an open mouth. They are rapt and say nothing to stop me from speaking, so I continue.

'Then Adelia has us moved out here. To The Rainbow Unit. She gives us all this nice shit and pretends she cares about us. We're so lonely we just lap it up. I lapped it up. She hypnotises us, and gives us one-to-one therapy, where she makes a Three-D avatar and pretends she's helping us, but really, she's learning everything she can to use against us.

'After that, she can enter posthypnotic suggestions into our minds and make it easier to hijack our brains after they discharge us.

'Oh, yeh - when we leave, Adelia has put these special laser beam lights in the Three-D avatar. The laser accesses parts of our brain so Adelia can control our behaviour. That's why when the patients return to the hospital, they are nothing like they were before. They don't remember the people they love or are close to. If Adelia can't turn them, then she kills them, and makes it look like an accident.'

Sophie. Derek... Marcie. They will not know me. My face crumples. I have to free them from the living hell they are stuck in. Poor Errol.

The inhabitants of the room are deep in thought, considering my words.

Adelia is not happy.

'*Shut up, you cretin. Shut her mouth at once, officer–we cannot allow her to roam free. She needs to be locked up*,' Adelia demands. Her voice is sharp as a wasp sting.

She makes to move towards me, but the man in plain clothes with the police officers steps towards Adelia, stopping her. He flashes a badge, identifying himself as police. The officer raises his hands, and the gesture is clear. *Stay there and do not move.* I take a deep breath.

Adelia folds her arms across her chest and taps one of her feet.

'Go on, Mary. I want to hear the rest. Can you tell me *why* Adelia would do *any of this*? She is a well-respected professional,' the plain-clothes policeman asks.

'I can guess why she did it.'

'Adelia was getting huge payments from people. I don't know who they are, but my boyfriend said there were at least two who were militia from different countries who put millions of pounds into her account.'

My eyes tear up. *My boyfriend.* Where is he? Who is he now?

'But the money is just a by-product. I think her actual aim is to rid the world of as many of "us" as she can. That's her proper work,' I explain.

'Adelia has recordings on her computers of all the people who have left. She wipes out their identities. She removes all the funny quirks and character traits that make them *"them,"* and then replaces everything they know and are with some kind of... *mind slave.* Someone who exists in body only, and who will do anything she inputs into their mind.'

'There are recordings you said. Can you show us?' Eileen asks.

I nod.

'Yes, I've seen them. I think I can show you. Adelia also had emails that showed details of her financial transactions.'

Thank God for Derek's computer knowledge. *Please, God, let Derek be OK.* Somehow.

Everyone in the room stares at Adelia, who shakes with rage. Oblivious to the police instruction to remain where she is, she takes a step towards me with her hand raised and her fingers curling into spiteful hooks. Her wrathful intentions are obvious.

I move back swiftly, and Little Mary detaches from the group to return close to my side, putting her small hand in mine.

Chapter 12

My body jerks.

I experience a sudden flash of insight, realising we have never touched before, and now I know why. As Little Mary's hand joins with mine, I feel a powerful jolt. My eyelids flutter as there is a transmutation of her memories. Then I relax, allowing them to flow. Soul osmosis. *Cool.*

Like a USB flash drive plugged into a laptop, I experience tragic scenes from Little Mary's short and painful life. Being shut into the cupboard by Adelia. Adelia towering over Little Mary, her face twisting in spite as she first taunts her, then lashes out at her daughter. Little Mary, hungry and alone, too exhausted to cry and too dehydrated to produce tears. Then she just stops breathing one day.

After that, *The Blue* calls to her, but so does my light, and she, Little Mary, chooses to come to me. Because she can see what will happen now. Despite all that she has suffered, my brave friend wants to help me and others, and feels a kinship with me. We are the same. Little Mary is not alone anymore, and nor am I.

My eyes swim with tears.

Sorrow for my friend's pain and suffering, for all she endured rises to the foreground, and I forget our onlookers, turning to confront Adelia.

'I know everything you did to her. *You bitch. You sick fucking bitch,*' I accuse Adelia.

Little Mary's second party suffering robs me of my remaining energy, and my words come out as a choked whisper.

I focus on Adelia, glued to the spot as Little Mary's emotions continue to blend into my consciousness.

'I know what you did to Little Mary, to your own daughter. You just couldn't have a daughter of yours that was anything less than perfect in your eyes could you, Adelia? Brown hair, brown eyes… a mental illness and a quirky spirit… Poor Little Mary just didn't come up to *your* idea of what was "acceptable," so first you tried your own methods to train her into what you wanted, and when that didn't work, you had to get rid of her - didn't you?' I gag, brimming with emotion.

I search Adelia's face for remorse. There is none. My dear friend endured so much at the hands of this monster, and she does not even feel bad about it.

'You're disgusting. It's *you* who's the broken one, not everyone else. You tortured all those people for money. Little Mary was the first one of us you got rid of. You told her you hated her because she wasn't good enough, but really, it was the opposite. Her goodness, her grace in the face of all your relentless cruelty. It showed you up for the evil psychopath bitch you know you are.

'After it was so easy to get rid of your own daughter, you realised that no-one cared about us, that we were expendable research subjects. You had free license to do whatever you wanted here; no-one cared. The contracts for the militia came after. Human robots for sale to the highest bidder. Slaves with their memory banks conveniently wiped clean before they were sold.'

The room lays quiet, and I sob.

'Stop speaking immediately, you ignorant filth!' Adelia enunciates into the silence.

As she scrabbles onto her bony knees, she slips, trying to get purchase on the shiny floor. Her nail breaks audibly, escalating her outrage.

'Argh! How dare you question me? Defective specimens like you, should not even be allowed to speak unless I allow it. You are a nothing. A nobody. A filthy bottom feeder. Just as my father taught me. You... "genetic rejects" should never be permitted to breed freely or to pollute our society with your substandard genes. You should be either put to work for the good of society or put to death so you can no longer be a drain on our society. All of you.'

The policewoman gasps out loud, and the impact of Adelia's hatred and disgust fills the room.

The noise makes Adelia's head snap in her direction, and her mouth chops shut. Her eyelashes flick. Adelia has said too much.

Her humanitarian veneer is slipping off in full view of the world, allowing a peek at her real perspective. In front of witnesses.

What will they do? I stop crying now and inspect them. One by one. When they take me, I will not fight. There is no point. I will just beg them to take me to another hospital. Section me again, anywhere but here please. Then I will try to convince whoever is in charge there that I am healthy again. I know what is "wrong" with me and I know how to hide it. I'll be able to pretend to be the same as everyone else.

Adelia stands silent and straight backed, her chin up, shoulders braced. She squints her eyes, then considers the others (not me) in the room with careful calculation on her face.

'How dare you hesitate? Who do you think you are dealing with here? I am extremely wealthy and have powerful friends. *I am a world-renowned neurosurgeon and psychiatrist*, and the founder of this elite institution. This *patient* has escaped from her treatment and has assaulted me. I demand that you arrest this girl immediately. She is a nobody,' Adelia says, as she pulls herself to her full height.

Her hair is loose from its style, but she still looks every inch the beautiful aristocrat. One slender finger points down at me.

My friends watch Adelia. Together, we wait for whatever will come next. I hold my breath, watching while the police officers get out their handcuffs and walk towards me. My heart sinks and I prepare to beg for a change of hospital. I would rather die than become one of Adelia's zombies.

The good doctor puts her hands on her hips, regarding me with a smug expression that says, "*Do you see? You are nothing, and the world knows it. There is no way you could win against someone like me.*"

The police officer continues on past me to hold Adelia with firmness. My mouth drops open as I watch.

The policewoman snaps wrist cuffs on the doctor, whilst she reads Adelia her rights under British law.

Adelia's expression changes from confusion, to incredulousness, to outrage, in a matter of seconds as the turn of events catches up with her.

'*How dare you!*'

'Nurse?' Adelia glares a warning at the CPN.

'I insist you tell these morons to unhand me at once,' Adelia tells Jo's wife.

Eileen looks at her with disdain.

'No, I won't. I believe in Mary. The patients *are* totally different people after they're discharged from here, and I always had my suspicions about what happened to wee Mary. I only saw her the once, but she was a lovely little bairn. She never spoke to anyone when she came here that time, and she was so thin. I cannee bear to think of what she went through,' Eileen says. Her Scottish accent is more pronounced, and I can hear the distress is clear in her voice as she remembers.

Adelia reacts with a venomous glare at Eileen, and then, chin tilting up, she falls silent. The neurosurgeon and renowned psychiatrist pulls herself to her full height, as she stands in the corner. It is obvious she recognises it is over.

Eileen clears her throat, blinking away tears, then stares at me.

'My Jo… he was my rock. A doctor. A beautiful, clever man, who was also a proud African man who stayed true to his culture in that he always did as much as he could for everyone he knew. Jo always kept me sane and took care of me. I would have loved to have children with him, but I would never have swapped being able to have a child with even one minute with him. Life with *Jo was enough*.' Tears drip down Eileen's face and she leaves them unchecked.

'He was always *more* than enough–can you tell him that from me please, Mary? Where is he - can he hear me?' Eileen's head turns from left to right as she tries blindly to direct her words at her husband's form.

Jo nods, going to stand close to his wife. His love for her shines a soft pink and blue in the gloom.

'He can hear you. Jo's standing right beside you, Eileen, and he loves you. For always,' I tell her. Jo did not need to tell me again. I can see his love for Eileen emanating from him.

Eileen turns to search for Jo, settling when Jo touches her face. Her hand rests against her cheek, tracing the movement. Then, Jo turns to me, his face set and peaceful.

'Mary… My little friend, daughter of my heart. It is time for me to go.'

I snap back to reality.

'What? No, Jo, please.'

'Adelia cannot hurt you now, and I have done what I needed to do. You are safe, Mary. It is time for you to live and let go of the past. Stay in touch with Eileen. Take care of each other. Make a new future for yourselves and enjoy it,' Jo bids me.

I look at my other friends. I did not notice at first, but when the police handcuffed Adelia, my crowd of supporters thinned out. Now, I am left with "the usual suspects." The motley crew of spectres that I have lived with on and off day and night for the last ten years. I see now that they are the family I had been yearning for all along, but now they are healed. It is time for them to go on the next step of their journey.

Will they *all* move on? Have they all achieved whatever outstanding debt they feel they need to pay in order to balance the scales and progress to the next part of their spiritual journey? No, not all of them were complete. I can sense my father is still remorseful about his treatment of my mum and me in his physical life and is expectant and longing for something.

Chapter 13

The police have stopped paying attention to us, and the plain-clothes officer speaks into a mobile, while the other talks into a personal radio, calling the custody of their suspect into the station.

They are training their eyes on Adelia.

When he gets off the phone, an officer speaks to me in a quiet voice. 'You mentioned the rest of the patients? Did this woman harm more of the patients here?'

I nod, swiping tears away with the back of my hand.

'So many... I think a load of patients didn't take to the re-programming, so Adelia killed them somehow. I'm not sure how many people it didn't work on, but I know she programmed at least a hundred. Including my friends Sophie, Derek, and Marcie. She just discharged them, and they weren't themselves. She changed them. Wiped their personalities out totally.'

'Wiped them out, how? And how did you find this out?'

'Derek... He was a computer genius and hacked Adelia's computer. I didn't believe him at first, I thought he might just be unwell... then, he disappeared and didn't get in touch- just like Marcie. It devastated me. Then I found a note Derek had left me and it had instructions on how to access Adelia's files and everything. I watched the videos he told me about for myself and read the emails. Then, I knew.'

My voice breaks and my bottom lip trembles. I suck it in. Different emotions are rolling through me, and my words mirror the feelings, running into one another with no separation.

Poor Derek, I had let him down, because I didn't listen to what he said. I had not given his words any credit, writing off everything he told me, just because of his diagnosis. This was what I hated most when people did it to me, and I had done the same. Now, my friends are zombies, but hopefully not forever.

'I hope they can go back to how they were before. Their new addresses are all on Adelia's system–along with the recordings. Please help them,' I beg the police.

I realise my attitude towards the law is a long way from where it had been at the start of this journey. My feelings towards *everything* were changed.

The man is middle-aged, with kind eyes and he nods, taking notes and asking questions. Half of my focus remains on Eileen. Jo said to take care of her, of each other. Eileen cannot see it, but The Blue is here, and its connection is filling me with serenity and love. I can now remember how good it feels to be immersed in it. My friends will become part of it, reabsorbed again. Tears well in my eyes, but I smile for them. It is not the end, and I will be OK if I let them go... They can leave this plane. The connection is eternal.

'Jo says he can go now. He wants us to take care of each other,' I tell her.

Even while I accept what will happen, I know my voice sounds forlorn.

Jo moves back to stand near me, his big rotund presence a comfort as always. He beams beatifically.

'Come now, Mary. You know it is a positive thing, and we will always be here,' Jo says. 'You are safe. Some of us are free, and you now know the truth about your gift. I could never have a child while I was here in my last form, but if I could have one, I would have wanted her to be exactly like you. I love you very much, child.'

Fresh tears brim at Jo's words, and gratitude swells inside me.

'I love you too, Jo. Thank you for everything,' I tell him in a gruff voice.

'Please tell Eileen I am at peace now, and our love will always be something that lives on with me. We will be reunited one day, in one form or another. Take care of her and yourself, Mary. Take care, everyone,' Jo says.

The other spirits look at peace, and salute Jo as he turns away to be reabsorbed.

Little Mary comes forward. She offers no words, but I know. It is time for her to return to source. I nod.

Little Mary has been my best friend for years, my soul compadre. She has achieved what she had come here to do and is now at peace. I close my eyes, allowing the warmth our shared love provides to shine between us.

There are no words, and we do not need any. We will always be connected. I glance back at her with a small smile. I know she feels my love projecting towards her, and the physical space between us does not separate us and never will. Jo, Dolores, and Lou wait for me to embrace them, and I do so, taking turns to savour their adoration as they blend with me temporarily. I breathe in. *Such love.* We shimmer with it.

My non-physical family takes a step back. They are going back to The Blue, but the gift of their love remains inside of me, and I know it will stay forever a part of me I can tap into.

Little Mary stares at me, and mouths, 'We will always love you, Mary.'

Dolores kisses her fingertips, no knitting in sight.

Jo bows, then holds one hand to his heart.

Lou waves one last time.

Then they leave, turning one by one towards The Blue.

All four will be at peace in joy, and they have given me the skill to understand I will be, too. I can use my gift without fear.

My attention returns to Eileen, who is scrutinising my face.

I tell her what Jo had said, and she nods. She accepts it as truth. Eileen walks back over to the police, beginning a quiet conversation with them.

I watch as Jo walks into The Blue until I cannot see him anymore, a smile on my face.

Chapter 14

The room thins out significantly, as the non-physical occupants of the room leave. Still, I sense straight away a new arrival enters, but cannot tell who. Could it be Derek? My heart leaps. Had he been able to respond to my call for help somehow, despite the programming?

No… It is not Derek. The smell of lavender makes me swing my head around, and I confirm who it is with a gasp.

'Mummy.'

I touch my hands to my cheeks, then feel my stomach and arms. Is this real? Am I real?

It has been so long. I fly into her arms, and she catches me. Inside, I can feel my father's joy as it merges into mine, amplifying it. This is also what he yearns for. His beloved wife. I know this is the reason she is here. My mum rests her chin on top of my head, telling me, 'I love you, Mary. I am so proud of you, mon coer. You remembered *everything* I told you, beautifully.'

'I did?'

She is still my biggest supporter.

'Mum, I love you- miss you. I hope you're safe and happy.'

'Of course I'm safe and happy darling, and I love you too, always and forever. Now, dear, let me speak to your father please.'

My dad's attention pricks up. He awaits my mother's next words on high alert. This means everything to him.

'I forgive you. The Blue is always waiting to accept you if you want it – can you feel it?'

I take momentary stock, as my father unmerges with me, and we examine each other. For over ten years, I had run from him, confused and frightened by the violence he had always wrought. Now, I understand he had been experiencing the same anger, frustration, and confusion I was. The moment he passed over, the sinister veil of desperation that had clouded his actions had gone away. And now, he was so sorry. Doing what my mum taught me, I allow myself to flood my inner being with love and understanding, absolving him. There is nothing left but his love, and mine. He is whole again, healed.

I nod in confirmation. He is realigned with source now. We both are.

'I'm sorry for everything, Mary. You're my little starlight and I'll always love you. Love never dies.'

My eyes well up, but I do not hug him as I had my mum. There is no need. We had already merged.

My mum stands in front of my dad, beckoning him with a smile on her face, then the two outlines become indistinct.

I take a deep breath. Love and well-being swell in my heart, making it feel as though it may burst. Now, I can allow myself to remember everything my mum had told me from my time with her in The Blue. That we all came from there, it is our source, and it is pure positive energy. We come into being, into this physical world, but we remain a part of it. Just as a person can take a bucket of water from the ocean and it will still be a part of the ocean. If we do not pinch ourselves off, we are always connected to source, and to unconditional love. I will never feel alone again.

I hold up my hand in salute as they leave. Together.

My parents and the rest of my non-physical family had left this plane, returning to The Blue.

Errol still stands beside me.

A police officer clears her throat, and I become aware once more of the physical forms in the room. Staring at me.

Oh, yeah. I grin. They grin back.

Epilogue...

'Good morning, I'm Sarah Nash. Thank you again for joining me today. I've been looking forward to meeting you for a long time, Mary. Is it alright if I call you Mary?'The sharp looking woman in her twenties begins our interview.

Something in her regard reminds me of an owl. Intelligent. Here I go again with my creature metaphors; I just cannot seem to help myself. I give a crooked smile as I nod my permission.

'Of course, and thank you for having me, Sarah,' I reply.

I gaze at the journalist, Sarah, sitting opposite me in the plush hotel room they had rented for our interview. Beyond her carrot red hair and wide green eyes, I can see Sarah's aura burns a bright orange. I know she is ambitious. I can also see lots of shimmering blue around her and read her honesty and compassion in it.

My shoulders relax. I see my reflection in the camera screens pointing at us, and know if I had bumped into this version of me two years ago, I would not have recognised myself.

I smooth my hair back into its shiny bob, lick glossed pink lips, then cross one silken leg over the other while I wait for the next question.

'So… it's been two years since you and your intrepid friends revealed the diabolical conspiracy from The Rainbow Unit. Because of your courage, they arrested Dr. Adelia Sinclair. They considered her as presenting such a high level of risk to the public they gave her an *indeterminate sentence*. This means they jailed her with no fixed length of time for release, for the murders and other atrocities she committed on the patients in her care over twenty years.

'Officials have traced some parties responsible for funding her horrific crimes against the people placed in her care, and their prosecution is in progress.'

I sigh, then nod my agreement. Yes, it is. The bastards, and I hope they are stripped of their riches, and thrown into the worst prison in the world.

'That's right, Sarah. The police were absolutely fantastic with the speed and thoroughness of their investigations. I believe in their last update, the MET police advised they now have details of eighty percent of those involved with funding Adelia's heinous experiments. I'm confident they will find the rest of them, eventually.'

Damn, I am good. I offer a wide smile to the journalist interviewing me, displaying my now perfect teeth.

'Unbelievable,' she says, shaking her head.

Aren't I just?

'And, before we go into the logistics of what exactly happened for the benefit of my viewers… can I ask? How have you all been? I read about the close friendships you made whilst admitted to The Rainbow Unit. What happened to *your* friends in particular since their discharge and in the wake of all this? I expect they're incredibly traumatised by Adelia's treatment of them. How are they coping two years on?' she asks me.

I smile as I consider my answer, but this time, my smile is natural.

'Surprisingly well, actually. Luckily, Sophie, Derek and Marcie were all amongst the discharged patients the experts successfully helped. They're doing amazingly. It also seems there were some positive side effects from Adelia's "treatments."

A knock on the door disturbs us both and we turn to see who is responsible for the interruption.

'Apologies, room service.' A spotty young man sticks his head 'round the door, then pushes a wheeled trolley in at Sarah's nod.

'I ordered us some fruit and croissants for breakfast. There should be tea, coffee, and juice there as well,' Sarah says.

My grin answers her questions. I have a sweet tooth and warm croissants with jam are my favourite. Sarah tips the man, and he makes for the door with timid speed.

She slips her purse back into her handbag, then gestures for me to continue.

'Sorry about that, Mary. Where were we?'

I wrinkle my nose and eyebrows. Shit, what was I saying again? Oh, yeah.

'I was just telling you about the positive side effect from Adelia's sessions we've found. Whilst my friends still have the diagnosis of paranoid schizophrenia, they're no longer considered "treatment resistant." Medication seems to work to keep them well, together with other strategies. They're all managing their conditions with a combination of healthy lifestyles, avoiding undue stress, and prescription meds. They've moved on from discharge and are now enjoying their lives. Marcie works in a children's creche as a play worker, Derek has an IT consultant company, and Sophie's art is doing fantastically well. She's now reunited with her lover, Rachel, and the two lovebirds were married last summer.'

'Oh, how lovely,' Sarah exclaims. 'And how would you say you're doing now?'

I mull her question over, pulling at the smart cuff of my satin blouse. I no longer dig my nails into the palms of my hands.

'Well… I can honestly say I'm content, happy.'

It is true. I am. Finally.

'That's great,' she says with a smile.

'And I understand after Adelia's arrest and subsequent imprisonment, they commissioned you to help the police with certain investigations? Could you tell me in what capacity that's in, please?'

How the hell does she know that? My smile falters and my eyes narrow. I will have to watch this lady. It would not be good if she dug around too much–and I can tell she is clever.

'I'm afraid I'm not at liberty to comment,' I say.

My tone is still polite, but it is clear the subject is not open to discussion.

Sarah's eyebrows raise. Although she looks intrigued, she catches her lower lip between her teeth, then nods. Sarah recognises my closed sentence and will respect it. For now.

'OK... well, how about a more personal update then? Can I ask if the rumours were true and there was romance between you and another patient at The Rainbow Unit, Derek? Can you tell us all what happened?'

My chest rises and falls as my heart rate increases. I know I cannot keep the grin from gracing my face at the mention of our relationship. Dishy Derek. He still gets to me. My Mr. Perfect.

'Yes. It's true. Derek and I are looking for somewhere to live together at the moment. We plan to move in with each other officially, as soon as we can,' I tell her.

We practically live together in Derek's small apartment already. Mine had too many terrible memories–*and it was fucking green*! So I gave it up. We both love the sea, so a coastal place somewhere is in the cards.

The journalist claps her hands together in delight.

'That's so lovely.'

Her pleasure for us is genuine, and my shoulders relax again.

'Derek had been discharged back into the community at the time of Adelia's attack, had he not? And am I right to understand it was *after* discharge that Adelia's programming really took a hold of the patients? What exactly happened with your friends, Sophie, Marcie, and Derek after discharge? The science behind it all may not have been clear to the public at the time,' she asks, leaning towards me.

I take a breath, my mind flying back to the terrible events of that last night at the unit.

'Yes, that's right, Sarah. Although Adelia would deliver some post-hypnotic suggestions while we were admitted to the unit, it wasn't until after they'd discharged the patients that Adelia fully erased our personalities. She used light therapy, hidden in the Three-D hologram to cement her programming. It's strange, and I don't completely understand the technology behind it, but these laser lights triggered something in the individual that automatically stimulated certain behaviours.

'Basically, she turned us into her very own robots, performing at her command. Adelia used all the information she learned during our one-to-one sessions against us. She recorded every key moment and feeling from our past she could during our time with her. Then, she systematically deleted them when we came back as outpatients, in order to erase our character and make us, in essence, a tabular rasa, a blank slate.

'At the point where Adelia believed the patient was stable, she would use the Inspiration Group meetings to test the strength of the new persona. Interaction with people they used to know and answering spontaneous questions would give her a good indication if there were any wrinkles she needed to iron out.

'Adelia had noted Derek was a "difficult patient," because he didn't respond to the programming as well as she wanted. Adelia kept very detailed records, and they showed she'd planned to deliver additional sessions to Derek, before she would allow him to speak to anyone from his former life.'

Sarah nods, her head tilting to one side.

'The whole thing is terrifying. This diabolical plot horrified the whole world. As soon as Adelia's conspiracy and her experiments at the hospital came out into the public light, I understand some of the top global neuroscientists stepped forward to help.'

It is my turn to agree and chime in.

'That's right, thank God for them, Sarah. They could use Adelia's own research to reverse what she had done to all her patients and overwrite the program she had inputted into most of us. Because she was so pedantic and proud of herself, she had recorded every instruction she gave us and every character trait she had overwritten.' I shake my head.

It still threatens to overwhelm me sometimes, the horror and cruelty Adelia's beauty had cloaked, although, now I am connected to source most of the time, I never feel alone or unloved.

'Luckily, the research notes made it possible to revoke what she'd changed for most of us. Although there are a few who were sadly too long entrenched in Adelia's program. We cannot reach them at the moment. There were also people Adelia had murdered over the years. Patients whose consciousness she could not erase, so she simply... *disposed of them.*'

Recently, I have wondered about trying to reach those who hadn't been helped psychologically, using my own gifts. I am also considering testing my medium strength, in order to help talk to spirits stuck at the hospital who have not yet passed over.

As I hear a familiar raucous laugh in the hallway, I turn in the direction of the noise. A huge smile chases away my frown. My peripheral vision informs me my friend Marcie is outside, and is bumping into something or someone with a clumsiness typical of her. I can hear her apologies to whomever she has become entangled with, punctuated by her trademark giggles. God, she is endearing. Eileen is out there too; we have planned one of our regular get togethers. I know my previous CPN well now, enough to be sure any friend of mine will be welcome to join us.

'It was a blessing I got my friends back though, all of them.'

Actually, I did not get *all* of my friends back. My non-physical friends had returned to The Blue, but that is OK. I know we remain connected, and at some stage, will be reunited.

My eyes move to the side of the journalist. Everyone except Errol. Errol stands beside Sarah, one hand half in his jean pocket, and the other hand waving in his usual understated way. He is staying with me for now, and I know there will be a few more friends who will join me along the way. When I need them.

I do not wave back. With Errol's help, I have trained myself not to respond openly to non-physical beings in company, unless I want to.

A smile spreads across my features. I can decide when to allow the receptive mode. Now, I am in control.

Coming soon!

Psychic Echoes: Book 2 in the Mary Jameson Supernatural Thriller Series

Mary Obosa Jameson is a young woman with a unique gift - the ability to communicate with the dead. But despite her powerful abilities, all Mary wants is a normal life. She has a loving fiancé, a beautiful home, and great friends, and she's determined to leave her paranormal past behind.

That is, until Detective Jay Santiago calls on her for help. Two boys have gone missing, and Jay is convinced that Mary's powers could be the key to finding them. With children and animals her soft spot, Mary is torn between her desire for a normal life and her deep compassion for those in need.

As Mary reluctantly delves back into the supernatural world, she realises the stakes are higher than ever before. Danger lurks around every corner, and she must use her powers to navigate a web of secrets and deception to uncover the truth behind the missing children.

Will Mary be able to find the missing boys before it's too late? And at what cost to her own safety and sanity? Find out in this gripping supernatural thriller, full of twists and turns that will keep you on the edge of your seat until the very last page.

Also by JP Alters

Psychic Training: Book 1.5 in the Mary Jameson Supernatural Thriller Series

When lost friends haunt the present, will Mary Jameson's newfound power be their salvation?

Having narrowly escaped the clutches of The Rainbow Unit and defeated the sinister Adelia Sinclair, Mary Jameson now stands on the brink of a new journey. Freshly aware of her psychic abilities, Mary is left unprepared and uncertain. Fortunately, her new spectral ally, Errol, emerges to guide her through mastering these newfound powers.

Can Errol equip her with the skills needed to rescue the friends she believed were lost to Dr. Sinclair's malevolent machinations? Embark on this riveting tale to discover what lies ahead.

The Twisted Fates: Unearthly Lessons in Darkness

Venture into the realm of the mysterious and macabre, with The Twisted Fates: Unearthly Lessons in Darkness, a heartwarming collection of supernatural and horror short stories that promise to both terrify and inspire.

From wolves in sheep's clothing, to whispers in haunted halls, The Twisted Fates steers you to chilling and spellbinding landscapes. But, as the darkness envelops you, glimmers of redemption peek through. It is here, within this delicate balance, that the characters-and perhaps you dear readers-encounter revelations that challenge and uplift the spirit.

This collection is perfect for fans of The Twilight Zone or Cabinet of Horrors. It invites you to delve into a world where fear and wonder intertwine, and the supernatural is never far from the surface. So, if you dare, grab a warm blanket, and lose yourself in The Twisted Fates, but be warned... once you enter, there's no turning back.

Printed in Great Britain
by Amazon

26138008R00195

So

It!

w/D

Sort It!

Everything a Teenager Needs to Know at the Click of a Mouse

Peter Hart

Piccadilly Press · London

First published in Great Britain in 2002
by Piccadilly Press Ltd.,
5 Castle Road, London NW1 8PR

A catalogue record for this book is available from the British Library

ISBN: 1 85340 702 X (trade paperback)

1 3 5 7 9 10 8 6 4 2

Printed and bound in Great Britain by Bookmarque Ltd.
Design by Louise Millar

Set in Legacy

Peter Hart is the editor of *It's HOT!* magazine.
He lives in New Cross, South East London with his cat, Santa.
This is his second book.

For David, Allen, Sam and all my friends who put up with me while I was 'writing my book!' – but especially John, who gave me unending encouragement and support. You can have the computer back now.

Contents

Introduction

Being a teenager can be pretty stressful. You've suddenly got countless niggling questions about hundreds of important subjects that sensible adults don't even seem to worry about . . . and they all need answers, now!

Take your body, for example. Why do you have stuff sprouting where you didn't even know things could grow? And why are things growing when you really wish they wouldn't?

On top of that, you have to deal with difficult parents, and the rows that seem to erupt from nowhere, or friendships and all the complex issues that seem to come with them. And what about all the scary stuff that relationships seem guaranteed to bring with them, just when you were least expecting it?

Then there are growing responsibilities like schoolwork, exams, careers and money. And did we mention any of the thousands of other questions, issues and desires that keep popping into your head – the individual things that are important to you?

In fact, with all this facing you like a bad dream you

just can't wake up from, it's a wonder you're not barricading yourself in your bedroom, refusing to come out except to go to the loo.

Aaarrgh! So what now?

Thankfully, help comes in the slightly unlikely shape of the internet. Did you realise just how much there is online to help you sort out your troublesome so-called life?

Whether you're looking to solve love dilemmas ('how do I kiss?') or body worries ('why does it look like that?'), conquer any school troubles ('I'm being sent threatening texts') or exam stresses ('how should I revise?'), or you simply want to make yourself more popular and meet new friends, all the answers you need are on the Net. If you fancy doing anything like saving the planet, winning Wimbledon or shaping up as a politician, you'll find help with all those issues, too!

There's stacks of fun in the shape of celebrity and entertainment websites, such as finding out where your idols hang out, fashion and beauty advice – get yourself a virtual makeover – and shopping sites to check out the cheapest CDs or funkiest fashions!). In fact, practically every area of your life is covered!

Chances are, you've already used the Net to discover some, or all, of the above. But you probably haven't seen the huge variety of brilliant websites out there, or realised exactly what they can do for you. So it's a good job you've picked up this book!

You're going to sort out my life?

This book has a simple aim, to help you solve the problems in your life (and have some fun!) by making the internet work for you. Explore some of the recommended sites, and you'll begin to see all the options available to help make your life happier. Take some advice, read the info, tools or tips on offer, or simply sit back and enjoy some fantastic entertainment! This really is the ultimate guide to everything cool on the web.

You'll also find help with designing or improving your own website. Just remember to follow the tips for keeping yourself safe online, and to behave as you'd want others to behave around you - then you'll be OK.

How have the websites been chosen?

You could search for helpful websites yourself, but search engines can be pretty unreliable - and who wants to wade through billions of irrelevant sites? That's why we've spent hundreds of hours searching through loads of them for you, so you don't have to. Only the very best are recommended here, in terms of the info they provide, their reliability and their reputation. Around five hundred made the grade!

We've checked out each and every one, highlighting their good and bad points, to help you. Also included in each category is one outstanding site that does stuff better than its rivals; we've voted this ☺ BEST ON THE NET, so look out for these words!

Most sites will be universal wherever you live, from Britain to Australia and everywhere in between, and some are available in a variety of different languages. The vast majority are also free – in fact, you can assume that no site listed will cost you a penny, unless we've stated otherwise.

The Net is changing every day, so sometimes you'll have to face up to a broken link or sites that simply no longer exist. But try putting some of the details into your preferred search engine first, before abandoning all hope, as the address may simply have changed.

So, what was that about barricading yourself in your bedroom? Soon, you'll be doing it for totally different reasons . . . you won't want to be dragged away from your computer!

Get ready to log on and get the life you really want. Your fun and trouble-free teens are just the click of a mouse away . . .

CHAPTER 1

Whose Life Is It Anyway?

Safety and netiquette online

Hanging out on the internet is brilliant fun – but you probably already know that! You can do so much online, and that's where this book comes in handy. But there are a few things you should bear in mind, before spending too long online – internet safety, netiquette and viruses.

(i) Safety

It's a big virtual world out there, and just as there are times you should watch your back in the real world, there are times you should be careful online. Even if you reckon you'll be all right ('I'm not a kid, I can look after myself!') you're more likely to run into a bit of trouble on the Net than a small child, who's actually much better protected from some of the dangers. See, teens are far more likely to venture off into parts of cyberspace that younger people would just avoid. You'll probably also talk to all kinds of people, not just those within your age group. There's nothing wrong with this – so long as you're careful – but it does leave you more at risk.

Here are a few things to consider:

- DO remember that there are certain websites, message boards or chatrooms where you could be made to feel uncomfortable.
- DO ignore any unwelcome messages in places like chatrooms, and remember that if you're harassed too much, you should report it to a responsible adult, such as your mum or dad.
- DO remember it's as important to be polite online as it is in the real world.
- DO only go as far as giving out your email address. Even then, you might want to set up a free address (such as MSN Hotmail at www.hotmail.com) that's different from the regular one you use with your friends.
- DO remember that going off into a private area in chatrooms can be dangerous as these aren't moderated (see page 26).
- DO beware of anyone who tries to turn you against your parents or friends online.
- DO choose a screen-name that won't give away your sex, e.g., Crazykid or sk8r rather than Kewlgirl or Flyguy.
- DO bear in mind that 15-year-old Claire from Cleveland could actually be 54-year-old Carl from California.

- DON'T forget you can remove yourself quickly from any place you don't like.
- DON'T post anything about yourself online that's too personal. Avoid giving out phone numbers, telling someone where you live, or posting your pic. In fact, avoid discussing anything that could identify you, such as the name of your school or any passwords. Your business is your business alone.
- DON'T forget that chatrooms are one of the internet's most dangerous places, as you never know who could be listening in to your conversation, possibly posing as a teen themselves. (Honesty might be the best policy, but not everyone respects that.)
- DON'T get involved in any 'get rich quick' schemes online – they're normally too good to be true, just as they are in the real world.
- DON'T ever enter any info about yourself unless you check with an adult first – even then, only do it on well-known websites.
- DON'T respond to emails from people you don't know. And don't open documents or files from mystery senders.
- DON'T discuss personal problems with anyone you don't know online unless it's through a registered organisation like ChildLine – the UK's free 24-hour helpline for young people in trouble or danger (www.childline.co.uk).

What if I want to meet someone I make friends with in a chatroom?

It's actually quite difficult for anyone you meet in cyberspace to hurt you in your own home, if you follow the guidelines above. However, the dangers get far greater if you actually want to get together with someone you've met online in real life. Sometimes, people aren't who they say they are. It's rare, but some perverts will pose as teens, using all the right language and subjects to be utterly convincing to you.

If you do decide you want to meet someone:

- Discuss it with a trusted adult (such as a parent) and make sure you take someone else with you.
- Tell your parents what time you'll be home.
- Arrange to meet in a public place you're comfortable with, such as a coffee shop or the local mall, where there are lots of other people around.
- It's actually a good idea to get your parents to talk to their parents first and, uncool as it might seem, to take them along to your first meeting.

Above all, remember that you're supposed to be having fun out there. Millions of teens go online every day, and only a minuscule percentage run into any dangers. Take care, follow these guidelines, and you'll be OK.

(ii) Netiquette

As you probably already know, people who talk on the internet, either by email, in chatrooms, on message boards or by webcam, have their own set of do's and don'ts – netiquette. It's there to ensure you don't upset anyone or do anything you shouldn't. But are you sure you know the do's and don'ts?

Take a quick look:

- DO picture entering a chatroom like walking into a party. Many people there will be very different to you, so wait on the sidelines to see what's going on. If you don't like it, you can leave and find another room. If it sounds good, join in!
- DO respect someone's opinions. It can take courage to chat on the Net, so listen and respond as you would if you met them in person.
- DO remember that people might want to talk in different languages. That's OK – they could be on the other side of the world!
- DON'T disrupt a chat channel, for example, by typing the same message repeatedly. Also, write in lower case, as CAPITALS are like SHOUTING!
- DON'T worry about correcting typos – the quicker you can get your thoughts on the page, the better.
- DON'T flame someone just because they've flamed

you (flaming is getting angry or starting an argument. It can also mean being told off). Instead, use humour, or just ignore it to defuse the row. It'll make you look good and them look bad – cool, huh?!

Net and mobile phone users have also developed hundreds of abbreviations and symbols to make things easier – you've probably even got a load of your own. You'll pick up more as you get experienced, so don't worry if you can't remember them. Some of the ones you might need are listed below:

:-) Smile
8-) Smile with glasses
;-) Wink
:-O Oh!
:-)) Big smile
:-(Frown
:-D Laughing
{{name}} A cyber hug

lol – Laughing out loud
rofl – Rolling on the floor laughing!
crbt – Crying real big tears
pmji – Pardon me for jumping in
brb – Be right back
bbl – Be back later
afk – Away from keyboard
cy – See ya
ttfn – Ta-ta for now (bye!)
wb – Welcome back/write back
ftbomh – From the bottom of my heart

afaik – As far as I know
btw – By the way
ty – Thank you
yw – You're welcome
imho – In my humble opinion
a/s/l – Age? Sex? Location?*
a/s – Age? Sex?*
*Remeber you don't have to reveal this info!

(iii) Viruses

It's great fun to download stuff from the Net – whether it's pictures, music clips, movie trailers, games or something else. But, when you download anything, you're running the risk of also downloading a virus – a program that infects part of your computer's hard disk and then makes copies of itself.

You run a far bigger risk if you're downloading stuff that has a questionable source – such as files uploaded on to fan sites. Protect your computer by only downloading from reputable sites, such as the official sites of your favourite pop stars or movies. Also, install anti-virus software, such as Norton AntiVirus (see www.symantec.com) which will help to detect anything dodgy. If you're really worried, don't download it in the first place!

Got all that? Right, then stop hanging around. Get ready for a good time online – turn to Chapter 2!

CHAPTER 2

Need a Friend?

Finding wonderful webmates

It's important to for all of us to have some good mates. After all, our friends are the people we share our lives with – our hopes and fears, the highs and lows, the best and worst of times. Where else would you go, if you wanted advice on how to ask out the school hunk or babe, if it wasn't to your friends? And whose help would you seek when the time came to dump them? They're there for so much more too, that life would be pretty boring without them!

Some people are lucky enough to have all the friends they'll ever need, but in reality most of us can do with a few more. With the Net, making friends has never been simpler – it's fast become the hottest way to meet new people who live anywhere from the next street to New Zealand.

The world has become a 'global village', as chatting to someone who's thousands of miles away is now as easy as shouting over the fence to your neighbour. As they say on the International Penfriends website (details on page 23), 'Have you ever considered that the greatest friend you may ever have, is someone you have never met, living in a land you have never seen?'

Still not convinced? Well, you could find someone who likes the same bands as you or who shares your unusual hobby, or who just wants to listen to what your day's been like. You could even choose someone from a country whose language you're learning – they might be able to help you with your homework! If you still haven't got over Sexy Simon/Susan Stevens, your number-one crush, blanking you in the lunch queue, you might just meet his/her alter ego on the Net!

If you've been unlucky in chatrooms or on message boards before, it's worth persisting and going back to some different ones. There are so many ways and places to meet people online that you're sure to find one, or more, that you enjoy.

What to do and say

So how do you successfully pick a new e-friend? Some penfriend and keypal websites will do it for you, matching your age and interests. Often you'll be able to do it yourself. So why not select someone from a country you never imagined you'd know anything about? Their culture will be fascinating.

Now, what do you say to keep them interested? That will depend on you, but most people talk about the things they find interesting – hobbies, the area where they live, friends and family. It's best not to give too much detail or send any photos of yourself until you're sure who you're talking to, but this can be fun later on. People are flattered when you ask them questions, too. If you're interested, you'll come across as an interesting person. Once you've had a few conversations, things will take off from there.

Remember, it's important to be honest. Avoid describing yourself as a gorgeous movie pin-up when you're just normal old Jane or James from Liverpool. It will only spell trouble later!

Make sure you take a look at Chapter 1 before you go online. Not only does it tell you the best ways to stay safe, it also helps you suss out some of the weird symbols people use when they're talking on the Net.

Finally, don't forget to relax and have a laugh – after all, meeting new mates should be fun!

(i) Penfriends and keypals

Although nothing is particularly slow online, making penfriends or keypals is perhaps one of the more time-consuming ways of finding friends. Why? Simply because it tends to be modelled on the way magazines used to put penfriends in touch. That means you never really talk to your e-pal in real time – instead, you exchange letters or emails.

Hundreds of sites exist, and they'll put you in touch with people from such far-flung countries as America,

China, Russia or Zimbabwe, as well as places much closer to home. But be warned that all but the best have a limited life, as they're run by amateurs who soon get overwhelmed by the numbers of people seeking new friends.

Some sites will automatically match you, according to various details you supply, while others will let you browse through by selecting from various categories including sex, age or location/language. Then you'll be faced with a list of possible friends to choose from, along with some info about them to help you decide!

Who knows, your new best mate could be waiting for you on the Net.

Top sites

☺ BEST ON THE NET

International Penfriends

www.pen-pals.net/ipf/ipf.html

With over 300,000 members in about two hundred countries, this is 'the oldest, biggest and best penfriend organisation in the world' for anyone from eight years upwards. They'll match you with people in your age group, and it operates with snail-mail only, for English, French, German, Italian, Spanish and Portuguese speakers. This is the only pay-site in this section, with yearly membership at $15 (about £10) for 8–14 year olds and $20 (about £13.50) for 15–20 year olds. It's guaranteed you'll receive ten letters in that time (or fourteen letters if you're 15–20), so it's worth it.

ePALS.com

www.epals.com

'The world's largest online classroom community.' Allows whole classes of students to register, then browse through and pick a class somewhere in the world that they want to write to. The site features versions in English, French, Spanish, German, Portuguese and Chinese.

A Girl's World.com – Penp Pal Club

www.agirlsworld.com/geri/penpal/index.html

'Where girls and teens rule the web.' Only for girls from 7–17, this is a brilliant site, as it doesn't even display your email address to other users. There are literally dozens of ways to search through the penpal database, using easy drop-down menus – it's the most detailed way of finding someone that we've come across! For example, you might just want to choose their age and country, but you can even check whether someone has the same dress sense, taste in music or attitude to boys as you!

Teen Chat International

www.iteenchat.co.uk

Easy-to-use, new British site where you get to choose your ideal new mate! Warning – don't give your mobile number when filling out the profile form.

KeyPals Club

www.teaching.com/keypals

Boasts 50,000 student users from nearly 80 countries. Search for a single student or a whole class to correspond with (handy if you want to share projects!)

Kids' Media Club

www.kidsmc.com/penpal

Cute-looking site with new friends from more than 140 countries. Only allows you to select by age, then browse a list of people.

The Penpal Network

www.penpalnet.com

Possibly the largest online penpal site in the world, boasting more than 100,000 members. Not strictly a teen site, but doesn't display the addresses of anyone under 18. Unfortunately a bit slow when you're trying to select your new friend.

Student Letter Exchange

www.pen-pal.com

Matches English-speaking penpals with students aged 9–18 across the USA and around the world, so you don't get to browse through yourself. Established for more than sixty years, containing more than 250,000 names.

Teens Most Wanted.com – Pen Pals

www.teensmostwanted.com/penpals

'The most wanted and the ultimate teens portal on the

World Wide Web.' Browse a very basic list of penpals (for example, '13/f Looking for pen pals' may be all you have to go by). Also includes dating advice (where to go and what to do) and snogging tips.

(ii) Chatrooms and message boards

Chatrooms are great if you want to speak to someone in real time, instead of waiting for emails to fly through cyberspace. Chances are, you'll have visited some already, whether it was one of the more general ones, where you can discuss anything you like, or one devoted to a more personal interest. There are music websites, for example, where you can gossip about your favourite star for the entire day! Chatrooms often get extremely lively with dozens of people voicing their opinions.

Most require you to register in some way before you're allowed to speak, but often they just need a username (either your name, or any 'handle' you fancy, like popfan or kewldude) and a few other details, such as your email address or a password.

In some chatrooms, you can even choose to 'go private' with a particular user, so only they can see what you're typing (handy if you're chatting up someone you fancy!).

Many teen chatrooms are 'policed' by a moderator, just to ensure there's nothing too naughty going on.

Where we've been able to find this out about a site, we've mentioned it, but don't assume a site isn't moderated, just because we don't say so! If you get too rude, moderators will boot you off the site – sometimes permanently, so take care!

Look out for hosted chats, provided by many of the major sites and advertised in advance. It's fun to talk to a celebrity for, say, half an hour, and makes a change from discussing your biology homework with your mate online.

If you prefer to have more time to consider someone's comments, you'll probably be using message boards (sometimes also called bulletin boards, notice boards, newsgroups, discussion groups or forums). There you can post a comment or opinion, which everyone can see and choose to reply to. You can reply to others, too. Keep checking back, as the busiest boards will have hundreds of comments added to them every day.

ICQ & Instant Messenger

Chatrooms are great if you want to talk to loads of people, but you can keep in touch with friends who are online at the same time as you, on a one-to-one basis. Just watch out for the instant email thingy that pops up on your screen. If you haven't got one already, download some instant message software, such as ICQ (http://web.icq.com), AOL Instant Messenger (www.aim.com/index.adp), or MSN Messenger (http://messenger.msn.com).

Top sites

☺ BEST ON THE NET

Dubit

www.dubit.co.uk

Enter this exciting virtual city, unlike anything you've seen before on the Net (you'll need a fast PC with Flash 5, which is easily downloadable, as it's got loads of cool graphics!). Save your details, then upload your image for others to see. Chill out in your very own apartment, and play 32 pre-loaded MP3s from some cool bands. Then get out and visit one of the city's four zones, go shopping in the virtual mall, play games, watch a movie at the cinema and much more! You can even chat to people you encounter on your travels and invite them back to your virtual apartment! There's a regular message board, too. Absolutely fantastic!

AAA Teen Chat

www.aaateenchat.com

'A growing online teen community.' Devoted to chatting and messaging, with rooms ranging from 'Preteen' to 'Teen' and 'The Hangout'.

ChatAway

www.chataway.com

Visit the singles café, create your own webpage, or post to the bulletin board.

Chat Mag

www.chatmag.com

Great chat site with help and advice, plus links to many other chat sites.

Fool Moon Family Community

http://foolmoon.com

Moderated message boards and chatrooms. As an extra safety precaution, under 13s must be supervised by an adult when using the chatrooms.

MaxiChat

www.maxichat.com

Hosts eleven MaxiChat sites from around the world – countries include UK, France, Belgium, Germany, USA and Italy.

MSN Chat

http://chat.msn.com

Microsoft's well-designed and easy-to-navigate chat site, with frequent celebrity chats.

Mykindaplace – Chat

www.mykindaplace.com/chat

Cool chatroom and messageboard from this online teen mag. You must become a **Mykindaplace** member first.

OnChat

www.onchat.com

Find a chatroom or create your own, and create or swap Avatars (cute little pictures that represent you online).

Teen Today.co.uk

www.teentoday.co.uk

Click on the menu for a huge choice of message boards, from pop music to sex, mobiles to movies, and a chatroom, too!

Trouble – Chat Zone

www.trouble.co.uk

Click on 'Chat Zone' for a choice of chatrooms and message boards.

Yahoo Chat

http://chat.yahoo.com

Thousands of people in hundreds of chatrooms, including loads of teen rooms, such as 'Europe', 'Teen City' (15–17) and 'The Mall'. Often hosts guest chats too.

(iii) Dating and romance

So you want to find love on the Net? Well, it does happen – you only have to open a magazine to find yet another true-life story of a couple who fell in love in a chatroom. Be warned, though, it's unlikely that you'll find the person of your dreams online, especially as they'll probably be a long way away. Still, it can be fun to try, and you should make some friends anyway.

Teen dating and romance sites tend to work in two main ways. Some offer a kind of matchmaking service, offering to pair you off with someone who has similar interests. Others offer chatrooms or message boards, where you can meet other people and flirt with them. For example, one 14-year-old American girl, mzstar14, left the message: 'Any guys 13–15: email me or im [Instant Messenger] me, see you later.'

And Limp_bizkit12, from Nottingham, UK, wrote: 'Hiya there. Lookin 4 a girl who likes Slipknot and Limp Bizkit and Staind. Preferably able 2 play guitar and into a wide range of different things! Hope 2 hear from ya!'

Some of these rooms or boards are moderated but some aren't. Be warned, they can get really offensive, and you might like to surf with adult supervision if you're unsure.

Most of the sites listed below are specifically for teens only, although some accept adults too. Remember, it's easy for an adult to pose as a teen on any site, so be careful with the information you're giving away, and never reveal anything too personal about yourself. If you do decide to meet anyone from one of these sites, check out the advice back in Chapter 1.

Top sites

☺ BEST ON THE NET

Teen Matchmaker

http://teen.matchmaker.com

'The leading online community enabling secure connections between teens with similar interests or needs.' More than five million people registered, with 50,000 more joining every week! Just check out the quote from one US user, Vicky: 'I've met the right man at the right time through your service. Thank you forever.' Part of the Lycos Network, so you know it's reliable.

Ace's Teen Chat

www.aceteenchat.com

Chatrooms and message boards for teens from 13–19. The teen chatroom claims to be one of the biggest on the Net, but there are bigger ones around.

Power2Youth – Power2Date

www.power2youth.com

Comprehensive teen site, with more than 14,500 teens registered and looking for love at Power2Date. This section boasts 'everything you'll ever need to find a date', from the 'Meeting Ground' to flirting tips. Very interactive and good fun.

The Student Center – Teen Matches

http://teenmatches.studentcenter.org

Excellent part of a much bigger American site which appears elsewhere in this book. Get matched to your perfect person, in a number of categories, or go totally wild and let the 'Random' option find someone for you!

TeenSpot.com

www.teenspot.com

Loads of chatrooms and message boards on a nicely designed site. Some are dedicated to dating or flirting, and others have enticing names like 'Party', 'Zone', 'Hangout' and 'Café'.

Teen Chat Zone

www.teenchatzone.com

Offers a 'Teen Dating' message board, a 'Teen Flirt' chatroom, and two more chatrooms for teens from 13–15.

TeenFlirt.com

www.teenflirt.com

Flirt in the moderated chatrooms, or post yourself on the message boards. Split into 13–15 and 16–19 years.

TeenFlirt Network

http://teenchat.pacer.com

'Dedicated to teen relationships.' Very basic, with four chat rooms.

Teen Singles Online

www.teen-singles.com

'The single teen's guide to finding love on the Net.' Created by teens, for teens, running since June 1999. Two chatrooms (13–15 and 16–19), message boards and more.

Teens Personals

http://teens.personals.net.au

For people from 13–20. Place an online ad, or enter the chatroom on this Australian site.

TeleBoards – Teen Personals

www.teleboards.com/teenpersonals.html

Very simple – just two message boards, one for girls and one for guys.

PlanetTeen

http://planetteen.com

'What teens want.' Sign up for your personal ID, then get prepared to check out this big teen site, including message boards and member pics.

(iv) Webcams

Want to be a TV star? Well, don't think that getting a webcam is going to turn you into one. There are some fairly famous sites where you can follow the daily lives of girls and guys who want to reveal everything to the world (a kind of Net-only *Big Brother*!), but these are few and far between.

These people tend to have their own websites, either dedicated to their cams, or with a section where you can view them. However, most casual users go through a larger host site, where you can browse some of the many cams online – featuring all kinds of people and places – and also download the software to get your own cam running on that site. After you feel comfortable with whom you've been talking to you can chat to people across the other side of the world, and see them at the same time.

These days, basic webcams are really cheap, starting at around £30 – so it is possible to see at least how your mug looks on the small screen, even if it doesn't quite get you a job reading the evening news!

Top sites

☺ BEST ON THE NET

EarthCam

www.earthcam.com

Hundreds of cams, showing all kinds of people and places – split into sections, from 'Arts & Entertainment Cams' to 'Weird & Bizarre Cams'. Browse the nine cams in New York's Times Square or the Waikiki Beach Cam, showing the idyllic, famous beach in Honolulu. Oh, and meet other teens and screen your own cam, too!

Camarades.com
www.camarades.com
Browse the 'Community Directory' to access thousands of cams.

Student Center – Webcam Portal
http://rankmywebcam.studentcenter.org/camportal
A small selection of American students' webcams, with links to their sites. Add your own cam to the list.

Webcamnow.com
www.webcamnow.com
View hundreds of live webcams, or broadcast your own images, by downloading the software.

WEBMATES Q&A

Web freak

Q: *I told my friends that I'd been looking for new mates online, and they started calling me a freak. They said they obviously weren't good enough for me, and started arranging to do things behind my back. What should I do?*

Cassie, 14, Stockport

A: You're right and your friends are wrong – they just have a bit of growing up to do. See, it's possible for us to have all kinds of friends who we do different things with, depending on our interests. Your friends are probably jealous at the thought of you having other friends, but they should realise there's room in your life for them as well. Make sure you spend plenty of time with them, but explain how important your webmates are, too. They'll see sense – just give it a bit of time.

Keypal KO

Q: *I wrote to some new keypals, and although I heard back from them, they only ever wrote once. I'm starting to get a bit paranoid, so is there something I'm doing wrong?*

Deepak, 13, London

A: Don't spend too long worrying about this – it's totally normal. Making friends is fun, but it can also be a difficult process as you have to find someone who is as interested in you as you are in them. Maybe the people you're writing to just aren't your kind of mates. Or maybe they've got quite a few keypals already and just don't need any more. Don't quit – keep writing to people and eventually you'll click with someone who wants to reply more frequently. You could also try chatrooms, to get a discussion going with someone first, before you start bashing out long emails!

Age gap trap

Q: *I've been writing to this lovely 21-year-old guy who really makes me laugh (I'm a 15-year-old girl). He really understands me, too. The thing is, he's recently told me he's actually 45. He still wants to write, but I'm unsure. What do you reckon?*

Jane, 15, Cardiff

A: Only a minute percentage of people on the Net are perverts, but you're right to question why a 45-year-old man would want to be talking to a 15-year-old girl. Why would he lie about his age? If he's been dishonest once, he could easily lie again. You might think he understands you, but you'll be better off sharing things with people your own age (and so would he!). Tell a responsible adult what's been going on and certainly avoid giving out any personal details about yourself, from what you look like to your phone number. There's more advice back in Chapter 1.

Phone peril

Q: *There's this 25-year-old woman in a chatroom who says she has my phone number, and that she'll be calling my parents to tell them what I've been talking about with her over the past few weeks. I'm terrified of what she might say. Help!*

Frank, 14, Norwich

A: OK, there's no way this woman could have your

phone number unless you actually gave it to her at any stage – and you should never give out details like that on the Net. Whatever you've been discussing, she has no right to threaten you, and you should tell someone about this immediately. Be wary of what you discuss online, especially in a chatroom, as you don't know who could be lurking there. This is probably just a silly threat, so try ignoring that chatroom for a few weeks and your problem will hopefully go away. If it's moderated, you could also tell the moderator and get this person booted off. If she persists, tell a responsible adult (like your mum or dad) about it before she does. You can explain things without giving too many details! Remember, they are *your* parents and ultimately they'll support you.

Cyber boyfriend

Q: *My friends laugh when I say I have a cyber boyfriend, but we've been talking to each other for nearly a year and I feel that we're really close. I live in England and he lives in America, but we're talking about meeting this summer. Should we?*

Kim, 13, Bournemouth

A: Having a cyber-relationship can be great fun, and you can certainly get close to someone, but it's impossible for this guy to be your real boyfriend, particularly if you've never even met. I'm sure you do feel quite close as you'll have shared a lot of online time together, but remember that meeting someone in real life can often be different to chatting to them on the Net. If you plan to meet, make sure that adults are involved, as I'm afraid you still can't be sure that he's who he says he is. And even if he's the real thing, it could still be a bit of a let-down!

CHAPTER 3

In a Bit of Bother?

Perfect love, brilliant body

The problem pages in teen magazines are popular for a reason. Girls and guys love reading about Simon from Shropshire's jealous girlfriend, or Tess from Tyneside's wonky boobs. And although it's a bit of a laugh, it's also reassuring to know that we're normal. If someone else has the same problems as us, then it makes a stressful time a whole lot easier.

Although you might have already used the Net to find out more info on a problem of your own, it's worth taking some more time to explore the websites which offer advice on teen love and body issues – there's a lot of useful information out there.

Some sites take a more traditional route, showing users' letters answered by online agony aunts. A lot of these archive their letters, so you can look back over several years' of questions, instead of being limited to the five or six posed in a monthly magazine. Others do things differently, with quizzes, games, fact sheets or diaries. Many sites cross over, answering relationship and body issues – but we've tried to split them up below to try to make things as clear as possible.

Nearly all of these websites are far more fun, colourful and lively than their magazine rivals. What's more, many are interactive, which is something you could never get from a magazine! And because the Net is anonymous, you can ask any question, no matter how stupid you think it might be, without worrying what people might think of you. Whatever your problem, you'll almost certainly find an answer to it.

Why not check some of the sites out now? They'll help you feel better almost immediately – we guarantee it!

(i) Relationships

Does s/he fancy me? Should I dump her/him? Why do they want me to do that to them? Find answers to relationship questions like these online.

You'll even find advice on getting on with friends and family, as falling out with your bigger sister every night can wear you down far more than a one-time brush off from someone you fancy at school. There are thousands of straightforward facts, too.

If quizzes are your thing, you'll find ones devoted to boys, girls, dating and mating! Enter an advice forum, to get helpful info from other teens. Read some relationship fiction, or discover a whole heap of relationship tips to ensure you never face a dating disaster again. You can also send fun, animated e-cards to let someone know you fancy them.

Top sites

☺ BEST ON THE NET

Yes No Maybe.com

www.yesnomaybe.com

'The internet's top teen advice and romance web forum.' Want to know how people rate your looks? Then submit a pic of yourself and other users can comment on it. (Scary, eh?) Play the 'Are We A Perfect Match' game – enter your name and the name of your crush to check your compatibility in dating – mentally and make-out wise. Plus, fiction, photos, games and a forum.

Kiwibox.com – Dating

www.kiwibox.com/dating.asp

Part of a massive site, 'built for teens by teens'. High school and college students write one hundred per cent of the content. Check out the 'ECupid Secret Crush' game, and some very comprehensive 'Dating Tips' – what to do, what to wear, how to act, and how to kiss. There's a love Q&A, too.

So . . . Loved Up

www.bbc.co.uk/so/lovedup

Part of the BBC's So . . . teen site. Split into lads and ladies sections, with quizzes such as, 'Is your ex still in your head?', plus dating disasters and e-cards. Match-make a friend or drop hints to your crush with the inspired and hilarious 'Make a Date Movie' game (a kind of online cartoon, where you decide on the characters and what they say) – then email it wherever you like!

Teenage Chicken Soup

www.teenagechickensoup.com

Submit your story and it could appear in the popular *Teenage Chicken Soup* books. A selection of forums and letters online, too.

TeenOutReach.com – Relationships

www.teenoutreach.com/Online_Help/relationship

Part of a much bigger site, with sections including 'Facts About Drugs', 'Homework Help' and 'Teen Pregnancy'. The 'Relationships' section is packed with useful hints and tips.

Teen Stuff

www.teenstuff.com

'America's favourite teen site, with more true stories and advice.' Select 'True Stories' or 'Forums', then send in your story or read others. Also available in French.

Teen Talk International

www.teentalk.com

Covers heaps of subjects, including dating and school, through message boards only.

TheSite.org
www.thesite.org
'Your guide to the real world.' Covering much more than simply relationships, this site features easy-to-understand info on everything from sex, health and drugs to careers. Plus discussion groups, polls and surveys.

(ii) Your Body

When your body bits start doing things you never imagined possible, it's easy to stress out. Like, should they really be that shape? Should it smell like that? Why does it feel so weird?

If you're ever worried about going to your GP for advice, you'll actually find that many of the answers you need are online. Plenty of websites are devoted purely to teens and their bodies, from head to toe!

Many sites let you look something up in an A–Z directory (like, 'What exactly is herpes?'). Others have chatrooms or message boards where you can link up with other teens who have got the same body worries as you. And, as mentioned in the intro to this chapter, some even offer you the chance to email your problem and get a personal reply.

Remember, though, if a problem persists, then see your GP – they'll have seen hundreds of people like you before, and there's nothing to be embarrassed about.

Top sites

☺ BEST ON THE NET

TeenGrowth.com

www.teengrowth.com

'All about your health.' Ask the experts a question and get a reply emailed to you. Find out loads of facts about your body, with quizzes and heaps of info. Plus get advice on friends, school and family.

Check Out That Body.com

www.checkoutthatbody.com

Even more teen health info, including 'Body Basics' and stories from other teens. Also has a database of past questions posed to the experts with their answers.

CoolMD.com

www.coolmd.com

'The cool place for health.' Masses of health news, with an A–Z listing, plus links to message boards and chat-rooms.

Doctor Ann's Virtual Surgery

www.dr-ann.org

Linked to the Teenage Health Freak site, this is a comprehensive guide to practically every health worry you could have as a teen, complete with A–Z listing, from 'Abortion' to 'Zits'.

Jellybean – Body & Looks

www.myjellybean.com/life/bodylooks.html

Part of a much bigger, cool site for girls. Three pages of advice, covering hundreds of body and looks problems from 'Obsessed with food' to 'Can a doctor tell if I've had sex?'

Lovelife

www.lovelife.uk.com

Heaps of info on sex and sexual health, split into cool sections: 'Become a Sexpert', 'Get It On', 'Check Up', and 'Emergency Info'.

Teenage Health Freak

www.teenagehealthfreak.org

The fictional, online diary of hypochondriac teen Peter Payne – his worries and traumas, plus those of his family and friends. Also includes health A–Z. Fun, colourful, well-designed and very popular site with more than six million hits.

TeensHealth

http://kidshealth.org/teen/your_body

From braces and diets to pimples and sleep problems, you'll find all the answers to your body queries.

Agony Aunts and Advice

Each month, teen magazines devote pages to relationship crises, body worries and mind matters. But they can only respond to a fraction of the letters that are answered online.

There are plenty of 'Agony' websites, with answers to hundreds of letters from worried teens. The agony aunts can be qualified professionals, or simply interested teens, like you, who want to help. After all, sometimes it's great to be able to hear some advice from someone who's around your own age.

As we mentioned earlier, most advice sites archive past letters, so you can look back through all the problems which have been posed over the years. You can even perform searches to check if someone's written in with the same problem before. As in Chapter 3, some sites offer the chance to email an agony aunt to get a personal answer to your problem – great if you want to stay completely anonymous.

However, don't forget that there can be no substitute for talking in real life to a trusted friend or adult.

Top sites

☺ BEST ON THE NET

Teenhelp.org

www.teenhelp.org

Get a personal email responding to your problem (they

answer more than a hundred requests every day!), check out the support groups on message boards, enter the chatroom or visit the archive, covering everything from 'Abuse' to 'Suicide'. Advice comes from 'peer mentors', a bunch of young (mainly teenage) volunteers aged between 12 and 23. Very helpful.

Advice 4 Teens

www.adviceforteens.co.uk

Submit your problems and get advice back from teen staff mentors, plus check out the archive of past questions.

Ask Heartbeat

www.askheartbeat.com/html/teenfaqs.html

Quizzes and FAQs (Frequently Asked Questions), for ages 14–20, such as: 'How can I tell if a person really likes me?', 'I just had sex for the first time', 'We are both in our teens but madly in love', and 'I have never been kissed by anyone . . . and I'm 17!' Although the advice comes from someone who isn't qualified in psychology or counselling, she has 12 years of experience giving advice.

ChildLine

www.childline.co.uk

Useful website of the twenty-four-hour helpline for children in trouble or danger.

Dear Lucie

www.lucie.com

Comprehensive teen-specific advice in all sorts of categories with a large archive of past questions and answers. Lucie (Walters) is a former teacher who writes a regular teen-advice column.

Mykindaplace.com – Reader Rescue

www.mykindaplace.com/agony/readrescue.asp

Part of the teen girls' website where readers give their replies to your agony questions. Also features a 'You And Your Body' section plus an online agony aunt.

Reach Out!

www.reachout.asn.au

Fun and lively Australian site with fact sheets and lots of helpful info.

Teen Advice Online – Dating

www.teenadvice.org/dating

The young volunteers on this site have served nearly 40,000 people since 1996, covering relationships, depression, school and more. Loads of relevant advice in the dating section.

Teens Helping Teens

www.bigteens.com

Not really an agony aunt site, but pages of advice from

other teens about what to do when faced with certain traumas.

Youth 2 Youth
www.youth2youth.co.uk
'The telephone, email and online chat helpline run by young people for young people.' Talk to people your own age about your problems – adults, keep out!

RELATIONSHIPS AND BODY Q&A

Stupid Cupid

Q: *My friends keep talking of something on the Net called Secret Admirer, but I don't know what they're talking about. When I ask, they just laugh. So, can you explain?*

Jasmine, 12, Erith

A: Many of the relationship sites feature a fun game you can play, sometimes called 'Secret Admirer', 'Love Match' or 'ECupid'. Here, you can secretly email anyone you fancy to let them know that you like them. Then that person goes online and types in the name of the person they think the email was from, to see if you're matched. If they get it right, you'll both receive an email to fix you up. Of course, it's easy for friends to 'fix it' if they're having a laugh. But friends like that – and any that take the mickey out of you – probably aren't great mates in the first place.

Itchy bits

Q: *My penis won't stop itching and I don't know what to do about it. I'm too embarrassed to tell my parents, and I don't want to go to the doctor. It's really driving me mad – help!*

Billy, 16, London

A: Having an itchy penis (or itchy vagina, for that matter) could be a sign that you have some kind of infection, possibly an STI (sexually transmitted infection). You could look this up on one of the body advice sites if you'd like more information – try **Doctor Ann's Virtual Surgery** at www.dr-ann.org for a complete A–Z listing. You'll also be able to find out how to protect yourself from STIs next time. However, you shouldn't use these sites as a substitute for seeing your GP. They'll have seen hundreds of cases like yours before, so there's nothing to be embarrassed about. Alternatively get yourself down to your local GUM clinic (Genito Urinary Medicine) where you can have a completely confidential check-up.

Down in the dumps

Q: *My girlfriend has just dumped me, and it's made me really depressed. I don't want to see any of my friends, and my family just doesn't understand. What should I do?*

David, 15, Newquay

A: Try visiting one of the many agony aunt/advice sites, where you'll be able to read letters from others who have been in your position. Although you're feeling low right now, hearing about others who have experienced the same thing can really help. Plus you'll be able to read a professional's advice on how to get over it. If you're still really down, you could try contacting one of the teen support lines, such as **Youth 2 Youth** (www.youth2youth.co.uk) where you'll find that someone's happy to listen to you.

CHAPTER 4

Won't School Rule?

Conquering a classroom crisis

Think of school, and you think of crusty, mumbling, corduroy-wearing, dandruff-shedding teachers with smiles like Hannibal Lecter. It can be pretty hideous and boring, can't it? But that's no reason to skip this chapter. Why? Because school is also about learning, bullying, homework, revision, exams and careers – and sometimes we all need help or advice in those areas.

Perhaps you're not very good at a certain school subject, or think you missed out on something in lessons. Then use the revision sites to fill in the gaps in your knowledge. The Net can help you conquer any classroom crisis, if you just know where to look. Maybe you want help in beating the bullies. You'll find it online. And do you know the best homework help sites? They cover loads of subjects, with experts sitting at the other end of your modem, just waiting to help you crack that question you've been scratching your head over since teatime.

There are also places where you can start thinking

about work – from summer jobs to your future. Although it's unlikely you're looking for a career yet, it's useful to see what qualifications you might need, or the most suitable job for you.

(i) Bullying

Bullying can come in all shapes and forms – verbal, physical and emotional. Although head teachers of UK schools have had to have anti-bullying policies for some years now, it still exists in nearly every school. It can be fairly minor, but sometimes it can affect someone's whole life. And with three-quarters of all children owning a mobile phone, a lot of bullying is now centred around threatening phone calls or texts, or even theft of the handset itself.

One big problem with bullying is that the victims are too frightened to tell anyone. But help is at hand with the Net, as there are hundreds of websites devoted to the subject. Because it's so anonymous, you can look up the advice without anyone finding out. So if you, or a friend, are being bullied, or if you're a bully yourself, but can't seem to stop, you can find out all the facts first. You'll also find answers to questions like 'What is bullying?'

Top sites

☺ BEST ON THE NET

Talk Helps

www.talk-helps.com

Also available in French, this site suits anyone from 5–14, and includes an online diary which you can fill in to track how happy or sad you are each day. Very interactive and very colourful, featuring characters like Bobby and Cindy Bully, Ian Intervener and Vicky and Victor Victim. Fantastic!

Anti-Bullying Network

www.antibullying.net

A Scottish site, with simple, easy-to-understand advice.

Bullying at School Information

www.scre.ac.uk/bully

Info from The Scottish Council For Research In Education. What you and your school can do, plus how to find out more. Not a very exciting-looking site, but useful all the same.

Take Action Against Bullying

www.bullybeware.com

This Canadian site answers lots of basic bullying questions like, 'What makes a bully?' and 'What happens to victims?'

Bully OnLine – Bullying by mobile phone

www.successunlimited.co.uk/bullycide/mobile.htm

Straight-talking info on what to do if you're receiving threatening texts. It'll show you how to log any threats you receive and how not to respond.

Bullying.org

www.bullying.org

'Where you are NOT alone'. Real-life bullying stories, from countries as diverse as Australia, Canada, Germany, Ireland, Mexico, South Africa, Sweden and the USA, give great inspiration and encouragement. Plus poems, music and drawings. Set up by a Canadian teacher after a high-school shooting in spring 1999.

Bullying Online

www.bullying.co.uk

Quite texty, but with loads of sections and good advice. Covers the usual, and contains helpful bits on mobile phone bullying, racist bullying and how to stay safe in cyberspace.

ChildLine – Bullying

www.childline.org.uk/Bullying.htm

Useful info to help anyone understand bullying.

Kids Health – Bullying

http://kidshealth.org/teen/your_mind/problems/bullies.html
Part of one of the Net's most visited sites for this kind of info, provides all the stuff you'd expect in small, easy-to-read chunks. Overall, the site contains the equivalent info of a twenty-five volume encyclopaedia!

No Bully

www.nobully.org.nz
Set up by the New Zealand police, the site covers bullying from Year 0 right through to Year 13.

Safe Child Bullies

www.safechild.org/bullies.htm
A little bit wordy, but more useful advice from this American site.

(ii) Homework

Homework sites are fantastic – they'll help you with info and advice on practically every school subject imaginable! So if you're stressing over Pythagoras' Theorem, or wondering about the role of the fool in *King Lear*, or anything in between, you can turn to the Net for a little bit of help. Some sites cover a whole host of subjects, in arts and sciences, while some are more subject specific.

Depending on the experience you've had with these,

you might already know that many sites do more than simply help to answer homework questions. The service where you can email real school teachers, to get help with tackling that question you've been worrying about is brilliant. Many will do this for free, although some offer a subscription service where you sign up and receive as much help as you want each month.

The essay sites are useful starting points to get you thinking, as they contain thousands of essays on many subjects. If you're looking to do a bit of research, then check out one of the online encyclopaedias, where you'll find a whole library's worth of information at your fingertips!

One thing to bear in mind – these sites are not designed to give you the exact answers you're looking for each time. Instead, they're intended to point you in the right direction, so you come up with your own answer. As the **New Aira** website explains: 'We are here to "help" with and not to "do" the homework for you!'

Many teachers are getting wise to the sort of assistance provided – particularly with the essay sites. Turn in perfect work containing stuff you'd never have thought of in a million years, and you could land in a whole lot of trouble!

That's why we strongly advise against using any of the sites that write essays for you. Word-for-word copying of essays is a bad idea, too. How will you survive when that dreaded exam time comes? You won't have a computer to help you then!

Be a little wary of any sites that don't originate in your home country – although they're good, the curriculum can often be quite different.

Top sites

☺ BEST ON THE NET

Homework High

www.homeworkhigh.com

Great fun, colourful, bright and lively, from the British TV station, Channel 4. Email questions to the online teachers and get an answer the same day! Plus, find rooms devoted to each subject, where you can chat online with teachers – for example, the English room is open three nights a week. There are even sound files to help you with foreign-language work.

About – Homework/Study Tips

http://homeworktips.about.com

Exactly how much advice do you want?! You'll find help with all kinds of homework issues – for example, how to handle handing it in late, and how to motivate yourself, plus polls such as 'How many hours of homework do you have each night?' There are loads of links to relevant sites – online encyclopaedias and dictionaries, and much more.

Academic Assistance Access

www.tutoraid.org

This American site claims to be 'one of the foremost

online tutoring services on the web.' Post your query – on any one of more than fifteen subjects – in the mailing list and prepare yourself for answers from qualified tutors and students.

A-levels.co.uk

www.a-levels.co.uk

OK, it's not quite homework, but we had to sneak this in. A very handy collection of links to the main A-level subjects.

Doctor Homework.com

www.doctorhomework.com

Building a Network of students who can help each other with their homework. Contains strong warnings that, 'this is not a cheat site – cheating will not be tolerated'. Too right!

Encyclopedia.com

www.encyclopedia.com

Just type what you're looking for into the search box and the you should get the answer from this free encyclopaedia.

Essay Crawler

www.essaycrawler.com

Search around 35,000 essays for the one you're looking for with this site, which searches eleven other essay sites, all at the same time!

GCSE Bitesize – SOS Teacher

www.bbc.co.uk/schools/gcsebitesize

Stuck on homework, revision or coursework? Use the SOS Teacher section of this brilliant site to send in your personal question. They'll try to get a reply posted on the site within twenty-four hours.

HomeWork Elephant

www.homeworkelephant.co.uk

Links to hundreds of brilliant websites to help with practically every subject you can imagine. Plus 'Ask Agony Elephant', for help and advice, with an archive of past questions.

Homework Help

www.startribune.com/homework_help

Email your homework questions to this American website and answers will be available on the site within twenty-four hours.

Homework Spot

www.homeworkspot.com

American links to literally thousands of helpful homework sites, from arts and crafts to Maths. Plus essay tips, advice on completing a college application and a bizarre collection of random facts – find answers to, 'Why do your feet smell?', 'How many body parts are spelled with three letters?' and much, much more!

Homeworkelp.com

http://service.homeworkhelp.com

First set up in 1993, this American pay-site costs around $40 (about £27) for six months which also gets you a free CD-ROM.

Kevin's Playroom

www.kevinsplayroom.co.uk

Award-winning, and produced by children for children. Stacks of information on loads of subjects. Plus, follow hundreds of links to other relevant websites.

KidsClick!

http://sunsite.berkeley.edu/KidsClick!/

'Web search for kids by librarians.' A kind of online encyclopaedia with links to loads of sites where you can find more specific info. For example, locate anything from a handful of sites on a subject such as 'puffins', or nearly a hundred sites on 'individual authors'!

Mega Essays

www.megaessays.com

This pay-site costs $19.95 (about £13.50) for three months and searches a database of 69,000 essays.

Netessays.net

www.Netessays.net

Intended for students, by students, this is updated daily.

New Aira

www.newaira.com

They call themselves the 'Student's Last Resort', and explain it's all about 'students helping students for a greater cause'. They say they'll attempt to reply to questions within twenty-four hours – but ours came in a flash, within one hour!

One Look Dictionaries

www.onelook.com

Look up the meanings of more than four million words in over 750 online dictionaries.

Planet Papers

www.planetpapers.com

A US database of student-written essays, designed to help other students write their essays. Divided by topic, contains (for example) around 1,500 literature essays, seventy religion essays and fifty geography essays. Use the search engine to look for your essay topic.

Term Paper Sites

www.termpapersites.com

Approximately 50,000 term papers (the American word for essays), with links to loads more sites.

Thesaurus.com
www.thesaurus.com
Is the perfect word on the tip of your tongue? Find alternative ways of saying things here.

Tutornet.com
www.tutornet.com
Also available in Spanish, this pay site costs around $40 (about £27) per month and offers 'unlimited tutoring from our Netucators' on all available subjects.

(iii) Revision and Exams

If you're stressing about revision and exams, then you've come to the right place. It's surprising how you can follow just a few tips and soon find yourself feeling much better. The sites that tell you how to revise, or what to do when you're preparing for and sitting the dreaded exams, give some great advice.

If you're looking for more detail as you actually do your revision, you'll find sites that can help you in virtually any subject, from Art to Physical Education. Many contain tons of revision notes, reminding you – and often explaining in a lot of detail – exactly what you should know. You'll also get the chance to test yourself, to see if your knowledge is up to scratch. Scary, but very useful too!

Help with revision

☺ BEST ON THE NET 1

Learn.co.uk

www.learn.co.uk

A massive site containing practically everything you need to help you revise for all those major GCSE, AS- and A-Level subjects, including English Language and Literature, French, Geography, History, Maths and Sciences. Each subject is packed with loads of important info you should know (revision notes) split into easy-to-understand sections. If you've studied it in class, then it's probably on this site! For example, click on 'Geography' and you'll be able to revise all the basic facts in areas from 'The Physical World' (Weather, River Processes, Glaciers, etc) to 'The Regional World' (UK, Mexico, Spain, Amsterdam, etc). Click on 'English Literature – Drama' and there are the major plays you'll need for this year's curriculum. Each section even includes a revision notes summary to help you remember everything. Then you can take the online mini-exams, complete with an automatic marker, to find out how good you really are. This is brilliant!

☺ BEST ON THE NET 2

GCSE Bitesize Revision

www.bbc.co.uk/schools/gcsebitesize

Covers more than fifteen GCSE subjects – far more than the **Learn.co.uk** site. There are all the regulars – such as

Biology, History and Maths – plus extras like Design & Technology, the newly added Music, and Physical Education. But just like **Learn.co.uk**, you can work your way through all the revision topics you need for each subject and take an online test in each area. Also includes hints on exam skills in specific subjects, helpful links to other sites and info on when GCSE Bitesize hits your TV screen. This site looks great too!

AS Guru

www.bbc.co.uk/education/asguru

A kind of GCSE Bitesize for AS-level students, concentrating on Biology, English, General Studies and Maths, with an additional section on Study Skills.

GCSE Guide

www.gcseguide.co.uk

Not as comprehensive as it might sound – in fact, it only covers GCSE Maths in detail, with a section on English coursework.

GCSEs UK

www.gcsesuk.co.uk

Links to past exam papers and exam/education boards. Plus a message board for students.

gcseVISE.com

www.gcsevise.com

Broad-based revision notes on English, Maths and Science for GCSE. You'll have to pay if you want more detailed info (it's £5 for a term's membership), but then you'll also get advice on how to revise, help with producing a revision timetable, and more.

Project GCSE

www.projectgcse.co.uk

Easy to use, covering the major subjects. Also includes the usual coursework, revision and exam advice.

Revision Central

http://revisioncentral.co.uk

Covers ten GCSE topics, but will also be expanded to cover A-levels and more. Presently contains only limited revision notes in each subject – nowhere near as comprehensive as some of the other sites. Also includes more than ten detailed tips on how to revise properly (like, did you know relaxation is just as important as sitting at your desk for hours? Try telling that one to Mum or Dad!). Hey, there's even an area where you can chill out online.

RevisionLink.co.uk

www.revisionlink.co.uk

Links to some of the most useful revision sites.

SAM Learning

www.samlearning.com

'For SATs, GCSEs and A-levels, SAM Learning offers comprehensive online learning that's proven to improve exam results.' Claims to be used by 600,000 pupils and more than 2,000 schools. Subjects can only be accessed on a limited, thirty-day free trial. You'll have to pay around £100 a year for a full subscription.

S-Cool

www.s-cool.co.uk

Contains GCSE, AS and A-level revision sections. The GCSE one covers a range of familiar subjects, plus Food Technology which isn't really covered much elsewhere. Contains the usual revision notes, revision summary and sample questions. Use S-Cool QuickLearn to swot up on unfamiliar areas you might have missed!

Help with specific subjects

Doc Brown's Chemistry Clinic

www.wpbschoolhouse.btinternet.co.uk

A bit hard to read, but packed with revision notes and sample questions for GCSE and AS-level students.

GCSE Physics Tutorials

www.gcse.com

Everything you need to know for your GCSE Physics exam . . . well, nearly! Also includes relevant exam dates, so you've no excuse to miss them, and links to individual boards' syllabuses.

The GCSE RE Site

http://re-xs.ucsm.ac.uk/gcsere/index.html

The usual formula of revision notes and exam help for Religious Education, plus a still-being-developed section on how to do the best coursework.

Mathslessons.co.uk

www.mathslessons.co.uk

Interactive Maths lessons and the chance to sit online tests.

PinkMonkey.com

www.pinkmonkey.com

Studying English Lit? This site contains more than 350 summaries of popular and obscure titles, including *Frankenstein*, *Great Expectations*, *Hamlet* and *To Kill A Mockingbird*. There's also a message board, study tips and essay help.

Help with exams

☺ BEST ON THE NET

Onion Street

www.bbc.co.uk/schools/communities/onionstreet

Where pupils get together to give each other online help with subjects including revision and exams. Offers online chats from professionals and chatrooms where you can discuss your worries. Check out the 'Revision Rollercoaster' for advice on how to revise effectively. Here, you'll also find advice on surviving exams, split into topics including, 'Handling Stress And Pressure', 'Music To Revise By' and 'Revision Recipes' (food to feed your mind!).

Exam Aid

www.examaid.co.uk

'Working against teenage exam stress.' Loads of links to sites which can help you through all the things that might affect your revision, or how you do in exams, including bullying, health issues, part-time work, relationships and sexuality.

Freeserve – Exam Revision

www.freeserve.com/learning/revision

Lots of links to help you with major GCSE and AS-level subject revision.

Pupiline – Exam Stress
www.pupiline.net/issues/examstress/toparticles.cfm
Useful page on preparing for exams and what to do when you're biting your nails and actually doing them!

TheSite.org – Blitzing Exams
www.thesite.org/info/careers/exams/blitzing_exams.html
Good advice on how to cope before, during and after your exams, from this massive teen site.

Tips Of All Sorts – Study
www.tipsofallsorts.com/study.html
A small but useful page of tips on revising for exams.

(iv) Careers

If you haven't already started thinking about your future, then now is probably a good time to begin. It might seem like ages until you enter the big world of employment, but decisions you make now about subject options and further education could affect what you do in later life.

The Net's great for helping you find out which careers are best for you, according to your interests, hobbies, and expectations. There are hundreds of sites listing thousands of jobs in all kinds of fields, including some that you didn't even know existed!

Whatever you want to be, you can find out the best GCSEs to take right now. Certain sites show the education and training courses you'll want to consider, offer advice on applying for a place at college, and much later, help you find the very vacancy you're looking for.

You'll even find a few sites giving advice on the best holiday jobs – spend your summer picking fruit rather than plucking chickens, for example.

Many sites give hints and tips on the whole job application process, from start to finish – this is useful even if you're only looking for that part-time or summer job right now. You can discover how to best present your CV, how to write a letter of application, what to do and say in those dreaded interviews, and even how to cope if you don't immediately get offered what you want.

Top sites

☺ BEST ON THE NET

Reach for the Sky

http://rfts.sky.com

'See what you can be – careers advice for teenagers.' Starting to think about your career? Then check out RFTS, with working tips from more than two hundred people, career profiles, careers agony aunts, celeb interviews AND advice on exam revision, work experience, going for interviews . . . in fact, just about everything useful you can imagine!

BBC Work and Careers

www.bbc.co.uk/business/work/index.shtml

Simple but effective work and careers advice and business info

Big Wide World

www.bigwideworld.com

'For babes and blokes with attitude.' OK, so how cheesy is that? Still, this UK site provides everything from UK news and entertainment to careers advice, a virtual Student Union bar and a section where you can flirt or find friends!

Careers Portal

www.careers-portal.co.uk

'The award-winning online careers service.' A gateway (a site containing loads of links) to higher education and careers info. Search anything from student finances to completing your UCAS form. Plus profiles on different careers, from accountancy to theatre and drama.

Careers A–Z

www.careersa-z.co.uk

A search engine for every career imaginable, plus CV-writing advice and more.

Careers Web

www.careers.lon.ac.uk

This might be the University of London careers service, but it's open to all. Mainly aimed at UK graduates, with plenty of info and advice. Visit the amazing virtual careers library for a directory of careers sites, useful if you're just starting to research your options.

CVCentre

www.cvcentre.com

'Home of the world-class CV!' Stacks of help on putting your CV together, even if you're only working part-time right now.

Cyber Teens – Work & School

http://www.cyberteens.com/wo

Part of a bigger teen site, contains hundreds of links divided into 'Careers', 'College' and 'Homework Help'.

Department For Education And Skills

www.dfee.gov.uk

A good place to start if you're looking for higher education advice (an A–Z of student unions, for example) or researching your job options. Check out the 'Young Person's Gateway' for links to other relevant sites. But be warned, this isn't the most exciting site on the Net.

Gojobsite

www.gojobsite.co.uk

Nearly 100,000 jobs in thirty-five industries, throughout the UK and Europe, were advertised in one month alone. Useful for seeing what's out there.

Monster.co.uk

www.monster.co.uk

'The world's leading career Network.' Directly available in twenty-two countries, including France, Germany, Spain and Italy as well as the UK and USA. Twenty-one thousand UK jobs, 60,000 in Europe and more than one million in total, world-wide. We love the specialist careers forum where you can ask an expert for advice.

Natives.co.uk – Summer jobs

www.natives.co.uk/summerjobs/summerjobs.htm

Search for jobs on yachts, barges, campsites, beach resorts and more, in countries including France, Spain, the UK and USA.

Reed.co.uk

www.reed.co.uk

More than 80,000 jobs online, from all over the world. Heaps of useful advice, even if you're at GCSE level or below.

SummerJobs.com
www.summerjobs.com
American-based, but still packed with useful info and ideas for earning that all-important cash during holidays.

Universities And Colleges Admissions Service (UK)
www.ucas.ac.uk
Studied at a British school or college? Then use the Tariff Calculator to turn your exam grades into points, then find everything you need to know about applying for uni or college in the UK and searching for the course to suit you.

YoungBIZ.com
http://youngbiz.com
Interesting American site full of fascinating stories of 'treps' (Net entrepreneurs, apparently!).

SCHOOL Q&A

Uncool school

Q: *My mum's just told me we're moving house from Cornwall to London. That means I'll be starting at a new school just as I'm in my final GCSE year. Now I'm not only worried about making friends, but also about messing up my exams. Help!*

Charlie, 14, Bude

A: The thought of doing something or going somewhere unfamiliar is always a worrying one, as most of us like what we know and we don't like change! However, scary as it might seem, you're being given an amazing chance to meet new friends and explore new opportunities in one of the world's most exciting cities! You'll probably find it easy to make new mates, but if you don't, then look at some of the tips on the friendship sites listed in Chapter 2. Also, use the homework sites listed in this chapter to keep on top of all your GCSE subjects, then look at the revision and exam sites to ensure you're fully prepared. You could even buy a small webcam to keep in touch with your friends back home, so you don't forget what they look like!

Homework won't work

Q: *My parents have been complaining at the amount of time I spend on the Net. The thing is, I'm mainly using homework help sites, but they say this could affect my schoolwork. Is this true?*

Gareth, 12, Manchester

A: Two out of three students with computers at home use them for homework help. However, as your parents have realised, it's important to use the Net properly. See, if you don't understand how to solve a problem because you've been handed the answer on a plate, you're going to find it tough going in exams. The best sites give helpful advice on finding the answer, leaving you to tailor it to the exact details of your particular assignment. Find a balance between online research and figuring things out yourself, and your parents will be far happier.

Terrible teacher

Q: *My teacher picks on me. I don't know why this is happening, but I think she's really got it in for me. What can I do?*

Kelly, 15, Aberdeen

A: Most teachers are too busy to waste time and energy on hating you. Instead, they might be behaving like this to get you to change something about yourself that they believe isn't helping you to progress at school. For example, you might be disruptive in class, or simply stare out of the window; maybe you're always late, or you turn up unprepared. You can find out more about the best way to behave by looking at some of the sites recommended earlier in this chapter. If you're struggling with classwork or homework, you'll find help with that online, too. If there seems to be no real reason why your teacher dislikes you though, this is really a kind of bullying – try looking at the sites dealing with bullying.

CHAPTER 5

Absolutely Fabulous!

The fashion and beauty low-down

If you look good, then usually you feel great . . . it's just one of life's little rules. And if you feel great, it probably means you'll have heaps of confidence, which can help you achieve virtually anything!

Looking good doesn't have to mean wearing expensive designer clothes or going to posh beauty salons. It simply means taking care of yourself and your appearance. So it's a good job fashion and beauty is pretty well represented on the Net (although there's a lot more for girls than for boys). Discover heaps of hints on getting a celeb look, and find out exactly what's in and what's out. Then, how about getting a virtual makeover by scanning in a pic of yourself?

You'll find the answers to hundreds of fashion and beauty dilemmas, and discover the beauty secrets of the stars. Like, did you know that actress Jennifer Love Hewitt gets rid of pimples by covering them with toothpaste? Or that *Friends* star Jennifer Aniston crushes two aspirin into her shampoo to prevent dandruff? Well, now you do!

(i) Fashion

Many of the web's fashion pages take the basics from magazines ('Get the look', 'Latest trends', etc) and simply adapt them for an online audience. Only the best sites provide something new, like **Fashion Nightmare**'s fantastic Personal Shopper, or **Cosmo Girl**'s nearest store finder.

Fancy yourself as a model? Read the diaries of fashion professionals at **Fashion Nightmare**, to see if you'd want to be in their shoes. Also check out a site called **Modelnews.com** (weirdly, its address is different – www.beamodel.com) for everything you need to know about getting into the business. Then, when you're done with that, check out some of the best model agencies.

None of this quite beats parading in and out of a changing room yourself, of course, but it's still worth a look . . .

Top sites

☺ BEST ON THE NET

Fashion Nightmare

www.fnmare.com

Sign up first, otherwise you'll get nowhere, then enter an amazingly colourful, interactive, fun site packed with advice and info. Find out how to become a model or designer and sort out your style nightmares, plus there are links to other fashion and beauty sites on the Net. This site even features a 'Personal Shopper'. Lively and great fun!

Allthegear.com

www.allthegear.com

'Fanatical about fashion and barmy about beauty.' Aimed solely at girls, packed with tips and info on topics like planning a girlie night in.

Better Than Fashion

www.fashionteen.com

The latest trends for boys and girls in a small but useful site.

Cosmo Girl – The Mall

www.cosmogirl.co.uk/mall/mall.jsp

Minimal fashion and beauty tips from the UK site of this teen mag, but includes a handy store locator to find your local branch of selected fashion chains.

Elle Girl.com

www.ellegirl.com

Website of the US/UK teen mag, split into sections like 'Shop Girl' (shopping!) and 'Pretty Girl' (beauty!), plus 'Global Girl', where you can send e-cards, exchange fashion ideas and find out what it takes to become a model.

Modelnews.com

www.beamodel.com

American-orientated site with info on breaking into

modelling, including 'Ask Geri', where you can get a personal reply to your email question. Includes inside truths and a guide to what agencies are looking for.

Premier Model Management
www.elitepremier.co.uk
Official UK site of the renowned model agency, and home to supermodel Naomi Campbell, with plenty of hot faces to inspire you.

So . . . Fashion
www.bbc.co.uk/so/fashion
Part of the BBC's bigger So . . . teen site, this includes ways to get a celebrity look, 'Off The Rails' – the latest looks for the season, and a tried and tested beauty section.

Storm Models
www.stormmodels.com
Browse the boys and girls to see the current model competition! Top names like Kate Moss and Jade Jagger can be found here.

Teen People.com – Style
www.teenpeople.com/teenpeople/style/home
Fashion, beauty and health pages of this American teen girls' mag.

(ii) Hair and Beauty

If you've ever wanted to give yourself a bit of a beauty makeover (and, let's face it, who hasn't?!) then the Net's the place to do it. You can also find answers to all those niggling beauty questions, plus enough hints and tips to fill a couple of encyclopaedias! There are even beauty sites that link you to . . . yes, yet more beauty sites!

Go on, take a peek! You'll never have looked so good!

Top sites

☺ BEST ON THE NET

Substance

www.substance.com

'Beauty on your own terms.' Not specifically teen orientated, but fab all the same. Includes a 'Hair & Nail Salon', where your hair questions will be answered by email, a 'Skin Clinic' and a 'Makeup Studio', all packed with articles and tips. We love 'Makeover-o-Matic' – simply scan in a picture of yourself, then choose an area to experiment on (eyes, cheeks, lips, etc). Create a 'look book' (save it!) then email your new look to your mates.

BeautyCare.com

www.beautycare.com

Links to tons of beauty sites. Check out the hairstyles section for around thirty male styles, and more than one hundred and fifty for women.

Beautynet.com

www.beautynet.com

'The virtual salon for beauty, wellness and style.' Yet more beauty hints and tips.

Beauty Guru

www.beautyguru.com

'I've scoured the web looking for hot beauty sites so you don't have to.' Nice illustrations and heaps of useful sites.

EZface

www.ezface.com

'The Virtual Makeover Experience.' Submit a photo of yourself, then the site's experts will adapt it within twenty-four hours, and you're then ready to use the site's 'Virtual Mirror' utility to experiment with all kinds of make-up and accessories. How you turn out is totally up to your imagination!

4Cosmetics.com

www.4cosmetics.com

Ask the 'Make-up Diva' for advice, and get loads more make-up hints and tips. A bit too texty.

Makeup 101

www.makeup101.com

Tells the secrets of professional make-up artists. Quite texty, but lots of interesting articles to read, such as, 'Ten beauty myths you need to know,' and 'What cleansers really work?'

Mr Joel's Beautychop

www.beautychop.pair.com

'Beauty secrets and beauty tips.' Packed with secrets on everything from shaving and waxing to self-tanning. Plus loads of fascinating celeb beauty secrets.

Online Makeup

www.onlinemakeup.com

Packed with make-up and cosmetics tips, featuring renowned brands including Cover Girl, Clinique and Bobbi Brown.

Shockwaves

www.shockwaves.co.uk

Having a bad hair day? Sort it with this site and investigate the Shockwaves styling range.

Vidal Sassoon

www.vidalsassoon.com

Opens with links to Vidal Sassoon sites in America, Canada, UK, Singapore and Japan. Get the low-down on the latest hair trends and meet the creative team.

World of Hair

www.worldofhair.com

Useful links to loads of hair sites world-wide.

FASHION AND BEAUTY Q&A

Getting personal

Q: *I've always used the internet for fashion and beauty advice, but sometimes I just can't find the answers to my questions. Is there anywhere else I can look for this info?*

Zoe, 14, Winchester

A: Most of these sites are packed with useful info, but it's frustrating if you can't find what you're looking for. Thankfully, help is at hand, as some sites offer you the chance to email them and receive a personal reply. For example, if you're searching for that elusive fashion find, tell the 'Personal Shopper' at **Fashion Nightmare** (www.fnmare.com) and they'll email you to let you know where you can find it. If it's beauty advice you want, try emailing the professionals at **Substance** (www.substance.com) and they'll get back to you within seventy-two hours.

Male musings

Q: *OK, so there's all this stuff for the girls, but there must be something for us guys. We sometimes want fashion or grooming advice too. What's out there?*

Darryl, 16, Liverpool

A: You're in luck . . . sort of! Some of the online men's magazines, like **FHM** (www.fhm.com) and **Maxim** (www.maximonline.com) feature small sections or items on their sites. You can also get shaving and grooming tips from **Mankind** (www.mankindonline.co.uk) with a shop offering world-wide shipping. And click on 'Sharp Grooming' at the male-orientated site **SharpMan.com** (www.sharpman.com) for heaps of grooming tips from the Q&A archive.

CHAPTER 6

I Need a New . . .

Money matters and shopping till you drop . . . from home!

Earn cash, spend cash. Earn cash, spend cash. Earn cash, spend cash. Hmm, when we're teens, most of us don't think about looking after the money we've got – we only think about buying as much cool stuff as we can!

With cash coming in from pocket money, paper rounds, part-time or weekend jobs, and holiday or summer work, you're making (and spending!) more money than ever. In fact, in 1996, teens earned more than $100 billion (about £68 billion) world-wide and it's probably even more now. Being a teen is certainly a big business! But it's easy to throw your money away without thinking about it, which is why you'll find sites telling you how to save, and how to make the most of what you've got.

That's not to say you shouldn't spend some of it though – and shopping online is so handy. Your mum and dad might still be a bit worried about it, ('Ooh, but I couldn't possibly send my credit card details down a phone line!'), and security was a bit of a problem in the past, but it's now much safer. In fact, teens are among the most likely groups of people to buy stuff online. In 2000, this age group spent $483 million (around £327 million) shopping on the internet, but this is expected to increase to an incredible $10.6 BILLION (£7 billion) by 2005.

Either begin shopping at a virtual mall, which provides links to many thousands of e-tailers from just one site, or visit the stores of your favourite high street names to pick up everything from CDs to trainers. You'll also find hundreds of 'internet only' stores which don't have premises in the high street, but still sell loads of great stuff, like hand-made beauty products or cool American clothes that you'd never get your hands on otherwise.

Internet shopping is often much cheaper than the high street, with things like chart CDs, DVDs, perfumes or books often priced several pounds cheaper than at some of the well-known stores. Plus, you are able to compare prices between several stores, which saves time AND money! Sometimes you'll pay extra for postage, but often it's included.

So how are you going to pay for anything, especially without a credit card? If you've been put off internet shopping because you don't have one, that's no longer a problem. There are several options for paying online, which you'll find a bit more about on page 93. Whatever you do, enjoy the online shopping experience – it's supposed to be fun!

(i) Money

Many of the teen money sites tend to be American, but that doesn't make them any less interesting or useful. They'll test how good you are with money (remember, it's not all about the cash you flash), show you how to make the best of it, and how to save for something you really want.

Set yourself a savings target and it's much easier to put some money away. Not only will you end up with those great new trainers/stereo/holiday, you'll also improve your self-confidence along the way.

Top sites

☺ BEST ON THE NET

There's Something About Money

www.yourmoney.cba.ca

Canadian site in English or French. Take the 'POP' quiz to test your money smarts (responsibilities), find out about credit and whether you're a good money manager, plus advice on planning for your future.

Children's Money World.com

www.childrensmoneyworld.com

More info and advice.

Fleet Kids
www.fleetkids.com
Quite young, but loads of money games to discover more about your cash capabilities.

A Girl Like U – Money & School
www.agirllikeu.com/money_school.asp
Part of a bigger teen girl website. Very American content.

Kids Bank
www.kidsbank.com
'A fun place for children to learn about money and banking.' Again, quite young, but lots of info.

Kids' Money
www.kidsmoney.org
In six languages, including English, French, German and Spanish. Ideas and links on making and saving money.

Moneyopolis
www.moneyopolis.com
'The place for money-sharp kids.' Find out about managing your money, and play the 'Moneyopolis' game, where you become a new resident of a virtual town, with a virtual $600 (about £400) to spend or save.

Young Money

www.young-money.co.uk

'The online gameshow where you can learn about money.' Earn points by answering questions and working out what to do with the money you 'win'.

Paying online

Many sites require payment by credit card, but these are only available to over 18s. However, some take the debit card, Solo, which you can get from the age of 11 in the UK. Others let you use a card, which is topped up with cash, a bit like mobile phone vouchers. And now you can even pay using your mobile (but again you must be over 18 for this).

Of course, if there's something you really want, but they don't accept these payment methods, then you'll have to persuade a responsible adult, like your mum or dad, to use their credit card for you . . . just don't forget to pay them back!

Paybox

www.paybox.co.uk

All you need is a current account at the bank and a mobile phone – but you must be over 18. Then simply pay for items using your mobile. This service is currently available in the UK, Germany, Austria, Sweden and

Spain. So how does it work? Simply enter your mobile when you come to pay. Your phone will then ring and you authorise payment by entering your Paybox PIN (Personal Identification Number). Paybox will then take the money from your bank account. There is a yearly charge for this service.

Smartcreds

www.smartcreds.co.uk

'Buy stuff online without a credit card.' Register for a card and top it up at any Post Office or any of 8,500 newsagents, convenience stores and petrol stations (PayPoint outlets) throughout the UK. Or buy a £20 Smartcreds scratchcard at selected Post Offices to top up by cheque or standing order from your bank account. Then shop online at around eighty registered stores.

Solo

www.solocard.co.uk

British debit card available from 11 years (with NatWest and Bank of Scotland) or 16 years (with HSBC and Halifax). Accepted by some e-tailers in the UK.

Splash Plastic

www.splashplastic.com

'Now you can pay as you go online.' Register for a card, then top it up with cash (minimum £10) at thousands of stores in the UK, including Carphone Warehouse and any PayPoint outlets – type in your postcode to find the store nearest you. Or you can use a standing order. Then check out the participating e-tailers, ranging from CD stores to gadget shops.

(iii) Virtual Malls

Find thousands of e-tailers that you never knew existed, plus plenty you already know about, by visiting a virtual mall. These sites link you to other online stores, and you can browse by category (so, if you're looking for CDs, you can check out all the listed stores).

The American malls unfortunately show a preference towards American e-tailers, but many ship world-wide, and if you're prepared to pay the postage, you could end up with some pretty fabulous stuff.

Top sites

☺ BEST ON THE NET

Deal Time

www.dealtime.co.uk

Not exactly a virtual mall, but lets you compare prices for all sorts of items at UK e-tailers – from CDs, DVDs and books to appliances and mobile phones – then make sure you get the cheapest! Simply type in what you're looking for. We found top chart DVDs up to £8 cheaper at one bargain site, compared with some of the others.

Cool Shopping.com

www.coolshopping.com

'The internet shopping channel.' Links to thousands of online stores – we found more than 120 under the heading Hip/Urban Clothing alone! Amy Strycula created this site in 1995 – click on 'Ask Amy' and she'll email you with gift suggestions for that elusive item, within twenty-four hours.

iWantToShop.com

www.iwanttoshop.com

'The UK's leading shopping directory.' Features around 4,000 shops, with sections including 'New Shops', 'Best Sellers' and 'Hot Gadgets'.

Mallpark

www.mallpark.com

Nearly half a million businesses, listed in fifty separate malls.

Student Center – Online Mall

www.shopcsni.com/studentcenter/

Fifteen different categories to browse, also with an A–Z search facility.

2020 Shops

www.2020shops.com

A UK-based virtual mall. It also allows you to compare prices of items at a number of online stores.

Yahoo Shopping
http://shopping.yahoo.com
Browse the wide range of departments to find the link of your choice.

(iv) Entertainment Shopping

Most of the high street 'entertainment' stores, like HMV or Virgin, also have websites where you can buy all the usual CDs, videos, DVDs, games and books. But the internet also boasts a whole load of names you won't find in the high street, sometimes selling the same products at cheaper prices. We found chart CDs for under £9, whereas some of their high-street equivalents in the UK were often up to £6 more expensive!

Books and video games are often cheaper, too, and many stores deliver world-wide.

Top sites

☺ BEST ON THE NET
CD Wow!
www.cd-wow.com
Ridiculously cheap CDs, including the latest chart titles at just £8.99 with free delivery within the UK. Now sells DVDs, too.

Amazon

www.amazon.com

The popular books and music e-tailer is now available in the USA, UK, Germany, Japan and France – just click on the links. Also find electronics, DVDs and much more.

Bensons World

www.bensonsworld.co.uk

DVDs and videos with savings of £4 to £5 and sometimes even £6, on UK high-street prices, with free delivery on DVDs world-wide.

BookBrain.co.uk

www.bookbrain.co.uk

You can't buy books here, but type in what you're looking for and this ingenious site will search fifteen book e-tailers and show you the cheapest options. We found a £20 (RRP) cookery book selling at £13 including postage in the UK.

Dividica

www.dividica.com

Cheaper-than-the-high-street prices for DVDs.

DVD Express

www.dvdexpress.com

Possibly the cheapest site on the Net for DVDs. But, be warned, they're Region 1, as this site's based in Canada (in Europe, we use Region 2). So, you'll need a Region 1 or multi-region DVD player to watch anything you purchase from this site.

Electronics Boutique

www.eb.uk.com

Online store of the UK's biggest games retailer. Shipping limited to the UK only.

Gameplay

www.gameplay.com

More games, with shipping to many countries worldwide (free in the UK).

Gamer

www.gamer.uk.com

Thousands of games for all formats, with free shipping in Europe and world-wide shipping available.

HMV

www.hmv.co.uk

Singles, albums, videos, DVDs, games – everything you'd expect from the online version of the popular high street chain.

Internet Bookshop

www.bookshop.co.uk

Book bargains galore, even when you add in confusing postage rates (£2.24 + 50p per item in the UK).

Jungle.com

www.jungle.com

'The UK's premier technology superstore.' CDs, DVDs and a whole lot more, such as computer hardware and sortware, gadgets and phones. You can also view the top sellers – just to make sure you're keeping up with the Joneses!

MX2

www.mx2.org

Cheap CDs, DVDs and much more, but postage is extra. Very slow to load.

Second Sounds

www.secondsounds.com

'Europe's no.1 online used CD store.' Thousands of CDs at prices that won't burn a hole in your pocket! Prices start at £1.99 and all CDs are supplied in new cases!

Streets Online

www.streetsonline.co.uk

CDs, DVDs, games, books and more.

Swotbooks.com

www.swotbooks.com

More cheap books. Postage is £2.40 per order in the UK.

Tower Records

www.towerrecords.co.uk

More of what you'd expect from the high street chain. Includes links to towerrecords.com in the USA and towerrecords.co.jp in Japan.

Virgin

www.virginmega.co.uk

Everything from the high-street store, online. Includes a store locator in case you still want to trek to a real shop.

(v) Fashion Shopping

Although you can't try something on when you buy online, fashion websites often offer extras that you couldn't find in-store, such as fashion hints and tips. And most have good returns policies in case you don't get it quite right. Don't forget to visit some of the cool, internet-only stores like **As Seen on Screen.com** (www.asseenonscreen.com) and **Go4soccer.com** (www.go4soccer.com) as well as your high-street favourites.

Top sites

☺ BEST ON THE NET

Topshop

www.topshop.co.uk

Very cool, easy-to-navigate, exciting site from the British high-street store. Shop by product or trend and check out the Fashion Clinic for essential advice. We also love the global clubbing message board. Delivery within the UK only, at £2.95 per order.

Abercrombie & Fitch

www.abercrombie.com

Fantastic website from the US high-street chain, featuring all their funky gear. Create a complete outfit on-screen in the 'Changing Room'. Delivery is $25 (about £17) for international shipping by airmail, however much you buy.

Adidas

www.adidas.com

Links to official Adidas sites in countries including France, Germany and Spain. Check out the latest ranges (unfortunately shopping online is only allowed in the USA).

As Seen On Screen.com

www.asseenonscreen.com

A brilliant site where you can buy the stuff you've seen the stars wearing – on stage, in films, or on TV. All sorts of departments, including novelty gift ideas and clearance. Browse by celeb (from Alicia Keys to Tom Cruise), movies or TV shows. Delivers world-wide.

Claire's Accessories

www.claires.co.uk

Very funky with cool sound effects and speech, plus the chance to select the backgrounds and music according to your mood ('Party!', 'Luvved Up' or 'Chilled'). But some sections take a while to load even on a fast computer. Worth the wait for fashion tips, a look at the Claire's range, ear-piercing info, and more.

Freemans

www.freemans.co.uk

The online home of this British catalogue - order online.

Go4Soccer.com

www.go4soccer.com

'The premier online soccer sports shop.' More than 22,000 different products for sale, including football equipment, clothing and other merchandise. Worldwide delivery available.

H&M

www.hm.com

Available in fourteen countries, including France, Germany, Spain and the USA. Unfortunately, you can't buy anything, but you can check out the latest stuff from this bargain retailer and then find your nearest store.

JD Sports

www.jdsports.co.uk

The UK sportswear retailer – shop by department, brand (including Adidas, Nike and Reebok), or style (such as Casual or Skate).

Look Again

www.lookagain.co.uk

Clothes for boys and girls from this British catalogue – order online.

Mykindaplace – Shop

www.mykindaplace.com

Shop for clothing, beauty products and other items, including gifts and gizmos.

New Look

www.newlook.co.uk

The latest looks, fashion tips, competitions and a store locator from the discount chain for girls. You can't buy online.

Next

www.next.co.uk

Browse and buy the complete range from the high street giant. Delivery within the UK only, £2.95 per order.

Nike

www.nike.com

Links to official Nike sites in countries including France, Germany and Spain. Some allow online shopping.

Sports Mart

www.sportsmart.co.uk

'The online sports shop.' All the sportswear you'd expect, plus find a bargain at 'Deals of the Day'.

Topman

www.topman.co.uk

The boys' version of Topshop, with everything you'd expect, plus a daily joke, an e-cards facility, and your chance to vote people in the news either 'topman' or 'prat'.

(vi) Hair and Beauty Shopping

You'd be hard pushed to find a cosmetics shop in your local high street that sells the variety of beauty products available on the Net. We'll bet you never even knew that you needed some of this stuff! There are loads of great gift ideas, too.

All your regular bits and pieces are also available online too, so whether you're just feeling lazy, or you want to pamper yourself at home, it's worth having a bit of a shop and then waiting for a beautiful-smelling package to arrive at your door!

Top sites

☺ BEST ON THE NET

Strawberrynet

www.strawberrynet.com

'The largest world-wide discounter of skincare, make-up and fragrance.' Established in 1999, serving more than a hundred countries, the site is available in seven languages. Free gift-wrapping and a five per cent discount if you buy three or more products. Free shipping world-wide – what you see is what you pay.

Beauty Shopping

www.beauty-shopping.com

American advice on hair care, nail care and skin care with delivery available world-wide.

The Body Shop

www.bodyshop.com

Global site of the cruelty-free beauty retailer. Check out the product range and locate your local store. No online ordering facility.

Boots

www.wellbeing.com

Buy everything you see in-store, with additional health tips and ideas for special occasions. Delivery from £2.50 within the UK.

Eyebeauty.com

www.eyebeauty.com

Only the cutest cosmetics (in the most colourful packaging!) available for delivery world-wide.

Fragrance Bay

www.fragrancebay.com

'The UK's leading e-tailer of fine fragrances.' Free gift-wrapping and shipping on UK orders, with world-wide delivery.

Fragrance Direct

www.fragrancedirect.co.uk

More top smellies delivered to your door, available world-wide.

HQ Hair

www.hqhair.com

Hair and beauty products, as used by the stars, such as Sebastian (Catherine Zeta Jones and Jennifer Aniston), Aveda, KMS and Tigi (Britney Spears). Plus celeb secrets and 'Ask Jayne', for professional products advice. World-wide delivery available.

Lush

www.lush.co.uk

Online home of the all-natural, hand-made cosmetics firm. You can almost smell the goodies coming off the screen! Delivery available to many countries world-wide – check the list.

P2U

www.pharmacy2u.co.uk

'Delivering health.' Everything you'd find in your high street pharmacy, plus all those products you may be too embarrassed to ask for, delivered straight to your door world-wide.

Space.NK

www.spacenk.co.uk

'Renowned for its unique mix of innovative, quality beauty products from around the world.' World-wide delivery.

ThinkNatural.com

www.thinknatural.com

'The UK's leading natural health website.' Thousands of all natural health and beauty products, with world-wide delivery.

(vii) And the Rest

Gadgets, gizmos and gifts . . . you can find them all on the Net, so you'll never be stuck for a present idea again! Whether you're browsing a store that sells toys for boys, bidding for something you really want on an auction site, or customising your mobile phone, these sites will give you stacks of fun. Most offer world-wide delivery, too, so the only limit is your imagination!

Top sites

☺ BEST ON THE NET

eBay

www.eBay.com

'The world's online marketplace.' Link to twenty-one global sites, including the USA and UK, and France, Germany and Spain. Gives you the chance to buy or sell anything online, by bidding for items, with several methods of payment normally accepted.

Alternative Gift Company

www.alt-gifts.com

Never be stuck for a present idea again! Use 'Ask The Expert' to locate the ideal gift . . . even if you have no idea what it is yet!

Big Boys Toys

www.big-boys-toys.net

Yet more gizmos and gifts with world-wide delivery.

The Carphone Warehouse

www.carphonewarehouse.com

Loads of mobiles and accessories from the online version of the UK high-street store.

Cody Gifts

www.sfcody.com

Great gifts for everyone, from a few pounds to blow-the-budget, such as 'The Astronaut Experience for Two' – a weekend at Alabama's Space Academy! Start saving!

Firebox.com

www.firebox.com

'The coolest, fastest, latest, greatest, hottest stuff you can get your hands on.' Select according to category, such as 'Gadgets', 'Bachelor Pad' and 'Kitsch'. We just had to buy an acre of the moon at £19.95, complete with Lunar Deed and Bill Of Rights (including mineral rights!) and loved the Snowmobile at £8,000! World-wide delivery.

Gadgetshop.com

www.gadgetshop.com

Weird and wonderful bits and bobs that could just transform your life! Use the gift selector to find gifts in various price ranges. We loved the ice crusher (£10), the walkie-talkie watches (£30 for a pair) and the home mix DJ kit (£230). World-wide delivery.

Gobazaar.co.uk

www.gobazaar.co.uk

Great gift ideas and gadgets with world-wide delivery.

MagicTricks.co.uk

www.magictricks.co.uk

'The UK's leading online magic tricks store.' Tricks for beginners and experts, plus magic videos and DVDs, with free delivery in Europe (spend over £20) and world-wide shipping available.

Make My Phone
www.makemyphone.com
Customise your mobile, selecting the colour and any design or images for the front and back – either those on the website, or your own. Free world-wide delivery.

Posters.co.uk
www.posters.co.uk
Thousands of posters, stickers, photos and art prints, with world-wide delivery.

Webswappers
www.webswappers.com
'Swap what you have, find what you want.' Swap anything you like for something else – so long as someone accepts your offer.

SHOPPING Q&A

Having a fit

Q: *I'm worried about internet shopping in case I buy something and it doesn't fit. Isn't it hard to get your money back?*

Dan, 14, London

A: Getting a refund on an internet purchase should be no more difficult then getting your money back on something you bought through a mail-order catalogue, so long as you stick with reputable retailers. After all, they understand that if you're shopping for something like new jeans, then no matter how good the pictures on a website, they can't beat actually being able to try something on in a changing room. It's not your legal right to be able to change it (unless it's faulty, for example), but most websites have goodwill policies that ensure you can. So, if you haven't got it right, simply follow their instructions for sorting things out.

Watch out

Q: *My parents keep telling me I can't shop online because of all the bad things they've heard about people being ripped off, or things not arriving through the post. But my friends have been visiting some really cool sites and I want to, too.*

Amanda, 12, Fife

A: Internet shopping has really changed in the past few years, and now it's just as safe as shopping on the high street, as long as you bear a few things in mind. Only shop in recommended places, or buy well-known brand names and make sure you read any small print for hidden terms and conditions. Always print off a record of your transaction, as you may need it later if your purchases don't arrive. And finally, keep a look out for hidden delivery costs – there's more on that below!

Signed, sealed, delivered

Q: *I don't want to end up paying a fortune to have something I've bought online delivered to my home. Can you tell me a bit more about postage costs?*

Dipty, 15, Birmingham

A: Postage (often referred to as 'shipping' or 'carriage') can be confusing. Some e-tailers don't add postage until the last minute, and if you're ordering from overseas, that can add a hefty amount to your bill. Others charge extra for each item you buy, which means prices can stack up. And some (the best ones!) make it clear that all prices you see on-screen include postage (depending on where you live). If you're really stuck, it's best to continue with your order, but to press the 'Proceed' button *only* when you've made sure you know exactly what you're paying for!

CHAPTER 7

Feeling Bored?

Music, movies and more!

The latest on your pop idol's love life! The cost of that TV star's new home! The scoop on that hot actor's latest movie! You can't escape the fact that we all love finding out what our favourite celebs are up to, then having a good gossip about it.

You're bound to have already marked some celeb websites in your 'Favourites' – anyone who wants to stay one step ahead of their mates when it comes to star secrets, knows to turn to the Net. Sign up for personal emails, which some of the sites offer, and you'll even receive the latest news and gossip straight to your Inbox.

As well as featuring some great 'all-round' entertainment sites, the Net is also home to thousands of other sites, focusing on all aspects of entertainment, including movies, music, TV and books.

Check out interviews with your favourite stars, from the big and small screens, and the charts. Find out all the latest news and reviews. Or even watch trailers for the latest movies. It didn't take long for people to realise that American sites are best for this as they contain movie reviews and interviews way in advance of their UK rivals, as the films are generally released there first. Music fans will know that you can hear clips of the latest music releases online.

But that's only the half of it. To find out what the Net can really offer you in terms of entertainment, it's about time you properly checked it out!

(i) Music

Pop, indie, rock, nu-metal, it's all represented on the Net, and there can't be anyone who hasn't looked up some info on their favourite band or artist, checked out the latest photos, or even wanted to listen to what's in the charts, online.

Music websites used to look quite boring – like online versions of magazines – but most are now as exciting as the bands they represent. Select one site alone and you can spend virtually all day visiting the different rooms, voting in polls, getting wrapped up in quizzes, and downloading the latest tunes – most usually as MP3s. But be warned – unless, you have a fast Broadband connection, the downloading can sometimes be a bit slow.

How do I use MP3s?

As most people know, MP3s are compressed sound files, which you can download on to your computer. All the bits that we can't hear with the human ear have been removed, to make the download time as short as possible (a four-minute tune takes about twelve minutes to download with a 58kps modem).

Most people use MP3s to download their favourite tunes from the Net. However, you should remember that the unauthorised distribution of MP3s is illegal. That's why sites like the infamous **Napster** (www.napster.com) have found themselves in trouble with record labels, as fans distributed MP3s to each other, via the Net. It's better to find an authorised tune at one of the specialist MP3 sites listed, and simply click to download.

Here's the good news – because MP3 files are so small, you can fit masses on your computer without filling up too much hard-disk space! Most sites will list their top downloads, so you don't waste your time listening to junk!

You can play MP3s using software on your computer (as long as you've got a sound card and speakers or headphones), download special software (such as **WinAmp** at www.winamp.com), or buy an MP3 player, which holds about an hour of music (some are built into mobile phones). You can also copy MP3s on to CD.

Top sites

☺ BEST ON THE NET

Click Music

www.clickmusic.co.uk

'Simply searching for music.' Search 250,000 websites and 20,000 pages of directory information, picked and evaluated by experts. Type in the name of the singer or band you're looking for, and find the official website, top fansites, the latest news from other websites, links to similar artists, MP3s and much more.

Emusic

www.emusic.com

Pay to download any of 200,000 licensed tunes.

Kerrang

www.kerrang.com

News, reviews, a message board and gig guide for the best heavy music around (rock, metal, nu-metal, punk and more!). Join Kerrang's virtual tribe for email updates.

MTV.com

www.mtv.com

Links to MTV all over the world. Get the latest news, view full-length vids, link to selected MTV shows and listen to MTV Radio.

NME

www.nme.com

Everything you'd expect from the online version of the UK indie mag, plus loads more special features including unique artist pages, video interviews, and online NME radio.

Popworld

www.popworld.com

'Where pop comes first.' Lively and interactive, with great sound effects and graphics, but if you've got a slow computer, you might get bored waiting for stuff to download. Wait around though, as it's well worth it. Hear clips of the latest chart hits in the 'Chart Channel' section, win celeb goodies, copy a celeb look on the 'Fashion Channel', and much, much more.

Pop-Music.com

www.pop-music.com

Feels a bit amateurish, but contains lots of gossip and reviews. Features an MP3 search of all the best MP3 sites.

Radio Locator

www.radio-locator.com

'The most comprehensive radio station search engine on the internet.' Links to more than 10,000 radio station web pages and over 2,500 audio streams from the USA and around the world. Choose by style, such as 'Dance' or 'Oldies', and by country, from Albania to Zimbabwe!

Radio 1

www.bbc.co.uk/radio1

Urban, dance, alternative and chart news, reviews and interviews, from the UK's leading youth radio station. Tune in online, or check out the on-air DJ, via the studiocam.

Rolling Stone

www.rollingstone.com

The top US music mag in its online form. All the usual, plus an A–Z artist search and access to 180,000 MP3s.

Smash Hits

www.smashhits.net

Links to artist homepages and all the other music info you'd expect from this UK pop magazine.

So . . . Pop

www.bbc.co.uk/so/pop

Part of the larger **So . . .** teen site, contains limited gossip and reviews.

Teen Music

www.teenmusic.com

News, interviews, features, quizzes, videos, polls, free stuff, trivia and fanclubs info – phew! Sign up for the weekly email newsletter.

Top of the Pops

www.bbc.co.uk/totp

Massive, great-looking site, from the UK's leading music TV show. News, interviews, features and competitions, plus the entire Top 40 with music and video clips to download. Have your say by voting for your favourite act from the previous week's TV show.

Worldpop

www.worldpop.com

'The global pop network.' Not just pop but also dance, urban and alternative music news, reviews and interviews from this established UK site. We love the 'Fonezone', where you can download ringtones and graphics for your mobile (there is a charge – see details online).

(ii) Movies

Cinema-going is big business again, as everyone from your little sister to your gran flocks to the movies. Despite a downturn in custom in the 1990s – and the rise and rise of DVD players – people are rediscovering their local Multiplex in a big way! After all, nothing can beat a big bucket of popcorn, a gallon of Coke, and your favourite actors up there on the big screen.

But use the Net to sort the fab flicks from the movie

mistakes and you'll certainly save time watching dud movies at the cinema. Most of the good film websites offer reviews, photos and interviews, but many go that important step further and will also let you view the latest trailers online, enter exclusive competitions, or check out what's on at your local cinema tonight.

Nowadays, most movie releases also have their own official website. They're often brilliantly detailed, with cast biographies, pictures, interactive elements and more. In the favourite sites listed next, you'll find the world's most fantastic movie directory, the **Internet Movie Database**, which you'll keep going back to again and again. Plus, look out for the sites like **Ain't It Cool News** and **Dark Horizons**, which bring you the latest inside info, and the fun-but-fascinating movie errors sites, listing hundreds of cock-ups in your favourite flicks. And if you're a real movie nerd, you'll want to check out **Drew's Script-O-Rama**, with hundreds of film scripts in full.

Blimey, this is almost as much fun as actually going to the movies! Sshhh now! And pass the popcorn!

Top sites

☺ BEST ON THE NET

Internet Movie Database

www.imdb.com

Visited by more than ten million movie fans each month, IMDB claims to be the 'biggest, best, most award-winning movie site on the planet.' Not an all-singing, all-dancing site, but instead the most info-packed movie directory around. Look up around 250,000 movies and more than 500,000 actors and actresses. Want to know about the new Elijah Wood film? Find it here. Want to read about every movie Gywneth Paltrow's ever starred in? Find it here. Want to see the latest trailers? Find them here. Also contains links to what's on at local cinemas, world-wide. Absolutely incredible.

Ain't It Cool News

www.aint-it-cool-news.com

Well-respected throughout the movie industry, this reveals the latest movie gossip and rumours. Still, it's more concerned with top gossip than looking good, and that means it's hard to read, with no pictures.

Dark Horizons

www.darkhorizons.com

One of the hottest sites to find the latest news, images, clips and reviews of current and upcoming blockbusters – it's totally packed with trailers! How did you ever do without it?!

Drew's Script-O-Rama

www.script-o-rama.com

Film and TV scripts galore for the nerd, or the actor in you!

Hollywood.com

www.hollywood.com

'Isn't it time you went Hollywood!' News, reviews and interviews. Click on the 'Multimedia' section for peeks behind the scenes of movies, the latest trailers, interview videos, premieres and photo galleries containing your fave movies in pictures!

Movie Mistakes

www.movie-mistakes.com

Established in 1996, providing a list of nearly 13,000 movie mistakes (continuity errors, etc) in around 2,000 films. Spot about 140 errors in *The Matrix* and over fifty bloopers in *Raiders of the Lost Ark*! Includes an A–Z search, a summary of the 20 best-ever bloopers, and the chance to submit your worn eagle-eyed observations.

My Movies

www.mymovies.co.uk

Even more reviews and trailers, plus competitions, a what's on guide and a 'Movie Mistakes' section.

Nit Pickers

www.nitpickers.com

Another A–Z movie errors site – spend a whole afternoon looking up your favourite vids and replaying the mistakes! Includes an incredible 430 cock-ups in *Titanic*.

Odeon

www.odeon.co.uk

Book tickets for your nearest Odeon cinema in the UK, and register for offers and film news. Plus, get your fave cinema's film times emailed to you each week.

Rotten Tomatoes

www.rottentomatoes.com

More statistics – nearly two million users check out some of the reviews of around 87,000 films each month. Not sure if you'll like the latest blockbuster? This site's a fun way to discover the reaction to the latest movies from America's top media critics, summarised via the Tomatometer (whole, or splatted!). By the way, the name comes from the days when theatre audiences threw rotten veg and fruit at the stage to show their disgust.

Screenit.com

www.screenit.com

'Entertainment reviews for parents.' Like it says, this is the low-down on the latest movies, videos and DVDs (plus a massive archive), but written for your mum and dad. So, each movie is examined in minute detail in categories such as, 'Blood/Gore', 'Sex/Nudity', 'Frightening/Tense Scenes'. Use it as you like (but probably quite differently to your parents!). This site is sometimes useful and sometimes plain hilarious – it even finds a load to write about a movie as innocent as *Stuart Little 2*!

The Slip-Up Archive

www.slipups.com

Yet more movie mistakes (about 9,000 of them), plus funny mistakes by celebrities, on the TV and in books. You can even choose to have the newest slip-ups emailed to you each week.

Teen Hollywood

www.teenhollywood.com

'Hang out with the stars.' Much more relevant than **Hollywood.com**, but the same idea. Lots of reviews, trailers, interviews and all the usual exciting stuff.

UCI

www.uci-cinemas.co.uk

No online booking, but the latest movie reviews, with links to official websites. Sign up for the weekly Cinemail for the low-down on the latest movies, plus listings for your UCIs throughout the UK.

UpcomingMovies.com

www.upcomingmovies.com

'Tomorrow's movies today.' Recently taken over by Yahoo!, this great site contains all the inside info on brand-new movies – months (and sometimes years) ahead of filming or release – ingeniously searchable by type of movie, cast or title. Lots of gossip, too.

Virgin.Net

www.virgin.net/movies

Search for what's on where in the UK, plus movie news and reviews.

Warner Village Cinemas

www.warnervillage.co.uk

Book for your local Warner Village Cinema in the UK, plus all the trailers and movie info you'd expect.

(iii) Games

If gamers can take their eyes off one screen for a second to look at another, they'll find the Net's got everything on games – previews or reviews; the latest news; cheats and hints, so you can finally finish that game that's been driving you mad; games you can play online or download to your computer.

Some sites act as games directories or search engines, while others are online games mags with all the stuff you'd expect from their newsagent equivalents but, of course, with far more interaction and cool downloads. Then, there are the sites where you can simply download a stack of games and, finally, there are sites devoted to all the major platforms (the official ones are listed next).

Warning! You might just get hooked.

Top sites

☺ BEST ON THE NET

GameHelp

www.gamehelp.com

'The web's no.1 search engine and community for gamers.' GameHelp claims to have everything you need for every game, and that means reviews and previews (from other sources, so you can see what a range of people think), handy cheats and helpful websites, plus free demos and the chance to meet other gamers. Certainly well worth checking out!

The Adrenaline Vault

www.avault.com

An American online games mag, with news, downloads, previews, reviews, features, cheats and hints and more. Hey, if you live in the USA or Canada, you could even become part of the reviewing and writing team.

Gamebrew.com

www.gamebrew.com

'The source for Java gaming.' The best Java games on the Net – which means great graphics and fun times!

GameHippo.com

http://gamehippo.com

Over a thousand freeware PC games to download, with a full listing of the newest games to make sure you don't miss any good ones.

Gamezilla

www.gamezilla.com

Online since April 1996, Gamezilla claims to be one of the most visited games review sites on the net. Sure, all the reviews are there, but we love all the cheats, hints and walkthroughs for PC games and major formats, with a handy A–Z listing.

Games Domain

www.gamesdomain.co.uk

An online games mag, with all the usual news, cheats and downloads, plus forums and a chatroom.

Game Spotter

http://gamespotter.com

'Tracking the best web games.' Established for over two years, the site claims to be the Net's premier web games directory, with over 1,000 games listed in various categories – '3D', 'Action/Arcade', 'Adventure', 'Classic', 'Humour' and much more.

GameZone Online

www.gamezone.com

'Your PC and video game connection.' The latest demos and downloads, plus a stack of cheats, and new releases reviewed, for all the major consoles in a variety of categories.

Happypuppy.com

www.happypuppy.com

'It's all games.' Stacks of games reviews for all the major formats – click on what you're looking for ('Xbox', for example) then access cheats and walkthroughs (everything you need to know about the game and how to play it – it literally 'walks you through').

Nintendo

www.nintendo.com

The official Nintendo site, so whether you own the GameCube, or any of the other systems such as N64, Gameboy or SNES, you'll find something useful. Also features web games and downloads, plus Nintendo e-cards.

Playstation.com

www.playstation.com

Whether you own a PlayStation or PlayStation 2, this contains all you'd expect from Sony's official PlayStation site, including news and features (with a handy archive). Unsurprisingly available in loads of languages, and we mean loads!

Tolkien Games

www.lysator.liu.se/tolkien-games/

More than one hundred different kinds of game to get you totally Hobbit mad, many available as freeware.

Xbox
www.microsoft.com/xbox
News and features on Microsoft's Xbox and its games, plus you can sign up for the Xbox newsletter.

(iv) TV

Nothing can quite beat curling up in front of the TV set, but you'll find a whole load extra about your favourite shows online. Most TV shows have their own official websites, or at least some pages devoted to them, so we've listed just a few of the good ones, and the most popular, below. Of course, there are also hundreds of other official sites and millions of fan sites to be discovered.

Official sites tend to give basic cast and character info, but many go a whole lot further. Some of the best are colourful, lively and interactive, letting you browse through exclusive clips, complete special quizzes and enter competitions. You can also find out what's on a TV near you, wherever you are!

Top sites

☺ BEST ON THE NET

Dawson's Creek
www.dawsonscreek.com
Everything the *Dawson's Creek* fan could need. Episode

updates, character pictures, clips of 'missing scenes', message boards and desktop secrets. Take a virtual tour of the set, plus buy all the *DC* gear you like! A great-looking, fun and interactive site.

Ananova – TV

www.ananova.com/tv

Find out what's on TV in your area, throughout the UK.

Buffy The Vampire Slayer

www.buffyupn.com

Cast and character info, an episode guide to every season, plus register your details to enter secret parts of the Slayer World. Choose your slayer alias with care!

CBBC

www.bbc.co.uk/cbbc

Lively site with links to the BBC's major teen shows, from *Blue Peter* to *Grange Hill*. Includes presenter fact sheets, competitions, and things to make and do.

CITV

www.citv.co.uk

Everything you need to know on ITV's teen programmes, with a whole heap of message boards.

Coronation Street

www.coronationstreet.co.uk

All you'd expect from the website of the British soap.

CulTV

www.cultv.co.uk

As much info as you can digest on hundreds of cult and classic TV shows.

EastEnders

www.bbc.co.uk/eastenders

Interviews, info, quizzes and much, much more on the popular British soap. Check out the 'Walford Cam' for a sneak peak at goings-on in the Square, view your favourite classic clips, contribute to the message boards, send e-postcards and download character wallpaper.

ER

www.ertv.com

Similar to the *Friends* site (see below) with everything you need to know about the top medical drama.

Friends

www.friendstv.com

The usual cast and character info, plus a 3D set tour, and current series episode guide. Subscribe to the *Friends* mailing list for exclusive 'Central Perks', including show news and gossip.

Hollyoaks

www.hollyoaks.com

A very advanced site, with lots of trendy moving graphics. Contains all the usual cast pics and info, plus lots more. Sometimes a bit slow to load.

Nickelodeon

www.nick.co.uk

Bright, lively and loads of fun – exactly what you'd expect from the kids' TV channel.

Radio Times

www.radiotimes.beeb.com

Online TV and radio listings magazine, with features, listings, competitions and more, plus the chance to personalise your listings to reflect your favourite shows.

The Simpsons

www.thesimpsons.com

Are you *Simpsons* mad? Then check out this site. Move your cursor over the Springfield map to explore the site. You'll love the entire episode guide.

Smallville

www.smallville.net

Read the 'Smallville Ledger', the fictional online newspaper for the US TV show covering Superman's teen years.

Television Heaven

www.televisionheaven.co.uk

'Preserving the history of classic television shows, both past and present.' Ask your mum about some of these!

Trouble

www.trouble.co.uk

Exciting, interactive and totally packed site from the British teen TV channel. Get a virtual date with the 'Flash Boyfriend' feature, listen to 'Trouble Radio', and check out your favourite shows. Great graphics, so sometimes a bit slow.

TV Guide

www.tvguide.com/espanol

Complete TV listings for Spain.

TV Guide.com

www.tvguide.com

Complete TV listings for the USA.

TV Mag

www.tvmag.com

Complete TV listings for France.

TV Today

www.tvtoday.de

Complete TV listings for Germany.

(v) Books

Nobody really wants to spend hours sitting on a hard chair in front of their computer reading a book (that's what the sofa was invented for!). Still, online books do exist, but, it's worth remembering that unless copyright has been granted, books cannot legally be reproduced in this way unless the author has been dead for seventy-five years or more. So, there's plenty of Dickens or Shakespeare, but very little current stuff, which is handy for homework, but not much good for anything else. Instead, check out the sites which recommend some cool teen reads. Then buy the book from your local shop, or simply get it online (see Chapter 6). Some of them also include interviews with your favourite authors and tips on writing a book yourself.

Top sites

☺ BEST ON THE NET

Reading Rants

http://tln.lib.mi.us/~amutch/jen/

'Out of the ordinary teen booklists!' Doesn't sound promising – particularly given the weird address! What's more, it's compiled by a middle-school librarian from New York City. But, this is actually a very interesting guide to some great teen books. See 'Boy Meets Book' for some cool boy reads, 'Historical Fiction That Won't Make You Snore', and 'Virgin Run' – books about falling in love and first times. If you like reading, you'll love this site!

Achuka

www.achuka.co.uk

'The chock-full, eyes-peeled, independent children's book site.' A bit hard to read, but packed with interviews, features, and loads of books reviews and information.

Bartleby.com

www.bartleby.com

'Great books online.' Similar to **The Literature Network** (see page 137), also with online encyclopaedias, dictionaries and thesaurus.

Books Online

www.books-on-line.com

An ever-expanding database of around 20,000 free books or extracts and 500 full movie scripts.

Everything Shakespeare

www.field-of-themes.com/shakespeare

The Bard's complete works online, along with essays, a message board, and links to other Shakespeare sites. English homework will never be the same again!

The Literature Network

www.online-literature.com

Access 200 books, including titles such as DH Lawrence's *Lady Chatterley's Lover*, Charles Dickens' *Oliver Twist* and Herman Melville's *Moby Dick*.

Teen Lit

www.teenlit.com

Set up by two teachers in south-east Michigan, USA, this is a place for teen writers to publish and discuss their own writing, and get tips in the 'Writer's Workshop'.

Teen Reads

www.teenreads.com

Recommended teen reads, with info and features about popular authors, series and characters. Established since 1996.

(vi) Showbiz

Even a single day is a long time in showbiz, so these general sites which cover all kinds of celebs, have plenty to write about, 24/7!

Click through the links and find yourself venturing off into page upon page of news, info, gossip and trivia. The sites linked to top US entertainment TV shows or magazines are highly recommended, but you'll also find some great stuff elsewhere, like on the online showbiz pages from the UK tabloid newspapers, *The Daily Mirror* and *The Sun*.

You might not realise that the contents of stars' suitcases are the most exciting things in the world, but once you've read about them, they will be. In short, be warned! These sites are one hundred per cent addictive!

Top sites

☺ BEST ON THE NET

E Online

www.eonline.com

'The number one entertainment website.' Established in 1996, this is the official site of America's E! Entertainment Television. Packed with celeb news, gossip, reviews and games, and it looks great. Includes excellent search facility – so, for example, you can find any mentions of Britney Spears, past and present (we found more than 850!). Check out the excellent multimedia section for movie trailers, star interviews and music downloads.

Entertainmentlink.co.uk

www.entertainmentlink.co.uk

Links to hundreds of other entertainment and leisure websites. Well worth checking out.

Entertainment Tonight Online

www.etonline.com

Official site of the massive US TV show. All the latest gossip and info on movies, music, TV and more. Sign up to 'My ET' for the 'latest breaking celebrity news, behind-the-scenes views and personal anecdotes', straight to your email, every day.

EW.com

www.ew.com

'The smartest link to entertainment.' This site, from American Entertainment mag, *Entertainment Weekly*, covers all the usual celeb stuff. Sign up for daily news, direct to your email.

Hello!

www.hellomagazine.com

Nose through posh celebrity homes, and sniff out the latest gossip, at the site of the popular celeb magazine. Also links to sister mags, *Hola!* in Spain and *Oh La!* in France.

Mirror.co.uk – 3am

www.mirror.co.uk/3am

Catty, funny essential reading – the online version of *The Daily Mirror* newspaper's 3am page. Miaow!

News.com.au – Entertainment
http://entertainment.news.com.au
The latest celeb news from Down Under.

Onlinesun – Bizarre
www.thesun.co.uk
Click on 'Bizarre' for 'The world's no.1 showbiz column.' All the latest from the showbiz page of *The Sun* newspaper.

Tiscali – Entertainment
www.tiscali.co.uk/entertainment
Loads of celebs, with a UK slant. Also, find out what's on near you – cinemas, clubs, theatre, etc.

MUSIC, MOVIES AND MORE Q&A

MP3 for free?

Q: *My friends say that downloading MP3s is illegal, but I've found loads of sites with tracks by my favourite acts like Madonna, Britney Spears and Destiny's Child. Could I really go to prison for doing this?*

Abdul, 13, Glasgow

A: Bad news – just as copying CDs by these artists and giving them to your friends is illegal, so is downloading them from the Net. You're unlikely to find the police knocking at your door, but it's illegal all the same. See, chances are the songs' copyright holders haven't licensed any websites to produce MP3s of these tracks (even if they're not doing it for profit). Of course, things are different if you download something at an artist's official site as this is legal and helps promote that artist.

Scream queen

Q: *I really enjoyed the* Scream *movies, and was wondering if there's a way of finding out about similar films, without trawling along the shelves in my local video shop? I know there are loads of movie websites, so maybe one of those can help?*

Karen, 15, Newport

A: One of those can certainly help – you'd be advised to start at the **Internet Movie Database**. Simply type in the name of the movie you like, such as *Scream*, then scroll down to find other recommendations rated for you ('If you liked this title, we also recommend . . .'). You can also look up info on all the cast, see how the movies did at the box office, add your own review and a whole lot more!

Download low-down

Q: *The other day, I wanted to watch a movie trailer on my computer, but when I clicked on the button, nothing happened. What should I do?*

Paul, 15, Ryde

A: Often, it's a good idea to save any downloads to disk first, as even the shortest movie or music clips can take a while to download, unless you've got a particularly fast connection to the internet. Most modern web browsers are already equipped with the software to let you download these short movie or music files. Sometimes you can watch video clips or hear sound clips without downloading them first. However, you will still need the right software, and should be pointed to a link to easily download a plug-in (which doesn't actually plug-in at all, as it's just another little piece of software) which will make everything work for you. Try **RealPlayer** (www.real.com) or **QuickTime** on a Mac (www.info.apple.com/usen/quicktime).

CHAPTER 8

Totally Addicted to Fame?

All about your idols

Everyone has an idol or two – people whose CDs they religiously buy, whose movies or TV shows they watch again and again, or whose sport they love watching. So it's no surprise that the Net feeds our star obsessions.

Most major music names have their own official websites, with stars as diverse as Britney, Limp Bizkit, 'NSync, Destiny's Child, Robbie Williams and Jennifer Lopez all covered. Unfortunately, the worlds of movies, TV and sport feature far less. Don't always expect to type the name of your fave star into a search engine and find an official site. However, even the most obscure celebs seem to have a few fans somewhere in the world, and you can virtually guarantee that someone will have set up an unofficial website or group in their honour. And, of course, a search on the more popular people can throw up thousands of results, and it can often be hard to pick the brilliant from the brainless. Using a general celebrity site as your starting point can help with this, as they'll list official or recommended fan sites.

Official sites are normally very well designed and

endorsed by the star themselves, while the unofficial fan sites vary wildly in quality. But all present similar information – biographical details, or pictures of the star in question. Many provide great extras, like downloadable music or movie clips, quizzes, chatrooms or lyrics.

There are many millions of celebrity sites and it's only possible to suggest a few here, to show what's on offer. Hopefully, it will help you begin to use the web more efficiently, sort the good sites from the bad, and hopefully give you a few surprises, too.

(i) General celebrity sites

Although the general celebrity sites can never be as detailed as any sites dedicated exclusively to our idols, they're a good place to begin looking for info and links. You'll also love the sites which can show you where to spot the stars, or give you their email addresses. And with the birthday sites, you'll never miss that special celeb's big day ever again!

Top sites

☺ BEST ON THE NET

Teen Idols 4 You

www.teenidols4you.com

'Your teen idol news source.' Search through past and current news on your favourite teen singers and actors. Pics of around 10,000 teen actors and 4,000 teen singers. Fancy yourself as a celeb journo? Then you can even submit celeb news yourself.

Absolutely Celebrity Network

www.absolutely.net

More female celebs than you can shake a stick at, with galleries, news and more.

Actor Archives

www.actorarchives.com

'One of the web's largest databases of pics and biogs of today's hottest actors.' Mini biogs, loads of pics, scans from magazines and more.

All Experts

www.allexperts.com

'The oldest and largest free Q&A service on the internet.' Pick a category, such as 'Movies' or 'Music' and click on a volunteer.

Best Celebrity Sites.com

www.bestcelebritysites.com

Not very comprehensive, but rates various celeb sites, ranks them and reviews them.

Celebhoo.com

www.celebhoo.com

'For everything celebrity.' Browse by category, such as

'Actors & Actresses' and 'Bands & Artists'.

Celebritybase.net
www.celebritybase.net
Search for celebs' official websites here.

Celebrity Addresses
www.celebrity-addresses.com
Find out where to write to your favourite stars, with a selection of addresses such as their record company, the TV station which makes their show, and even the occasional home address! Costs $12.95 (about £8.30) per month.

Celebrity Desktop
www.celebritydesktop.com
Lists nearly two hundred actors, and over four hundred musicians, with the chance to download images and sound clips, plus send postcards.

Celebrity Email
www.celebrityemail.com
Charges a monthly fee of $9.95 (about £7) for celebrity addresses info.

Celebrity Link
www.celebrity-link.com
Around 6,000 celebs listed at nearly 23,000 websites.

Celebrity Palace

www.celebritypalace.com

Lots of celeb info, although not very comprehensive. Includes biogs, pics and links.

Celebrity Zone

www.celebrityzone.co.uk

Great-looking site which claims to be the fastest-growing celeb site on the Net. Unfortunately, not yet that detailed, as searches on some well-known British celebs came up with nothing.

Cinema Stars

www.cinema-stars.com

Limited to female celebs, but includes biographical info, filmographies, links to related websites and pages and pages of pics to ogle at.

Famous Birthdays

www.famousbirthdays.com

Discover who was born on your birthday, plus send virtual cards, and check out the jokes and trivia.

Fansites.com

www.fansites.com

Pretty basic, but contains a good listing of celebrity sites, and auction items currently available on eBay (www.eBay.com) that relate to the stars.

The Male Celebrity Archive

www.spacesurfer.com/mceleb

Quite amateurish, for pics only, but a good combination of pics and screen-grabs from movies, which fans have uploaded. Has a sister site for female celebs at www.spacesurfer.com/wceleb.

Seeing Stars In Hollywood

www.seeing-stars.com

Want to spot a star in LA? This brilliant site contains a calendar of Hollywood events and lists hundreds of places where you can spot the stars. For example, movie premieres or filming locations, plus restaurants owned by the famous, and where the stars live, dine or shop. Plus a celeb addresses search facility.

Starpages.net

www.starpages.net

Similar to **Celebhoo.com**.

Today's Birthdays

www.todaysbirthday.com

Tells you which celebs were born on this day, and lets you search for your fave celeb's birthday.

Young Celeb.com

www.youngceleb.com

Links to more than 400 stars under 25 years old.

(ii) Official sites

It's impossible to list many official sites here, but a few of the good ones are recommended. Official sites are sometimes better than fan sites, as they contain exclusive content or give you the chance to buy merchandise. However, many are let down by the fact that stars like to control their image, so you'll only see their most recent pics, or be able to hear their latest singles, or see their current movie trailer. Still, they're well worth a look.

Top sites

☺ BEST ON THE NET

Leonardo DiCaprio

www.leonardodicaprio.com

'A portal into Leo's past, present and future.' One of only a handful of A-list actors to have their own, official site. Features fan art, news on Leo's latest movie projects and trailers for all his films to date.

Britney Spears

www.britneyspears.com

All the usual, plus a sickly section from Britney's mum – 'Lynne's Corner' – and news on the Britney Spears Foundation, set up to help children in need.

Destiny's Child

www.destinyschild.com

Available in lots of languages, including French and German. Check out the Destiny's Child chatrooms.

Elvis

www.elvis.com

'Home of the undisputed king of rock and roll.' He might have been dead for years, but The King still gets his own website.

Janet Jackson

www.janet-jackson.com

Check out the fantastic 'create your own dance video' section!

Jennifer Lopez

www.jenniferlopez.com

Available in English, French and German. Everything you'd expect, such as news, interviews and pics, plus JLo Radio.

Kylie Minogue

www.kylie.com

A diary section, written by Kylie, plus the latest vids, lyrics, an awesome screensaver and a shop where you can exclusively buy the 'Love Kylie' lingerie range.

Mary-Kate and Ashley

www.mary-kateandashley.com

Fun and funky site from America's favourite Olsen twins, stars of *So Little Time* and *Two of a Kind*. With entertainment, fashion, gossip, e-cards and heaps more.

Mis-Teeq

www.misteeq.com

Home of the UK garage girls, with exclusive, web-only competitions.

'NSync

www.nsync.com

Packed with info on the world's biggest boy band, including a section for fans to post poems, comments or their own pictures of the guys.

Pink

www.pinkspage.com

One cool American lady gets one cool site, with everything you'd expect, plus a secret look into her life with Pink's diary.

Robbie Williams

www.robbiewilliams.com

Online home of the British star.

S Club

www.sclub.com

Available in English, Dutch, German and more, with message boards.

Will Smith

www.willsmith.net

Focuses on the music side of Mr Smith's career, with all the usual stuff.

(iii) Fan Sites

The love and devotion put into many fan sites is unbelievable. In fact, you wonder if some of these fans have time to do anything other than run their website, as they sometimes look more professional than the official equivalents! You'll find a lot of detail in fan sites (particularly the obsessive ones), with info, pics and more covering the star's entire career, not to mention rare clips, magazine or TV interviews and jaw-dropping rumours!

Many have annoying pop-up ads so the people hosting the site can make some money, but you can't expect to get something *completely* for nothing, can you?

Top sites

☺ BEST ON THE NET

Limp Bizkit

www.bizkitmusic.com

Fantastic site with loads of brilliant bits, including rare/live sound clips, song meanings and so much more.

Ben Affleck

http://katieweb.com/ben

Tons of info and gossip from a very dedicated fan – find out what Ben's up to, almost before he does!

Brad Pitt

www.bradpittfan.com

Seven thousand Brad pics in this well-designed site.

Britney Spears

www.britneyfans.com

'The number one source for Britney fans.' Fantastic-looking, very comprehensive site, with a complete discography, music and video downloads, lyrics and Britney wallpaper for your computer. What more could you want? Watch out for the annoying pop-up ads.

Cameron Diaz

www.celebs.cz/cameron/main.shtml

Thousands of photos of the *Charlie's Angels* star, including movie images, plus nearly 200 audio clips and interviews, plus Cameron quotes and a photo of the week!

Destiny's Child

www.dc-unplugged.com

'The official Destiny's Child fan site.' Looks very flashy (so it takes a while to load), with all the bits you'd expect.

Elijah Wood International

www.thatsyours.nl/elijahwood

Great-looking site, packed with everything you ever wanted to know about the *Lord of the Rings* star.

Jennifer Aniston

www.geocities.com/Hollywood/Hills/8495/jennifer.htm

Pictures, e-cards, chat, news and a mailing list.

Josh Hartnett

www.josh-hartnett.org

'The ultimate fan site.' Amazingly professional tribute to the *Pearl Harbor* star, stuffed with Josh news, interviews, clips and more. Looks almost as good as the actor himself!

Linkin Park

www.linkinpark.org.uk

UK-based site with heaps of essential info for the hardcore fan, including tour dates, fan quizzes (how dedicated are you?), plus cool mobile phone ringtones to download.

S Club
www.sclub7online.net
'The most popular S Club fansite on the Net.' Massive site with heaps of up-to-date news and gossip, photos, lyrics, wallpaper and a chatroom.

(iv) Groups and Communities

Want to talk about a topic that's close to your heart? Then do it on one of the web's groups and communities. You'll be able to chat with others from all around the world who share your interests – whether it's for school work or pleasure.

Although these groups cover virtually every subject you could imagine, they're especially cool for chatting about your favourite stars, with some letting you post and download photos, sound or video clips. You'll probably need to register, for free, to get involved.

Of course, if you can't find one devoted to the person you like, or you think you could create a better club, then there's nothing to stop you – anyone can easily create a club, you then just need to wait for some members to join up.

Top sites

☺ BEST ON THE NET

Yahoo

http://groups.yahoo.com

Join thousands of groups where you can share photos, files and gossip with others, and even create your own group. There are around 150 groups devoted to Brad Pitt, and nearly 3,000 featuring Britney Spears. Simply register, and you're away!

Domeus

www.domeus.com

'The largest online community platform in Europe.' Available in many languages. Register to join groups or create your own.

MSN Communities

http://communities.msn.com/home

Part of the world-wide Microsoft organisation, these communities are a bit like mini-websites, and therefore contain everything you'd expect of a website, from news and gossip to pictures of your favourite stars. Register and create your own, or share your photos with others online at My Photo Center.

FAME Q&A

Posh idols?

Q: *I've been able to find loads of official sites for my favourite acts like 'NSync, but I don't seem to be able to find official sites for my actor idols like Brad Pitt and Josh Hartnett. Do they think they're too good for the internet?*

Sarah, 13, Bury

A: Although record companies will set up official websites for their acts, to help promote them online, film or TV companies tend to set up websites devoted to particular movies or TV shows, rather than specific actors. Very few celebs from the worlds of movies, TV or sport have so far bothered with their own sites, as they see them not as a useful promotional tool, but an invasion of their privacy. However, slowly more and more stars are coming round to the idea of setting them up, with big Hollywood names like *Friends* actress, Jennifer Aniston, and *Gladiator* star Russell Crowe now jumping on the bandwagon.

No to newsgroups

Q: *You mention groups and clubs, but say nothing about the thousands of newsgroups that exist on the internet. Why is this?*

Patrick, 14, Belfast

A: Newsgroups (they're rather like the message/bulletin boards in Chapter 2) look a bit outdated these days. They're like the online information equivalent of an early-1980s computer, which filled a whole room, when you can now fit something far more powerful in the palm of your hand. Still, if you're looking for info on someone, or want to find something out, then post it to the appropriate newsgroup, or run a search, and you'll be pleasantly surprised by the results! Try **Google Groups** (www.google.co.uk/grphp?hl=en), a traditional newsgroup service, which lets you access more than 700 million messages dating back to 1981, should you really want to! If not, then browse the text-only newsgroups for discussions on any subjects that take your fancy. One word of warning – try to avoid getting 'flamed' (told off!) for asking a stupid question (one that has been asked a whole load of times before). Most discussion forums have a Frequently Asked Questions (FAQ) section where common questions are answered. Read this first when entering a new group to avoid trouble.

CHAPTER 9

And Now for Something Completely Different – Sport and Politics

Exercise your body and mind

One great thing about the internet (apart from everything we've already seen!) is that you can guarantee that it will feature stuff that interests you, from the day-to-day to the totally obscure.

When it comes to sport, you'll find websites devoted to practically every one imaginable – from Athletics to Wrestling. Sports sites let you follow events happening just around the corner, or on the other side of the world. Whether you support Liverpool or the Miami Dolphins and want to know the latest scores, catch up on team news, or read some great sports features, it's all online. You might even want to try a new sport – use the Net to check out the equipment you need or the rules to follow, before you get involved.

There are also some great sites listed covering other

things that loads of teens are interested in – things like politics, green issues, vegetarianism or animal rights. Whether you want to know what organisations you can join or you want to polish up your arguments, the Net can help.

(i) Sport

Want to find out about your favourite sport? Then the super sites, like **Sports.com** or **Sportingnews.com** are good places to start. They contain all the latest news and results on all the major sports, and many also feature video clips, interviews, player or competitor profiles and even fantasy leagues. Just remember, there tends to be bias towards the 'main' national sports (such as football in the UK), depending on the home country of each site.

Official sites tend to come under the umbrella of each sport's official organisation, but some of the best are independent sites set up by fans. Unlike the more news-based super sites, many of these also contain hints and tips on improving your game.

Top sites

☺ BEST ON THE NET

Sports.com

www.sports.com

This doesn't just provide sports results, it includes contests, fantasy leagues and so much more. There's a big football focus on the UK site. Available in different languages, including French, German, Spanish and Italian, as well as an American version.

Adrenaline Sports
www.adrenaline-sports.net
Thinking of taking up an extreme sport? Find all the easy-to-understand info you need, including good and bad points on each sport (dangers, start-up costs, etc) and some tips to get you started.

Athletix
www.athletix.org
All the athletics news you could want.

Autosport
www.autosport.com
'The world's best motorsport website.' Packed with motorsport news and features from around the world.

BBC Sport
http://news.bbc.co.uk/sport
News, interviews, info, even sporting weather forecasts are covered on this very comprehensive site from the BBC. Test BBC *Match of the Day's* footballing expert in 'Ask Albert' – pose your tricky footy teasers and wait for his reply.

Bike Magic

www.bikemagic.com

Cycle news, reviews, features and a marketplace.

Boxing.com

www.boxing.com

'The internet's number one boxing forum.' Plenty of news and info – pulls no punches!

Bungee Zone

www.bungeezone.com

'The most comprehensive guide to bungee jumping on the net.' Features world-wide club listings, equipment info, types of jump (now, this bit is scary!) and a disasters section which the faint-hearted should avoid at all costs!

CricInfo

www.cricket.org

'The home of cricket on the internet.' Massive site with all the usual stuff, plus a massive info database, a news archive and even the rules of the game!

ExtremeSports.com

www.extremesports.com

Surf, skate, snow, bikes – they're all covered here, with the latest news and cool 'Video Vault' of impressive stunts.

Football 365

www.football365.com

'Football news, football fun, football fast.' British football news, features and fun – one site you'll definitely score with! Visit the homegrounds section to find out all the latest news and gossip on your club, from the Premiership to Division Three and the Scottish Premier League.

Golf Today

www.golftoday.co.uk

'Home of Europe's premier online golf magazine.' Tee off with stacks of golfing stuff. Also available in an American version.

Kidstuffadventure.com

www.kidstuffadventure.com

Created by young people, this has info on destinations, activities, experiences and products that excite them, including all kinds of sports.

LTA Online

www.lta.org.uk

News from the UK's Lawn Tennis Association, plus a fantastic 'Fans Zone' with factfiles on the top British players and helpful advice for anyone wishing to improve their game.

Martialinfo.com

www.martialinfo.com

'Voted the hottest martial arts site.' Packed with news, info, expert advice, who's who of martial arts, even an e-cards section. Then join 41,000 others and subscribe to receive your online magazine and updates by email.

NBA

www.nba.com

Home of America's National Basketball Association.

NFL.com

www.nfl.com

All the news, info and interviews from America's National Football League on its official site. Find out more about the players and even join the fantasy league.

Racingpost.co.uk

www.racingpost.co.uk

All you could want on British horse-racing.

Snooker.net

www.snooker.net

Stacks of snooker news, but a very dull-looking site.

Soccernet

www.soccernet.com

More stuff on British football, plus a European and Global focus.

Sportinglife.com

www.sportinglife.com

All the latest news on all the major sports from this UK-based site. Seems especially strong on football, horse-racing, cricket and rugby.

SportingNews.com

www.sportingnews.com

US-focused site, covering baseball (MLB), basketball (NBA), football (NFL), hockey (NHL) and more. Try also www.sportsnetwork.com for similar stuff.

Swim Info

www.swiminfo.com

'The world's leading independent resource for swimming.' News, features, results and a shop, so dive in!

World of Rugby League

www.rleague.com

Stacks of stuff with links to British, Australian and New Zealand sites.

WWE.com

www.wwe.com

All the excitement of World Wrestling Entertainment with news, videos and more.

(ii) Politics

Whether you're into animal welfare, politics or saving the rainforests, you'll find plenty of like-minded teens on the Net. Some sites just provide news and info, others let you join up, but all will give you the info you need to get involved and take action.

The sites listed below are just the tip of the iceberg, and many will give you a whole host of links to other related sites. Happy hunting!

Amnesty International
www.amnesty.org
'Working to protect human rights world-wide.' Information on human rights (for example, facts about the death penalty), latest news and ways you can help, such as getting involved in freeing a prisoner of conscience.

Animal Aid
www.animalaid.org.uk/youth/home.htm
Campaigns peacefully against all forms of animal abuse. Features an A–Z listing, covering topics including animal experiments, products to avoid, and heaps of info on endangered species.

The Conservative Party
www.conservatives.com
Official home of the Conservative Party.

FITteen

www.fitteen.com

'You're the only one standing in the way of your success.' Advice on keeping fit and eating healthily, with recipes, routines and a chatroom.

Generation Rising

www.generationrising.com

'Where YOUth get connected.' American website for responsible, community-minded teens who want to get heard. Sections include 'Take Action' (get involved in saving the rainforests); 'Sound Off' (your chance to take a stand against teen violence); 'Go Global' (get connected to people, events and organisations).

The Green Party

www.greenparty.org.uk

Official home of the Green Party of England and Wales.

Habitat For Humanity

www.humanity.org

Habitat For Humanity builds houses for people in need. Loads of celebs have already got involved and now you can, too.

HumaneTeen

www.humaneteen.org

'Where young people make a difference for animals and

their world.' Features important issues and a section on how you can help.

The Labour Party
www.labour.org.uk
Official home of the Labour Party.

Liberal Democrats
www.libdems.org.uk
Official home of the Liberal Democrats.

Teen Hoopla – Activism
www.ala.org/teenhoopla/activism.html
Useful list of websites for any teen who stands up for something they believe in, from civil liberties to the prevention of crime.

Teen Ink – Environment
www.teenink.com/environment/index.html
More than four hundred thought-provoking articles written by teens about the environment.

Teens For Animals
http://teensforanimals.wiew.org
Links to animal rights and environment sites, under headings including 'Animal Cruelty', 'Circuses', 'Fur', 'Hunting', 'Rainforests' and 'Vegetarian Info'.

Vegetarian Resource Group
www.vrg.org/nutrition/teennutrition.htm
Useful nutrition advice for veggie teens. Click the link for recipes, too.

The Vegetarian Youth Network
www.geocities.com/RainForest/Vines/4482/index.html
Useful info, plus links to other veggie sites. Find veggie penpals, take a look at the recipes and check out reasons for going veggie if you're not already converted!

World Wildlife Fund
www.wwf.org
'Take action for a living planet.' News and info on the work of the WWF.

AND NOW FOR SOMETHING COMPLETELY DIFFERENT Q&A

Driving mad

Q: *I'm nearly 17, so I'm interested in finding out more about driving. Where should I look?*

Jurep, Southampton

A: The UK might have one of the best international road safety records, but any extra help you can get with learning to drive, outside of the driving school, is invaluable. **Driving Online** (www.driving.co.uk)

contains heaps of tips on passing the UK driving test. It's packed with other driving info, including driving issues (drink- and drug-driving, road rage, etc) and funny motoring stories. **WorldDrivingSchools.com** (www.worlddrivingschools.com) is another great resource for the learner driver, whether you're in the UK, USA, or Australia, with a register of more than 5,000 driving schools – simply click the appropriate link for your country. In the virtual driving school you can find all the info you need to start learning, then later take the online theory test (on the UK site), which is different every time!

Finally, once you've got the learning out of the way, visit **Top Gear** (www.topgear.beeb.com), 'the independent guide to buying and enjoying your car'. Find out about issues including security and servicing, plus learn how to tell a brilliant motor from a dodgy old banger. Bet you're now itching to get mobile!

Fitness fanatic

Q: *I can't say I'm really into any sports, but I do like keeping fit. So which sites can I visit for that kind of advice?*

Dan, 15, Tunbridge Wells

A: There are plenty of health and fitness sites to keep you going, such as **Health Fitness & Tips** (www.health-fitness-tips.com) with its health and fitness news, daily exercise suggestions, info on tracking your fitness levels, and more. Guys will also like

Men's Health.co.uk (www.menshealth.co.uk), a cool site, based on *Men's Health* magazine, covering fitness, sports, health and girls. However, a favourite must be **Workoutplan.com** (www.workoutplan.com), which calls itself 'the flexible, free, personal exercise planner'. After you've registered, this clever site helps you create and follow a personal fitness schedule, whether you want to work out at home, in the gym or with friends.

Get your skates on!

Q: *I'd like to become more involved in politics, but I don't know where to start. I get frustrated by all sorts of things in my town, such as the state of the local skatepark, but I'd also like to make a difference on a national level, too.*

Will, 14, London

A: Getting involved in politics can be very rewarding, as it's great to be able to make a difference. Sometimes it can be frustrating too, so you should be prepared for this, remembering it can take a while to change things for the better. You can find out more about your local council online, to discover their plans for your area, or even track down your local MP and drop them an email with your complaints. You could also see if there's a local youth offshoot of the political party you'd like to be involved with. Getting involved at this level could eventually have far wider-reaching consequences. Simply use your search engine and type in key words to find all of these.

Conservation crazy!

Q: *There are quite a few 'green' schemes in the area where I live, such as a tree-planting initiative and can and bottle recycling. However, I'm interested in more global green issues, like the extinction of animals or the destruction of rainforests. How can I find out more?*

Jessica, 13, Birmingham

A: The internet is fantastic for being so relevant to everyone, wherever they live. So while someone in Brazil should be able to find out about your local tree-planting scheme, you can get all the info you need about their rainforest's destruction. Some of the sites listed in this chapter will link you to the relevant web addresses. It's worth remembering that everything happening overseas might sound more glamorous, but – as your mum might say – 'charity begins at home'. Saving those bottles and cans for recycling is just as important as saving the lesser-spotted tree coyote from extinction . . . after all, the environment is important wherever you live!

CHAPTER 10

Still Not Sorted?

Do it yourself – in minutes!

So you've scoured this entire book, yet you still can't find the site you're looking for. Or you've found some sites that interest you, but you reckon that you can do them better. Then why not build your own website and make people come to you?

You've probably already had a go at getting yourself online with a homepage (you know, cute family pictures, info about the dullsville town where you live, pics of Aunt Maud quaffing too much sherry at Christmas). Loads of people have also set up tribute sites for their idols. If you haven't, why not try? Or create a site about your hobby or interests. This chapter shows you where to begin.

Many of the best websites are designed by teens (mind you, there are some really appalling ones out there, too!). But even if you haven't tried creating a site before, then don't be put off – it's not at all difficult, as everything you need is there for free on the Net. However, building a good site depends on how you build it, what you want it to do and, of course, how much effort you're prepared to put into it. Just make sure you don't put up too many personal details about yourself.

Where do I begin?

Start by working out what you want your webpage to do, as this will help its design. Loads of people just decide they want to produce a site about themselves, but if they don't think it through properly, it ends up being pretty messy, and pretty boring, too! However, well-planned fan sites are often better than their official 'rivals' as a dedicated fan has decided in advance what all the brilliant elements on that site are going to be.

Why not sketch your site first, so you know how it will look and how all the links will work together? Think it through at this stage, and we guarantee it'll be more interesting (and get more visitors) than about 500 million others out there!

OK, so what next?

Think a bit more about the design and content. Will the design be simple or complicated? It's worth remembering that cluttered pages don't stand out, but ones that are simple, while still being interesting, will encourage someone to read on.

Also, remember that some people might have a slower computer than you, and what takes seconds to appear on your screen could take far longer on theirs.

Here are some more tips:

- 👍 DO keep backgrounds simple – white, black or muted colours are normally better than the bright ones that give you a migraine.
- 👍 DO keep pages short – nobody wants to keep scrolling d-o-o-o-o-w-w-n-n for ever!
- 👍 DO use tables to make your pages look a bit like newspaper articles. Too much text will just be boring.
- 👍 DO make your site easy to navigate. Split it into simple, easy-to-understand sections with lots of obvious links to other pages.

- 👎 DON'T bother with background images – magazines don't have them, and neither do good websites.
- 👎 DON'T use loads of graphics – they take ages to download, and often text will do. The same applies to pictures, music or moving images. Remember, many pics and music are copyrighted so you'd be better off using free images or sounds.
- 👎 DON'T bother with a hit counter – they're a sure sign of a beginner's site.
- 👎 DON'T just copy someone else's site – yours should be one people want to come back to, so make it different. There might be thousands of Britney fan sites out there, but how many get regular visitors? There's no point in putting a lot of effort into a site nobody visits, or one which someone browses and then never returns to.

Fine, but how do I actually create it?

At this stage, there's no point in worrying about complicated HTML programming. There are so many site-building packages around, there's just no need to bother. Hmm, now all you need is some webspace to host your site.

Well, good news. Chances are, your internet account comes with some webspace or even a site building program. If not, then try one of the sites that lets you build and host your own site, such as **Yahoo!** and **GeoCities.**

If you're still stuck, you could also use the programs that come with Netscape Navigator (Composer) or Microsoft Internet Explorer (FrontPage Express). You'll then just need someone to host your site (it's easy to find someone suitable at www.freewebspace.net).

Although most of the site-building programs also enable you to upload what you've created on to the web just by clicking a few buttons, sometimes you'll need a hand. If you do, then simply use a File Transfer Protocol (FTP) program to do this – again, they're readily available on the Net (and recommended!).

How can I take things further?

If you're really serious about having a strong presence on the Net, then think about buying your own domain name which people will easily be able to identify with your site, and find when they're running a search! You could also look at some of the many online guides to creating your own website.

Top sites

☺ BEST ON THE NET

Webmonkey For Kids

http://hotwired.lycos.com/webmonkey/kids/

'The fun way to build web sites.' Probably a bit simple, but a good place to start if you're new to all this. Features 'Lessons' (design and layout, learning HTML, etc), 'Projects' (make an online birthday invite or a slide show) and 'Tools' (such as how to get your site online).

ABCs Of Building A Website

http://webdevelopersjournal.com/columns/abcs_of_building_web_sites.html

'A web design tutorial for rank beginners.' The very basics on creating your site – packed with useful info.

AskTheRabbit.com

www.asktherabbit.com

'Put the power of the rabbit to work for you.' Er, right. Cute name, cool site – type in the info you're looking for (about building your site, promoting it, whatever) and the rabbit will guide you to hundreds of reports, publications, services, weblinks and more, to ensure you're totally sorted out.

CuteFTP

www.cuteftp.com

Using a PC and needing a hand getting your new site

uploaded? Experts recommend CuteFTP as a really easy way of doing it. Download a free trial here and find out how to buy the full version.

DHD Photo Gallery

www.hd.org/Damon/photos

Over 8,000 free images and more than 300 sounds for you to use on your website – everything from toilets (hmm, now they'll come in handy on your pop music website!) to food and drink.

Fetch

http://fetchsoftworks.com

Just like **CuteFTP**, but for Mac users instead. Again, there's a free version to try out. After that, you have to buy a cheap licence.

1st Page 2000

www.evrsoft.com

Fancy learning a bit of HTML after all? 1st Page 2000 is 'the world's no.1 free HTML editor', and lets you start off all simple, while building your skills. Use this if you haven't got, or don't want to use, any of the web page builders discussed above.

Homestead

www.homestead.com

Another build/host site. The software works just like

Windows. There is a charge of around $5 (less than £3.50) per month for personal use.

IMS Web Dwarf

www.virtualmechanics.com/products/dwarf/index.html

If the thought of HTML makes you feel sick, then use this wysiwyg (what you see is what you get) builder – it works a bit like a word processor.

An Introduction To Publishing On The World Wide Web

www.pathcom.com/~kujira/web.htm

More hints and tips for the beginner.

Mediabuilder.com

www.mediabuilder.com

Over 3,000 backgrounds, photos and more for use on your websites.

Quick Draw Co.

www.quickwebpagedesign.com

Stacks of tips, plus sign up for a page-building and site design 'zine by email.

Tripod

www.tripos.lycos.com

Another build/host site, but this one, like **Yahoo! GeoCities** is totally free.

Webmonkey

http://hotwired.lycos.com/webmonkey

'The web developer's resource.' More news for the webmaster (hey, that's you!) with stacks more stuff on making your site better.

Webreview

www.webreview.com

Sorted your site? Now find out more about making it better – although some of this went over our heads!

Web Design Guide

www.dreamink.com/beginners

Small bites of info on building your site, plus a useful Webopedia to help you with all the terms you might not understand.

Yahoo! GeoCities

http://geocities.yahoo.com

Lets you build your site, then hosts it for you. The excellently simple 'Yahoo! PageWizard' will assist beginners, or flashier types can use Yahoo! PageBuilder.

Index

Also available from Piccadilly Press, by
FRANK McGINTY

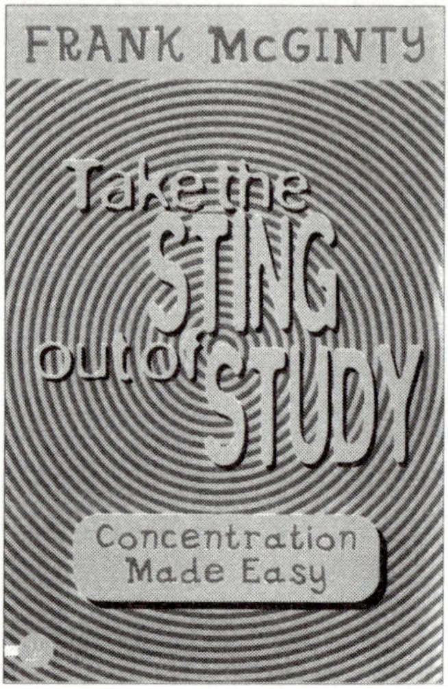

Students have more than ever to learn at school these days, and there seems to be an endless succession of exams and assessments. This book aims to help you not only to master the skills of concentration, but also to relax. It may even help you to enjoy your studies!

Learn how to:

- get organised, work to a routine, yet be flexible and adaptable;
- work in your preferred learning style and with the eight forms of intelligence;
- recognise and overcome the limits you put on yourself;
- avoid the effects of dehydration, lack of oxygen and caffeine sensitivity;
- get into 'The Flow';
- and much, much more . . .

By the author of *Smart Thinking*:
"It's an engaging, clear and positive exploration of the nature of self-belief. Well worth making available – and reading yourself." *The Guardian*

Also available from Piccadilly Press, by
KERRY PARNELL

Street Smart is about safety. With practical guidelines, tips for common sense and advice on how to handle difficult situations with confidence, it can help you live your life safely and independently. The message is *be aware*, rather than *beware!* Kerry Parnell covers the issues teenagers face, such as:

- drugs and alcohol;
- dating and sex;
- safety on the street and on transport;
- peer pressure and bullying;
- streetwise know-how – cash machines, pick-pockets, strangers;
- internet, email and phone savvy;
- avoiding or coping with abuse, harassment or assault;
- dealing with crime;
- and much more.

By the author of *Bliss - The Smart Girl's Guide to Sex*:
"This accessible and straightforward book . . . provides facts, reassurance and invaluable advice." *Publishing News*